# LOL: LAUGH OUT LOUD

AN AFTER OSCAR NOVEL

LUCY LENNOX

MOLLY MADDOX

Cover Art by: Cate Ashwood at Cate Ashwood Designs

Cover Photo: Eric McKinney at 6:12 Photography

Beta Reading by: Leslie Copeland at LesCourt Author Services

Editing by: Sandra at One Love Editing

# ACKNOWLEDGEMENTS

We'd like to thank the following:

Leslie Copeland, Sloane Kennedy, Shay Haude, Victoria Rothenberg, and Chad Williams for invaluable beta feedback.

The Lucy's Lair FB Group for answering the question (quite thoroughly) about whether or not a horse can fit through a front door.

Cate Ashwood for fast, talented design work.

Eric McKinney and Dustin McNeer for a stunning cover photo.

Sandra Dee for speedy, thorough editing.

Lori Parks for eagle-eyed proofing.

Our father for "forgetting" to put in his hearing aids the days we worked on LOL at his house. Dad, you missed all the good stuff.

*We'd like to dedicate this book to a group of people who make us LOL every single day. To the members of Lucy's Lair on Facebook, thank you for your support, your humor, your patience, and your zany comments. You are all so deliciously crazy. Don't ever change. You are our people.*

# 1

## SCOTTY

*Cop Commandeers Horse Carriage For High-Speed Chase Through City!*

Wʜᴇɴ ᴀ ᴄᴏᴘ ᴄᴏᴍᴇs ʀᴀᴄɪɴɢ out of a building on Fifth Avenue, hops in your horse-drawn carriage, and screams, "Go!"—you go.

You don't stop and ask for paperwork. Or a badge. Or an explanation of who you're chasing. You simply follow his shouted orders about where to turn.

At least, that's what I did when it happened to me.

After the uniformed man jumped in shouting, I snapped the reins on Nugget's big brown ass and felt the carriage lurch ahead into the park. Playdate moms and iBanker joggers leaped out of the way, spilling Starbucks mocha lattes and missing key points from their podcasts about the volatility of the yen in today's bear market.

Onward we surged. It was a race against injustice, or so I assumed. I hunkered down in my seat and sallied forth up Cedar Hill toward the obelisk. There were definitely people racing after us both on foot and in those tricycle hackney things I'd never quite understood. But whether those people were other police officers or just lookie-loos, I wasn't sure. And I certainly couldn't take the time to swivel around to see them when I was trying to keep Nugget from cardiac arrest in front of me.

"Are we heading to the Park Precinct?" I yelled back, assuming his closest brothers in blue would want to help him continue his pursuit on the back of a faithful NYPD steed instead of my plodding carriage horse. Poor Nugget was running for glory, but there was no doubt my girl's stamina was going to run out if we kept this up.

"No! Keep going!" the cop barked from behind me. His commanding voice brooked no argument, so I continued spurring Nugget past other carriages, ignoring the calls of "WTF, Scotty!" and "Dude, etiquette, man!" from my fellow drivers. It wasn't usually cool to shoot ahead of everyone else, but didn't they realize I had a situation on my hands?

"Left! Shakespeare's Garden," the man called out.

I hung a quick left, leaning the opposite way to keep the high-sprung carriage on four wheels. There was haste, and then there was stupidity. Whoever we were chasing wasn't worth me losing a limb, for god's sake.

As we approached Central Park West, I either had to turn left to stay in the park or get confirmation there was a dire emergency that justified my breaking any number of laws by driving my carriage on a city street away from the Central Park area.

"Where to now?" I called over my shoulder.

"South! Left!"

Just as I was about to swing us in that direction without thinking, I noticed none of the traffic was heading south on Central Park West. Only north. Duh, one-way street the other way.

"South on Eighth isn't happening. Have to go down Sixty-Sixth to Columbus." Belatedly, it occurred to me that was the type of information a cop should know. Unless he was super new to the city. But still.

We continued through the intersection, horns blaring and people shouting, before weaving in and out of traffic on the cross street. I spotted a Starbucks and spent a solid thirteen seconds wondering if I had time to duck in and grab an Americano to help warm me up. It was fucking cold as shit today.

But unfortunately for my frozen toes, the pursuit of justice took precedence. I urged Nugget onward, hanging a left on Columbus when we reached the end of the block. Finally, we were heading south. The speed had lessened, and I tried to pick up the pace. My heart was hammering in my chest as the reality of our situation sunk in. Were we in danger? Was there someone with a weapon behind us? Or... in front of us?

The cop barked more orders out, turning us east and then south and then west again. As we crossed the same street for the second time, but from a different direction, I began to wonder just what kind of emergency we were dealing with here. It wasn't until we were fighting traffic on West Fifty-First that I began to question whether maybe this guy had just wanted a ride to Anthropologie for something trendy but unique.

"Um... Officer?" I called over my shoulder. "Are we... following anyone in particular?" There were definitely still people behind us, only now it seemed like yellow cabs more than anything.

"Yeah. Uhhh... that... that black car there." He waved his hand vaguely. "Go!"

Three black cars idled in front of me. "Can you be more specific? The Honda or the SUV?"

"Never mind. Up there—make a right!" he barked. "Head to the Chelsea Piers as fast as you can!"

Well, that clarified things. Not much, but at least a little. Now I knew the officer had a destination in mind and that we weren't in the middle of an actual horse-and-buggy low-speed chase through central Manhattan.

By this time we were kind of, sort of on our way to the stable where my horse, Nugget, lived. So this route wasn't entirely unfamiliar to me. It was just odd, and at this time of day, very illegal. Normally, I spent my day driving tourists through Central Park. Besides the drive to and from work and a quick U-turn in traffic between customers, I didn't normally drive poor Nugget through the city streets.

And people were staring.

"When you say the Chelsea Piers," I began, "is there some kind of sting operation happening down there, or...?"

I noticed the cop seemed to be breathing just as heavily as he had when he'd hopped in the carriage. And we'd been going long enough that he should have been able to catch his breath by now unless he was horribly out of shape. I cast a quick glance over my shoulder. He didn't look out of shape. In fact, despite the bulk of his winter uniform, he looked like he had a pretty fine shape.

But the color of his face concerned me. The bits of skin I could see between his turned-up collar and pulled-down hat appeared pale. And the way he had a hand pressed against his stomach didn't bode well.

"Are you okay? You're not going to be sick, are you? Nugget really hates vomit. Like seriously, the results aren't pretty. Trust me. This one time—"

"I'm not going to be sick, all right?" the cop said gruffly, cutting me off. "Just keep going. It's urgent."

It was times like these I wished for a rearview mirror so I could get a better look at the man. When it was just a stroll through the park, I could swivel around in my seat to chat with my customers while I trusted Nugget to keep her nose on the horse butt in front of her.

But this was city traffic—stoplights and pedestrian crossings. And we were going at a pretty decent clip which meant less time to react to the unexpected. I had to keep my focus on what I was doing.

"You know I'm not allowed to be driving on city streets like this right now, right?"

"You have my permission," the officer called from the back. "Stop asking so many questions. Jesus."

Not going to happen. Ever. Not asking questions wasn't my thing.

"Are you from the Seventeenth?" I asked, ignoring him and wondering why he was heading so far out of his precinct. Not that I really had a good handle on how NYPD cops handled jurisdictions. It was more that I was hoping to pry information from him about what the hell was going on. "Or Eighteenth maybe?"

"Mpfh," he grunted. "Again with the questions."

A group of tourists with their noses buried in a guidebook suddenly darted into the street in front of Ellen's Stardust Diner, frightening Nugget and scaring the bejeezus out of me. Nugget snorted and veered away from them. Directly toward a sidewalk crowded with street vendors.

I yanked on her reins, but the horse wasn't having it.

The cop let out a curse behind me. "Take Seventh—up there on the left."

"I don't think that's a good id—"

"Do it," he barked.

"If you say so," I said on a sigh. I tugged on the reins, following his directions.

Almost immediately we ground to a halt.

"Can't your horse go any faster?"

Oh hell no. I wasn't letting brave Nugget get blamed for this man's poor decisions. "Not to be a front-seat driver or anything," I said, pausing to cluck my tongue to keep Nugget from nosing the back of a taxi, "but we might get there faster if we didn't head straight into the heart of Times Square."

"What? Oh, god, why? For the love of all that's holy, just get me to the piers."

As soon as I got to Forty-Ninth and turned right, I swiveled back to get a better look at my cop. Or my potential carriagejacker. I wasn't sure which he was at this point.

It seemed like the sort of thing I should probably find out. "So I think perhaps it's time we have a chat, mmkay?"

He looked up from where his face had been buried in his hands. His pallor was ghostly white, and the poor man still appeared a little too close to vomiting for my taste. I took in the bulk of his winter uniform over body armor, dark beard scruff above the black NYPD turtleneck. I couldn't see much of him other than his face, but that was all I needed. He was hot enough to answer the question of whether or not I'd press charges against my kidnapper (no) and whether or not he was worth the loss of income I was experiencing while on this jaunt (also no, because gorgeous didn't pay rent).

I sighed and turned back to face the road, nearly tipping sideways when a couple of tourists jumped into the carriage with their cameras out.

"Get out!" I barked. "Police business! Go!"

"What the hell, dude?" one of the young men asked when the carriage suddenly lurched forward. Nugget must have seen a break in the traffic and taken advantage of an open passing lane. I was pretty sure it was for bicycles only. Regardless, she put on the gas, sending one tourist spinning off the bench to the street and the other one grasping at the reins in my hand.

"Let go," I warned, shoving him off with a shoulder. "You don't want a piece of this, man. We're in the middle of something here."

"Waylon!" the other man shouted from behind us. "Jump off, dude. That man is fucking insane."

"He's right," I growled, trying again to keep the tourist from grabbing at me to stay on the carriage bench. "*Crazy.*"

"Get the hell off of him," came the now-familiar voice behind us.

My knight in navy body armor.

"My parents were right. This city is full of crazies," the tourist muttered before scrambling down at the next red light.

I yelled after him. "Says the man who double-hijacked a fucking horse and buggy!"

"Double-hijack? What does that even mean?" muttered the cop.

I swiveled and waved a hand between us. "What the hell do you call this? First you carriagejack me; then those idiots pile on. This shit is illegal as I'm sure you know. I'm not even allowed to be on this street right now. Section 20-381.1 of the code states that horse-drawn cabs shall not be driven except for that area inside or immediately adjacent to Central Park between the hours of ten in the morning and—"

He gave an exasperated groan. "Like I give a crap about the horse code. Just drive and stop talking!"

Wasn't there a saying about all the hot ones being crazy? Or was that only about women? Either way, it was just my luck. I finally got a hot, presumably single man in my horse carriage and he was either a real cop, which meant most likely straight, or a fake cop, which meant soon-to-be incarcerated.

"Hey, listen," I said over my shoulder. "Before I drop you off, can you come with me really quickly to the nearest precinct office just to verify—"

He shook his head, vehemently. "No deal. I'm undercover. Forget it."

I glanced back at his very obvious uniform. "I'm not sure you know what the word 'undercover' means."

He looked down at himself and cursed. "Never mind. You don't understand. This is important."

I rolled my eyes and made the hand gesture to indicate taking a right on Eleventh, but as soon as I did, the cop-type-person barked out another order. "Left! Go left. It's... it's a matter of life and death."

"Is it though?" I asked while turning left just in case. I'd never been one to disobey the boys in blue. "Is it really?"

"Yes. It really is. If I don't get off this fucking island right now, someone's going to die."

"Is there a getaway boat waiting for you at Chelsea Piers?"

"Don't be ridiculous."

I smothered a chuckle. I didn't want the guy to think I was disrespecting him. Neither cops nor psychos appreciated disrespect.

"Then you're hoping the Circle Line or Liberty tour to Ellis Island is the best bet?"

There was a pause before he spoke up. "Um. Wait. Isn't that where you get the ferry to New Jersey?"

Well, if I wasn't sure before, I certainly was now. No way this man was an NYPD cop. Which meant he was an imposter. Which meant I was probably in way bigger trouble than I realized. Just my luck.

"No, baby doll. That's where you get one free drink ticket while snapping pics with Lady Liberty. I believe you're talking about the Midtown ferry terminal."

"Oh. Yeah. That's it. Take me to that one, then. Thanks."

Seriously? "You do realize I'm not a cab, right?"

He grumbled something in response, but I couldn't hear what. It didn't matter; I was done with our little joyride. Hot or not, this dude wasn't worth me getting in trouble. I started to turn right onto Seventieth, intending to take us back to the park. The fake cop could find some other conveyance to jack if he wanted a ride to the Midtown ferry terminal.

"Hey, wait, where are you going?" he asked as he realized we were headed the wrong way.

Before I could answer, I heard the whoop of a police siren behind me.

"Your friends are here," I singsonged back at him. "Maybe they can take you the rest of the way."

"Fuck, keep going! Don't stop." He stood up and leaned over my shoulder, reaching for the reins and snapping them on Nugget's butt.

Nugget jolted through the turn, throwing the cop back into the carriage bench and me nearly off the side of the driver's seat.

"Woah, woah, girl," I called to Nugget. But apparently, as soon as we were heading east again, she'd spotted the corner of the park and decided she was done with this stupid jaunt and wanted to return to familiar territory.

There was no stopping her. Even when the cops turned on all flashing lights, loud-as-hell sirens, and called for immediate backup.

I was so fucking screwed.

# 2

## ROMAN

*Hollywood Hottie Roman Burke Hijacks Central Park Carriage!*

As I sat in the back of the cop car wondering what the heck my agent was going to say, I glanced at the carriage driver. I'd overheard one of the officers calling him Scotty, but then again, he might have been referring to the horse.

An officer approached the car, and I couldn't help but eye his uniform. Mine was an exact replica and I made a mental note to give the costume designer props for being so accurate. The cop opened the door and ducked his head inside. "Mr. Burke, my supervisor would like to speak to you at the station house. Would you mind coming with us?"

I tried to read his expression to figure out if I was in trouble. "Am I being charged with a crime?" I wasn't an attorney, but I'd played one on TV plenty of times. I at least knew the lingo.

"No, sir. Not yet." He gestured to the carriage driver. "Mr. Pinker doesn't seem inclined to press kidnapping charges at this time, and we remain unsure about whether or not we're going to charge you with impersonating an officer of the law."

My eyes bulged. "Wait, what? Kidnapping?" I cried. "Are you crazy? I didn't kidnap anyone."

Scotty must have overheard me because I could see him over the cop's shoulder. He deftly raised one smartly plucked eyebrow at me.

*Didn't you though?* the raised brow seemed to ask.

I sighed. "I commandeered a vehicle," I explained. "There's a difference." At least I hoped there was.

Now it was the cop's eyebrow's turn to be judgy. "Under what authority?"

"Mine."

He actually rolled his eyes, muttered something about how he wasn't even supposed to be on shift today, and shut the cruiser door in my face. Of course the paparazzi had already arrived. I never understood how they did it, but the moment anything salacious happened, they managed to show up practically within the minute, cameras flashing.

They surged around the sidewalk and street, trying to get photos of me in the back of the cop car. I could already see the headline now: *Is Casting Roman Burke a Recipe for PR Disaster?* My agent would be apoplectic. I sighed and pressed my fingers against my eyes. Filming on the movie was almost wrapped, only a few days left. I'd been so close to making it through without any trouble.

"Directors like working with actors who don't end up in the news for things like mistaking his wife and his daughter. On the red carpet during premiere night. That kind of press tends to reflect poorly on the movie," my agent had told me when I'd signed on to my current project. "So maybe try not to cause trouble this time around?"

I'd swallowed a number of choice retorts, knowing it wouldn't matter what I said. He knew as well as I did that I wasn't that much of a troublemaker. I just had a penchant for being in the wrong place at the wrong time and putting my foot in my mouth when I got nervous. Somehow the paparazzi always captured it on film. Like the time I accidentally drove the wrong rental car off the lot and was charged with grand theft auto or the time I got seasick all over the president of the Motion Picture Academy during a fund-raising party on a yacht.

Then there was the time I thought I was giving money to a single mom, but it turned out she was both a single mom *and* a high-paid escort.

It had gotten to the point that I was such a magnet for stupid, easily misinterpreted moments that I'd become almost a recluse when I wasn't actively filming.

And now here I was again.

As the paparazzi swarmed, trying to push around the cop car, I did my best to keep my face scrunched down into the collar of my thick winter coat so they couldn't get a clear shot of me. No picture, no headline, no scandal. Or so I hoped.

Just in case, I pulled out my phone to dial Oscar. Better he hear it from me than someone else.

He picked up after the first ring. "This better be good. I'm naked and waiting under a sheet for Paulo."

I double-checked the phone to make sure I'd dialed the right number, even though I recognized Oscar's voice. "Who the hell is Paulo?"

"My masseuse."

"Why do you have your phone on the massage table with you?"

"Why are you asking me questions right now?" Oscar countered.

"Oh, right. Well, you see... I might accidentally be in the back of a cop car." I tried to quickly sum up what had happened.

"Um, Ro-Ro?" Oscar interrupted in a high-pitched voice. He seemed overly concerned.

"Don't call me that," I grumbled. "I thought we talked about this."

"Romaine Lettuce, are you telling me you're in the back of a paddy wagon right now in custody of the po-po?"

"I'm not sure I know what any of those words mean."

"Why did you call me instead of your lawyer?" he shouted.

The loud noise made me jump and grab at my chest. "Dammit, Oscar, did you not hear the part about me having a panic attack on the set? Don't scare me like that."

"Call my friend James. He's a lawyer. Oh wait. He's the money kind."

"I have money," I assured him. "That's not a problem."

"No, I mean, he lawyers stuff related to money. Or business... or something. I don't know if he does violent crimes."

"This isn't a violent crime," I snapped. "I just... made a mistake."

"You know who else says that?" Oscar asked with a sniff. "Violent criminals. Just sayin'."

I sighed. "Fine. Give me his number."

"Whose number?"

I hung up on him. Maybe instead of calling the last guy I'd dated, I needed to call my crisis manager instead. I let out a breath and dialed again.

"Why'd you hang up on me?" Oscar asked. "I was trying to help you."

I reminded myself that despite our disaster of a date, the man was a PR genius.

"I know. I need you to run point for me with the producer and director. They're probably freaking out right now. And with how many freaking photographers are here, there's no chance this isn't already hitting the internet big-time."

Finally Oscar seemed to pull his shit together and take me seriously. "I already texted the director. The producer is probably too busy crying to be much help. Every minute you're not on set is costing them thousands."

"Don't do that, dammit," I hissed. "That doesn't help my anxiety."

"What happened on set?" Oscar asked gently, sounding genuinely concerned. "Did something trigger the panic attack?"

Thankfully, I was saved from having to answer by the return of the cop. My panic attack and what caused it wasn't something I particularly wanted to dive into right now.

"Just smooth things over with the director and producer, okay?" I told him. "I gotta go."

"But wait—"

I hung up on him again and let out a breath. I was an actor for god's sake. One of the best, if past awards and box office numbers were any indication. I should at least be able to act like a man who wasn't on the verge of a panic attack. I closed my eyes, trying to remember what it felt like to be calm. Not on edge. No pressure, no stress. Usually I could pull on another character like a change of clothes. Right now, however, I was finding it difficult.

The cop opened the door and leaned in. I gave him my best Hollywood smile. "This has all simply been a misunderstanding... you see, I'm playing a cop in the new *Deep Cut* film. We were shooting over by the Park when... ah... something happened."

"Wait... wait..." He peered closer at me. I waited, knowing exactly what came next. I'd experienced it a thousand times. Recognition hit and his face went slack. "You're *that* Roman Burke? Like from the movies *Death Pawn* and *Back Passage*?"

I would have paid back *years* of lucrative royalties to get them to have changed the title of that movie. But you didn't always choose which ones hit it big, and that movie had helped launch my career.

I amped up the wattage of my smile. "Yes, that was me. And I really need to get back to the set as soon as I can. I'm sure you understand."

He frowned. "Is that why you jumped into Mr. Pinker's carriage? To hitch a ride to the set?"

I wondered if I would be in less trouble if that was the case. But I wasn't really comfortable with lying to a cop, so I hewed as close to the truth as I could. "That's the direction we were headed in when we were pulled over."

He tapped a pen against the citation booklet he'd been scribbling in. I tried to get a glance at what he'd written to see what kind of trouble I was in.

"There's still the issue of impersonating an officer," he pointed out.

I held up my hands, giving him my most earnestly innocent expression. "I didn't impersonate an officer. I never said I was a cop. How can that be impersonating an officer?"

The officer opened his mouth, paused, and closed it again. Then he blew out a breath. "Well, I guess it was really Mr. Pinker who broke the law here with his unlawful drive through the city during these hours." He brought up his citation pad again and glared over at the carriage driver. "We can't let these people jam up city streets and scare the tourists."

I stared at him. I didn't really appreciate the tone of voice he'd used or the implication behind the words. It made me want to jump to Scotty's defense. "I'm not sure *these people* scared much of anyone," I snapped.

The officer frowned and I realized my tone probably hadn't helped either of our cases. Belatedly, I realized what Oscar always called my "Hollywood Charm" might come in handy in this situation. The paparazzi were going to get their shots regardless, so I might as well stage a few that would be flattering.

I stepped out of the vehicle and reached out my hand to shake his. My height immediately dwarfed the officer, and the breadth of my shoulders cast a shadow across the side of his face. He peered up at me, and I grinned, removing my hat and raking a hand through my hair. I tipped my mouth into a lopsided grin.

Oscar called it my "aw shucks, I'm just the awkward boy from next door who grew up to be hot" move. It had graced the cover of dozens of magazines and sold millions of movie tickets. It was my signature look and made me instantly recognizable to anyone who hadn't been living under a rock for the last ten years..

Two or three women squealed from the nearby crowd while the paparazzi scrambled to snap photos. Several people screamed my name trying to get my attention, but I tried to block them out of my mind. Instead, I glanced at the carriage driver, wondering how he would react to the news of who I was.

For a moment he didn't react at all and I felt an odd twist of disappointment. Then he seemed to recognize me and his eyes widened. My grin grew. I wondered if he'd want an autograph. At least that would give me the opportunity to talk to him again. Now that my panic attack had eased and I wasn't so emotionally raw and ragged around the edges, maybe I could even charm him into agreeing to grab coffee.

He was cute as hell, after all. And pretty funny as well, now that I thought about it.

The moment the thought went through my head, Scotty's face snapped back into a scowl. It was obvious he was pissed as hell at me. Which was a shame because I really liked the idea of spending more time with him.

But first, I had to make sure neither of us got arrested. I returned my focus to the cop. "I'm so sorry to be causing such trouble for you today, Officer Maltman," I said, reading the name tag quickly before shaking the officer's hand. "I'm sure you have much better things to do than press charges against this poor man. We can hardly blame him for racing away from the pursuing crowd of reporters," I said, tilting my head toward the swarm of photographers and people holding up phone cameras. "I'm sure he was concerned for his safety."

The carriage driver—Scotty—balked. Twin spots of red rose in his cheeks, making him look even more adorable. "What? Are you freaking—"

I cut him off with a look. "Besides, he was being compensated by the production company. I'm sure they have all the proper paperwork in hand." While Oscar was no miracle worker, he was a sly fox when he needed to be. I was sure he was already on top of things in the background, Paulo or not.

The officer looked unsure. "But—"

I spotted an angry-looking man approaching us with a no-nonsense expression on his face. He seemed to be Officer Maltman's superior because Officer Maltman began kissing ass. "Captain Baker, this is—"

"I know who this is. Mr. Burke, sorry for the misunderstanding. You're free to go. Officer Maltman, why don't you give Mr. Burke a ride to his set so we can start clearing the crowd away?"

The officer shrugged and started toward his car. I smiled at the captain and opened my mouth to thank him, but he stopped me before I could get it out.

"I think we can both agree it's in our best interest to call this a misunderstanding and get the hell out of here, correct?" he said low enough that he couldn't be overheard by the press.

I blinked. "Yes, sir," I immediately responded. "Thank you."

He nodded. "Good day." He began to walk away, but I stopped him.

"And the carriage driver?" I asked, sneaking a peek at the young man in the gray scarf who'd ferried me through the city streets. "I would hate for him to get into trouble because—"

The captain turned to the young man. "Mr. Pinker, you're free to go. Your medallion owner would like a word with you at the stables."

Scotty's face dropped, the color in his cheeks draining. He spun and climbed back into the carriage without saying a word. His entire demeanor had changed. I wanted to call after him, but I was acutely aware of the cameras snapping. I didn't need to drag him into my mess, and if I made a big production of going after him, that's exactly what I'd be doing. Instead I made a mental note to have Oscar follow up with him to make sure he didn't get in trouble.

I followed Officer Maltman to his car and was just climbing into the passenger seat when one of the reporters broke through the line of cops trying to hold them back. "Mr. Burke, is this at all related to Polly Macari's claim that she's carrying your love child?"

I froze and snapped my head around, trying to find out where the question had come from. It was breaking the cardinal rule that one should never feed the paparazzi, but I couldn't help it. The question had come out of nowhere.

Before I could locate the reporter, another one called out, "You look surprised. According to her agent's press release a few minutes ago, you're the father of her child. Are you denying her claim?"

Surprised was an understatement. What the hell was Polly thinking? A press release? Claiming I was the father of her child?

She and I hadn't even dated for fuck's sake. Much less slept together. In what world would Polly and I have a "love" child?

But I knew better than to say anything. All my years of public relations training to keep a neutral face were put to the test as I schooled myself not to react. If Polly had told the world I was the father of her unborn child, there had to be a reason. And it had better be a good one.

I just needed to find out what it was before saying anything publicly. "No comment," I ground out between clenched teeth before slipping back into the cop car.

# 3

SCOTTY - TWO WEEKS LATER

*Sorrel Spotted Stalking SoHo!*

I HATED alliteration with the heat of a thousand suns. As I strode up West End Avenue in the predawn hours, I tried not to notice the stupid tabloid headline screaming at me from every newsstand. You'd think two weeks would be long enough for everyone to forget about my little jaunt through the park with Roman Burke, but apparently not. And every single headline was a reminder of just how much my life had been fucked the day that man jumped into my carriage.

When I finally found the brownstone I was looking for—which wasn't difficult since a handful of die-hard paparazzi were camped out in front of it—I wrapped Nugget's lead around the handrail and raced up the few steps to the front door before pounding on the thick wood with my fist.

"Open up, asshole!" I barked. I gave exactly zero shits about what his neighbors thought, or the photographers for that matter.

I found the doorbell and laid on it with my thumb, pressing in and out over and over until it was time to bang my fists on the door again. My steel-toed boots found the kickplate and taught it a few lessons too. This motherfucking asshole was going to answer to me.

And Nugget.

After many minutes of sustained attack upon the entry to Roman Burke's residence, the door finally opened, revealing the man himself in all of his gorgeous, albeit angry, glory.

So... so much glory. He was tall. So tall. And had thick, bed-rumpled dark hair that begged for my fingers. And there were... muscles and... stuff.

I sighed and reminded myself I was here on a mission.

"What... what's happening?" he grumbled, rubbing his eyes over dark, delicious stubble. He stood in the entry in low-hanging pajama pants and absolutely nothing else. Which was unfortunate, because it meant I had to spend a good two or three minutes just gawping and drooling before I could give him what for.

When he finally seemed awake enough to recognize me, his eyes widened. "You."

"Yeah, me. I've come to bring you a horse," I said as assertively as I could. "Asshole," I added under my breath, because, c'mon. It was needed, if only to remind me why I was there.

He blinked.

I flapped my arms toward Nugget. "A horse! That horse. You know, the one you completely fucked over when you went on your merry chase through the city? The poor girl who was nothing but an innocent pawn in your game. The mare who's been maligned by the press as a—"

He held up a hand. "I get it." His eyes darted to the photographers, who'd stirred and begun snapping pictures. "Do you think maybe you could keep your voice down?"

The nerve of this man. "No. I cannot," I said, raising my voice instead. Just to be ornery because Roman Burke deserved it. "Thanks to you and your little jaunt, Nugget and I are homeless. I can handle it, but she can't. She needs a roof over her head and decent feed. If she gets caught roaming the streets, they're going to take her away from me and do god only knows what to her."

Roman winced and blinked again. "I think maybe I haven't had any coffee yet?"

I hopped down the steps, untied Nugget, and led her back up the stairs to the double doors. My every movement was followed by a riot of camera shutters snapping around me like the jaws of hungry crocodiles. I ignored them. I'd gotten good at it after a few of the paparazzi had tried following me for a few days after the fake-cop joyride incident.

I reached the top of the stairs, horse in tow. "Then let's get you some coffee. Move out of the way." I shouldered past him, opening up the second part of the double door and leading Nugget through it. The floor of the entry hall had a nice, glossy tile which assured me the movie star's household staff wouldn't have a difficult time cleaning up Nugget's indiscretions.

"Where's the coffee maker?" I asked over my shoulder. When there was no answer, I looked back and found Roman staring at the back end of Nugget.

"Is... is there a horse in my house?"

"She's very well mannered. Don't worry about it."

"I... but... I don't think there's supposed to be—"

I cut him off. "I said don't worry about it."

"But the paparazzi." He ran a hand down his face. "They just saw—"

The man really needed to focus. I snapped my fingers, hoping to break him out of it. "They saw a polite man invite a guest in for coffee."

His brows furrowed. "I'm not sure they'd agree with that characterization."

I rolled my eyes. "Fine. It was either let us in or have this conversation in front of the tabloid press. I assume the horse in the house is the lesser of two evils, yes? Now, where's the coffee?"

He thought that through for a moment, ultimately coming to the same conclusion. "Right, in the kitchen," he said. I stared at him, indicating that his response had not been helpful. "Oh, um. Upstairs on the next floor," he added. His eyes slid to Nugget again. "But surely she can't join us."

"Don't be ridiculous. She doesn't even like coffee. You don't happen to have a terrace out back or a fenced-in... yard or anything, do you?"

Roman looked around as if the answer was hanging next to one of the landscape paintings on his perfectly styled wall. "Um... no? I mean, there's a small patio, but it's..." He blew out a breath and raked a hand through his messy hair, revealing dark armpit hair that wanted to be sniffed and licked by... people. "It's open to the street right now because the paparazzi pulled part of the fence down last week."

I shook myself out of the stupor. "Is that how they caught that photo of Polly on your couch?"

He crooked an eyebrow, a slow grin starting to tilt his lips. "You been reading the news about me?"

Yes. But he didn't need to know that. I lifted a shoulder dismissively, hoping he didn't notice the flush heating my cheeks. "It was on every newsstand. Impossible to live in this city and *not* see it."

It was time to change the subject. "If the patio's off-limits, we'll just let Nugget hang out here for now." I shrugged and let my over-stuffed backpack drop to the ground, before gesturing toward the stairs. "Lead the way to the kitchen."

Roman reluctantly started making his way around the edges of the foyer, keeping his body facing Nugget as if the horse might suddenly turn feral and bite him on the ass.

I ignored him and gave a stern warning to Nugget. "Behave. Your new daddy isn't going to treat you well if you make a mess in here. Don't fuck this up for us."

She made a *pppbbbttt* sound and began to nibble on the corner of one of the landscapes. Good enough.

When I turned to start up the stairs after Roman, I came face-to-face with a Hollywood-perfect ass. His low-slung pajama bottoms sat low enough that the twin divots above each cheek were clearly visible, and the material of the pants was thin enough that I could almost, *almost*, see through them. There was no way I couldn't *not* watch the way the muscles contracted as he took each step. The movement was mesmerizing.

*Don't look at his ass*, I scolded myself. That led me to look up at his back instead, the smooth expanse of skin rippling over sculpted muscles. Was it suddenly hot in here, or was it just me?

I scowled. *It's irrelevant*, I reminded myself. *Even though the man is bi, he's way out of your league, jackass.*

And that was a fact. Roman Burke was arguably the hottest star in moviedom these days. Sure, he'd had an unfortunate dip in his career due to some not-so-flattering news stories, but he was already on track to get an Oscar nomination for his recent role in *The Last Blue Curve*, so I had to assume he was doing just fine.

Fine enough to stable a horse anyway.

"Don't suppose you have a chef in this place who could whip me up a hot meal, do you?" I asked, trying to remind myself of my priorities. Number one, take care of Nugget. Number two, take care of me. And if I didn't get at least a little food today, I was going to be in trouble.

"You like eggs?" he asked when he reached the top of the stairs. He glanced back at me, and there was something so casual about the movement, so familiar, as if I was a friend rather than a stranger who'd just barged my way into his house. With a horse.

It set me a little off balance. I'd expected him to try to get rid of me as quickly as possible, not offer to cook for me. "No, but I'll eat them anyway," I said, not really quite sure how to react to the unexpected hospitality. "I'll take anything you're willing to part with."

He nodded and led me down a hall and into a space-age kitchen, something fresh out of a fancy magazine. It was huge, with a wall of windows along the far side and countertops that seemed to stretch for miles.

"Holy fuck," I blurted, looking around. "You must be really serious about your food."

"Mpfh," he grunted, making his way to a high-tech coffee machine of some kind. "Espresso? Cappuccino?"

"Um... coffee? Would be good?" I wandered through the room, running my hand along the cold marble surface of the counters. "I've never seen a kitchen like this in real life."

He paused in the middle of pouring coffee beans into some sort of shiny bullet thing and glanced at me. "What do you mean?"

I shrugged. "It's huge, for one. I don't even know what all those appliances are for." I gestured toward a space-gray box built into the cabinetry. Right next to it was a small flat-screen panel the size of a cell phone. "Like, what's that for?"

He blinked. "It's a microwave," he said in a deadpan voice. "Surely you've seen a microwave before."

I narrowed my eyes at him, careful not to let them lower to take in the expanse of his smooth bare chest. Which was very, very tempting. "I know what a microwave is. I've just never needed to call one before."

He wrinkled his forehead. "Huh?"

I pointed to the cell phone screen next to the microwave.

"Oh." He chuckled. "That's not part of the microwave. That's the smart fridge." He said it as though it were obvious. When in fact, it very much wasn't.

I looked around, noticing the lack of fridge. "Is it smart because it's not here?"

He laughed again. "It's here. But you can tap on the screen to see what's in it instead of opening the door and letting all the cold air out." He turned back to the task of making the coffee.

I thought about the night spent curled up in Nugget's crowded stall at the stables last night. How I'd been lucky to have access to cool, clean water for me and horse feed for Nugget. "Right," I said softly. "Good. Wouldn't want to spoil all that food by looking at it too much."

Roman glanced at me with the crinkled forehead again, but I cleared my throat and barreled ahead. After all, we had business to discuss.

"So, she gets clean alfalfa hay at night and horse feed during the day. Right now she's been on—"

Now Roman looked really confused. "Who does?"

"Nugget," I told him. The *duh* was silent. "You know, the horse. You may remember her from such things as flinging you across Manhattan and being downstairs in your entry right now."

Roman threw up his hands. "Whoa. *Whoa.* Hold on. I am *not* taking care of your horse. I don't have a place to put a horse. Don't be ridiculous. I don't even want a horse."

And, with that, I lost whatever final thread had been holding my composure together.

I slammed my hand on the counter. "Oh! You don't want a horse?" I asked in a high-pitched screech. "Well, why didn't you say something? Here I thought you needed a horse to round out your fucking celebrity status. You know the one? The one where you're the baby daddy of Polly's unplanned pregnancy? The one where you've vowed on every fucking news outlet to support her financially even though she's a megastar in her own right and has millions of dollars? So, just to be clear, you're happy to support a baby who doesn't need shit from you but not an innocent horse who never fucking asked for this and whose worst crime was taking your scammer ass across town for shits and giggles?"

When I finally paused long enough to suck in a breath, I realized he was staring at me with his dark stubbled jaw on the floor. He slowly closed his mouth and swallowed.

"I'm sorry. Remind me of your name again?"

That was when my hunger and stress from the past couple of days caught up to me and I sank like a dirty lump onto his pristine hardwood floors in a dead faint.

# 4

## ROMAN

*City Courier Claims Equine Enters Burke Brownstone*

I POKED at the guy with my bare toes.

"Um, sir? You... you seem to have lost your feet, there."

He didn't move. Shit, I was going to have to touch him. Which was fine, except he was a little bit filthy. And by that I meant a lot bit.

I squatted down and reached for his neck, easily finding his pulse under his dirty-blond scruff. As I came closer to him, I noticed smudges of dirt in his skin and the recognizable scent of hay and the outdoors. Had he been *sleeping* with his horse?

"Carriage driver man," I said, nudging him gently now that I knew his heart was still beating. His coat was worn and stained, and his boots were dirty enough I should have asked for him to remove them downstairs.

But the man under the dirty and worn clothes was unexpected—at odds with his outward appearance. He had fine features and a delicate, youthful complexion. That surprised me considering he spent all day in the sun driving his carriage through the park. I would have thought he'd have sun- and wind-roughened skin.

Maybe he hadn't been doing the job very long. Or maybe he was diligent about applying sunscreen.

"Scotty," he mumbled.

"No. I'm Roman. Roman Burke," I corrected before remembering Scotty was the name the cops had used for the carriage driver.

His eyes opened and then narrowed, but not before I noticed how blue they were. "I know who you are." His snappish tone caused me to wince.

"Shit, sorry. You meant that *you're* Scotty. Right. I remember that now."

His nostrils flared. I wasn't really helping things by babbling. "I think the first order of business is to get you some food. Let me help you to the table." I reached under his back and helped him up, catching another whiff of horse with an underlying scent of a man in need of a shower. It wasn't really unpleasant, just... wrong, somehow, as if he was normally quite put together.

As I gripped one of his hands, I realized I remembered these same long, slender fingers from that day in the carriage. I'd noticed them holding the reins gracefully since it had been so different from how I would have clutched at them for dear life. His nails were meticulously clean and trimmed despite the outward appearance of the rest of him.

"I'm sorry," he said, adding more apologies to the general air of remorse in the room. "I haven't really eaten."

I frowned. I didn't like hearing that. "In how long?"

He shrugged, not quite meeting my eyes. "Since yesterday morning maybe? Or the night before?"

He hadn't eaten in over twenty-four hours? No wonder he was light-headed. "Why?"

He glared at me. "Because I got fucking fired after an asshole forced me to drive my carriage through Manhattan, and I had to spend all my fucking savings on keeping my horse fed and stabled while I tried to find another job."

Oh.

After mumbling yet another apology while helping him settle on a stool at the center island, I returned to the stove to figure out what to cook for him. Wait. He'd said he didn't care for eggs. "You like pancakes?"

Scotty's head came up, and I was struck again by his clear blue eyes. I didn't remember those from the carriage ride day. But then again I hadn't really been in the best mental state at the time.

He smiled. "Are there people who don't like pancakes?"

He had a point. I pulled a package of strawberries from the fridge and rinsed them under the tap before placing them in a bowl in front of Scotty along with a cup of coffee and the fixings for it. "Get started with this," I told him.

He wolfed down the fruit and coffee before I even had the pancake batter mixed. I paused to refill his mug before returning to the stove and pouring out the first batch. He chucked in a bunch of cream and sugar before starting on it like it was his first cup. When the first batch of pancakes was ready, I put a fat stack in front of him with butter and syrup.

"Thanks, man. I really appreciate it," he said before digging in. He swallowed his first bite and hummed in appreciation. I tried not to notice the drop of syrup clinging to his bottom lip. Or to think about how badly I wanted to lean across the counter and lick it off. How sweet his mouth would taste right now, a mixture of strawberries and butter and sugar and coffee.

I cleared my throat and turned back to the stove, trying to get my thoughts under control. The man was a stranger, I reminded myself. And he literally smelled like a barn.

And he was sweet and funny and adorable and had the kind of body that I would love to—

No. I would *not* allow my thoughts to go there. Scotty was a complication. A rather huge one given the horse that was doing god knew what in my entry downstairs. Not to mention whatever photos the paparazzi had gotten of them coming into my house. I was surprised I hadn't already gotten a call from Oscar or my agent.

Shit. Oscar. He was going to be furious when he heard about this. I was supposed to be leaving town today—supposed to be going to his cottage in Vermont to lie low while the Polly Pregnancy Scandal raged.

But Scotty had been right. It would have been career suicide to allow him to let loose in front of all the reporters camped out in front of my house. If I hadn't let him and his horse in, he'd have thrown his fit in front of dozens of video cameras and cell phones, and it would be trending online within minutes. And I was already in enough trouble for my jaunt through Central Park without even more press coverage of the eventual fallout.

Scotty forked another mouthful of pancakes into his mouth with another appreciative groan. I tried not to let the sound make me think of other things that might make him groan.

"Didn't know you had it in you," he said, adding another glug of syrup to his plate.

I glanced over at him and frowned. "What's that supposed to mean?"

Scotty studied me while he chewed. "Figured you for someone who had his meals brought in."

I thought about how I normally had my meals brought in.

"I can cook," I protested. *I'm not defensive; who's defensive?*

"Mm-hm," he said, waving a bite through the air. "These aren't half-bad."

"High praise indeed," I scoffed. "I'll have you know I won a prize for my apple pie in the county fair in fifth grade."

Scotty stopped chewing and stared at me. "No."

"I sure did." I unpuffed my chest from where it had accidentally gotten braggy. "Just ask the Hamilton County judges from the year Juanita took the Prettiest Sow Award in the Nebraska—"

Scotty began choking on his pancakes. I scrambled over and whacked him on the back. When he finally regained his composure, he smirked at me. "I stand corrected. I'm eating the work of a master chef."

"Shut up," I grumbled before turning back to my own batch of pancakes. "My point is, I can cook a damned pancake."

"You used pancake mix."

I fisted a hand on my hip. "I added my own special flair."

He didn't seem as impressed as he should have been. "Was the flair vanilla extract?" he asked. "Because that suggestion is right there on the box."

I narrowed my eyes at him. "Would you like your pancakes to go? Because that can be arranged. And I'm sure your horse won't mind the citations she gets on the city streets this time of day. Not to mention the attention from the press when you're spotted leaving my house."

I'd meant it as a joke, but Scotty didn't take it that way. His face fell, his eyes cutting away and then down to his lap. "Fuck you."

My heart climbed into my throat. I'd struck a nerve, and a raw one at that. He looked so suddenly sad and dejected, the complete opposite of how he normally was. It was wrong and weird, and all I knew was that I needed to fix it.

I reached across the island and placed my hand over his. His skin was softer than I'd expected for a man who handled leather reins all day. "Hey," I said. He didn't look up. I squeezed his fingers. "Hey," I said again.

Finally Scotty's eyes met mine. There was a slight sheen to them, and I noticed a muscle ticking along his jaw, as though he were clenching his teeth to keep from crying. Something inside me threatened to break at the thought of this man spilling any tears. Especially if I was the one to cause them.

"I'm sorry," I said softly.

He held my eyes a moment longer, and I found myself unable to breathe. Then Scotty looked away again and I could finally draw air.

"S'okay," he said.

"It's not," I said.

He pulled his hand out from under mine and placed it in his lap, shrugging. I pressed my palm against the cold marble of the counter, missing the soft warmth of him.

Scotty the carriage driver might be all smiles and jokes, but I wondered if maybe part of that was a defense mechanism, a way to protect himself against the world. Perhaps I'd let his good humor distract me from the severity of the problems he was facing.

I pulled the remaining pancakes off the stove, piling several more onto Scotty's plate before fixing my own. I took the stool kitty-corner from him at the island so I could at least see his profile while we ate.

"Did they really fire you?" I asked.

He nodded. "That same day."

"But it wasn't your fault!"

"Tell that to them."

"I will." And I meant it too.

He rolled his eyes at me.

"No, really," I insisted. I noticed that Scotty hadn't touched the new stack of pancakes. I pushed the butter and syrup closer to him. "I'll tell them they have to hire you back."

"No offense, Roman, but not everyone listens to you. Especially my homophobic boss who was already looking for an excuse to can my gay ass."

The mention of his gay ass got the attention of my own bi ass, as well as other parts of my anatomy that were perfectly happy to hear the news of his sexuality. But my blood was too busy boiling with injustice to spend much time on that new piece of information. I'd have to come back to it later.

"That's illegal," I bit out.

"Right. Let me call my attorney real quick." He patted at his pockets like he was looking for something. "Oh wait, I don't have one. Oh wait, I don't even have a phone anymore to make that call with."

My stomach dropped. "You don't have a phone?"

Scotty barked out a laugh. "Why do you sound more surprised about that than me being hungry?"

"Everyone gets hungry," I said before realizing he hadn't meant hungry. He'd meant *hunger*. As in, *can't* eat, not *didn't* eat. "Oh."

He flapped his hand at me. "Go back to your Nebraska naiveté and eat your damned pancakes."

With that he snatched the bottle of syrup, pouring it liberally over his plate. As I watched him return to his own food, I realized how far apart our lives were. My biggest problem right now was my reputation. Sure I had a small army of paparazzi waiting outside my door for me every morning, but I also had millions of dollars in the bank and a staggeringly successful career in film.

This guy didn't have a phone or even food, and here I was worried about a little celebrity gossip? It wasn't fair. Especially since I'd been responsible for him ending up in this situation.

"What do you need?" I asked as gently as I could. "I'd like to help you."

Scotty took a breath and looked over at me. I expected him to refuse the offer out of some misplaced sense of machoism or something and that I was then going to have to convince him. But he surprised me by saying, "I need somewhere safe to put my horse. And I need another job so I can find a place to live and afford feed and hay for Nugget."

His honesty was refreshing. Even if the vulnerability in his eyes twisted at my heart.

I frowned. "Wait. I assumed the horse was owned by your boss. But you're saying it's yours?"

"*She* is mine. Yes. It's a long story, but she's mine." He blew out a long breath. "And as of last night, we're both homeless. Being homeless in the city is one thing. Being homeless on horseback in the city is another."

I bit my tongue hard to keep from laughing. It wasn't funny, but the image of him wandering the streets on a horse with bags and ratty sleeping bags hanging off the saddle horn made me want to chuckle.

As if to hit home the point that his situation wasn't funny, Scotty added, "If they catch her, they're going to take her away from me, Roman. She's all I have left."

Those words, the way his voice cracked saying them, the pain in his expression, it was like he was laying himself bare to me, right there in my kitchen. He was desperate, that much was obvious. And he'd come to me for help. Probably because he had no other options, but still.

The way Scotty held his chin in a defiant tilt made it clear he wasn't a man who asked for help often or easily. But he was asking me. Somehow, that he was willing to entrust me with this part of himself felt like a rare gift.

I placed a hand on his arm. "I'll figure something out," I told him. "I'm not going to let you lose your horse."

His chin wobbled and he glanced away for a long moment before clearing his throat and looking down at his empty plate. "Can you make some more pancakes first?"

I laughed and whipped up another batch. As he ate I cleaned the dishes, trying my hardest not to notice the faint smell of horse poop wafting up from downstairs. I was going to have to find another place for that horse to stay sooner rather than later.

When Scotty finished devouring his fourth stack of pancakes—even though he was small, the man could eat—I suggested he take a shower upstairs while I researched nearby stables.

"Yeah, okay," he said, glancing over his shoulder at the stairs. "You're not, like, going to call the police and have them come arrest me while I'm naked in the shower, are you?"

I pictured him naked in the shower. I couldn't help it. I imagined the water hitting his shoulders and sluicing down his slim, naked body. Curving around lithe muscles and catching in hair as it traveled lower and lower and—

"Dammit, Roman." He snapped his fingers in my face, bringing me back to reality. "Are you going to report me the minute I'm out of your sight?"

I shook my head and blinked at him, realizing I must have taken an unusually long pause while considering what it would feel like to rub the soap between my palms and then slide them down his bare back, how they would curve just perfectly over his ass. Ungh.

"Roman. Focus."

"Huh? No. No. Of course not." I cleared my throat and gestured vaguely toward the stairs leading to the entry. "I'm going to try and find somewhere for the horse."

"Nugget," Scotty corrected.

"Nugget. For Nugget. Yes."

Scotty narrowed his eyes at me again and crossed his arms over his chest. "Don't fuck me over, Roman Burke. I have friends at the *Wall Street Journal*."

He was so obviously lying, I almost laughed. For some reason, this little street urchin made me feel a strange kind of bubbly giddiness. Just having him feisty and real here in my house made me want to shout with joy. Finally, something besides the depressing situation with Polly and the paparazzi and my career to concentrate on.

"I'm not going to fuck you over, Scotty," I assured him. "Lord knows I can't handle the *Wall Street Journal* coming at me with... what? Accusations of horse thievery? Of feeding the homeless?"

The edge of Scotty's mouth curled, but he tried to maintain his air of annoyance at me. "What about carriagejacking? And impersonating an officer? You never even got charged with those things."

"If I recall," I shot back, "that entire episode was captured on video and broadcast all over the damned internet. In fact, because of that little jaunt through the city and the situation with Polly, I'm supposed to be packing up and fleeing the city right about now. So do your worst, carriage boy. You don't scare me."

Just then we heard the sound of liquid splattering onto tile downstairs. It took about half a second to realize Nugget was voicing her displeasure with a stream of powerful horse urine.

I locked eyes with Scotty, but before I could express my own displeasure at him, he shot up the stairs to the guest room and bath.

"Yeah, you'd better run!" I shouted after him anyway. "And don't think I'm cleaning that up!"

It wasn't until I turned back to my laptop that I remembered what I'd said about promising Oscar I'd be leaving the city today. The moment filming for *Deep Cut* had wrapped, he'd insisted I take time away from the city and the constant presence of paparazzi in order to give the recent news stories a chance to die down. "No photos, no scandals," he'd reminded me.

He'd offered me his cottage in Vermont and said it would be a great place to relax, get my head on straight, and figure out what project I wanted to work on next. I'd agreed. Living under the constant eye of the press was exhausting. It would be nice to go somewhere I could scratch my balls without it becoming national news.

Just then my phone buzzed with a text. It was from Oscar, of course. He had a preternatural ability to know when someone was thinking about him. Honestly, it was unsettling at times.

He got straight to the point.

**Oscar:** *There's a horse in your house.*

Well, that answered the question of when the photos from this morning would get out.

**Me:** *Yes.*

**Oscar:** *A horse.*

**Me:** *Yes.*

**Oscar:** *In your house.*

**Me:** *Yes.*

**Oscar:** *I did not know this was a thing that could happen.*

**Me:** *Apparently it is.*

**Oscar:** *I can see that. In great detail. In fact, I'm looking at several pictures of it right now. On Twitter. Where the horse in your house is trending.*

**Me:** *LOL?*

**Oscar:** *Or something.*

**Me:** *Her name is Nugget.*

**Oscar:** *Well that clears everything up.*

**Me:** *I thought it might.*

**Oscar:** *Hey, speaking of things that shouldn't be in your house right now: you. Aren't you supposed to be on your way to my cottage in Vermont this very moment?*

**Me:** *I was packing when Scotty came with Nugget.*

It wasn't exactly a lie. Sure I'd been in bed when Scotty started waging war on my front door, but I'd at least been mentally packing.

**Oscar:** *Scotty would be that adorable street urchin who accompanied said horse?*

I felt myself smile. I couldn't help it.

**Me:** *Yes.*

**Oscar:** *Well, seems like you have everything under control so I'll just go back to doing Reiki.*

**Me:** *Energy healing?*

**Oscar:** *Ricky. Stupid voice to text.*

**Me:** *Wait. Your cottage in Vermont — you said there was some land around it. There wouldn't happen to be a barn up there, would there? I find myself in need of a place to store a horse.*

# 5

## SCOTTY

*Burke's Blunder Gets Carriage Driver Canned*

I STEPPED out of Roman Burke's palatial shower feeling like a new man. I'd stood under the steaming spray for at least twenty minutes, letting it scour away several days' worth of dirt and grime. Most of that time I'd also been acutely aware of the fact that I was standing naked in the same place Roman stood naked every morning.

Of course it hadn't been difficult for my imagination to make the leap between that thought and the image of Roman standing there naked now. With me. Both of us naked together. He was so much bigger than I was—so much taller and wider, and I'd wondered if that meant other parts of him were bigger as well, and if so, what kind of size were we talking about?

I swallowed, the thought setting my blood on fire and sending it south. But as much as I wanted to indulge in the thought of Roman Burke running massive soapy hands over my body, that particular fantasy was going to have to wait. I was pretty sure someone like Roman would have an unending supply of hot water, but I didn't want to test that theory. There was nothing worse than having a good shower stroking session interrupted by a literal douse of cold water.

Plus, I had to remember that Roman was the reason I was in this mess to begin with.

Once I was out of the shower and dry, I reached for my backpack only to remember that I'd left it, and therefore my one remaining set of clean clothes, in the entry foyer. I started to pull on the clothes I'd been wearing earlier, but the stench and filth of them was too much. Wearing those, even just to sneak downstairs and back, would put me back where I was before: smelling and feeling like a barn.

Instead, I wrapped the thick towel around my waist and snuck into the hallway, sticking to the edge of the staircase in hopes of not drawing attention. As I reached the bottom of the steps and tiptoed past the door to the kitchen, I overheard Roman on the phone. He sounded exasperated.

"Why does it matter what kind of horse it is...? ... how many hands? She doesn't have hands. She's a horse. She has paws, or whatever. Hooves."

I glanced around the doorframe. Roman paced the length of the kitchen, waving a hand as he talked. "No... I don't know... listen, let me let you talk to the horse's owner. He's busy right now, but..."

I decided to save the poor man.

"I'm here," I said, wandering into the kitchen as confidently as possible like I'd meant to only be wearing a towel. I wasn't intimidated by this movie star seeing my little scrawny body at all. Not one single bit. It didn't matter. At all.

The moment he saw me, Roman's eyes bugged out and his jaw dropped for a split second before he shook his head. He glanced away, then back at me, then away again. "Hi. Oh... hi. You're... here. With a towel. On. With a towel on."

I raised a brow and smirked at him. "Did you want me to talk to the person on the phone?"

He looked at me blankly. "What person?"

I gestured to the phone. "I thought maybe you were talking to someone on the phone. Perhaps I was mistaken, my bad." I turned to walk out of the room.

"Oh! Yes. The person on the phone. Here." He thrust the phone toward me without an explanation.

"I assume it's about Nugget?" I asked with a grin. "You were saying something about a horse?"

"Yeah. You need to talk to a man about a horse. Wait. The man about the horse. Yeah."

Roman bit his lip as if to stop himself from blurting out more nonsense. It made him fucking adorable as hell, which was not something I needed to notice. He was already hot enough without being cute on top of it. I needed to remember he was an ass. A job-ruining ass of the highest order.

*Even asses needed a good fuck...*

I took the phone and turned away, wiggling my hips to calm my excited dick down. "This is Scotty," I said, trying to ignore the faint trace of Roman's aftershave on the phone.

The man on the other end asked me a bunch of questions related to transporting Nugget to a barn in Vermont. When I realized just how far away she would be from me, I asked the man to hold for a moment.

"Vermont?" I hissed, spinning to face Roman. "There are stables in New Jersey for god's sake."

Roman held up his hands. "Calm down. The barn is at the farm where I'll be staying for the next few weeks. I figure Nugget would be better there since I'll be able to keep an eye on her myself."

A small part of me swooned at the fact that Roman cared enough about Nugget to want to keep an eye on her rather than ship her off to some random stable. But the rest of me was pretty ticked off about him taking my horse so far away.

"And what about me?" I asked. "I'm just supposed to trust you? I'm supposed to let you take my fucking horse and, what? Hope I'll hear from you someday?"

"I'm going to give you money to help tide you over," he said calmly. "But first we need to get Nugget out of my house. This is the best solution I've found, and it's the one I'm offering. If you have a better one, I'm willing to listen."

"Yeah, how about a barn somewhere closer?" I knew beggars couldn't be choosers, but still. The thought of being that far away from Nugget made my heart hurt.

Roman's expression was sympathetic. "I called every barn in an hour's radius. None of them can stable a new horse right now. Not on such short notice."

I pressed the heel of my hand to my forehead. He was right. There were no other options. I should be grateful Roman was willing to help at all. And that he would be there to check on Nugget personally would be a relief.

Then I remembered that Roman was the reason I was having to ship Nugget off in the first place. If it hadn't been for his carriagejacking, I'd still have my job and Nugget would be tucked in her stall at the Clinton Park Stables.

But anger at Roman wasn't going to solve this problem. I needed to be reasonable about the situation. At least five weeks on a farm in Vermont would satisfy the regulation for carriage horses' annual vacations. And it wouldn't cost me a thing.

"Fine," I sighed before turning back to the man on the phone and finishing the arrangements.

While I wrapped things up on the call, I studied Roman from the corner of my eye. His gaze meandered over my bare skin like a curious and arousing fingertip. His cheeks flushed and after a minute, he shifted in his seat like he was rearranging something annoying in his pants.

Hm. Interesting. After hanging up, I decided to test the waters a little bit with a surreptitious butt wiggle as I sauntered toward the stairs. I felt the towel slip lower around my hips as I moved and wondered how well the twist would hold together. When I got downstairs, instead of slipping immediately into the clean clothes, I readjusted the towel lower, even allowing some of the blond curls at the base of my happy trail to show above the edge of the cotton. Then I sauntered back up the stairs and past the kitchen door.

A plate crashed to the floor and a muttered curse rang out, but he didn't come after me or say another word. I made it back to the bedroom unscathed and changed into my last clean clothes. I tried not to be too disappointed by that fact.

Two HOURS later I was footloose and fancy-free, meandering down Broadway with a fat stack of cash in my backpack and a spring in my step. Just that morning I'd been facing the very real prospect of losing my horse and my best friend for good, and now I'd not only found a place for her to stay, I had enough money to tide me over while I searched for a new job. For the first time in two weeks, I felt optimistic about the future.

I also had a carefully printed Vermont address on a scrap piece of paper in my jeans pocket so I at least knew where Nugget was if I found a new carriage medallion owner to take us on. I debated about whether or not to head to the park right now to see if I could get any leads, but I'd just done it the day before and I worried about annoying people.

Instead, I ducked into the nearest place and bought a cheap phone. My mother was probably going crazy trying to reach me even though I'd told her I'd be out of touch for a few days before I'd sold my iPhone the week before.

But then I'd had to pay an unexpected vet bill at the stables for Nugget to stay current on her vaccines. In the end, that had only given us six more days, which wasn't nearly enough for me to find another job that could pay enough for the stable fees.

But now that Nugget was on vacation, I could focus on earning some money.

I headed to the public library on Fifth Avenue and settled in to do some internet research. Before I started that, though, I pulled up my email account and shot my mom an email to her Corrlinks account in prison, giving her my new number and telling her what time to try and call me the next day. After clicking Send, I opened a new tab and pulled up a few job boards.

There were several restaurant gigs that looked promising as well as a janitorial service hiring overnight help. If I could work overnight, it'd be much easier to catch some naps in the park or a library during the day. That way my money would go a little further. Not having to spend it on rent or transportation would be huge.

I clicked the link to send in applications to three restaurant jobs and the janitorial job, crossing my fingers most for the cleaning position.

Then I spent a few minutes indulging in a little online research about my new horsey daddy. I typed *Roman Burke* into the search engine and was immediately met with a page of headlines about his most recent scandal. I ignored all the stupid bullshit ones, and clicked on the *Us Weekly* article that had come out shortly after the incident in the park.

*There may be more to the story of Roman Burke's wild ride through Manhattan the other day than meets the eye. While his representatives initially blamed the stunt on a misunderstanding due to his filming for the upcoming action movie,* Deep Cut, *sources present at the time claim a more personal reason for his hasty escape.*

*A witness claims Burke had a panic attack after a scaffolding collapsed on set. Whether or not that panic attack is at all related to the timing of actress Polly Macari's paternity claims is unknown.*

*Despite confirmation that Roman Burke was dating Columbia literature professor Peter Navine as recently as last summer, there have long been rumors of Burke and leading lady Polly Macari involved in a secret liaison due to their on-screen chemistry in* Infinite Payback.

*Burke, who has always been open about being bisexual, is frequently spotted around town with both men and women, but has only ever confirmed a serious relationship with Navine in recent years. According to Burke's spokesperson last fall, Burke and Navine parted amicably.*

*Did Roman Burke leave Navine for Polly Macari?*

*When asked directly whether Burke and Macari are in a relationship, Macari spokesperson, Jennifer Coleman said, "We will not divulge any information about Ms. Macari's personal life at this time, only that the child she is carrying was fathered by Roman Burke." However, Burke's spokesperson has had a different response to our query.*

*Immediately after the incident, which concluded with Burke's now-famous jaunt through Manhattan in a horse carriage, Burke's spokesperson said, "It is well-known that Roman Burke and Ms. Macari are friends after having starred in several films together. However, Mr. Burke is not in a romantic relationship with Ms. Macari, nor has he ever been."*

*But quickly after the incident, the Burke team seemed to change their story, saying, "We neither confirm nor deny the paternity of any child Ms. Macari may or may not be carrying at this time."*

*It's not quite clear why the change in stories nor why neither side is willing to clarify matters. Meanwhile, Macari and Burke both seem to be avoiding the spotlight by staying home or, in Burke's case, on a closed set. There has been one confirmed sighting of Macari visiting Burke's Manhattan brownstone for several hours, but no one knows what happened behind those closed doors.*

I clicked away from the article, my gut twisting with annoyance. I honestly had no idea what I was more upset about. Was it the carriage incident itself? That made the most sense since it had led to my own predicament. Or was it the idea of a famously bi actor ending up with a woman? I knew that was unreasonable and selfish of me, but it would be a great loss to my team in some odd way. Fine, a great loss to my fantasies maybe. Or could it be that I was pissed Roman Burke was romantically involved with someone else? Because, we all knew if it looked like a duck and talked like a duck, they'd probably fucked.

Which really pissed me the hell off.

I grunted. It was none of my business. What was my business was finding a damned job. I clicked out of the article and back over to my email account. Nothing.

After blowing out a deep breath and scrubbing my face with my hands, I had to face a harsh reality.

There was no way in hell I could keep Nugget in the city.

I'd already begged the other medallion owners for a job and

casually asked around to see if any drivers were planning on quitting or retiring soon. No luck. And now I was looking for a cleaning or restaurant job? In what reality would that pay enough to cover stabling fees, vet bills, and horse feed on top of rent and food for me?

My back teeth began to ache from clenching them against the emotion that wanted to come out. It all felt futile. I couldn't come up with a solution that worked. Even if I could find a job that would pay enough, I'd be working so many hours I wouldn't have time to give Nugget the care and attention she deserved. And how fair would that be for her?

My mother's words about spending "less time bitching and more time fixing" echoed in my head. Feeling sorry for myself wasn't going to solve anything. It never had in the past.

Out of curiosity, I clicked around on the internet searching for horse-related jobs in and around Stowe, Vermont. Maybe if I couldn't find a job in the city, I needed to expand my search. Sure, I'd lived my entire life in New York, but that didn't mean I had to stay here forever.

One of the first results that popped up was a company that offered sleigh rides. I sat and thought about it a minute. It would be a change from the hustle and bustle of Central Park, but it would mean Nugget and I would still be able to work together. I sent out polite emails to three different sleigh ride companies in Vermont in hope that one of them might have an opening.

I drummed my fingers against the table as I waited for a response. It was ridiculous to think they'd respond so quickly, but I was anxious. And desperate. Plus, it wasn't like I had anything else to do with my time. Except of course peruse just a few more of the stupid bullshit articles about the Roman/Polly situation from the melodramatic tabloids.

Those were certainly more entertaining, and juicier.

Time must have passed more quickly than I expected—and the half-naked photo spread of Roman was more distracting than I'd realized—because my third forty-five-minute session ended after about two minutes. I glanced up and looked around, realizing the people sitting near me were all different from the ones who'd been there when I'd sat down.

I sighed and checked my email one last time. Nothing. Which meant I was ending the day in an even worse place than I'd started it. Sure I'd found a place for Nugget to stay, and I had money in my pocket, but I was still homeless and jobless with no prospects on the horizon.

I remembered another of my mother's expressions: "stop waiting for life to hand you things and go take them for yourself." Perhaps she'd been a bit liberal with the "taking" part of that particular maxim, but that didn't make it any less true. If my best prospects for a job were in Vermont, then I had to figure out a way to get there and apply for them in person.

With a renewed sense of purpose, I stood up from my chair and reached for my backpack.

The backpack that was no longer anywhere to be found.

# 6

## ROMAN

*Polly Spotted At Sak's Sans Baby Daddy Burke*

WHEN I PULLED down the long driveway of Oscar's Vermont property, I was expecting to see a little cabin in the woods—someplace nice and cozy where I could play mountain man hermit and pretend I was a broody hero from a depressing British novel.

But then I saw the "cottage" and quickly realized the word cottage had to be used in quotation marks when referring to Oscar's Vermont estate.

It was a mansion. Like, millions and millions of dollars' worth of vistas and outbuildings, decorative fountains, and what had to be at least a twelve-car garage. And the entire thing was backlit by the setting sun like some kind of monument to wealth and perfection. I'd always known Oscar had money, though he took great pains to keep the source of his wealth to himself, but this house was unbelievable

"Jesus fuck, Oscar," I muttered to myself. "I'm paying you too much for crisis management."

I knew that wasn't the case, especially since I wasn't actually paying Oscar at all. Mostly because he wasn't really a crisis manager at all; he'd just been through enough crazy crap himself that he always knew exactly what to do. The man was unflappable.

I pulled up to one of the garage bays and clicked a button on the smart-home app Oscar had made me download on my phone. The garage door slid up smoothly, exposing a pristine interior. After pulling in I noticed several of the other bays held gleaming, expensive-looking vehicles. I wondered how often Oscar came up here. He'd made it sound like he wasn't here very often, but I couldn't imagine wanting to ever leave.

I left the keys in the car since the place was so secluded and made my way into the spacious mudroom and beyond to the enormous open kitchen. Everything was covered in warm colors from the hardwood floors to the wood-paneled walls to the upholstery on the sofas and chairs. It wasn't too fussy or modern, and I knew right away that despite the place being about ten thousand too many square feet for just me, I'd be able to relax here just fine.

Except, after spending less than an hour wandering around and familiarizing myself with the layout of the place, I had to admit, I was already a little lonely. Not for the first time, I wondered why I hadn't pressed the issue for Scotty to join me. I'd offered, thinking that it would make sense he'd want to stay near his horse and take care of him. But he'd been adamant that he needed to stay in the city to look for a job.

"I'll take your help," he'd told me. "But I don't need your charity."

Frankly, his refusal had left me feeling a little dejected. I wasn't used to being turned down. In fact, usually people jumped at the opportunity to spend time with a star like me.

At least his rejection confirmed Scotty wasn't impressed with my celebrity status. Though it also meant he wasn't impressed with me as a person either. Not enough to want to spend a few weeks in a secluded cottage with me.

Which was a shame. Because Scotty's personality was big enough that it would make the house feel less empty. Plus, it would have given us ample time to get to know each other. And by get to know each other, I meant fuck each other's brains out.

Because I'd been spending a *lot* of time fantasizing about that as well. Every bedroom I peeked my head into in Oscar's manse, I imagined Scotty on the bed naked and waiting. Every shower I pictured him beckoning me to him with a crooked finger. And forget what the sauna had made me imagine—it involved a lot of sweat-slicked skin.

Thanks to his little stunt wearing just a towel as he sauntered around my kitchen that morning, I had a very good idea what Scotty would look like naked. The memory of it had kept me half-aroused for most of the six-hour drive up here.

I groaned. I needed a cold shower to cool my libido and clear my head. Instead I opted for a walk outside, figuring I should probably check to make sure Nugget arrived safely and was settled in to her new home.

The transportation company had texted me to confirm delivery of Scotty's horse a couple of hours earlier, but I wanted to see her with my own eyes. The last thing I needed was for something to happen to Nugget, especially under my watch. I'd seen how important that horse was to Scotty, and I took my responsibility of taking care of her seriously. Oscar had assured me a local man would come in every day to feed and care for her, but just to be safe I'd asked him to track down a local vet who would come check on the horse once a week as well.

Bundling back up in my coat and yanking a wool hat down over my ears, I left the "cottage" to go in search of the barn, trying desperately not to think about how I was going to pass several weeks of solitude like this without anyone to talk to.

I wondered if Nugget would be open to a little conversation.

As I walked down the snowy path through a stand of evergreens, I began to feel the tension in my shoulders recede and my pace slow. I breathed deeply, reveling in the sharp, cold air that filled my lungs. It was beyond silent here. Every now and then, I heard a clump of snow fall from a tree or the rustle of a small animal under a bush somewhere, but compared to the city? It was heaven.

This was exactly what I'd wanted, I reminded myself. Peace and quiet. Room to breathe. And not a single paparazzi camera anywhere in sight.

Thankfully, finding the barn wasn't that difficult. It was painted red and shaped like any stereotypical barn out of a children's book, and I imagined Oscar designing his "cottage" on his "farm" and ordering a "barn" to go on it.

From the hoofprints and tire tracks in the snow, I could tell there'd been recent activity here. I pulled open the heavy wooden door and peered inside. Sure enough, a familiar brown horse nose poked over the gate to one of the stalls.

"Hey there, Nugget," I called softly. "You made it here okay? Did you get carsick? Well, I guess it would be trailer sick, wouldn't it?"

I approached slowly and gave her time to get used to the idea of me being in her space. I wasn't really a horse person, but I knew better than to do anything near a large animal that might take them by surprise.

"Do you miss your daddy, hm?" I asked, spotting a pail of raw carrots hanging from a nearby hook. I took one out and offered it to her. "I hope he's found a good job already and has a nice warm place to sleep tonight."

The horse nibbled the carrot out of my hand and nudged my arm with her nose for another. I rubbed the short hair on her forehead. She reminded me of the horses my sister, Diana, and her husband, Earl, had on their farm back home.

"Maybe I should have brought Scotty with us," I murmured. "He could have kept you from getting lonely. Kept me from getting lonely." I chuckled. "I've been here less than two hours and I'm already talking to the animals. Maybe this wasn't such a good idea."

Nugget made some scoffing sounds and continued bugging me for more treats. I gave her another carrot and scratched the side of her neck. She looked good—healthy and clean—and I reminded myself that next time I visited her I needed to bring my phone so I could snap a photo of her to email to Scotty. It would put his mind at ease to see her so well cared for.

"G'night, sweet Nugget," I said before turning around. As soon as my back was to her, Nugget somehow managed to pull my wool hat off. I turned and stared at her before barking out a laugh. The beanie hung from Nugget's front teeth.

"You thief!" I said, lunging to grab for it. "Give me back my hat."

Nugget jerked her head away before I could wrap my hand around it. Laughing, I tried again, but the horse took several steps deeper into the stall as if deliberately trying to play a game of keep-away.

When I slid open the door to the stall to wrestle the hat back, out tumbled a man—a very familiar and adorable man I hadn't been able to get out of my mind all day.

He landed on his back and blinked up at me for a moment before offering a smile. "Surprise?"

"Scotty? What the fuck?"

He scrambled up onto all fours before standing up and leaning casually against the side of the stall as if to chitchat. "Oh, yeah, hey."

I lifted my eyebrows incredulously. "Hey? What about, 'Hi, Roman, let me explain why you don't want to press charges for stalking and trespassing.'?"

I was being harsher than I meant to be, but I was just surprised. Scotty wasn't supposed to be here. In fact, he'd specifically rejected the idea of coming with me. So what had changed? Being a celebrity had made me wary of people who popped up unexpectedly. I'd heard horror stories from friends about fan situations turning real bad real fast.

Still, I couldn't keep my heart from hammering with excitement at the sight of him. Scotty was here! Fun and sassy, fiery and sexy as hell.

His eyes dropped to the ground where he used the toe of his boot to push a stray piece of hay out of the way. "Um. Yeah, about that..."

I crossed my arms, waiting.

"You see, I was at the library, right? And, um, I was applying for some jobs. Which, let's be honest, isn't fucking easy when you have no address to put down on the application. And how fair is that?" he asked, waving a hand through the air. "I mean, really. Do you know that the New York Coalition for the—"

"Focus, Scotty," I reminded him.

"Right, well, anyway, I didn't realize how much time had passed, and when I reached down to grab my backpack..." He trailed off.

My stomach dropped. I saw where this was probably going.

He lifted a shoulder. "Someone had taken off with it."

"Shit," I told him. "I'm sorry."

"Yeah, so was I." He winced. "Especially since that's where I'd put all the money you'd given me."

"Did you call the police?" I asked him. "Alert the security people at the library to check the cameras?"

Scotty looked at me like I was an idiot. "Of course I did. And guess what? It turns out that *they* wanted an address for me too. Imagine that."

"So what did you tell them?"

He cleared his throat and looked at the floor, the stall door, the ceiling. Anywhere but at me.

"Scotty."

He let out a sigh that sounded more like a huff. "I told them I was staying with you."

"Here?" I asked incredulously, noticing Nugget approach out of the corner of my eye. She no longer held my hat in her mouth.

He rolled his eyes. "No, dumbass. I gave them your brownstone address. One of them felt sorry for me and offered to give me a lift home, and I couldn't say no without looking suspicious. And when he dropped me off, I saw them loading Nugget onto the trailer, and at that point I had nowhere to go and no fucking money, and the thought of having to stand there while my horse was taken away just broke me."

Nugget rested her chin on the top of Scotty's head, and the man didn't even seem to notice. His hand came up automatically to scratch at her chest while he spoke.

"So, I... uh... hopped in."

I stared at him. There were so many questions, I didn't even know where to start.

Before I could say anything, Scotty held up a hand and said, "And before you tell me how stupid I am, I know that already, okay? Don't forget this homeless shit is new to me. Up until last night I had a place to stay, even if it was only a fucking horse stall in a stable for the last few nights."

As he got more and more defensive, his cheeks flushed and his eyes widened. I could see the fear close under the surface of his bluster, and I remembered how he'd tried to distract me from his problems this morning through humor and jokes. He didn't like being vulnerable. Didn't like asking for help. Yet here he was.

"Why didn't you come up to the house?" I asked him.

Scotty shrugged, looking down and toeing the same piece of hay.

"Or say anything when I was talking to Nugget?"

He shrugged again and it almost broke my heart. Did he not think he deserved better than camping out in a stall? Especially when I had that massive estate all to myself. All he'd have had to do was knock on the door and I'd have welcomed him in instantly. Happily.

Eagerly.

Then a thought occurred to me. Maybe that was the problem. "Is it me? Is that why you didn't want to come up here initially or why you stayed hidden when I came out here? Because you don't like me or—"

He started laughing. Like honest to Jesus, hands on his knees because he couldn't stay standing guffawing. "Oh my god, seriously?" Scotty asked, wheezing as he tried to catch his breath. Finally he straightened and wiped at an eye, still chuckling. "You're funny, you know that? You should star in more comedies. Something like *Clueless* meets *Mean Girls*. But gay. *Super* gay."

I frowned. I still wasn't sure what he'd been laughing at. "That sounds like a terrible movie."

"It would *kill* at the box office," he said seriously. "Trust me."

I opened my mouth to protest, but Scotty cut me off with a hand in the air. "And also, just to get back on topic, per your earlier question, no, I can unequivocally say that me not announcing my presence had absolutely nothing to do with my feelings for you." He paused and tilted his head to the side as if reconsidering.

"Well, maybe it did a little," he amended. "But only because I didn't want to disappoint you."

That shocked me. "How in the world could you disappoint me?"

He stared at me like it was obvious. "By losing the money you'd given me? For being back in the same position I was before: homeless, jobless, and out of options? And all of that after you'd been so... so..." He gestured toward me, flustered. "So *you*."

"So me?" I asked. I couldn't hide the smirk creeping across my lips. "Care to elaborate on that?"

Scotty narrowed his eyes. "I'm sure you have enough people in your life kissing your ass, Roman Burke, that you don't need me doing it as well."

I tried to formulate a witty comeback, but all the words got trapped in my head. Because my brain was too busy picturing Scotty on his knees behind me, his hands on my hips and his lips ghosting across my cheeks as he kissed my ass. I let out a small grunt.

His eyes met mine, and I wondered if he could tell what I was thinking, because suddenly he'd gone quiet as well. His tongue darted out to lick his lips, and I swallowed a groan.

"Come back to the house with me," I said. It came out rougher than I expected, more a command than offer. I thought about all the fantasies I'd had earlier. All the ways he and I could tangle our bodies around each other in that massive house.

He glanced toward the stall, shifting his feet. "You mean... the house, like the big house? Because I can totally stay here. I don't mind. Nugget's used to me and—"

I shot him a look. The very idea of leaving him alone to sleep in the barn with the horse was abhorrent. "You're not staying out here with the damn horse," I told him.

Scotty was quiet for a second, and I noticed that his chest rose and fell rapidly, as if he'd just finished running a race. Or as if he was scared. We stood only a few feet apart and it was suddenly so starkly apparent just how much larger than him I was. I towered over him, his shoulders barely as wide as my chest.

Not only was I larger, I held all the power. He was homeless. Penniless. And without me, his horse likely would have already been taken from him. Plus, even though I felt like a normal guy, I was a celebrity. Lately the news had been overrun with stories of celebrities using their status to pressure others into bed with them.

I swore that would never be me.

I blew out a breath and shoved a hand through my hair, taking several steps back to give him space. I needed to slow things down. Make sure he was fully on board before anything happened between us.

Because I fully intended something to happen between us. It just had to be Scotty who made the first move.

I let out a laugh that I hoped came across as disarming. "What I meant to say was, there's no need for you to stay out here. There's plenty of room—the house is big enough to put up the entire New York City Gay Men's Chorus. Come on."

I nudged him away from the wall and toward the door to the barn before scooting past the horse to retrieve my soggy hat. After securing Nugget back into her stall, Scotty slipped her one last carrot before bidding her good night with a pat on the nose. When we stepped outside, the sun had fully set, turning the air frigid. I glanced toward Scotty, making sure his coat was thick enough to keep him warm during the walk back.

"So, this isn't your place?" Scotty asked. He had his hands deep in his pockets and shoulders hunched against the cold. I made a note to look for some warmer clothes for him. It wouldn't have surprised me if Oscar didn't have entire wardrobes of winter gear in every size imaginable.

"Nah. It's a friend's vacation home," I told him. "I've never been here before. Honestly, I was expecting a little cabin in the woods."

We rounded a corner to see the giant house lit up like a proud display of the Crown Jewels.

Scotty froze and then laughed. "You weren't kidding. That's quite a cabin," he muttered. "If this is his vacation home, I'd love to see his real place."

I smiled. "Yeah, Oscar's a bit of an enigma. I can tell you he has an apartment in Brooklyn that's super normal."

Scotty side-eyed me. "I'm not sure your idea of normal and mine are the same."

I nodded. "Point taken. I just mean... you never know what you're going to get with Oscar. But he's an amazing guy. Very loyal friend. And funny as hell. You'd like him. He's sweet. He'd probably baby-talk Nugget like I did."

Scotty lifted an eyebrow. "You sound half in love with him."

I barked out a laugh, remembering my disastrous date with Oscar. "No. Definitely not," I said adamantly. "Been there, tried that. It did *not* work, trust me."

Scotty's lips turned up in a grin. "That sounds like a story."

We entered the house through the door to the mudroom and took off our winter coats. After flipping on the lights in the kitchen, I made my way to the fridge with an overwhelming sense of déjà vu from this morning.

I took stock of what Oscar had on hand. The fridge was stuffed as was the pantry. He must have called ahead and had the place prestocked for me. I needed to remember to thank him. I turned to Scotty, rubbing my hands together. "So, eggs are off the table," I said, remembering this morning. "But how do you feel about pasta?"

"I feel agreeable toward pasta. Do you..." He glanced up at me from under blond lashes. "Do you want me to cook it? I feel bad about... you know. I'm happy to work for—"

I cut him off before things got any more awkward. "Absolutely not." I stepped over to him and put my hands on his shoulders, ducking down a little to meet his eyes. They were so fucking blue. "You do not have to work for your keep. You do not owe me anything. I recognize that this is a shitty situation for you, and I don't want to make it worse with things being awkward between us, okay? So let's just... can we maybe pretend that we're two friends taking a break from the city for a few days? How about that?"

He studied me a moment, and then his mouth twisted into a smirk. "That's not very believable when it's widely known you don't have any gay friends. How could you, after starring in a movie called *Back Passage*?"

I let my head fall back with a groan. "Don't remind me. I will never live that down."

"As well you shouldn't," he mock scolded.

"Hey!" I protested. My eyes met his and I saw gratitude shimmering in the depths of that impossible blue. Reluctantly, I let my hands drop from his shoulders when what I really wanted to do was squeeze them tight and drag him toward me.

Instead I moved back to the fridge. "Tell you what, why don't you get a pot of water going on the stove, and I'll get started on the sauce. Do you like wine? I think that might help tremendously. We've both had a very long day." I glanced over at him. "You more than anyone."

"I love wine. Thank you. But..." He bit at his lip for a moment as he considered his words. "One more thing before we pretend I'm not homeless and penniless." He reached into the pocket of his jeans and pulled out a mobile phone, holding it toward me.

I glanced at it dubiously before plucking it from his palm. "Is this some kind of antique flip phone?" I teased, dangling the cheap pay-as-you-go device between my thumb and index finger. My intention had been to lighten the mood a bit, but Scotty's face remained serious.

"Shut up." He cleared his throat and shuffled his feet. He was adorable when nervous. "Besides Nugget and my coat, it's my only worldly possession. I want you to hang on to it for me."

I stared at him. "Why?"

He held his arms out to his side and spun around. "I just want to make sure you know I don't have a phone or a camera or anything else that can—"

"Stop," I blurted, finally understanding. "Just... stop. I don't..." I'd intended to say I didn't think he'd sell me out, but that was stupid. I didn't *want* to think he'd sell me out. But experience and my own history proved that was a foolish assumption to make, especially with someone I didn't know very well and hadn't vetted.

"Please, Roman," Scotty said quietly. "I can't bear the thought of you stressing about when I'm going to betray you. And I wouldn't blame you at all for worrying about it anyway, but giving you that phone is the only way I know to prove to you—"

"Okay," I said quickly. Whatever it took to make him stop because he was clearly uncomfortable, and I'd do anything to put us back on equal footing "Fine. I'll... I'll hang on to it. All right? And... when you need it to make a call, just tell me and I'll give it right back." It seemed like a ridiculous arrangement, but if it made him feel better, I'd play along.

He nodded and smiled. "Thank you. I'll, ah, need to check it tomorrow in case I get any job leads, but tonight we can be off the grid. Now, did you say something about wine?"

After I picked a bottle from Oscar's extensive collection and opened it, I poured us each a glass and returned to chopping vegetables for the pasta sauce. Scotty set a big pot of water on to boil and turned to me with a sneaky grin. He grabbed his wine and hoisted himself up so he was sitting on the counter next to the cutting board. Close enough that I caught the faint scent of hay drifting from his clothes. I found I was beginning to like that smell. Especially because it was pure Scotty.

He took a swallow of his wine and then crossed one slim leg over the other. "You were saying something earlier about a disastrous date with the enigmatic Oscar? Dish. If I'm staying in his house, I feel like I should at least know a thing or two about the man."

I looked up, catching Scotty's eye. "Only if you promise to share a disastrous date in return."

He leaned forward and placed a palm against the side of my face, giving my cheek a pat. "Oh honey, you are just too adorable if you think any date with me could ever be considered a disaster."

I couldn't help but laugh. "No man is that lucky."

Scotty waved a hand down his body. "Lucky enough to have all this?"

My grin widened. "What I meant was lucky enough to avoid disaster in the dating world. But you're right, any man who gets all that," I said, my eyes following the path his hands had indicated, "would be lucky indeed."

When he didn't immediately respond, I wondered if I'd gone too far. The expression on his face was fleeting, just a moment of surprise and a quick furrow between his eyebrows like maybe I'd caught him off guard. He took a swallow of wine and then smiled. "I believe you were about to tell me about Oscar?"

I took the hint and returned to the earlier topic. Oscar himself had told this story a hundred times, so it wasn't like I was sharing state secrets or anything. "It started when I tried a matchmaking app for the first time. I mean, anonymously, of course."

Scotty leaned forward, cackling. "This is going to be good, isn't it? Go on."

I nodded and grinned. "It involves frogs, a porcupine, helicopters, and the surprise appearance of my date's entire extended family. So... yes."

# 7

## SCOTTY

*Research Reveals White Wine Reduces Men To Tears*

HE'D ONLY JUST BEGUN to describe the date with Oscar and already my stomach hurt from laughing. "Wait," I cried through tears. "Start over. And don't leave out a single detail."

Roman lifted an eyebrow at me, but his full lower lip curled up in a smile nonetheless. "Pay attention, young Padawan, for I cannot ever speak of this again without initiating a vengeance sequence."

"I'm listening," I told him. "I totally promise." I took another healthy glug of my wine. Since I hadn't eaten much in the past several hours, it went straight to my head. I already felt a warm buzz tingling through me, though a part of me wondered if that was due to the wine, the relief of having a safe place to spend the night, or being in the presence of Roman Burke. Because honestly, the man was almost too good to be true: smart, funny, clever, and hot as fuck.

I wondered if you could see little heart-shaped bubbles floating above my head. Shame about him being a movie star and completely out of my league. But hey, a man could daydream, couldn't he? And flirt.

"So at first my date with Oscar seemed to be going well. He was friendly and charming and interesting and definitely good-looking. Pretty much the whole package."

I ignored the small knot that formed in my chest at that last bit. I had no reason to be jealous, especially since this was a story about an ex and a disastrous date. It was more that I didn't like the reminder that I wasn't the whole package and never could be. At least, not for Roman.

I guzzled more wine and grabbed the bottle, sloshing more in my glass and topping his off in the process. "How the hell was a helicopter involved? Did he pick you up for your date in one?"

He laughed. "That would have been a sight. The paparazzi would have loved it."

I spread my hands through the air like I was announcing a headline. "*Movie Star Mingles with Mysterious Mogul.*"

"More likely, *Actor Known for Being in Wrong Place at Wrong Time, Even on Dates.*"

That sounded much worse. "Yikes."

He kept his focus on cleaning the seeds from a bell pepper. "The paparazzi doesn't really like me so much. I've learned to ignore it."

His words were saying one thing, but the tension around his eyes and the frown furrowing his forehead said something else entirely. I wanted to press him on it, but it was clear from the way he held himself that he didn't want to discuss it.

"So you're telling me he didn't pick you up in a helicopter? Shame. I was just beginning to think that this Oscar fellow knew how to make an entrance."

"Oh, he does, trust me," he said, chuckling. "But our first date started off pretty innocently. The guy invited me to something called the Reptile Experience because apparently he'd learned through my profile that I liked the movie *Jurassic Park*. Which," he said, raising a finger in the air, "I would just like to point out, is not the same thing as wanting to touch reptiles."

"Oh god," I groaned. "Hence, the frogs."

"You might think so, but no, actually. Believe it or not, that's where the helicopters came in."

My eyes widened. "Seriously?"

"Unexpected, right?" He cut several slices of the bell pepper and pushed them toward me to snack on before dicing the rest for the sauce. It was a small gesture, but one that reinforced the kind of person he'd already shown himself to be. Thoughtful. Considerate.

"So it turned out that the Reptile Experience was a special exhibit at a wildlife park out in Jersey. You know one of those 'get up close and personal with the animals' type of things. Oscar picked me up—in a car, not a helicopter," he pointed out, grinning at me. "And drove us out there on a beautiful Sunday afternoon. We strolled around, talking and getting to know each other as we made our way to the center of the park to where the reptile exhibits were."

I took another sip of wine. I didn't particularly like imagining Roman walking arm in arm with another man. Thankfully, he didn't dwell on that detail.

"And then... some kind of glitch happened in the computer system that controlled the locking mechanisms for all of the enclosures. Every single one of them failed at once."

My eyes widened. "No!"

He laughed. "Yep. Elephants, lizards, snakes, a troupe of orangutans, several flamingos, a couple of ostriches. You name it, it was loose in that park. And there we were stuck right in the middle of it all."

I couldn't help joining his laughter. "Oh my god, what did you do?"

"Took refuge on the roof of a nearby gift shop with several employees and the rest of the guests who'd been too deep in the park to evacuate."

My eyes widened. "You're kidding?"

"No!" He was laughing hard enough that his eyes gleamed with tears. "You can't make this stuff up. After four hours, they finally determined they had to extract us using helicopters like we were on a

sinking ship of some kind. It was seriously the most bizarre experience of my life."

"How have I never heard about this?" I asked. "Famous movie star
choppered out of a wildlife park run amok with wild animals? That's
paparazzi gold right there."

His eyes widened like he couldn't believe it. "That's the best part!
No one, and I mean *no one*, realized who I was. And that included
Oscar."

I shook my head. "No way. Not possible."

He lifted an eyebrow in my direction, smirking. "Oh really? You
can't think of a single situation where someone might mistake me as
someone else?" He reached out and squeezed my knee playfully. "You
yourself thought I was a cop."

I squirmed under his touch. "Shut up. That was... extenuating
circumstances."

He left his hand on my knee a second longer. I swore I could feel
the heat of him through my pants. And then it was gone and he was
reaching for his wineglass, tipping it to his lips. I tried not to watch
him swallow. Tried not to think about what the skin under the corner
of his jaw would taste like.

I cleared my throat. "Anyway, continue."

It seemed to take him a moment to get his bearings. He set a pan
on the stove and poured in a drizzle of olive oil before returning to
prepping vegetables. He noticed that I'd already devoured the pepper
he'd cut for me, so he grabbed a couple of carrots and sliced them
into sticks, pushing them my way.

"Right, they deposited us at a landing pad several miles away from
the wildlife center. By that time it was late afternoon and Oscar
informed me we were close to his aunt Dahlia's house and suggested
we pop in for tea since we'd had to miss lunch what with being
trapped on a roof during the reptile rampage."

I stared at him while taking a bite out of one of the carrot sticks.
"During the middle of your date?"

Roman nodded. His eyes twinkled merrily, and I was glad to see him so relaxed. It convinced me he truly wasn't too put out by my unexpected appearance. And that perhaps he even liked having me here with him.

"I think I just blinked at him," he continued, "but he must have taken it as a yes, because suddenly there we were at Aunt Dahlia's house surrounded by at least twelve of Oscar's extended family members including his parents. That's where the frogging happened."

I blinked at him, my lips pursed as I tried to hold back a laugh. "I'm assuming you don't mean the yarn unraveling kind of frogging?" I asked.

He laughed. "I don't know what that is, but no. Uncle Vinnie— and no, I'm not making that up—asked if I'd like some frogs to take home. Stupid me assumed they were some variation of the chocolate turtles that had been served on a platter with the tea, so I accepted politely. Um, no. Out comes a giant mason jar with three actual living frogs in it and a giant plaid bow around the top."

"No!" I shouted.

"Oh yes. And it gets better. 'We're so happy you're part of the family,' Uncle Vinnie says. 'Here's your welcome frogs.' Apparently, these are spawn of an important familial frog that—"

At this point I was laughing hard enough to snort my wine. "Welcome frogs?" I gasped.

Roman snickered and held up his hand. "Stop. Don't make me laugh more, or I'll never get to the part about the porcupine."

"Porcupine?" The man had to be pulling my leg at this point. "Do you get one of those when you join the family too?" I asked.

"No. As it turns out, Oscar has a porcupine, incidentally also named Oscar, he keeps in his pocket. Which I only discovered—"

Carrot pieces shot out of my nose. I was going to have to stop eating and drinking completely if I didn't want to choke and give him an even bigger story to tell his next date.

I grabbed a napkin and spoke, halfway hyperventilating and with tears streaming down my face. "I'm so sorry for interrupting, but it had to have been a hedgehog. A true porcupine would have been too big to fit in the man's pocket."

Roman stared at me before losing it completely and putting his hands on his knees in the middle of the kitchen.

"Is it..." I tried asking between choking breaths. "Is it his little Oscar? Like his tiny..." More sputtering as I pointed at the crotch of my pants. "Prick?"

"Prick. Stop," Roman begged. "Stop so I can breathe."

"No, keep going," I squeaked. "I need to know about the porcuhog."

Roman waved his hand in front of his face while tears streamed from his eyes. "Hold on, hold on," he said. "Let me just get the sauce going so it can simmer first."

He chucked onion, garlic, and the bell peppers into a pot on the stove and the room filled with the smell of deliciousness. I closed my eyes, inhaling deep. I wanted to store this memory forever: sitting on this counter, Roman with his sleeves rolled up, chopping vegetables as he talked, his laughter echoing in my ears while the buzz of wine in my veins turned everything warm. It was so easy being here, with him. Like I belonged.

It was the closest to perfection I could ever imagine life being.

A tiny voice in my head was sending off alarm bells, warning that this wasn't my life and never would be. But I hit snooze on it. Fuck reality. Fuck tomorrow. Tonight this *was* my life, and I was damn well going to revel in it.

I let out a sigh.

He glanced my way. "You okay?"

I smiled at him. I was better than okay, I was content. "Yeah," I told him. "Thanks for that. I needed a good laugh."

He went back to his sauce, dumping in a couple of cans of tomatoes and then fishing around the spice cabinet. "Then you really need to meet Oscar. He's got a million stories just like that. The man collects bad dates like baseball caps. I'm beginning to think he's cursed."

"He definitely sounds like a character," I said.

"Totally." He opened a few tins of spices and added pinches of several to the sauce. "So now it's your turn."

"My turn to what?" I asked, even though I was pretty sure I knew the answer.

He grinned at me. "To share. You know, crazy dates? Psycho exes?"

I reached for the wine bottle and topped off both of our glasses. We really didn't need to talk about me. There honestly wasn't anything there to share. "But you never finished telling me about the date with Oscar. What happened next? Was that the end of it? One date and it's over?"

"You'd think," he chuckled. "But no. He was a pretty good sport about the whole thing, and once I got home and figured out what to do with those fucking frogs—"

I nearly choked on my wine. "You mean you actually took the welcome frogs?"

He looked at me sheepishly. "What else was I supposed to do? They were a gift."

I couldn't believe it. I had to set my glass down I was afraid that I would spill it from laughing so hard. "They were practically livestock!"

"Their names are Beep, Peep, and Mayweather. They live happily on a horse farm in Nebraska with my nieces. Anyway," he said pointedly, "as I was saying, Oscar and I actually dated for a bit after that. I was worried he might be freaked-out when he found out who I really was, but he didn't even bat an eyelash."

He continued adding spices to his sauce, but from the angle of where I was sitting, I could see that the tops of his ears had turned pink. Was he actually blushing? And what kind of guy travels from New Jersey to Nebraska with a jar full of random frogs to give them to his nieces? A good guy.

I cleared my throat. "Then what happened? Why did you break up?"

Roman adjusted the temperature on his sauce and then grabbed his wineglass and leaned his hip against the counter. "It just didn't work out. Oscar's a great guy, but he's not the right one for me."

*Who is the right guy for you?*

The question hung in the air. I wanted to ask it so badly, but instead I chugged another gulp of wine. Unless he was going to say "a narrow-hipped carriage driver from the city with a wicked sense of humor and a horse named Nugget," I didn't want to hear it.

"What about after Oscar?" I asked instead. "Did you date a lot after you two broke up?"

He shrugged. "Not really. It's not really that easy to date me."

I wouldn't have minded accepting that challenge. I cocked an eyebrow. "You high-maintenance? Do you turn into an asshole if you get fed after midnight?"

A small smile crossed his lips at the *Gremlins* joke. But it was temporary. "I just come with baggage. My life isn't private. Which means anyone who dates me doesn't get a lot of privacy either. That's a lot to ask someone to take on in order to go out with me." He lifted a shoulder. "Some people can't handle it. And I can't really blame them for that."

I thought back to when I'd been in the library looking up articles about Roman. All the headlines that had screamed back at me. So many of them laughably ridiculous but repeated over and over again. Articles about what he'd eaten, what he'd worn, what an ex-lover had said about his performance in bed. He was right. There was nothing about his life that was private. I'd even been one of the shmucks who'd gobbled those stories up like a starving fan without realizing that I'd been feeding the paparazzi's need.

His eyes met mine. The carefully crafted movie-star exterior was long gone. This was the real Roman, the guy who'd let a practical stranger bring a horse into his home and then cooked him breakfast. The man who'd accepted a jar of frogs because it was the polite thing to do, but then instead of tossing them aside, he named those frogs and gave them a home. The man who'd talked to Nugget earlier that evening because he'd had no one else to talk to.

And it was clear from his expression that this Roman—the real Roman—was lonely.

I wanted to launch myself off the counter and throw myself into his arms. I wanted to thread my fingers into his hair and wrap my legs around his waist and do whatever it took to erase the pain and loneliness from his expression.

But then he let out a laugh. "Poor me, right?" He shoved a hand through his hair. "Sorry, no one likes to hear a celebrity complain. I'm one of the luckiest human beings in the world." He turned back to his sauce, giving it a stir.

"That's way more than enough about me," he said. "Now it really is your turn. Any good stories from the dating trenches?"

I shrugged and toyed with a ragged fingernail. "I don't date, really. I mean... I hook up, I guess."

"You guess?"

I looked up at him and saw his furrowed brows.

"No, I mean..." I shrugged. "Yeah, I hook up. But the last person I actually dated was in high school."

The spoon in his hand clattered to the counter and he turned. "High school? Fuck. How young are you?" he asked, stepping back like I was infected with a plague.

I rolled my eyes at him. "I'm twenty-eight, Roman. Jesus."

He cocked his head to the side. "Really? You look younger than that." Then he did the math and his eyes widened. "Wait, you haven't dated someone in like ten years? Why not?"

I set my wineglass down again and rubbed my hands over my face. God I hated telling this story. But Roman had opened up to me. It was only fair for me to do the same. "He changed his mind," I said simply.

"About you?"

"About being gay."

Roman's eyes widened. "Oh."

I shrugged again. Apparently that was becoming my signature move. I was Don't-Give-A-Fuck Man. "It's fine." I hadn't thought about Ian in a long time. So why was it suddenly making me feel depressed?

"Obviously it's not fine if you've never dated anyone since," Roman said. "I assume it made you gun-shy about relationships?"

I forced myself not to shrug. "Dunno. I guess. Relationships are a crapshoot anyway. It's kind of hard to trust that the person's going to stick around, you know? I can't..." I struggled to figure out the best way to explain it, which made me realize I'd never really had to before. I'd never known anyone well enough to share this with, so I'd never needed to find the right words.

I blew out a breath. "I don't want to rely on someone and then have them pull the rug out from under me like that again. It's not worth it."

One moment Roman stood by the stove, and the next he was in front of me. He set his wine on the counter and placed his hands on my knees. Without thinking, I spread my legs so he could get closer. He stepped between them automatically. I could smell the scent of fresh garlic and basil coming off him.

I looked away, nervous whispers skating along my skin where his hands seared my skin through my jeans.

"Scotty," he said softly. "Not everyone is like that. Plenty of men know what they like, what they *want*." His words held a deeper meaning that sat between us like a living thing.

"Mm," I hummed nervously. Because what I wanted to say was, "And what do you want?"

But if the answer wasn't me, I would sure as hell regret asking.

He reached up to nudge my chin until I looked at him again. From this close, I could see the late-evening whiskers on his face, the pale oval scar along one cheek, the lone slash of tawny gold in one of his warm brown eyes. He was close enough to kiss, close enough to lay my head on his shoulder and simply rest, knowing I was safe in his care.

I hadn't been safe in someone's care since I was nine years old and my grandfather had died. After that, it had been just my mom and me, and it had always been clear that I'd been the one caring for her. Which I'd done a shit job of because she'd ended up in prison.

More proof of just how awful I was at relationships.

Roman leaned in a little and I held my breath, terrified I was going to accidentally do something to ruin the moment or scare him off.

He continued moving in, but instead of lowering those lush lips onto mine, he slid his arms around my back and hugged me.

Just hugged me, as tightly as he could.

"I'm sorry," he whispered into my hair. "I know what it's like to be alone for so long, and it's not great."

And it was true. I could tell by the sound of his voice, and by the memory of the loneliness in his eyes, that he knew exactly what it was like to be alone. We both tried to mask it, but it was always there beneath the surface.

My entire body began to tremble, and my eyes smarted. Was this really happening?

I carefully slid my arms around his neck and held on just as tightly. For some reason, I felt completely comfortable letting go around him.

"No," I breathed. "It's not."

And then I felt warm tears slide down my face and into his collar. He didn't say another word, simply stayed there with his arms wrapped around me until I was done crying.

When the timer went off for the pasta, I pushed him away gently and quickly wiped my face off with my shirt. "Saved by the bell," I said, letting out a watery laugh. "I'm starving."

After that, we were both content to let the conversation pop back up to shallow depths. Strangely, I didn't feel as awkward as I expected after being so vulnerable around him. We joked while we ate. Roman asked me questions about Nugget and then told me a story about working with a horse on a movie set. Clearly he was trying to cheer me up, and it made me like him even more.

By the time we were done with dinner, I was stupidly half in love with the man. And I'd even somehow convinced myself that he might feel something for me as well.

Which was a one-way ticket to disappointment and blue balls. I needed distance from the man. I needed to put on the brakes before I fell even harder for him.

"I'll clean up," I said quickly, hopping up and reaching for our plates. Suddenly, I felt like if I didn't get away from him, I was going to jump in his lap and beg him for more touching. "You cooked most of it, and I'm really good at doing the dishes. I once had a part-time dishwasher job at the Cracked Egg," I said as I carried everything into the kitchen. "Do you know it?" I called over my shoulder. "Probably not, it's in Queens. They have this chef there named Bobby G, and that guy was crazy. He—"

His warm hand landed on my lower back as I set down the stack of dishes on the counter. I almost fumbled the entire stack into the sink when I felt his touch. I sucked in a breath at the feel of him.

"Leave them," he said. There was a gruffness to his voice.

My eyes fluttered shut. "I really don't mind," I told him, my own voice sounding breathy and strange. "If you let them sit too long, they'll be a bitch to clean and then—"

"I don't care." His fingers curled against my lower back. I had to clench my hands to keep from turning and grabbing him.

"But—"

He leaned closer. Heat radiated from his body, searing the length of me. His breath tickled the back of my ear and I shuddered. "I'm only going to ask this once because this has to be your choice, Scotty. And I don't want you saying yes out of any sense of obligation for what you think you might owe me because you don't owe me a thing. You understand that?"

He paused. Belatedly, I realized he was waiting for an answer. I nodded my head, not sure I could actually form words right now.

"And I don't want you saying yes because you think I hold some sort of power because I'm a celebrity because I don't. I'm just a man with a job that's more visible than most," he continued. "Okay?"

I nodded again. I realized I was holding my breath, but try as I might, I couldn't force myself to exhale. If he didn't get to the point soon, I was afraid I was going to die. Which was a shame because I was pretty sure I'd want to be alive and conscious for what I hoped was coming next.

Roman lowered his head so that I could just barely feel the scrape of his jaw against the side of my neck as he spoke. "I can't pretend anymore that I don't want to kiss you pretty fucking badly, Scotty. So I need you to think about whether or not—"

Halle-fucking-llujah. Before he could say another word, I turned around and launched myself at his face.

# 8

## ROMAN

*In Bizarre Turn Of Events, Burke Bottoms... Or Does He?*

FINALLY I HAD Scotty in my arms. And it was every bit as amazing as I'd hoped it would be. The moment he jumped in for the kiss, I grabbed the back of his head and held him to me, taking in the feel of his lips, his warm breath, his soft skin. Within seconds, we were tangled around each other, dishes forgotten. He climbed up my body until his arms were wrapped around my head and his legs around my waist. I held him under the ass and kneaded his cheeks with a groan.

"Jesus fuck I want you, Roman," he moaned into my mouth. "So much. Please."

The words sent a shudder through me. "I've been thinking about you all day," I told him between kisses. And it was true. Scotty was so vulnerable and sweet, nervous and sexy. Something about him called out to me more strongly than anything I'd felt in a long time, if ever.

I wanted him so badly, I'd spent the entire mealtime with my fist closed under the table so tightly, my nails making painful crescent-moon marks in my palm. I was surprised dinner was even edible given how distracted I'd been cooking it.

The number of times I'd wanted to turn and pin him against the cabinets and kiss him senseless was ridiculous, but I hadn't wanted to scare him. And I sure as hell hadn't wanted him to feel obligated out of some kind of weird sense of payback for me taking care of him and his horse.

Which is why I'd tried to lay it out there in words. To give him the chance to think, to say no, to protect himself from doing something stupid. Because being with me was stupid as hell. Anyone who even looked at me funny wound up on the cover of a magazine with accusations and rumors spinning wildly around the world. The most serious relationship I'd ever experienced had ended because of the invasion of privacy involved in dating me. Pete had loved me, I knew he had, but it hadn't been enough in the end. The paparazzi had been brutal.

I couldn't bear for the same thing to happen to Scotty. The thought of all that vibrance leeching away under the constant pressure of the press was too much to bear.

But the press wasn't here, I reminded myself. We were alone, protected for now. And I'd given Scotty the chance to choose, and he'd chosen this. *Me.* "God I've been wanting to get my hands on you."

He smiled against my mouth. "Me too. Tried to tease you in the towel back in the city," he admitted breathlessly. "Didn't work."

"It worked," I growled. "Drove me crazy."

Scotty kissed me again, deeper and longer. "You didn't come after me. I thought maybe it was because you were with Polly." He hesitated a beat before adding, "Or that you just weren't interested."

I rested his ass on the counter and pulled back until I could meet his eyes. They were semi-glassy, and his skin was flushed pink. He looked so kiss-drunk, I wanted to devour him, but I needed to make a few things clear.

"Scotty, first of all, I am definitely very, very interested. Like can't-take-my-hands-off-you-against-my-better-judgment interested. You got that?"

He frowned. "Against your better judgment?"

"I don't really know you yet, Scotty, but nevertheless, I've brought you into my residence. Twice. You could have an ulterior motive."

"I don't," he told me. "I swear. My motive is mostly wanting Nugget to be okay... and, well, a little bit of wanting to put your cock in my mouth."

I wondered if I was grinning like a fool. I felt like I was. "You're welcome to do that anytime. You're sexy as fuck, and I don't want to stop touching you."

Scotty nodded, a grin parting his slightly swollen lips. "I like hearing you say that."

"Then I'll be sure to say it often." I couldn't help it—I leaned in to brush my mouth across his before pulling back again. "Second, I'm not with Polly. I'm not with anyone right now."

His eyes sparkled. "Good."

I leaned closer to him. "Third, the reason I didn't come after you and drag that towel from your hips is because I couldn't make a move on you and then hand you a stack of cash."

Scotty blinked, and then the words seemed to sink in. "Oh."

"And I still worry that you think—"

His eyes widened. "No! I don't think that. I know this isn't... this doesn't have anything to do with that."

I let out a breath. "Good. Because me being attracted to you is completely separate from the situation you're in. I need you to know that. I'm happy to put you up here and leave you alone if that's what you want or what you need."

He shook his head slowly, not losing eye contact with me. "It's not what I want or need." Scotty reached out, curling his hands around my hips. "I want you. I need you."

I cupped the sides of his face and leaned in for a soft kiss. "Thank fuck," I whispered against his lips. "I need you too. Let's go upstairs."

After helping him down from the counter, I threaded our fingers together and led him from the kitchen, through the wide open living space to the stairs beyond. The cold winter night outside the windows seemed miles away from the warmth and excitement inside.

I managed to find the bedroom I'd claimed and shut the door behind us once we were inside.

We stared at each other for a moment before Scotty stepped closer, brushing the stiff bulge in his jeans against my upper thigh. I let out a groan and reached for his hips to pull him closer. Scotty's hands came up to my stomach and ran up to my chest and out to my shoulders, squeezing each muscle as he went. With every touch of his hands, my dick filled even more.

"Take your shirt off, Roman," he said in a low voice.

My eyes widened in surprise. For some reason, I was used to being the dominant one in bed. But I kind of liked hearing him assert what he wanted.

After pulling back just enough to remove my shirt, I lifted an eyebrow at him. "What about yours?"

Scotty grinned and yanked his shirt over his head, tossing it on the floor before putting his hands back on my bare chest. They began to move and explore again immediately. I put mine on his shoulder blades and slid them down. So much warm, smooth skin. Just as I was wondering whether or not to sneak my hands down into the back of his pants, he leaned in and latched his mouth on one of my nipples, firing all the nerves between my chest and my dick.

"Fuck," I hissed. I ran my fingers into his hair and held him there. Scotty's own fingers moved down to undo my pants. As soon as he got them open, he pressed a palm over my swollen cock and squeezed, eliciting another shudder from me. "You're driving me crazy," I groaned.

He pulled off my nipple and grinned up at me, eyes half-lidded and nose pink from being pressed against my skin. I pulled his face in for another kiss and then deepened it, more, more, until I could barely breathe and still wanted more.

By the time we came up for air, my pants were around my ankles and Scotty was wrapped around my waist again. I loved how small and tight his body was. He was little but strong and not at all frail. I moved us over to the bed and laid him down on it. Within seconds, I had his pants off, revealing a tight little pair of pale pink boy shorts that almost made me shoot all over him.

"Gnfh," I grunted, reaching out to run my hand along the outline of his hard cock through the fabric. "Me like."

"Mm-hm, he's reached the caveman stage of horny. That's a good sign. C'mere."

Scotty grabbed my wrist and pulled me down on top of him, wrapping those sexy legs around me and arching his cock up into my belly. I found his mouth with my own and returned to my new favorite thing: kissing the fuck out of him. His lips were already puffy, but that only made me want to nibble on them some more.

I reached under him and wrapped my arms around his back before rolling us both over so he was on top of me. He writhed around a little more, making me absolutely crazy, before sitting up on my dick and holding a finger up.

"Not so fast," he said through panting breaths.

His short blond hair stuck up in chunks from where I'd run hands through it. It only made me want to get my hands in it again as soon as possible.

"What's wrong?" I asked, grabbing his hips and grinding up under his balls.

"I'm strictly a top," he said, almost aggressively.

"Yeah, fine. Whatever you want," I urged. "Just get back here and lose the shorts."

Scotty's eyes widened. He pressed a hand to my chest, stilling my movements. "Really? You'd let me top you?"

Granted, there was no blood to facilitate my brain function, but I was still confused. "Of course," I told him. "Why wouldn't I?"

His face softened and his hands ran gently up my chest. "You're the sweetest thing ever."

"I don't... I don't understand. I want to have sex with you, want to see you lose it and climax all over me, or in me, or near me. However that happens is super awesome with me."

"I prefer to bottom," he said with a cheeky grin.

"Wait, was that a test?" This was so fucking confusing. I just wanted to have an orgasm, preferably with my hands all over this beautiful man.

Scotty wiggled his butt over my dick again before pushing up on his knees and doing a sexy slow reveal of his hard cock.

The blush-pink tip appeared before the nest of dark blond curls and a pair of dusky balls high and tight. I reached out to fondle them, keeping my eyes locked on his for his reaction. His eyes slid closed, and he hummed in pleasure.

This was going to be so much fun.

# 9

## SCOTTY

*Surefire Ways To Satisfy Your New Partner In Bed*

I WAS NERVOUS AS FUCK. Being in bed with Roman Burke, *the* Roman Burke, had suddenly gotten real. There were so many things I wanted to say, to ask, to clarify. Was this just a quick, meaningless fuck? I had to assume it was. Was I going to be expected to keep it a secret? Again, I assumed so. Was I just the nearest, easiest person for him to screw, or was there anything special about me that attracted him?

I tried to remind myself it didn't matter. Why couldn't I simply enjoy the moment without staging a mental lightning round of *Jeopardy*?

I remembered what I'd decided in the kitchen earlier: that I would give myself tonight without second-guessing things. And maybe tomorrow morning as well if he was up for it.

Roman wanted me; he'd made that clear. That's all that mattered. I needed to stop questioning it and enjoy myself. There was no doubt in my mind I would kick my own ass down the road if my only memory was the second-guessing rather than the touching and fucking.

After shimmying off my underwear, I lay back down on top of him and kissed him on the neck, the jawline, his cheek, and finally his lips. I felt the warm strength of his large hands go immediately to my ass cheeks and begin squeezing. I fucking loved it when men played with my ass. I didn't do a million squats before bed every night to have the thing ignored.

"Your ass, I swear to god," Roman murmured. "Want inside it. Want to finger it, eat it, everything."

I nodded enthusiastically which almost caused me to break his nose since we were still lip-locked. He pulled back laughing. "Get on your stomach before you kill me."

I scrambled off him and lay facedown on the bed. Roman's hand came down in a light slap before grabbing my ass again and mumbling more curse words. He moved away for a moment before returning, and within seconds, I felt him spread my cheeks and press cool lube to my hole.

"Nghh." I drooled into the pillow as he teased me with his fingers. Roman pushed my knees up under me until my ass was propped in the air. He dropped openmouthed kisses on the skin of my lower back as he slid a finger inside me. I felt my body squeeze around him and heard the sharp intake of breath behind me.

"So hot, Scotty," he murmured against my back. "Tight as fuck, Jesus."

He pushed in another finger, and I literally mewled like a damned cat in heat. "*Roman.*"

His mouth moved in a line of searing kisses up my spine while his fingers found the bundle of nerves and dragged across it.

"Oh god, Roman, fuck!" I arched back into him, pressing my ass toward his stomach and driving his fingers in deeper. "Again, more. Please."

He moved his fingers in and out, stretching and pulling and pressing my gland until I was desperate and begging for him. My head spun and my nerve endings twitched everywhere. But when Roman suited up and pressed the tip of his cock against my ass, I nearly blacked out.

I wanted him so badly, my dick ached and my ass squeezed. I had to force myself to slow my breathing in order to relax enough to let him in, only because I was so damned needy and desperate.

Finally, he pressed into me, stretching out again along my back and kissing the nape of my neck before whispering in my ear.

"You okay? Tell me to stop if—"

"Don't stop." I reached for one of his hands and held it next to my face, kissing his knuckles and turning it over to hold his palm against my face.

He pulsed in and out of me until he was balls-deep and my ass was pressed all the way back against his body. He groaned, the sound of it sending shudders through me.

"You're so sexy, Scotty," he said, trailing his lips across my shoulder. "Want to stay inside you all night like this."

I felt his other hand slide under me to reach for my dick. It had been leaking precum steadily into the bedding the entire time he'd been teasing me with his fingers and mouth. So when he began stroking it, I knew I wouldn't last. I was already way too primed to blow.

"Roman," I warned, sucking in a breath. "Roman, I can't—"

His pace picked up, both in the thrusts of his hips and the slide of his grip around my shaft. I felt him everywhere. His lips on my ear, his hand on my face, his stiff cock grazing just the right spot inside.

It all came together and exploded into a vision of sparks. My entire body contracted and then expanded in waves of shock and pleasure. I cried out his name as I spilled all over his hand and the bed. My body squeezed his dick even more, and he grunted in my ear before pushing in one last time and holding me tight through his own release.

Even after he was done, he held me firmly to him. My hand still pressed his palm to my cheek, and my other hand was threaded back into his hair behind my head. Our heartbeats thumped wildly as we came down from our orgasms, and our skin stuck damply to each other.

I couldn't remember the last time I'd ever had sex like that. *If* I'd ever had sex like that—hot and tangled and desperate and shattering. That had been some kind of "going off to war" sex. Or "I've wanted you for twenty years" sex. Not "we're alone and horny for tonight" sex. Certainly not "one and done" sex.

At least, that's how it had felt to me. But it was entirely possible he hadn't had the same experience I had. Wasn't it?

Roman began to move. He pressed a long, chaste kiss into my temple before grasping the condom and pulling out. He moved away from me, presumably to clean up, but it felt awful. Cold, lonely.

The wetness of my release cooled uncomfortably between my stomach and the bedding, and the air in the room did the same to the sweat on my skin. I pushed up onto my hands and knees and then sat back on my heels in the middle of the mattress, wondering if I was supposed to get up and find another bedroom.

I wrapped my arms around my chest, holding myself as a chill worked its way across my damp skin. It occurred to me that Roman had to be used to people throwing themselves at him for quick fucks. He was a movie star for Christ's sake. Which made me wonder if that made me the equivalent of just another notch on his bedpost, or whatever the saying was?

I let my chin drop. I'd gotten carried away in the moment. I'd allowed myself to believe the fantasy that Roman Burke was actually interested in me. How absurd was that?

And then he was there. Standing in front of me with a wet wash-cloth and a clean hand towel. Looking at me like I was the most trea-sured thing on the planet. "Baby, lie down," he murmured.

Without thinking, I shifted onto my back. Roman leaned in and went to work with the hot cloth, wiping me down while telling me how amazing I was and how hot the sex had been. His voice was gentle and reverent, and not at all the way someone who was only interested in a quick fuck would behave.

I began to wonder just how much of my stupid assumptions had come from stereotyping him as some kind of entitled superstar instead of giving him the respect of judging him based on his actions and words.

When he was done with the wet cloth, he tossed it away and began going over the same body parts on me with the dry hand towel, all the while still nattering on about how great the sex had been and how good I'd felt underneath him.

He was so fucking sweet. I simply watched him in awe as he took care of me with such tenderness. When he was done, he finally caught me staring.

Roman actually blushed. It was fucking adorable. "What? Am I rambling? Sorry."

I reached out and hauled him back on top of me, wrapping my legs around him and pulling his face in with my hands so we were eye to eye. I shivered at how deliciously warm he was, how instantly the chill in the air disappeared under his weight.

"That was amazing," I told him. "And anytime you want to ramble about how good I am in bed, I'm totally here for it," I added.

His face opened into a happy grin. "Good. Because I might not be able to stop. It's been a long time since someone made me feel that way."

Roman leaned in and kissed me sweetly and slowly, lingering inside my mouth before gently tugging at my lower lip with his teeth. When he finally let go, his face was serious. "Stay with me tonight?"

I was so giddy at the invitation, I took a second to keep from blurting out, "Hell yeah," while pumping my fist in the air.

Roman must have mistaken my pause for hesitation. "Or not." He started to pull away. "Obviously you don't have to. Just pick any of the bedrooms…"

I clapped my hand over his mouth. "Don't be ridiculous. I'm using your ass like a furnace."

His face lit up again like a little kid as we both scrambled under the covers. Immediately, Roman reached for me and yanked me against his side. "Get over here."

I laid my head on his shoulder and wrapped my arm over his broad chest, running fingers around the contours of his muscles. One of his hands toyed with my hair while the other rubbed up my arm.

"How did you get into horses?" he asked after a few minutes. It was clear from our wandering hands on each other that neither one of us was quite ready to sleep just yet.

"My mom used to have a job cleaning apartments," I told him. "When I was like five, she cleaned three different apartments in this one building, and right next door were the stables where the carriage horses lived. So a few times if I didn't have school or it was summer break or whatever, she'd have to take me with her. But she couldn't take me into the apartments, so she told me to play in the park across the street until she was done. De Witt Clinton Park on Eleventh and Fifth-Third, you know it?" I lifted my head to look at him, but he shook his.

I was careful not to include any of the uglier parts of that time in our lives, especially my mom's attempt to teach me how to grift while I was at the park.

I settled my head back on his shoulder. "Well, anyway, there's a playground, but it's pretty little. After a while, I'd get bored and sneak back across the street to the Clinton Park Stables. An old guy there took pity on me and let me in one time to see the horses. After that, whenever Mom took me to work, I'd visit Arnold and the horses."

I drew a finger down the center of Roman's chest and into his belly button, playing around with different shapes on his skin.

"Love at first neigh?" he asked.

I chuckled, tweaking his nipple at the bad pun. "Definitely. When I finished middle school, Arnold offered me a job and helped me get working papers. I mucked stalls and did general shit work after school and on weekends." I smiled, remembering how pissed off my mom had been that my schedule at the barn meant I wouldn't be available to seek out new marks for her schemes. Working at the stable had been my refuge in more ways than one, but I didn't plan on sharing that little detail from my past.

"I fucking loved it," I continued. "I had all kinds of daydreams about owning my own farm or ranch one day where I could have my own horses and teach kids to ride. When I saved up enough money for my own riding lessons, I found a place in the Bronx I could get to by taking a train and two buses. I wanted it so badly. But then my mom lost her job. So all my money went to the usual—rent, food, heat."

I shrugged. "I still haven't taken riding lessons, if you can believe it. And that was almost ten years ago."

"You've never learned to ride in all that time?"

"Nope."

Roman's hand slowed in my hair. After a beat of silence, he gently turned my chin until I was facing him again. "I'm sorry you never had the chance to take lessons." He brushed his lips against my temple.

He sounded so sincere, so concerned. I didn't know how to respond and was afraid that if I said anything my voice might crack, so I buried my face in his neck instead.

Roman returned to threading his fingers through my hair, but after a moment he paused again. "Wait," he said, frowning. "If you don't know how to ride, how the hell did you come to own your own horse?"

"Well, I never took riding lessons, but I did take a carriage-handling course in order to get certified, but that meant I also had to get a driver's license. Which is a total bitch when you're born and raised in the city. Took me a full year to complete that course and get my certification."

I wiggled over until I was lying on top of him. There was no way to keep my hands off his body. Just lying next to Roman Burke naked was making me hard again, so I pushed my dick into his lower belly.

Roman's mouth curved up on one side. "Finish the story." But his hands cupped my ass, so how exactly did he expect me to have words?

"Then I got a horse. The end." I leaned down to kiss him, but he turned his head to the side, laughing so hard I practically bounced on his chest.

"Seriously, how did you get the horse?" he pressed.

I sighed and sat up, making a point of sitting so that his dick slid between my cheeks. Roman's nostrils flared and his hands twitched on my hips, fingers pulling my cheeks open just enough to settle his length snugly between them.

"Arnold hooked me up with a medallion owner who was looking for a driver. The driver said he'd hire me if I had a horse. I think it was his way of saying no since he knew I didn't have a horse. But Arnold called his bluff. Said I could use his horse. So I did."

The spot between Roman's eyes furrowed into a frown. "Scotty, did I just steal someone else's horse?"

# 10

## ROMAN

*When Your Love Nest Gets Pests*

I SMIRKED, making sure Scotty knew I was just teasing. I didn't actually think he'd tricked me into stealing a horse.

He tweaked one of my nipples, causing me to wince. "Don't be silly. Arnold died almost four years ago. He left me Nugget and a little bit of money for her care."

My smile fell. "I'm sorry." I reached up to cup my hand around his cheek. "It sounds like Arnold was someone very special."

He pressed his face against my palm, turning slightly so that the edge of his mouth brushed the tip of my thumb. "Thank you. He was. He drove every day for like forty years before retiring. After two weeks of retirement, he came back to work as a stable hand. He just didn't want to leave the horses, you know?"

While he spoke, he dragged his fingertips up and down my arms while I held on to his hip. The press of his ass cheeks along my dick was making my brain spin off into many different directions—none of which was a horse stable in Hell's Kitchen.

Scotty seemed to sense it, because he squeezed his ass and reached back to cup my balls in one hand. "Want to talk more about this? Or did you maybe want to stop the talking for a few minutes?"

"*Gnf.*"

"Thought so," he said with a low chuckle. He leaned down to take my mouth with his and used the momentum to straighten out his body on top of mine again until our cocks were nestled against each other. "Where's the lube?"

I slapped a hand blindly around the edge of the bed until I felt the bottle and handed it to him. Within moments, he'd slicked us both up and turned dry friction into something utterly intoxicating.

"Jesus fuck," I groaned. "Move your hand."

I replaced his smaller one with mine and clasped both our cocks together in my grip as best as I could. When it wasn't good enough for me to get good thrusting speed, I brought my second hand around. Scotty braced himself above me, fucking into my fists and making obscene noises in the process while I jacked us and humped up into him.

God, it was dirty and awkward as hell but hot as fuck. Wet sucking noises came from the lube; Scotty whimpered *please, please* over and over again; and I even heard my own deep grunts bouncing around the room.

It took no time at all before I was ready to paint Scotty's chest with my release. I gritted my teeth and held out as long as I could, twisting my grip around the most sensitive part of his cock in hopes it would drive him over the edge before I lost the rhythm to my own orgasm.

It worked.

Scotty shouted, thrusting one last time through my fists. Tendons stood out on his neck, and his skin flushed deeper red. There was no more holding back for me.

My grunts were replaced by a roar until I was out of breath completely and Scotty had thrown himself off me and onto the bed beside me, trying to catch his own. When I could move again, I grabbed for one of the discarded towels and repeated the cleanup routine before settling back next to him.

"I've decided I'm keeping you," he said between deep pulls of oxygen. "Hypothetical question. What size handcuffs you wear? Did they tell you that day in the squad car?"

I coughed out a laugh. "Hypothetical, huh?"

I reached for his hand that lay between us and pulled it up to press a kiss to it before holding it against my chest. "I think probably size *manly man*," I mused. "Unless they do superhero sizing, in which case... hmm."

Scotty's blue eyes danced when he turned to meet my gaze. "Never ask a man ego-based questions after he's had an orgasm."

I flashed him my best grin. "Good point."

I manhandled him around until his back was snuggled against my front. Within seconds, he was already asleep. I couldn't resist pressing a kiss to the back of his head. He smelled faintly of horse and hay, a scent that could only belong to him. A scent that was quickly becoming intoxicating to me.

I thought about his earlier comment that he'd decided he was keeping me. I knew it was offhand—just an expression. But still, something in my chest had fluttered at the thought. A sudden jolt of pleasure at the idea of us.

Obviously I couldn't imagine him fitting easily into my life back home. The press would tear him apart, and I wasn't willing to put him through that. But I could easily see him fitting into my life *here*. I wondered how much convincing it would take to get him to stay for a while.

And I didn't just want him to stay for my sake. He'd had an awful couple of weeks and needed time to rest and get his bearings. Since it was my fault his life had taken a turn for the worse, it seemed only reasonable I could give him the space and time to figure out how to turn things around. Plus, I couldn't imagine forcing him to leave his beloved Nugget.

And really, what was the hurry?

My thoughts were interrupted by the buzz of my phone on the bedside table. I grabbed it quickly before it could rattle again, waking Scotty. It was a text from Polly.

**Polly:** *U free to talk?*

I glanced at Scotty. He was so warm and cuddly, one of his legs hooked around my own like it was the most natural thing in the world. I didn't want to leave our comfortable little nest and was about to tell Polly that when she added:

**Polly:** *Please?*

With a sigh I typed back.

**Roman:** *Gimme a sec.*

As carefully as I could, I disentangled myself from Scotty, pausing to inhale the scent of him one last time before slipping from bed and pulling on my pants. I tiptoed to the door and closed it quietly behind me before making my way down to the kitchen.

I punched in the autodial for Polly's number while I rummaged around in Oscar's liquor cabinet, looking for a nightcap.

"How's mamma-to-be?" I asked as soon as she answered.

"Fuck you, Roman," she spat before hanging up.

I stared at the phone, eyes wide. "Wrong question I guess," I mumbled under my breath before redialing her number.

She answered on the first ring. "I'm bloated, my breasts are ginormous, I can't keep a goddamn thing down, and yet that doesn't seem to matter because I'm putting on weight like a bear hibernating for winter. So don't fucking try me, Roman."

"Sounds like pregnancy agrees with you," I teased, smiling.

"You say that to my face next time and we'll see how that works out for you," she grumbled.

"Oh, I know better than that, trust me. But seriously, though, how are you?"

She let out a long sigh. "Tired," she said. "Really, really, tired." I could hear the exhaustion in her voice, and I had a feeling it wasn't just from the pregnancy.

I poured myself a glass of scotch and carried it into the living room. It was full night, but the sky was awash with stars, the moon reflecting off the snow. "What's going on?" I asked her.

"I realized I kind of want to put the father's name on the birth certificate," she said. "I know that's a totally duh thing, but I just hadn't thought about it before today."

"Medical records are pretty well protected, so the paparazzi shouldn't be able to get their hands on that if you don't want them to find out who the father is," I told her.

"That's not the problem," she said. "The problem is that the father doesn't know he's about to be a father."

"Oh." When Polly had told me about the pregnancy, she hadn't said anything about the father and I hadn't asked. It was her business, I figured, and if she wasn't ready to tell me yet, I wasn't going to push her. But I didn't have to know who the father was to know what to tell her. "You should probably tell him."

"No shit, Sherlock," she snapped back. "It's just... it's not that easy. He... uh... doesn't know who I am."

Words escaped me for a long moment. "What? How? I don't understand."

She let out another long sigh. "It was when I was on location in North Carolina. We'd been filming for two weeks straight and we had a long weekend and I just wanted to get off set and escape all the shit with the movie and I went out to a bar in one of the suburbs and I met this guy and I kept waiting for him to recognize me and he didn't and I went home with him and..." Her voice warbled and she broke off.

"So it was a one-night stand?" I asked gently.

"We didn't leave the house the entire three-day weekend."

"A three-night stand, then."

"And we've been texting every day since," she added. "And talking on the phone. And video chatting. His name is Howard. He's a regular guy, a businessman. Owns a small architectural firm. And he's a widower and has three kids, twin girls who are in college and a son who's in law school, and he's kind and sweet and fucking amazing in bed. He does this thing where—"

"Zzzzttt!" I said, cutting her off.

Other than the TMI about their sex life, I'd never heard her talk about a man like that. All gushy and melty and breathless. I smiled. "It sounds like you like him."

"I do," she admitted.

"Then what's the problem?"

"Oh, I don't know. What do you think will happen when I call him up and am all like, 'Hey honey, been to the movies recently? I'm guessing not because if you had you might have recognized your long-distance girlfriend on the big screen.'"

"He refers to you as his girlfriend?"

I could hear the blush in her voice. "Yeah."

"Though seriously," I continued. "How has he not figured out who you are? Your movie is killing it at the box office, and the poster for it is basically your face with crosshairs over it. Plus you've been on the cover of every tabloid for the past two weeks. Is the man dense? 'Cause if so, I'm not sure about the viability of a long-term relationship."

"He's a fifty-two-year-old widower. He spends his weekends at home reading spy novels, and I doubt he's ever given any of the gossip magazines a second glance, especially with his daughters out of the house."

I gave a whistle. "Older man, huh, Pol?"

"Can it, Roman."

I turned serious again. "You're going to have to tell him."

"I know. I just... I'm scared to. He's so normal and stable and solid and good and so outside all the crap and bullshit of our world and this is going to freak him out." She let out a long breath. "I don't want to lose him."

"You'll lose him if you don't tell him," I told her. "Relationships can't work without honesty and open communication."

"Why do you have to be so fucking reasonable, Roman?" she grumbled. "You make it sound so easy."

I laughed. "Yeah, it's super easy. That's why I'm holed up in my ex-boyfriend's 'cottage' with—" I was about to tell Polly about Scotty but caught myself at the last minute. It wasn't that I didn't want her to know, or that I didn't trust her, and it certainly wasn't that I was embarrassed to be shacking up with the carriage driver. It was more that I felt a need to protect him. Shield him. If he wanted to tell people he'd hooked up with me, that was his decision to make. But I wouldn't make it for him.

"With?" Polly pressed. "Is there something or someone you're not telling me about?"

"Without anyone to warm my bed," I finished. "That's what I was about to say."

"You know how easy it would be to fix that," she said. "Head to the nearest town and flash that grin of yours and you'll have your pick."

*Or I could just go back upstairs*, I thought to myself. I immediately pictured Scotty the way I'd left him, cuddled under the covers all soft and warm. I couldn't wait to slide back in behind him and draw my arm around his middle and pull him close.

"Call Howard, Polly. Give him a chance," I said, already making my way back upstairs. "And let me know how it goes."

"Fine," she grumbled. "Good night."

I hung up the phone and slipped back into the bedroom. We hadn't taken the time to close the drapes and the moonlight on the snow reflected in through the window, casting the room in a soft glow. I shucked off my pants and crept onto the bed, sliding under the covers and scooting until I could feel the heat radiating from Scotty's body. With a sigh I closed my eyes and let myself sink against him.

Half-asleep, he reached back and grabbed my wrist, dragging my arm across him, shivering when the cold of my chest pressed against his back. "Chilly," he mumbled.

"Sorry," I whispered into his hair.

"S'okay. I'll warm you up." He hooked a foot behind my calf, pulling me closer.

I fell asleep exactly where I wanted to be.

I KNEW it was a dream because there was an orange-feathered snake tickling my nose and giggling. And there was no such thing as a laughing orange-feathered snake in real life.

I sneezed and batted it away.

It came right back.

"Fuck off."

"Mommy, the naked man said a bad word," a little voice shouted in my ear.

My eyes shot open to see two huge brown eyes right in my face and a long feather dancing by my nose. "Holy god," I cried, scrambling back. Where the hell was I?

"Aunt Goldie!" the little girl screamed. "He's awake!"

In my haste to escape the child, I ran right over a dead body in my bed, further freaking me the hell out.

"What?" I tried in vain to figure out where I was and what was happening.

I sucked in a breath when I saw the dead body was a blond-haired man with very nice muscles lying underneath me.

"Oh god, wake up," I begged, poking him and pushing him. "Don't be dead, oh my god."

He moaned and told me to stop.

Good, one dead man back alive. That was something at least.

My brain was so mixed up from the sudden wake-up, the strange location, the unknown child, and the—was that a car alarm going off?—that it took me a second before I remembered Scotty.

His eyes blinked up at me. "Why are you on my face?" he choked. "Can't breathe."

I moved to the far side of him and shoved him toward the kid, making sure the bedding stayed pulled up above our shoulders. Maybe he knew who it was. "We're under some kind of attack."

Both of us stared at the little girl. She was probably around six years old with a good four or five ponytails sticking out at all angles and enormous brown eyes blinking at us in curiosity.

Scotty stage-whispered out of the corner of his mouth. "Do you think she's the distraction while her accomplice steals the car?"

I wondered why I'd thought he was dead. "I think I watch too much *Forensic Files*," I muttered.

"Relevance?" he said, poking my side. "Who is that?"

Why was he asking me? "How am I supposed to know? Maybe she stowed away in... oh I don't know... a horse trailer?"

"That's rude," Scotty scoffed. "I thought we were past that."

I grinned. "That's not something you get past. It's something you bring back up over and over because it's flipping fantastic."

"Mpfh."

I leaned my chin on Scotty's shoulder but didn't get any closer to the girl. "Sweetie, where's your mommy?"

Just then a wild-haired woman in denim overalls and neon green rainboots came tearing into the room. The moment she spied the little girl she came to a stop, fisting her hands on her hips. "There you are. I told you to leave him alone."

"You said just the one, though," the little girl said, pointing. "Technically I wasn't breaking the rules."

The woman looked up and realized there was more than one "him" here. "Oh Christ on a Christmas tree," she muttered. "There's two of 'em."

"Ma'am," I began, as politely as I could. "Would you be so kind as to—"

"We're naked here," Scotty said bluntly. "Unless you want to start her education young, maybe you could give us a minute to get some clothes on? That'd be super fantastic."

The woman actually snorted. Which made her laugh, which only set her off more until she was full-on giggle-snorting as she led the girl from the room.

I heard her call out as she closed the door behind her, "Oh by the way, my jackass boyfriend just stole someone's black SUV. Hope it wasn't yours."

I lay back and put my hands over my face, but Scotty pulled them off. Wrinkles of concern on his forehead warred with a smirk on his swollen lips.

"*Your* SUV?"

"Yep."

"You have any idea who that was?"

"Nope."

# 11

## SCOTTY

*Ten Tips For Hosting A Killer Brunch On Short Notice*

AFTER ROMAN and I quickly pulled on clothes and made our way downstairs, we—or at least I—were surprised to see more than just the woman and the little girl. Six people stood around the kitchen making merry with mimosas.

"You didn't tell me it was a house party," I said under my breath. Roman's hand held mine in a vice grip for some reason, which surprised me since it was a kind of semi-public claiming I wouldn't have expected from him.

"I didn't know it was. I'm supposed to have the place to myself."

That's when they noticed us hovering in the doorway. A younger man in a pink polo with a popped collar and pastel madras pants looked up, and his eyes narrowed when they landed on Roman. "Do I know you? I swear you look familiar."

I felt Roman stiffen beside me.

Pink Polo tapped a finger on his lips. "You from Harry's Hot Wax? The guy who gives out the bottled water and ointment?"

Roman shifted from one foot to the other. "Um... no?"

I didn't know why he was suddenly so unsure of himself. It was the complete opposite of the Roman I'd seen on the street after the police had pulled us over for our joyride through Manhattan. That Roman had given everyone his Hollywood smile and practically preened under their attention. This Roman appeared awkward and uncomfortable and at a complete loss for words.

I decided to step in and help the poor man out. I clapped my hands to get everyone's attention. "Okay, who here knows Oscar?"

All the hands shot up and everyone in the room cheered. Well, that was at least something, but it didn't narrow down who they were or what they were doing here. I tried a different tactic. "Who here has the key code to get in the door and was specifically given permission to come today?"

The only person who raised her hand was the lady we'd seen in the bedroom.

"And who might you be?" I asked.

She gave me a knowing smirk and seemed confident as hell. I liked her already. "I'm Marigold," she said matter-of-factly, as if that was supposed to mean something to me.

"Marigold..." I drew out her name and then paused, hoping she'd fill in the blank, but she just raised an eyebrow at me.

"Oscar's sister," Roman murmured to me the same way I'd imagine a stage manager would feed someone forgotten lines.

I turned to him in surprise. "Wait, you know her?"

"No. She lives in Nebraska."

"You're from Nebraska," I pointed out. I mean seriously, how many people actually chose to live in Nebraska voluntarily? They had to all know each other.

He rolled his eyes. "It's a big place."

"Not really," Marigold piped up. "Not in terms of population anyway. Hey, do you know Dan and Trish—"

"Stay focused," I said, snapping my fingers. "Why didn't Oscar tell Roman you'd be stopping by?"

She grabbed a strawberry from a basket on the counter and

popped it in her mimosa before taking a chug. "Oh, we're not stopping by. We're staying."

Roman choked beside me. "You can't."

She raised an eyebrow. "Oh?"

"Seriously, dude, you are really, really familiar," Pink Polo interrupted, oblivious to the conversation we'd been in the middle of. He kept tilting his head from side to side as though looking at Roman from a different angle might jog his memory. I ignored him.

"What he means to say," I said to Marigold, placing a hand on Roman's arm to calm him, "is that Oscar told us—" She quirked an interested eyebrow the moment I said the word us. I cleared my throat. "I mean Oscar told *Roman* that he'd have the place to himself."

She gave a dismissive wave. "Oh, we're not staying here, we're staying at the spa, and screw Oscar if he thinks he can dictate otherwise."

I felt a small bit of relief at that information. Beside me, Roman seemed to also relax a tiny bit. "Good," I said.

"Roman... Roman... Roman..." Pink Polo guy muttered as he stared up at the ceiling. "That name. I feel like I should know it."

We ignored him. So did everyone else in the kitchen. Most of them seemed to be raiding the fridge and chugging mimosas as though the house belonged to them.

I tried to focus on what was important. "So what was that you said about someone stealing Roman's car?"

Marigold rolled her eyes. "Yeah, that's just Cyan being Cyan." She pulled another carton of orange juice from the fridge and started pouring it into a crystal pitcher.

I blinked at her. "And Cyan would be... I mean, other than a color?"

"My boyfriend. He does that sometimes—takes off when the muse strikes. Artists, am I right?" She said it so casually as if this was a totally normal thing.

"Does he usually use other people's cars?" I asked incredulously.

She shrugged, completely unruffled. "Sometimes."

I didn't even know where to begin. "Is he going to... bring it back?"

"Of course," she said, seeming a little affronted by the question. "But—"

She put her hands on her hips and narrowed her eyes at me. "Who the hell are you? Roman's naked spokesperson?"

I returned to our side-of-the-mouth whispering. "Is that a thing? Because I happen to be looking for work…"

"God, it's like right on the tip of my tongue," Pink Polo said, shoving his hand through his frost-tipped hair. "This is going to drive me crazy."

"Oh for fuck's sake, Collins," Marigold said, whirling on him. "It's Roman Burke. The movie star. You know, the lead in the movie you've watched like seventy billion times?"

Collins's jaw dropped. "Oh. My God. That is totally who it is."

Beside me, Roman practically vibrated he was so tense. Which didn't make sense—he got recognized all the time; this couldn't be anything new for him.

"Dude," Pink Polo, aka Collins said, skirting around the kitchen island to approach Roman. "You have *no* idea what a *huge* fan I am."

"Such a fan you didn't even recognize him," I muttered.

"Like seriously, bro," Collins continued as if I hadn't even spoken. "*Back Passage* is totally my favorite ever."

I snorted. He did seem like the kind of guy who would like some *Back Passage* action. I elbowed Roman, expecting that he'd be thinking the same thing, but he didn't even flinch or show the slightest hint of amusement. Something was seriously off with him. "You okay?" I asked under my breath.

He nodded, but I noticed the muscles straining along his neck. He tried to smile, but it looked like a corpse gone into rigor mortis. Not pretty at all.

"I've totally gotta document this," Collins continued, pulling out his cell phone. "The guys in my polo squad are going to shit themselves when they find out."

Roman's eyes had gone wide. He looked like a deer in headlights. It was pretty obvious he wasn't down with getting his photo taken, and even if he was, I wouldn't let him. No one as pale and sweaty as he was at the moment needed to have that look captured for posterity.

I stepped in between Roman and Collins. "How about we save photo time for later, m'kay?"

Collins looked crestfallen. "But—" He tried to lean to the side to continue pleading his case with Roman, but I mirrored his move, keeping myself firmly between the two.

Just then, someone opened a champagne bottle with a loud *pop* that sent the cork flying across the room to plink against the window and tumble to the ground. Roman jerked, his breath catching in his throat. I glanced at him. He'd grown paler and more sweat pebbled his forehead.

"I'm gonna... I have to..." he swallowed. His eyes jerked around the room, like he was desperately searching for an exit. I'd seen the same expression on a panicked horse before it rampaged through a barn, and we did not need that happening here with Roman. Not while there were strangers watching and while Collins still had his phone out and was able to start recording in a moment's notice.

I needed to get him out of there before this entire situation imploded. I held up a finger to the group. "Give us just a mo, m'kay? Maybe fix up a couple of those drinkie-poos for the road so you can be on your way. Thanks."

Then I turned to Collins. "Hey, lemme see your phone real quick?" I held out my open palm, and Collins automatically started to hand it over. I snatched it from him before he could think better of it. "Awesome. It'll only be a sec."

I shoved Collins's phone in my pocket and looped an arm through Roman's, leading him from the kitchen. Once we were out of earshot, I turned and put my hands on his shoulders. "What's going on?" I asked him. "You're not acting like yourself."

His eyes met mine, then glanced away. "Sorry. I'm just... there was... a lot of noise." Roman rubbed at the center of his chest. "And I don't... I don't handle the unexpected well. I'm sorry. Give me a minute and I'll be fine."

I tilted my head at him and cupped his neck. "You're pale."

"It's winter."

"No, I mean, something's going on. What is it, Roman?"

He clenched his jaw and glanced down. "I sometimes have anxiety issues. Usually if I'm mentally prepared, I can keep my anxiety in check, but when something unexpected happens and I'm not prepared, it can throw me." He blew out a breath. "It's not something I like to talk about. Please don't tell anyone."

"Of course I won't, Roman," I promised him.

I felt his pulse thundering under my palm. I began smoothing my thumb over it. He closed his eyes and stepped forward into my embrace. It reminded me of the hug from the kitchen the night before when he'd sensed me needing comfort. Did that mean he needed the same now?

I held him tightly and didn't say anything for a little while.

"It's okay," I whispered.

Roman buried his face against my neck, his breath hot and warm along my shoulder.

"I'm just not ready for this to be over."

For a brief second I thought he might mean the two of us and my pulse tripped into overdrive. But then he continued, saying, "This vacation," and disappointment flooded my veins. I mentally kicked myself for even getting my hopes up in the first place.

"It's just, the more people who know where I am, the more likely it is someone's going to say something and it's going to get back to the press and then that's it—vacation over, back under the microscope." I could hear the resignation and exhaustion in his voice. "I was just hoping I'd have more time before it happened."

"Do you want me to reach out to Oscar?" I asked.

I felt him shake his head. "It's fine. I don't think they'll be staying long anyway."

Seeing as how we'd just left them mixing a second pitcher of mimosas, I wasn't so sure about that. But I didn't want to stress Roman out any more than he already was.

"Why don't you go lie down and I'll see if I can hurry them along," I offered. "Or at the very least keep them out of your hair."

He pulled back so he could meet my eyes. A frown crinkled his forehead. "You'd do that?"

What kind of question was that. "Of course. Why wouldn't I?"

"You don't even know them. Why would you want to spend time with them?"

I shrugged. "That doesn't bother me. I meet strangers all day long."

He hooked his hand around the back of my neck, pulling my forehead against his. "You're a good man, Scotty. Thank you."

His words warmed my heart. Enough that I felt like I might never be cold again.

Now I was the one whose chest needed rubbing. The last thing in the world I needed right now was an unreciprocated crush on this man. I was homeless, jobless, and bordering on hopeless. There was no chance in hell this ended well for me. I was lucky to have his kindness long enough to fill my belly and get a ride to the nearest town for a job.

I cleared my throat and moved away from him, looking down at the wide planks of the hardwood floor. "You go," I said, nudging him away. Afraid if I didn't let go now I never would, and that train of thought led to danger.

"Keep an eye on Marigold," he warned. "She's flighty and tends to make bad decisions, like walking off a job one time because she didn't like the way her coworker parted her hair. Or the time she saw a painting she didn't like at their uncle's house and donated it to Goodwill without telling anyone. It was a Monet. They assumed it was a reproduction painting and sold it to some lucky thrift store shopper for forty bucks."

My eyes widened. I couldn't even imagine. Not just the part about Marigold donating her uncle's Monet just because she didn't like it, but even having an uncle who owned a Monet in the first place. It was another reminder just how different Roman's world was from my own.

"I'll make sure not to let her near my fine-art masterpieces," I promised him.

The corner of his lips curled up. I liked that I'd been able to make him smile.

He pressed a kiss to the tip of my nose with a murmured thanks and retreated toward the master bedroom. I blew out a breath and returned to the kitchen.

"Okay," I said, clapping my hands as I returned to the party. "Someone said something about everyone going to the spa? Sounds great. Awesome plan. I'm totally in favor. Manis, pedis, facials, massages. All things you can't get here, which is why you should totally go ahead and go before someone else takes the best time slots. Why don't we go ahead and make that happen?"

I realized at that point that the number of people in the kitchen had swelled. There was now an older couple who didn't seem to fit with the vibe of the rest of the crowd. As soon as the older woman saw me, she beamed like we'd known each other for ages and came gliding toward me.

She took my hand in both of hers. "You must be Roman's *friend*. Marigold was just telling me *all* about you."

"Um." I cut my eyes toward Marigold. She smirked at me. The woman had known me for all of five minutes—what exactly could she say about me? Then I realized the emphasis that the older woman had placed on the word *friend* and *all* and realized exactly what Marigold had probably told her. I was guessing it involved me and Roman and finding us in bed together. Great. The last thing Roman needed was to have that little tidbit of information find its way to the press.

"Yeah, about that... Roman is kind of a private person, so if you could keep that bit of info—"

"Oh posh." The woman waved a hand. "If you think I don't have better dirt on Roman Burke than that!"

"Yeah," Marigold chimed in, reaching for another strawberry and popping it in her mouth. "Oscar isn't exactly discreet when it comes to sharing details of his sexual exploits with his family."

"I..." I didn't know what to say to that. Sexual exploits? Family?

The older woman patted me on the shoulder. "Never you fear, dear, Roman's secrets are safe with us."

"And you are..."

"Oh dear me, so sorry," she said, pressing a hand to her chest. "I'm Gladiolus. Oscar and Marigold's mama."

This was turning into a regular family reunion. Or a garden party —I wasn't sure which. "Are you going to the spa as well?"

"No, no, of course not. That's more Marigold's thing. Birch and I are taking Rosette to the Sugar Shack," she said, nodding to the older man, who I presumed was her husband, and the little girl who'd awoken us. I wasn't sure I wanted to know what the Sugar Shack was, but so long as it didn't involve them staying with us, I was cool with it.

"We just dropped by to pick up the package," she continued. "We'll all be out of your hair in two shakes of a lamb's tail."

I looked around the room. "And the package is...?"

Marigold snickered next to her mother. "She's kidding about the package."

"Hush, dear. He doesn't need to know." Mrs. Oscar's Mom sniffed.

"But Mom..."

"Zzttt," she said, elbowing her grown daughter in the side. "Snitches get stitches, Goldie."

Apparently that wasn't enough to scare Marigold, because she didn't stop. "The package is Oscar's vodka stash. He's always got the good stuff you can't find anywhere else."

I thought about Roman saying that I needed to be careful Marigold didn't make off with anything important of Oscar's, but I wondered if vodka fell under that category. "And if you get the vodka, will you leave?"

Marigold drained the rest of her mimosa. "Yep."

I clapped my hands together. "Excellent. Let's go find some vodka."

Half an hour later, the kitchen was a mess, Oscar's vodka stash was seriously depleted, and the house was once again blessedly empty. I retreated to the bedroom to find Roman on his side under the covers. "They're gone," I said, collapsing on the bed next to him.

"Finally. Marigold said something about going to the spa? Or the sugar shack? I never could quite figure it out. But so long as they're gone and stay gone, I don't much care."

"The spa and the sugar shack are both on the property," he said, voice muffled by the covers.

"Shit. So they could be back after all."

Roman rolled to face me. "I'm sorry, Scotty."

"For what?" I asked, genuinely not sure what he was apologizing for.

He glanced away. "For being lame."

I stripped down to my boxer briefs and nudged him over so I could lie next to him. "You're the opposite of lame, Spartacus."

He turned onto his side to face me. "Spartacus?"

"I think Roman sounds a bit... serious. Don't you?"

"But I—"

I put two fingers over his lips. "You're going to go with it. Because you're Go-With-The-Flow Man."

"I thought I was Spartacus," he said with a grin after pulling my hand away.

"That too."

I nudged his legs apart with a knee and slid closer until we were tangled together. "I say we hide up here for a bit and then we go downstairs and make a feast to take to the movie room."

"Movie room?"

I grinned. "This place has to have a home theater. And we can spend the entire rest of the day pigging out and watching Roman Burke movies."

He shook his head vehemently. "No way. Uh-uh. I can't stand watching myself on screen."

Even with an expression of mock horror I could tell he was feeling better. Lighter, more quick to smile. His anxiety from this morning fading into the past.

"What's your favorite movie?" I asked him. "Besides *Jurassic Park*. That's stupid, by the way, especially for someone in film."

He laughed. "I only put that down on the dating site because it was the first thing that popped into my head." He paused and thought for a moment, letting his head fall back on the pillow. "Let's see... my favorite movie... I like old Doris Day movies. Which, I mean, makes me hella gay, right?"

I nodded. "Natch."

"And I also love cheesy romantic comedies. *Fifty First Dates* is one I get sucked into every time it's on. But I like unique ones too. Did you ever see *Life of Pi*?"

"Yeah. Sad as hell. We're not watching that. Or *Castaway*. Or anything scary for that matter," I told him.

"What do you like, then?"

I thought about it. "I like the rom-coms too. And I fucking love teen movies even though they're also cheesy as hell. I'm a sucker for Hallmark movies at the holidays, but once Christmas morning rolls around, boom. I'm done. No more till next Thanksgiving. And don't test me on that."

Roman smiled and ran his hand through my hair. "No Christmas movies, then. Do you like spy films?"

"Love them. I have a huge crush on the guy who was in... what was it called...?" I pretended to search my memory for the name and then snapped my fingers. "Back Pass—"

"Don't say it!" Roman barked, tackling me and shutting me up with his mouth. I laughed through the kiss, squirming happily underneath him as he pinned me to the bed and tried to keep me quiet with his mouth on mine.

There was no telling how long we spent wrestling and rolling around, jerking each other off and then showering together. When we finally came back downstairs clean and in comfortable sweats, the house was empty and quiet.

But not for long.

# 12

## ROMAN

*Cooperative vs Competitive: Choosing The Right Video Game For A First Date*

SCOTTY WAS A MOTHERFUCKER. We did find Oscar's home theater, but we also found his PS4 and its fat stack of accompanying games. It turned out, Scotty was a ringer on absolutely every game we played.

"How much time do you spend on this shit?" I finally muttered after my little chef dude fell off a moving truck to his death for the one-billionth time. I tossed aside my game controller and reached for my bottle of water.

"You mean before I had to sell my gaming system to pay for horse feed?" Scotty asked absently while he navigated through the game screens to set up our next match.

It was a stark reminder of his dire financial situation.

I toyed with the cap to my water bottle, unsure how much he would appreciate me prying into his life, especially since his current situation was my fault. "Are you going to try and get another job driving a carriage?" I asked him. "Is that something you can do?"

He finally set down his controller and looked at me. We were sprawled out on a big stack of floor pillows and surrounded by bags of snacks. Scotty wore a pair of sweats and a plain T-shirt we'd scrounged in a closet stuffed with clothes of various sizes, all brand-new with tags still on them. Apparently Scotty wasn't the first guest to arrive at Oscar's house without an overnight bag.

In response to my question, he pushed himself up straighter, and even though the dim light in the room set his face in shadow, I could still make out the crinkle in his forehead.

"Sorry," I said, glancing away. "I didn't mean to spoil the mood."

Scotty tilted his head to the side, eyes narrowing slightly as he considered me. "If we're bringing the mood down anyway, tell me what you were running from that day in the park."

I blinked at him, surprised by the question. We'd told the media that I'd been running from a crowd of aggressive paparazzi, but Scotty would have known that was a lie. He'd been there, after all. He knew there hadn't been cameras chasing me when I'd first jumped into his carriage.

But I wasn't sure how much of the truth I was ready to share. Actually, that wasn't true. I wanted to share it all with him. And that was the problem. As a rule I didn't trust people, yet I kept wanting to trust Scotty against my better judgment. I was used to keeping so much of myself locked away and out of sight, aware that some people viewed my most personal stories as currency that could be used to their advantage. And because of that, I knew better than to trust someone I barely knew.

I'd been burned before, trusting too easily only to turn around and find my secrets splashed across glossy magazine covers the next week. I didn't want to make that same mistake again.

When I didn't immediately respond, he waved a hand. "Never mind. I knew I shouldn't have asked. It's none of my business anyway."

He turned away from me to reach for his Coke, and the movement revealed a sexy strip of skin between the bottom edge of his shirt and the waistband of his pants. Without thinking, I reached out and drew my fingers across it, wanting the reassurance of his physical presence.

Scotty stilled. "That feels good," he said softly. "I like being touched."

I ran my full palm up under his shirt and across the narrow expanse of his back. His skin was smooth and warm. "Take off your shirt and lie on your stomach."

Without hesitation, he put his drink back down and did as I'd said, offering me a pleased grin in the process. My chest fluttered at the sight of it. So did my cock.

As soon as he was settled comfortably on a pillow, I began to rub his back, letting my fingers splay against his muscles. Enjoying the strength and curves of his body.

"You know I was filming *Deep Cut* that day," I began, caving to my selfish, emotional desire to confide in him. Maybe there should have been the usual warning bells clanging in my head, but there weren't. And if I was making a huge mistake by opening up to him, well, then I'd deal with the consequences later just like I had before when old partners and friends had sold my stories to the tabloids.

"Mm-hm," came his muffled response.

My eyes moved down to his adorable bubble butt sticking up in the gray sweats. *Focus, Roman.* I wanted to get this story out. I wanted to open up and share this part of myself—to show him I was more than just a face on a movie screen.

So I continued. "That day we were filming a scene where... wait. Do you know how my father died?"

Scotty twisted so he could look up at me over his shoulder. "Wasn't he killed in some kind of farming accident?"

My chest tightened, remembering. I tried to make sure I took slow, steady breaths. "Not really. We didn't have a farm. My dad sold insurance."

He frowned. "Oh. I thought it was something to do with a farm. Sorry."

I shook my head and ran a hand through his blond locks, messing his hair up again the way I liked. "It's fine," I told him, trying to keep my voice from wobbling. This wasn't a story I told often. Or at all, really. "And he did die on a farm, but it wasn't a farming accident. He was struck by lightning while changing a flat tire on the side of the road."

Scotty's eyes went wide. "Jesus, Roman."

"Yeah. We were driving back from a day trip to a nearby town when Dad recognized a neighbor of ours on the side of the road with a flat. I was thirteen and my older sister, Diana, was fifteen. A thunderstorm started and Mom begged Dad to get back in the car and wait out the storm, but he was too stubborn to listen. Said he wanted to get home in time for the baseball game on TV."

Scotty reached out a hand to squeeze my leg. "I'm so sorry. I can't imagine what that must have been like for you."

I let out a rueful laugh. "Shitty. Really fucking terrible. I can't say I was super close to my dad, but being there when it happened..." I had to pause a moment to keep my voice from cracking. Memories of that moment began swimming to the surface, and I forced them away with a shake of my head. "And losing my dad right when I was starting middle school—it was all just awful. I, um, joined the drama club after that because I couldn't bear to spend too much time at home, you know?"

The concern on Scotty's face was amazingly sweet. He looked at me the way he looked at Nugget—protectively, affectionately, devotedly. It stirred feelings deep within me, and I basked in the warmth they created in my chest.

"Is that how you got into acting?" he asked.

It was a common question, one I was asked in almost every interview. And I almost gave him my practiced answer that drama club had opened a world of possibilities and shown me I had a talent that an enthusiastic and supportive teacher had helped nourish.

But there was a deeper, more complicated answer, and that was the one I found myself sharing with Scotty. "I liked that being on stage allowed me to become someone else, even if just for a few minutes or hours. Because if I was someone else, I could forget about what happened with my dad. I didn't have to be angry and sad and lost. It gave me an escape."

There was a moment of silence after I finished. I was afraid to meet Scotty's eyes, not sure what I'd find. His hand on my leg tightened. "That makes sense," he said softly.

"Anyway," I said, clearing my throat. "I've had a hard time with loud, sudden noises since then. Because of the... the accident."

Scotty let out a breath. "Understandable."

"Yeah," I continued. "So that day on set—the day I met you— there was... and I even knew it was coming... there was a gunshot. It kicked off like this... adrenaline response in my body and I began breathing heavily. My heart raced and my skin started pouring sweat. I tried keeping it together, tried focusing on my job and my role, but then a gaffer bumped into a scaffold, knocking a stack of metal poles and wooden slats down onto a cement floor. The loud bang of each pole and slat hitting the ground was too much." I clenched and unclenched my hand into a fist. "I freaked and bolted outside."

Scotty reached over and took my fist, pulling it open and threading his fingers through mine. "To me."

I kept my eyes on his and nodded. "To you."

He drew his thumb softly across my knuckles. "And you picked a carriage because...?"

"I just wanted out of there as fast as possible. And when I saw you there..." I had to pause and swallow. I didn't know how to explain it to him. At the time I hadn't been thinking—not really. I'd just seen him and the carriage and the word *safe* played through my head. But somehow that seemed too much to confess, so I lifted a shoulder.

"I knew you'd be the quickest way across the most distance. I couldn't just stand there and wait for a cab. And my legs were shaking so much, I knew I couldn't take off running. But you... you could get us all the way across the park."

Scotty shifted until we were cross-legged in front of each other, our hands tangled together between us. "You must have been really upset," he said softly. And he sounded so sincere. There was no judgment, no laughter that Roman Burke, the man who played badass spies and Navy SEALs on the big screen, could be freaked-out by a few loud noises.

"I was," I told him. "I don't even remember some of it. It was like this... physical thing."

The corner of his lip kicked up. "Yeah, I kind of noticed at the time. I totally thought you were going to hurl in my carriage, and then we really would have had a situation on our hands."

I smiled as well. It was nice to have a bit of humor to temper the seriousness of the conversation. But I could tell there was something still on Scotty's mind in the way his forehead remained crinkled. "Was there something else you were wondering about?"

He glanced down at our hands, at the way our fingers intertwined, and nodded. "I'm curious about Polly."

I blew out a breath. "You and everyone else," I muttered.

It was the wrong thing to say. Scotty reacted instantly, stiffening and trying to pull his hand from mine. I tightened my grip, not letting him escape.

"I'm sorry," I told him. I dipped my head, forcing myself into his line of sight. "Scotty." I used my voice that commanded attention and his eyes snapped to mine. "I'm sorry," I told him again.

There was a flash of indignation in his expression. "I'm not here so I can learn your secrets and sell them," he told me.

"I know, I didn't think that you were," I said. "If I did I wouldn't have shared any of that with you," I added, loosening my grip on his hand and giving him the chance to pull away if he wanted. Thankfully, he didn't.

A muscle ticked in his jaw. "I don't want you thinking I'm using you."

I wanted to cup my hands around his cheeks and kiss his concern from his lips. "I don't think that. I promise. Otherwise you wouldn't always be so stubborn about accepting my help."

His eyes narrowed playfully, the previous indignation gone. "You like that I'm stubborn and you know it."

I couldn't resist dragging my knuckles along the line of his jaw, my thumb coming to rest on his bottom lip. "If you hadn't been so stubborn, you wouldn't be here now. So yes, I do like it."

Scotty drew in a sharp breath. His tongue darted out, just tasting the tip of my thumb. I was about to let out a growl and pounce on him, but he held up a hand. "The Polly story first. I want to make sure I'm not moving in on someone else's man."

I sat back, needing some physical distance if I didn't want to jump him. "I found out Polly was pregnant not long before the media caught wind of it. The moment she found out, she came to my house really upset and wanting to talk. I had no idea she was going to release a statement naming me as the father. When the paparazzi bombarded me after the carriage ride—that's the first I'd heard of it."

He frowned, started to ask a question, thought better of it, and closed his mouth. Then opened it again and hesitated. "But... I mean... are you... you know... like..." He made a motion with his hands that I assumed was meant to approximate sex.

I laughed. "No. I'm not sleeping with Polly."

Scotty glanced away. "But did you... like... are you... its... you know, the um.... parent?"

"No."

He met my eyes, his expression relieved. "Really?"

"Really."

His frown was back. "Then why did she say you were?"

I took a breath, knowing I couldn't tell him Polly's secrets. But I could tell him my own part of it. I'd at least made that clear with Polly when I'd agreed to this ridiculous scheme. "She was desperate and panicked. She needed to protect the real father's identity, and she knew if she gave the media a salacious alternative, they wouldn't have any reason to question it. Since there's been so much speculation about the two of us and we're good friends, she knew I was a safe bet and that I'd go along with it."

We stared at each other for a minute before Scotty moved closer and crawled into my lap to straddle me. His blond happy trail immediately attracted my attention, and I ran a finger through it to the elastic band of his pants. There was movement under the cotton of his sweats.

"So you're not having a baby," Scotty murmured, running his hands up under my shirt and across my stomach.

"Nuh-uh." I leaned in and ghosted a kiss next to his mouth.

"And you're not having sex with a beautiful woman."

"Nope. Am having sex with a beautiful man. A sexy-as-fuck man," I promised, sliding my hands around his sides and down into the back of his pants to cup his bare cheeks. "At least I'd like to."

"Mmm," Scotty hummed before latching onto my Adam's apple and sucking lightly. His hands began to lift my shirt off me, and he pulled away long enough to let it come all the way off. "Lie down on your back, Spartacus."

I did as he said and made myself comfortable with him stretched out on top of me. Our semihard dicks nudged each other through our pants, which only served to plump them up even more.

Scotty reached for my wrists and moved them above my head while his mouth continued to move and suck and lick down my neck to my collarbone.

I was a sucker for that and made appreciative noises accordingly.

"Like that, hm?" he purred.

"Nhgh."

Scotty released my hands and began moving down my body, kissing along my chest and belly until his stubbled chin was nudging down the loose band of my pants. I couldn't wait for him to do it, so I reached down and shucked everything off, revealing my excited dick and the strings of precum it was releasing steadily now.

I caught sight of his smirky grin when he noticed how excited I was. "Proud of yourself?" I teased.

"Little bit, yeah."

Before I could respond, he gave my slit a lick and then immediately took my entire cock down his throat.

"Fuck!" I barked as he swallowed around me. "Oh god, Scotty, *fuck* that feels... yeah, babe, please keep... doing that, please."

He pulled off, leaving my shaft dripping wet. He jacked me with his hand a minute before lowering down over my cock again and repeating the deep-throat maneuver.

I grunted and tried to focus on not coming right away. It felt too good to let it end.

My hands made it into Scotty's hair and held on. When he pulled off again, I saw tears in his eyes and saliva all over his flushed mouth and chin. He looked utterly debauched as he peered up at me through his lashes as if wondering if he was doing okay.

He was. He was doing an incredible job.

He didn't even have his mouth on me when I blew. The look of him kneeling next to me, servicing me, trying to please me, was enough to finish me off. I grabbed him by the back of his neck and pulled him to me for a crushing kiss while I stroked my cock with my other hand twice.

I cried out into his mouth as we kissed and the warm fluid from my orgasm coated my hand and stomach. When I leaned back from the kiss to catch my breath, Scotty moved back down to lick up the remains of the cum on my skin. It was sexy as hell.

I threw my head back on the pillow underneath me with a groan. "You're going to kill me."

"Don't die," he said, smiling. "I'm going to need you to reciprocate after another round of *Overcooked*."

Scotty sat up and licked his lips before leaning away from me and coming back with two game controllers. He plunked one on my still-heaving chest. "This time, don't drop the burgers," he told me. "It's a cooperative game, dumbass. If you lose, I lose."

I blinked up at him. My head was still spinning with "Scotty is a sex god" chants and general feelings of kick-ass well-being.

"What?" I asked, trying to figure out why he was talking about burgers when we'd just spent the last few hours eating our body weight in snack food.

Before he could answer, a strange male voice came from the direction of the stairs leading up to the main level of the house. "Yo, anyone here?"

I stood up and fumbled for my clothes, glancing over at Scotty to see him pulling on his own shirt.

"Who the hell is that?" Scotty hissed. "The infamous Oscar?"

I didn't recognize the voice, but I knew who it wasn't. "No. I don't know who it is, but it's not Oscar."

"Do you have a weapon?" Scotty asked.

I glared at him, gesturing to my 100 percent nude body. "Yes, Scottsman Pinkerton. I have all kinds of weapons up in this bitch."

Scotty broke into a laugh. "I'll have you know it's Scotland Pony Pinker."

My eyes widened. "No way."

"Of course not. Shut up and get dressed. You're going first. Think of yourself as a human shield of sorts."

We made our way upstairs carefully, Scotty holding on to the back of my pants with a vice grip that gave me a terrible wedgie.

"Let go of my underwear," I whispered. "You're chafing my crack."

"Shh, we can't hear the bad guys over the sound of your bitching."

Even though we were about to face our own deaths, I couldn't help but think of how much fun I was having hanging out with Scotty.

He yanked the back of my shirt, choking me. "Wait! Do your police thing!" he hissed.

"What police thing?"

"Like you did with me. Obviously it works. Try it."

I turned back and gawped at him. "Dude, I'm wearing sweats and a Snickers Bar T-shirt."

"What does your shitty fashion sense have to do with anything?"

We were hovering at the top of the basement stairs, staring at the closed wooden door.

"Open it," Scotty urged.

"We're going to be shot. You know that, right?"

"It's Vermont, for god's sake. At the most, we're going to be offered Ben & Jerry's ice cream and lectured on greenhouse gasses."

Suddenly, the door opened away from us, revealing a huge mountain man with a giant beard the size of a serial killer...'s giant beard.

"Fuck," I blurted. "We weren't ready."

"He's a cop," Scotty squeaked from behind me, pushing me forward. "You're under arrest!"

The two of us glared at the stranger for a beat before something became painfully obvious. The giant mountain man was dressed in a police uniform.

"I think you have that the other way around," the man said calmly.

*Motherfucker.*

# 13

## SCOTTY

*Does Roman Burke Have A Cop Fetish?*

MAYBE I WAS GOING to have to wait and get my reciprocal blow job in jail.

And also maybe I needed to stop hanging out with Roman fucking Burke since he was the common denominator in the sum total of police problems I'd had lately.

"Just for this, you're paying for riding lessons when we get out of prison," I muttered under my breath as we followed the cop to the kitchen. "And you're paying my attorney's fees too."

Roman responded by turning to me with an indulgent smile on his face and leaning in to kiss me on the lips. "You delight me," he said.

I stared at him in shock. "Even though I'm getting you arrested again?"

He reached for my hand and held it between both of his. I'd noticed he liked to be touching me most of the time we were near each other, which I loved. I was a touchy person anyway, and around Roman I was practically a salivating skin whore.

He chuckled. "You're not getting me arrested. That's one of Oscar's exes," he said, nodding toward the hulking man who'd met us at the top of the stairs.

As I watched, Officer Beardy McBeardson helped himself to a beer from the fridge. He was very obviously comfortable in the house as he didn't even hesitate before grabbing a bottle opener from one of the drawers and tossing the cap into the hidden trash can.

"Careful about glass houses, Roman," the cop said, tipping his beer bottle toward him. "You dated Oscar too."

I was very, very confused. "So wait... have you two met before?"

The cop turned his attention my way, his eyes sweeping over me. A slow smile spread across his face. "Nah. But we all know about each other. We're like a club."

"And not a very exclusive one apparently," I pointed out.

His grin widened. "I'm Trevor, by the way," he said, reaching out to shake my hand. "Nice to meet you, gorgeous," he added with a wink.

Before I had a chance to fully extend my arm, Roman reached around my waist and pulled me back against his chest with a little growl from his throat.

Trevor threw his head back and barked out a laugh. "What, I can't appreciate this jewel just because you're currently wearing him?"

I assumed I was the jewel in question and wasn't sure how I felt about the description. On the one hand, jewels were pretty and fancy, and I never minded being considered as such. But on the other hand, jewels were items to be owned and possessed, and I wasn't really down for the idea that I belonged to someone like that. I'd spent too many years being independent to be willing to be considered nothing more than someone else's possession.

Though the idea of belonging to Roman wasn't that disagreeable. In fact, I rather liked the idea of decorating his body with my own. Before my mind could get lost in that delicious fantasy, Roman dropped his arm. I wondered if it was because he didn't want me to feel like someone's arm candy or because he didn't want Trevor to get the wrong idea about us.

"Why are you here, Trevor?" Roman growled.

Trevor lifted a bushy brow. "Someone reported a stolen vehicle?"

Now it was my turn to bark out a laugh. It seemed we'd both completely forgotten about Marigold's boyfriend taking off in Roman's SUV.

"Touché," Roman mumbled, nudging me toward one of the stools at the counter. "You want a beer, Scotty?"

"Sure, but I can grab it." I started toward the fridge, but he shooed me away. "Sit."

I slid onto the stool, admiring Roman's ass as he bent to look in the fridge. It was a nice view. "I think I saw some clementines in there earlier way in the back," I said, "You want to grab them? After all that junk, I feel like I have scurvy." Roman bent further and I sighed at the way his pants hugged the muscles of his legs. The man really did have an amazing ass.

As Roman foraged, Trevor took another swig of his beer and looked me up and down like a tasty treat. "Scotty, hm? Where're you from, sweet Scotty?"

"Nunya," Roman grumbled over his shoulder. "Nunya beeswax."

"He's practicing for a role in the remake of *The Godfather*," I said with a laugh. "And I'm from Queens. What about you?"

"Burlington."

"The coat factory?"

"Yes," he said with a straight face. "All my friends were jealous growing up since I always had the latest in winter wear."

"Is that where you met Oscar?" I asked, subtly—or not so subtly —trying to shift the conversation toward the man who was beginning to take on a larger-than-life vibe.

Trevor's laughter was like a storm—deep rumbles that vibrated the air around him. "If I told you where Oscar and I met, it might be considered contributing to the delinquency of a minor."

I leaned my elbow on the counter and cupped my chin in my palm. "Oh? Tell me more."

He reached out like he was about to fluff my hair, but Roman intercepted, shoving a clementine into the cop's open hand. "Paws to yourself, Officer Bad Touch."

There was something that sounded almost like jealousy in his voice. Not that he had any reason to be—Trevor wasn't my type. He was a little too large and... bearded... for my preference. Plus, I'd had enough interaction with the law in my life that I didn't need to invite it into my bed.

I found it interesting that Roman might be jealous of Trevor's obvious flirting with me, but seemed to have no problem with the fact they'd both dated the same man. Maybe it was because both their relationships were in the past?

"If you won't tell me how you met, what about why things didn't work out between you two?" I asked him.

"Christ, where do I even begin?" Trevor said, rolling his eyes. "The man is insane, god love him."

As Trevor answered, Roman pulled a stool closer to mine and sat, fingers tearing into the rind of a clementine. When he had it peeled, he held it out to me before starting work on another.

"Aw, thank you," I murmured to him.

He gave me a grin and shrugged like it was nothing.

"Jesus, you two are going to send me into sugar shock," Trevor grumbled, sliding off his stool and moving to toss his empty bottle in the recycling.

"You were saying about Oscar?" I prodded around a mouthful of clementine.

"It was his family more than anything that scared me off."

"Mm-hm," Roman echoed. "Preach."

I remembered the story about his first date with Oscar and snorted. "Did they offer you welcome frogs as well?"

Trevor's eyes went wide. "No. Though that's both weird and not at all surprising."

"It's kind of an eccentric family," Roman added.

"Oh?" I asked sarcastically. "I hadn't noticed."

"So you've met them?" Trevor asked, helping himself to another beer.

"One of his sisters and his parents dropped by this morning." I caught myself. Had it really just been that morning? Being with Roman seemed to make time stop—I felt like I'd known him much longer than just a day or two. "They're staying somewhere else on the property, though."

He grinned. "Yeah, you have me to thank for that. I'm the reason Oscar exiled them to the outbuildings."

"I will definitely thank you for that," Roman said, placing another peeled clementine in front of me.

"Wait," I said, holding up a hand. "Wait. What do you mean he exiled them to the outbuildings? Like the barn?"

"No. The spa. And the kennel. The hutch."

"Why does everyone keep talking about the spa?" I asked before the other words hit my brain. "He made them sleep with the dogs or... rabbits? What the hell?"

"No," Trevor laughed. "They're his family's other houses on this property. There are a total of six of them."

While I tried to wrap my brain around that, Trevor continued his story. "Anyway, Oscar and I were going at it in the kitchen when—"

"Eugh!" Roman said, shoving his stool back and picking up his beer like it had been tainted by the countertop. "Gross." Then he noticed my peeled clementine and let out a squeak of horror before slapping it across the kitchen. It splatted against one of the floor-length windows and fell to the floor in a sad, pulpy mess.

We all just stood there, staring at it.

"Um, what was that for?" I asked.

"I was saving you from the sex fruit."

Trevor started giggling. It was unexpectedly high-pitched and entirely at odds with his bulky frame. "Sex fruit," he repeated under his breath, sending himself into more giggles.

I managed to keep my own laughter at bay long enough to place a kiss on Roman's cheek. "My hero."

"Anyway," Trevor said loudly, interrupting the moment. "We were fucking on the kitchen floor and suddenly his family was standing in a circle around us chiming in with helpful feedback. I think one of them was chanting a spell or something. What's a chanted spell called?"

"An incantation?" I glanced over at Roman, but he was busy spraying the counter with bleach. "Do you honestly think they haven't cleaned this place since then?"

He grunted, distracted by his search for sex cooties.

"Yeah, an incantation," Trevor continued. "I think they did that to us. Ever since then, my dick is actually bigger. Want to see?"

Suddenly, Roman's attention was back with a vengeance. He held up the spray bottle as though it were a dangerous weapon. "He does not want to see your dick."

"Speak for yourself, Bossy-Pants Man," I corrected. "If the big sexy policeman wants me to look at his nightstick, I'm going to look at the man's nightstick." I was teasing him, of course, because I relished this little possessive streak he had going on.

Roman's jaw dropped, but he snapped it closed again and turned away, taking the spray bottle back to where he'd gotten it from under the sink. "Yeah, of course. Good."

Trevor winked at me like we were coconspirators and then started fiddling with his duty belt. "Come here, sweetheart."

I started across the room, but instead of heading toward Trevor, I climbed on Roman's back and placed a kiss behind his ear.

"I only want to see your nightstick right now, Sparty," I said quietly into his ear. Roman's entire body shuddered.

"You're playing a little fast and loose with nicknames, Scotch Tape," he said with a chuckle. He reached back to keep me from falling off.

"Give the nice man his police statement so we can get back to me creaming you at—"

"Hey, whoa there," Trevor interjected. "No need to be explicit. Don't make a man want something he can't have, cutie."

Roman smirked. "He means beating—"

Trevor held up his hand. "Stop it right there, cowboy."

I hopped off Roman's back after noticing the time on the microwave clock. "Speaking of cowboys, I need to go see a horse. Be back in a few." I kissed Roman long and deep on the lips, making it clear he had nothing to fear about my interest in him.

"Want me to come with you?" he asked.

There was something about the way he said it that made my chest warm. There was nothing sexy or fun about mucking out a stall and feeding a horse—there was no reason for Roman to offer to join me at all unless it was because he wanted to spend more time together. As if it was just a given that he might join me. It was such a casual offer, but that was what made it feel so special.

I wanted to say yes, but I couldn't. Because the real reason I was going out to the barn was in case my mom called. I didn't want to risk Roman overhearing our conversation. I loved that he'd been so willing to open up and share the story about his father's death and how that had impacted him, but I wasn't so sure I was ready to tell him about my own past.

People tended to look at you differently after they found out you had a criminal past.

I brushed a kiss across Roman's lips. "No, it's fine. I just want to check on her before it gets dark."

"Do you have your phone? Just in case anything weird happens."

"Weird?" I asked.

He shrugged. "With Oscar's family at the spa..."

"I still don't think I understand what that means."

"Just text or call if you need me, all right?"

The concern in his eyes caused my chest to tighten. "Yes, Spartacus, but you have my phone in your pocket."

Roman's eyes narrowed at me as he patted at his pants until he found it. "I've tried to return this to you all day. Why do you keep slipping it back in my pocket? I trust you, okay? Stop giving me your phone. If I didn't take a chance on people from time to time, I'd live in an awfully lonely bubble."

I leaned in again and kissed him softly. "Thank you," I told him. I wanted to warn him that he shouldn't trust people so easily. That he was too nice and one day someone was going to take advantage of him and I didn't want to see him hurt.

Which I knew from experience. My entire life had been steeped in the art of people taking advantage.

But I liked that despite everything Roman had been through, he still had faith in people. He was still willing to trust. Especially me.

I just hoped that in the end I was worthy.

Roman's forehead creased in confusion, but I didn't stick around to explain what I knew about people taking advantage. After donning my winter gear, I headed out into the frigid air. My breath turned to clouds, the air otherwise still and quiet, sound dampened by the thick coating of snow still blanketing everything. I kicked my feet against the path as I cut my way through the trees, trying to ignore the cold seeping through the old cracked leather of my boots. It was well past time I replaced them, which was another reason I needed to get a job and start earning money again.

The few times that day I'd checked my phone, I'd been disappointed but not surprised to see a whole lotta nothing. Then Roman had set me up on his laptop to check my email, and it had been even worse. Two of the three sleigh ride companies had said they were adequately staffed for the season, and the third, which had been the closest to Stowe, hadn't even responded. I was shit out of luck.

The thought caused my stomach to squeeze with anxiety. I felt a sharp spike of guilt. I'd spent the day lounging and gaming and sexing instead of submitting more resumes and beating the pavement looking for work. I knew I should be heading back to New York, but the idea of leaving Nugget behind was too painful.

The thought of leaving Roman behind hurt just as much.

It was a ridiculous concern. I knew that. I'd only known Roman a day. But it had felt longer than that. And I knew that once we returned to the city we'd go back to our own separate worlds. Leaving him would mean letting go of him forever. I wasn't ready for that just yet.

I wanted to stay in our little hidden Vermont bubble just a little bit longer. At least for one more day.

When I approached the barn, I saw movement to the right in the closest fenced pasture. It was Nugget and she was rolling on her back in the snow like a giddy little kid, kicking up fluffy chunks of white as she stretched her legs. I leaned on the fence completely entranced. I'd never been able to watch her have fun like this. Every time she'd had her mandated trips out of the city, I hadn't been able to go with her because of the money.

She stood up and shook herself off before sneezing and moving through the snow toward me. Her large frame was so familiar and comforting, I felt my throat tighten.

It became blazingly obvious in that moment that I couldn't give her what she needed. What she deserved.

As I stood there waiting for her to reach me, I was overcome with the sudden realization I couldn't keep her. The thought almost brought me to my knees.

"That your horse?" a voice called from behind me.

I steadied myself with a hand on the fence and turned to see an older teenage boy moving soiled straw out of the barn door to a pile near the edge of the trees. He let go of the cart he was pushing and came over to me with a friendly grin, pulling off a work glove to shake my hand.

"Kip Dawes. I'm the neighbor looking after your girl here." He glanced around as if looking for someone. "I was expecting to meet Roman Burke, but that's not you."

"Not even close," I admitted. "I'm Scotty Pinker. I'm Roman's—" I froze. I had no idea how to finish that statement. I wasn't his boyfriend. I didn't even know if I qualified as a friend. But acquaintance felt too formal and distant. And lover was way too much information.

I heard Roman's deep chuckle from behind me. "He's Nugget's owner."

Heat spread across my face as I turned to greet him. "And this is Roman Burke, but you can call him Smart Ass."

Kip kept the friendly smile and nodded, clearly not overly impressed with being in the presence of a famous movie star. I wondered if he was used to seeing celebrities in his fancy ski town. "Well, that's a mighty fine draft horse you have there," he said, nodding at Nugget. "If you're ever looking to get rid of her, my dad would probably do just about anything to add her to our sleigh ride program."

I stared at him, my heart leaping with excitement. This had to be the sleigh company I hadn't heard back from. "I'm definitely not interested in selling her, but I'd love to hear more about the program. Does your dad happen to own Stowe Sleigh Rides?" This was too good to be true.

He nodded. "My dad and three of my brothers run it together. One of my dad's original Clydesdales is getting ready to retire. He's looking for a replacement. Oscar told him Nugget here was a Central Park carriage horse. That would be a boon, wouldn't it?" His grin was contagious. "Tell the tourists they can get their sleigh ride with a famous carriage horse?"

"Are you hiring, by any chance?" I asked excitedly. "Like I said, I'm not looking to sell, but I am looking for work. I—" I stopped talking when I saw the answer on his face.

"No, sorry. There's not even enough work for me to join them when I graduate." He lifted a shoulder. "I was hoping my dad would be ready to retire and give me his spot when I got my degree, but I finish in May and he's not budging. Equine jobs around here are slim pickings to be honest."

My heart dropped. I tried to think of something to say to cover up my crushing disappointment. "Oh."

"Yeah, I'll have to move after I finish my equine science degree in a few months. Maybe find a hippotherapy program or teach riding lessons after school. Not sure I want to go to vet school, but we'll see."

I smiled at him, trying desperately not to be jealous of this kid who had the world at his feet. "That sounds amazing. I'm sure you'll find something great with a degree like that."

"As long as I can work with these beauties, I'll be happy," he said, reaching out to stroke Nugget's long nose.

Roman shifted his weight until his shoulder was pressed against mine. I couldn't feel his warmth through the layers of our coats, but I appreciated the solid presence of him while I still felt so unsteady.

Maybe I'd been too hasty in saying I wasn't interested in selling Nugget.

I scratched Nugget's chin, distracted with unpleasant thoughts of her happily pulling a sleigh with someone else holding the reins. "Thank you so much for taking care of her," I murmured. "She's really important to me."

Roman's strong arm came around my lower back and pulled me closer against his side. Part of me wanted him to let go and return to the house. I didn't want to feel this raw and scared in his presence. Instead, I stayed quiet. Roman brushed a kiss across my temple.

"No problem," Kip said, turning back toward the cart and sliding his gloves back on. "Oscar's sister Hyacinth sometimes brings her horses when she visits from Pennsylvania, and I take care of them too. Anytime you want to visit with your girl there, I'll be happy to look out for her. And if you change your mind about selling her, my number's posted on the corkboard in the barn."

I attempted to smile and nod my thanks, but I probably looked like a psychopath instead.

Roman ran a hand along Nugget's neck while I cooed at her and let her nuzzle into my hair. He must have sensed my need to be quiet, because he simply stayed with me while I lavished Nugget with attention and baby talk. When we headed back to the house, he held my hand and kept his eyes on the path.

"Nice kid," he said.

"Yeah."

"I'm sorry about the job."

"Yeah." I shrugged, trying to keep my chin from wobbling. "It was too good to be true, you know? What're the chances I turn up and the one person I meet has a dream job for me and my horse? Ridiculous."

"Still sucks."

I snorted softly. "Yep. Still sucks balls."

We walked for a few more beats of silence until Roman broke it.

"Know what else sucks balls?" he asked, a suggestive quirk to his lips.

I turned to him, thankful for a reason to stop obsessing over Nugget and my future. "Please tell me it's you."

Before he could answer, my phone rang. I recognized the number as the central prison exchange my mom called from. My stomach clenched. I came *this* close to ignoring the call, but I couldn't bring myself to turn my own mother away when I was all she had and she was stuck behind bars.

I started to tell Roman I needed to take the call, but he was already giving me a big "fingers crossed" sign before retreating toward the house to give me privacy. Clearly he thought the call was a job lead.

When I answered, I was greeted with the familiar robotic voice of the prison phone system before my mother came on the line.

"Where the hell have you been?" she hissed.

I waited until Roman was far enough away so he couldn't hear me before I answered.

"Long story," I told her, not wanting to get into it with her. If I did, I wouldn't be able to stop from blaming her for my situation. It was because of her schemes that I no longer had the money Arnold left me to help with Nugget. It was because of her getting caught and sent away that I hadn't been able to make rent by myself anymore.

And what I hated most about it, was that it was my fault for relying on her in the first place. If I'd just stood up to her the first time she'd roped me into her schemes... if I'd just left home when I turned eighteen and never looked back... But I couldn't forget all the times my mother *had* been there for me. The lengths she'd gone to keep a roof over our heads and food on the table.

The real problem was that I couldn't bring myself to believe the worst about my mother. She wasn't a bad person—she was never cruel or evil. She just had issues with morality. And theft. And fraud. And a whole collection of other misdemeanors and felonies. But she was still my mother. And, in a way, everything she'd done, she'd done for me. Even if she sometimes picked a shitty way of going about it.

"Well, you can tell me when you come pick me up tomorrow," she told me.

I sucked in a sharp breath, the frozen air searing my lungs. "Tomorrow?" How in the world could I have forgotten that? I thought she had another two months at least.

"Yeah, early release. Overcrowding and whatnot," she said. "You woulda known that if you'd have bothered calling me in the last two weeks."

Was she serious? "I didn't have a fucking phone," I snapped. "Or a place to stay or food for that matter."

"Christ, Scotty. What the fuck?" Her voice started rising. "You get your ass fired? Shit! Now what're we supposed to do?"

I felt my entire body begin to shake, and I knew it wasn't because of the cold. "I'm working on it. I've already applied for some jobs in the city, and when I get back from Vermont, hopefully—"

"Vermont?" She practically shouted the word. "What're you doing in Vermont?"

Crap. There was no way I could let her find out about Roman. If she knew I was hanging out with a millionaire celebrity, her brain would explode with any number of awful extortion schemes. "Following a lead on a job," I told her.

She paused a moment, giving me room to say more. It was a tactic that had worked on me in the past, but this time I refused to budge. "So you're not going to be here to pick me up?" she finally asked.

I closed my eyes. The thought of leaving caused my stomach to plummet. But I knew it had to happen at some point. And my mom was family. I couldn't abandon her.

"I won't be back by then," I told her.

"Then I'll just let myself into the apartment and I'll see you when you get home."

I squeezed my fingers against my forehead in frustration. "I don't have an apartment. I told you—I lost it after I lost my job."

"Oh for the love of—" She cut herself off and let out a long breath. "Then where am I supposed to stay, Scotty?"

I felt my shoulders tense, the pressure of her expectations that I fix this for her squeezing around me. "I don't know."

"I don't have a lot of money," she said.

I gritted my teeth. "Join the fucking club. I don't have *any*."

"Scottybear," she said, shifting automatically from commanding to sugar sweet. This was the woman who could charm the wallet right out of your pants in the middle of a Broadway lunch hour. "I need you to hurry up and get back here so we can share a place again. I don't know how long my money's gonna last if I can't find a job right away and don't have anyone to split rent with."

"I'm trying to find a job," I told her. How did she not understand? "I can't magically make one appear out of thin air."

"Remember that time after Jingo left and I had to work the streets?"

My stomach turned over. I was ten, and my mom had done that because she'd caught her boyfriend looking at me with a little too much interest. "Yeah, Mom. Of course I do."

"You want your mama to end up back on the streets?"

It was a low blow. But an effective one. And it wasn't like she was telling me anything I didn't know. I *did* need a job, and both of us needed someone to share rent with in order to have any chance at getting our feet back under us. The sooner I got my head out of the clouds and realized my life wasn't some dreamscape of sleigh rides in Vermont, the sooner I could get my ass back to the city and find work.

"Of course not," I said, mentally packing away my dream. My stomach continued to churn, and I felt my chin begin to tremble. I couldn't let her hear my emotion over the phone. I had to end the call.

"Of course not," I repeated, trying to sound more sure of myself. "I'm working on it."

"That's a good son." It sounded perfunctory, but the little boy inside me still preened at the statement. "Now give me a mailing address where you are. I gotta give it to the paperwork people in the morning so they can let me out of this place."

My brain was only halfway engaged when I rattled off the address for Oscar's place. The rest of my thoughts spun from the rapid shift between thinking about any way I could beg for work from Kip's family and knowing I was heading back to Queens to find a minimum-wage job instead.

I ended the call and trudged back to the house, struggling like hell to think of a solution that didn't involve looking at this multimillion-dollar home like easy pickings. When my mom had gotten me busted for petty larceny at thirteen, I'd gotten off with probation. The next year, I'd started working at the stables. But then she'd roped me into another one of her schemes when I was sixteen. That one ended in juvenile detention and a record. Thankfully it was sealed, but it still freaked me the hell out enough to keep me from ever doing anything to wind up back there.

And that was also part of the reason the medallion owner had immediately fired me at the stables. When you had a reputation for being a punk kid with juvie shit in your history, you weren't given the benefit of the doubt when you returned to the stables with a police escort.

I opened the door to the mudroom and kicked off my boots.

"That you, Scotty?" Roman called from the kitchen.

"Yeah, it's me." I shucked off my coat and hung it on a hook.

Suddenly, Roman appeared in the doorway between the mudroom and kitchen. "You okay?"

I looked up at him and noticed concern etched in his handsome features. "Why do you ask?"

"You don't sound right. What happened? Was it bad news about a job?"

"Oh, no. It's not about a job."

"Shit. Is it Nugget? Is she okay?"

Suddenly I realized I wasn't going to be able to keep this from him, and my stomach plummeted. He would insist on helping. He'd insist on giving me money. I couldn't let that happen.

"Roman." My voice came out shaky and unsure.

The furrow between his eyebrow deepened. He took a step toward me. "Fuck, Scotty, whatever it is, we'll fix it okay? Oscar probably knows a vet or—"

I walked right into his chest and slid my arms around him for one last hug. Because there was no doubt in my mind, my ugly past was going to mean having to say goodbye to this sweet man.

"Nugget's fine," I mumbled into the soft cotton of his shirt.

Roman's arms came around me and held me tightly the way he had before when I'd needed comforting. He was solid and steady. A good man. Sincere, sweet and thoughtful. How the hell could I lie to him? I couldn't. But I was so embarrassed. Of my past. Of my present. Of what I was about to ask him.

I pressed my face into the hot skin of his neck above his collar because I couldn't bear to look at him when I said the next part. "I think I'm g-going t-to have to s-s-sell her."

# 14

## ROMAN

*Roman Horsemanship Throughout The Ages*

SCOTTY'S entire body was shaking, and I was sure I'd misheard him.

"You don't mean that," I said into his hair. It was still chilled from the outside and smelled of woodsmoke and winter air.

"I do," he said on a watery breath.

The pain in his voice caused my chest to tighten. I tightened my arms around him for a moment before finally relenting. "Let's sit down and you can tell me what happened."

I pulled his face out of my chest and noticed his tired eyes. Gone were the sparkling baby blues I'd come to appreciate in such a short time. In their place were limpid pools of murky blue gray. I leaned in to kiss his lips softly in comfort and reassurance. Scotty's hands clutched at my shirt as I kissed him longer and deeper than I'd planned.

"Come on," I said, forcing myself to pull away. "I started a fire in the other room."

I led him down a hallway to a small den with wood paneling and a stone fireplace. A dark leather love seat and chair sat in front of the blazing fire. I pulled him down next to me on the love seat and sat facing him. "Tell me."

Scotty sat with his back against the arm of the couch, his knees pulled tight against his chest and his arms clasped tight around them. His bottom teeth scraped at his top lip enough to make me want to soothe it with another kiss. But I knew that would only lead to more fooling around, and he was clearly upset. I knew how much he loved Nugget, so if he was considering selling her, he was truly desperate, which really shouldn't have come as a surprise to me considering his situation.

"The, ah, the kid who..." Scotty cleared his throat. I noticed his knuckles were white where he clasped his shins. "The kid who's taking care of Nugget says his dad might want to buy her. They run a sleigh ride company here in Stowe, and... ah, well... it would be a great situation for Nugget."

I frowned. "But you told him no. You didn't want to sell."

He just looked at me with those sad eyes until I thought I wouldn't be able to take it anymore. "I have to."

I stared at him and saw every bit of raw emotion just under the surface. He was trying so fucking hard to be brave. "But... Nugget is your—"

His blue eyes were bottomless pools of sadness. "Please, don't," he whispered. "*Please*, Roman."

My heart felt like it was one of the clementines from earlier, being pulled apart and swatted across the room. "But why? What happened between then and now?"

Scotty's chin trembled when he spoke. "A reality check. I already tried to get another carriage-driving job in the city, Roman. And there was nothing. If I can't find a job with Nugget, that means I have to find one without her. And I don't have a degree. I can't afford to keep her on a dishwasher's salary. And even if I could, she'd be trapped in a barn most of the day without anyone to give her the attention she deserves. It's part of the reason I came to Vermont. If I can sell her here, she'll have a better life, you know?"

"But why now?" I asked, still struggling to understand. "Why all of a sudden? Who was on the phone?"

"Um, it's..." Scotty took a breath. "It's my mom. She..." His eyes closed for a minute, and when they opened, he looked everywhere but at me.

I reached out and took one of his hands, scooting closer so I could hold it in both of mine. "Tell me," I said again softly.

"You're going to hate me," he spoke so quietly, I almost didn't hear him.

My immediate inclination was to reassure him that he was wrong, but I stopped myself. I hadn't known Scotty long enough to have any idea if he was right or not. It seemed impossible to imagine him doing something that could make me think so ill of him, but I'd been burned before. All I could do was hear him out.

"What about your mom?" I urged.

He slipped his hand out of my grip. It was the only time I could remember him not wanting to be touched. A part of me wanted to hold on to him tighter, to reach for him and pull him closer, but I didn't want to push. Even though we sat next to each other, in that moment he felt impossibly out of reach.

He cleared his throat and kept his eyes downcast. "She's been in jail, and um... she gets out tomorrow."

I blinked, taking in the information. It hadn't been at all what I'd been expecting.

"I should have told you earlier," Scotty continued quickly, not making eye contact with me. "I'm sorry. And it wasn't for anything bad. I mean, not that there are really any great ways to end up in jail. But she didn't hurt or kill anyone—it was a money scam and she got caught. I mean, obviously she got caught since she ended up in jail. But that's not the point. Or rather it is the point since I'm telling you my mom is a convicted felon."

He cut himself off, clenching his teeth together before continuing. "I know the last thing you need is for the tabloids to find out you've been hanging out with the son of a convicted felon, but I just figured

since we were so far in the country and there was no one around..."
He blew out a breath and added another "I'm sorry" in a soft voice.

Scotty wasn't wrong about the tabloid stuff, but he seemed so torn
up about it—way more than he needed to be. "Hey," I said, reaching
again for his hand. "Don't worry about that. We're safe here."

He looked up, his eyes meeting mine. "You're not... mad?"

I brushed my thumb over his knuckles. "We can't be held responsible for other people's actions."

He let out a bitter laugh. "Oh, god, you have no idea how much I
wish that were true."

"It *is* true," I told him.

Scotty squeezed his eyes shut, and I noticed his eyelashes were
damp with unshed tears. I ran my hand up his arm, squeezing his
shoulder, then the side of his neck so that my thumb traced his jaw.
He automatically leaned into my touch. "Thank you," he whispered.

"Your mom made bad decisions," I continued. "That's not your
fault."

He squirmed slightly, shifting so that my hand could no longer
reach his face. I dropped it onto one of his knees, still craving the
touch of him.

"Here's the thing..." He blew out a breath and then met my eyes.
His chin trembled while he tried to stay steady. I could tell it was
taking all of his courage to tell me this. "She has nothing. We usually
live together to save money, and now she has no job and no place to
stay. I need to go home and get a job. I need to face reality, Roman,
and reality is me not being able to keep Nugget."

I opened my mouth to offer him help, but he didn't let me speak.

"Before you say it, *no*. I know you're incredibly kind and generous,
but..." Scotty shook his head and cursed under his breath before
looking back at me with pleading eyes. "Please, Spartacus. Please
don't offer to give me more money. I don't want to be that guy. Especially not with you. I just... I need help selling Nugget because it's my
only option. I can't afford to keep her, but I don't really know what
price to ask, and how to make sure they'll take good care—"

I'd had enough. He was trembling now, his eyes shining with

tears. It was too much for me to take. He was too vulnerable and in too much pain. I couldn't bear it. I yanked him into my lap and enveloped him in a giant hug. It seemed to be our thing all of a sudden, and I was 100 percent cool with that. If there was any way I could use my body to provide this man comfort, I would do it in a heartbeat.

"I'll buy her," I growled into his ear.

"No way," Scotty said angrily, trying to wriggle out of my hold. "I told you—"

I held him firm. "Shh. I've always wanted a horse. In fact, just yesterday someone told me I needed a horse to round out my, and I quote, 'fucking celebrity status.'"

My comment worked to elicit a small smile. Scotty snorted. "I was just pissed at the situation. I know you don't really want a horse."

"I do," I told him earnestly. "I totally want a horse. And not just any horse. A Nugget. She's grown on me. And I already know she'll fit in my house, so it's a match made in heaven."

Scotty kept himself rigid a moment longer, and my mind spun with other ways to get him the money he needed while still allowing him to maintain his pride. Honestly, if he'd really wanted easy money, all he'd have had to do was call one of the tabloids and tip them off to my location. If he'd wanted big money, he could have snuck a photo of me naked and sold it.

He could have easily sold me instead of his horse. But he hadn't.

My heart tightened at the realization. At the statement it made about how much he respected me and my privacy.

Ever since my first movie hit number one at the box office, I'd had people vying to get close to me so they could profit off me. At the time I'd been so naive and trusting. It had never occurred to me the lengths that someone would go to use me to get what they wanted. It had only taken a few breaches of my trust for me to learn my lesson.

I'd had no reason to doubt Scotty's motives when it came to me, and I hadn't needed proof that he wasn't using me. But I'd gotten it nevertheless.

"I'm not selling you my horse," Scotty said with complete annoyance. "Stop trying to make this okay. It's not okay. Nothing about this is okay! I'm selling her to Kip's dad."

"It will break my heart if you take Nugget away from me," I told him. And it was true. Because it would break my heart to see Scotty have to let go of something he loved so dearly. "And if you sell her to Kip's dad, I'm going to have to offer him even more money to buy her back. Please don't do that. Let me buy her for cheap direct from the source."

I was trying to lighten the mood in hopes it would keep both of us from shattering.

Scotty snorted through his tears. His smile made my heart sing. "Don't be ridiculous, Save-Everyone Man."

"I don't want to save everyone," I murmured, catching his eye. "Just you. And Nugget."

Scotty's body sunk against mine as he let out a breath. "I'm so sorry, Roman. I told you you'd hate me."

I ran a hand through his short blond waves. "And you were wrong. I don't hate you. In fact, I like you more and more with each passing moment."

Scotty pulled back to give me the side-eye. "Did Marigold leave you some magic mushrooms by any chance?"

I tried to ignore the fact that I'd just told him how much I liked him and he hadn't said anything about his own feelings in return. As much as I wanted to press the issue, however, I let it go. If Scotty wasn't ready to talk about the issue, me pushing him wasn't going to help.

"Oh my god. Because that's something we need to add to this situation," I said with a bark of laughter. "The carriage ride, the cop impersonation, the horse in the house, the stolen vehicle, and now magic 'shrooms. Christ. Oscar's going to fire me as a crisis management client."

Scotty let out a little giggle that was cute as hell. "He can't blame you if they came from his sister. Oh my god! Did you know he has another sister named Hyacinth? She has horses."

"Yep, and Lily, Jasmine, and Rose—that's Rosette's mom I think.

And another brother named Heath and one named Sage. It's a veritable garden."

Scotty scrunched up his forehead. "Then where the hell did the name Oscar come from? It's not a flower, is it?"

"Believe it or not, it is," I told him.

"You're right. I do not, in fact, believe you," he said.

"It totally is," I said. "Look it up. The Oscar plant has a giant papery seed ball, and it's also called butterfly weed. And don't ever ask him or his mother about it in person, or be prepared for a diatribe, complete with graphic sketches of the wrinkly seed balls."

Scotty's smile was so fucking cute, it set my heart racing. I was quickly realizing I'd do almost anything to get that smile on his face as often as possible.

Including, it seemed, buying a goddamned horse. I was going to have to call my money manager in the morning to see about buying a barn or some place to actually store the thing.

"Say, uh..." I began, running my hands into his hair again like it was iron and my hands were magnets. "I might need to hire someone to take care of my horse... Do you know of anyone?"

His smile disappeared. "Roman," he said, hitting the *en* sound hard.

"Scottsman," I replied, doing the same.

He lifted his chin, staring me down. "I'm a hard worker. I'm willing to find work in town or back in the city. I don't want charity." His jaw was set, and his slender nostrils widened.

I took his chin between my fingertips, my thumb fitting neatly over the edge of it. "I understand. But lest you've forgotten, my SUV was stolen which means we're stuck out here." I didn't mention the handful of other cars Oscar had in his garage, and besides, I didn't know where the keys were to any of them. "And since you're stuck here with me for the foreseeable future, it makes sense that instead of paying Kip to take care of Nugget, I can pay you. See? It's not charity."

Scotty narrowed his eyes for a moment, considering the proposition.

"I'm going to be paying someone to take care of my new horse," I pointed out. "It might as well be you since you know her best."

Scotty scraped his teeth along his top lip again. Then he nodded. "Okay. Thank you." He placed his hand over mine on his knee. "You're a good man, Roman."

The words caused my chest to tighten. I wasn't sure anyone had ever said that about me before. They'd called me a good actor, or a good friend, or a good brother. But never a good man. And coming from Scotty made it even more meaningful.

"Of course. Does your mom need a place to stay? Or... do you need to go to her? Do you want me to book a car to take you back to the city?" As much as I didn't like the idea of Scotty leaving, I couldn't expect him to stay just for me. Not if his mom needed him.

He shook his head frantically. "No. I mean no. *No.* I don't need to go to her. She... she's not... she'll be fine staying in Queens. But... really, thank you for asking. I'll just send her some money and she can find a cheap place to stay while she gets on her feet again."

I ran my hand alongside his face to make sure he was still looking at me. "You know I'll sell Nugget back to you the minute you're ready for her, right?"

Scotty's eyes filled quickly, and I could tell he was fighting the emotion. He nodded and clenched his jaw together for a second before speaking. His voice was rough. "Yeah. I do know that, but I don't know why. I don't deserve your generosity. But I'm grateful for it. You need to know just how grateful I am, Roman."

"I'm the one who got you fired. And even if I hadn't been, my parents taught me that when people need help, you help."

Scotty's eyes opened wide as if he was remembering what I'd said about my father changing our neighbor's flat tire. Or maybe it was just me remembering. Either way, I didn't want to think about it. I needed to change the subject.

"Can we stop talking about money and horses and maybe you can let me suck your dick instead?"

If it was possible, Scotty's eyes widened even more and the corner of his mouth turned up in a sexy curl. "Um... yeah? Like... is that a trick question, or..."

I tackled him onto his back and proceeded to strip him naked without either one of us saying another word. It quickly became clear the love seat wasn't going to work, so I slithered us onto the plush burgundy carpet in front of the fire. The warm light from the flames made his fair skin look more golden. I feasted on all that bare skin as I pressed myself against him until finally making my way down to his leaking cock.

"Yeah, suck me," Scotty murmured under his breath. "Fuck. So good."

I teased him with heavy, wet passes of my tongue along his shaft until he was begging and gasping. Finally I sucked him down and pressed his cock into the roof of my mouth with the flat of my tongue. His hands grabbed my head, and his legs crossed over my back. When I looked up at him, all I saw was the expanse of his slender neck with his head thrown back. The deep groans coming out of him were enough to make my balls tingle, and the taste of his dick in my mouth was not helping me stay in control.

I pulled off long enough to tell him to come for me, and then I used a finger to brush lightly over his hole. His entire body arched up, his hands tightened in my hair, and he sucked in a loud breath as his salty release hit the back of my throat. As he came down from his high, I continued licking and sucking him gently until he looked at me with glazed eyes and pulled my face up to his for a kiss.

We made out for a little while longer, but I could feel Scotty relaxing into half-consciousness. After slipping my clothes back on, I found a throw over the back of one of the chairs and put it over his bare body to keep him warm while he dozed.

"Stay," he murmured when I leaned down to press a kiss to his cheek.

"I'm just going to start on dinner and check in with Oscar, okay?"

"Mm."

I left him sleeping in front of the fire and made my way to the kitchen. The house was so quiet and peaceful, but I realized it was different than the night before when I'd just arrived. With Scotty in the house, it felt warmer, less lonely. I didn't feel itchy and restless. I felt closer to the relaxed state Oscar had been hoping for when he'd encouraged me to come to Vermont.

After shooting Oscar a quick text to ask him to call me when he had a few minutes, I rummaged through the fridge, mentally thanking him for arranging to have the kitchen stocked before my arrival. I found chicken breasts and some vegetables that I pulled out in hopes I could figure out what to do with them. Google suggested something called Chicken Garden Medley which I kind of hoped made me look like a superstar in Scotty's eyes.

After putting water on to boil for the pasta, and chopping peppers and zucchini to sauté, I was already feeling like a stud in the kitchen when I came face-to-face with the package of raw chicken. All I could think about was the commercial on television years ago that showed bacteria from raw chicken ending up all over the kitchen because of mishandling by the cook.

"Fuck," I muttered, eyeing the package like it was a little plague bomb waiting to detonate. I imagined poor Scotty wracked with stomach cramps and winding up in the hospital from my mishandling of the toxic stuff.

The trilling of my phone caused me to jump a mile high and drop the wickedly sharp knife I'd been holding.

"Shit fuck shit!" I yelped, jumping out of the way to avoid severed toes. "Fuck!"

My heart was thundering and the pot was boiling, throwing out giant mounds of steam in my face. My phone continued to ring, and I scrambled to answer it before the noise woke Scotty.

"What?" I barked into the handset.

"Smooth," Oscar said dryly. "I don't know why you've been accused of having an attitude problem on set when you're perfectly chill with me."

"I've never been accused of having an attitude on set," I snapped, leaning down to pick up the wannabe murder weapon. "You're thinking of Dalton Orr."

"That guy is an ass," Oscar muttered. "But he gives good head, so he's forgiven."

The famous, *straight* actor was notorious for getting his gay on after a few drinks at parties, but I was surprised Oscar had ever let the man near him. "Tell me you didn't," I said.

"Just the once. He'd found out you and I dated and couldn't stand the idea of you having something he didn't." I could hear the grin in his voice. "He was *very* persuasive. Eloquent even."

"I thought you were looking for Mr. Right, not a closeted cock-slut," I reminded him.

"That's presuming a Mr. Right exists for me," he said. Before I could say anything in response, he changed the subject. "You sound unusually testy tonight. What's up?"

I sighed. "How do you cook chicken without killing people?"

There was another pause, this one longer. "Is this what you called me about?"

"I mean, not necessarily, but it's the most pressing question I have at the moment."

"Easy," he said. "You hire professionals to do it for you."

"Not helpful at the moment," I pointed out.

"I hear my sister turned up. Did she steal anything while she was there?"

"You mean besides my inner peace?" I peeked into the cabinet under the sink in hopes of finding dish gloves or something to protect me from the chicken.

"Or my vodka."

I paused, thinking. "Yeah, she did take that. I believe the phrase she used was 'purloined for compensation for past injustices.'"

"Huh. She's not wrong on that. But you'd think the spa would be enough," he grumbled. "Anyway, she told me you had a boy there."

I bumped my head on the frame of the cabinet. "Shit. A boy? Fuck, Oscar. I don't have a boy here. I have a man. I mean... yeah, he's kind of young but... Jesus. You make it sound dirty. He's a good guy."

There was a long pause. "You brought a man to Vermont?" His opinion on the matter was clear in the tone of his voice.

"No!" I protested. "Well, yes, sort of. I mean, not really. I didn't invite him or plan it, but I guess technically you could say I brought him since I paid for the conveyance in which he—"

"Who is it?" Oscar cut me off. "And why didn't you tell me?"

"Um..." I knew it wasn't going to go over well when I told him about Scotty. If the tabloid press discovered I was sleeping with the same guy whose carriage I'd jacked, especially when I'd all but admitted to fathering Polly's child... well, let's just say that would make for a very exciting day in the news media. Especially once you threw in the little detail about Scotty's mother being a convicted felon who'd recently been released from prison.

"Fuuuuck," Oscar said with a resigned sigh. "Fine. I'm coming up there."

# 15

## SCOTTY

*The Clorox Guide To Safe Chicken Handling*

I WOKE to find myself alone, the fire reduced to ember and the afternoon sky faded to evening outside the windows. I could hear the sound of Roman's voice coming from somewhere in the house, and while I couldn't pick out what he was saying, the rhythm and cadence of his tone made it sound like he was likely on the phone. I figured it would be best to give him a bit of privacy and stretched, luxuriating in the feel of my sex-sore muscles.

A stupid grin spread across my face when I noticed the blanket tucked around me. Roman must have pulled it over me before leaving me to nap. He seemed to enjoy doing things like that—little tasks to take care of me like getting my beer and peeling my clementines earlier. And I had to admit, I didn't mind being taken care of. Though it was a new experience for me—even when I'd been a kid, my mother hadn't been the most nurturing of parents and I'd learned early how to take care of myself.

It was what caused my fierce independent streak and was one of the reasons it had been so difficult to accept Roman's offer to help. I refused to allow myself to become reliant on someone else because I didn't want to deal with the consequences when they inevitably left. Because they always did.

At least with Roman I already knew there was no future. Somehow that made it easier to accept his little acts of kindness. I didn't have to worry about whether they would last because I already knew nothing about us would last outside this tiny bubble of Vermont.

The real world with its responsibilities was still waiting out there for me in the same way the paparazzi was probably still camped out in front of Roman's house waiting for him.

The thought caused an ache in my chest, and I rubbed my fist against my sternum as though that could somehow ease the pain. It wasn't just that I would miss Roman once this bubble popped, but I would miss the potential of us. In another world, if Roman wasn't a movie star and I wasn't a nobody with a criminal record, maybe we could have seen if something might work between us. But the idea of dating—I didn't even want to fantasize about the possibility because there was no way it could happen. It would be too much of a risk for his reputation, and I couldn't bear the thought that my past might harm his future.

*Stop thinking of what you don't have and enjoy what you do have*, I scolded myself. Right now that was Roman, and suddenly my desire to see him, to touch him, and be reassured by him, overcame any concern about interrupting his phone call. I slipped out from under the blanket and shucked on my clothes before following the sound of his voice to the kitchen.

He was standing barefoot by the stove, ignoring a large pot belching steam to concentrate on the phone conversation. He seemed to be begging someone not to come, and I snorted, unable to think about how that was the opposite of what he'd said to me earlier when he'd been begging me to come. Roman's eyes snapped up to meet mine, and he grinned, clearly realizing what he'd said. His cheeks pinked and his free hand reached out for me in a *come here* gesture.

I wandered over to him and slipped under his arm. He wrapped it around me, his hand cupping my shoulder and pulling me against him with my back to his chest. I let myself sink into the feel of him. He was so much bigger than I was—wider and taller, his muscles more bulging. And he was warm from the heat of the stove. He felt safe, like he could protect me from the weight of the world.

If only that were the case.

I pressed a kiss against his bare wrist, and he squeezed me tighter before releasing me. I turned to help myself to a drink from the fridge. When I turned back to see if he wanted something, I caught him staring at my ass. He was still arguing with someone, so I lifted my eyebrow in silence. He winked.

I grabbed a second beer, wondering if the kind in the fridge was a brand Roman particularly liked or something that Oscar just kept stocked in his house. Either way, I could tell by the fact it came in glass bottles and had a name I'd never heard of that it was way out of my price range. I tried not to think about how much cheap food I could have purchased with the cost of those two fancy beers.

"Oscar, dammit, stop," Roman said with a big melodramatic sigh. "Seriously. I'll let you know if we need you. No! I mean, if *I* need you." His eyes flicked to me and away, his cheeks growing even redder. "Gotta go... *Don't come here.*"

He clicked off and chucked his phone down on the counter like it was on fire before shoving his hands into his hair. "I swear that man," he grumbled.

"Did you ask him where that spa is?" I asked, handing him the beer. "Because you could probably use a massage, to be honest."

He snorted and reached for my waist, drawing me closer and pressing a kiss to the top of my head. "No. And if I need a massage, I have someone right here with magic fingers."

Even though the move felt nice and boyfriendy, Oscar's call had reinforced my earlier thoughts of just how bad things could go for Roman if the media found out about me shacking up with him. And the idea of there being anything other than shacking up involved was... ludicrous. The man was a movie star for god's sake. No, I was going to lie super low and enjoy the little time I had in this dream bubble until it burst.

"Do you need some help with dinner?" I asked him, eyeing the half-prepped ingredients scattered across the countertop.

He laughed. "Unless you like poison chicken, yes I do. Turns out I'm just as bad at playing a chef in real life as I am in video games."

I pulled away from him, frowning. "Wait, I thought you knew how to cook. The two meals you've made for me so far have been delicious."

His cheeks turned pink, and he dipped his head, glancing away. "Yeah, those are the only two recipes I actually know how to cook. I kinda learned them to impress dates."

I raised my eyebrows in surprise. "Seriously? Like you need to cook to impress people. You're kind of impressive all on your own, you know. Though why pancakes and pasta—seems like an odd combo?"

If possible his cheeks burned brighter. He cleared his throat and shifted his feet. "One for dinner, and if it's successful enough..." He shrugged.

It took me a minute to follow, and I started laughing. "The other for breakfast. Oh my god, you whore."

"Hey, it worked for you, didn't it?" He grinned and ran his fingers over my ribs, tickling me. "You ate my pasta and ended up in my bed."

I swatted his hands away, trying to dance out of reach. "It wasn't your pasta that got me into your bed, trust me," I said, winking.

He caught me and pulled me against him, pressing a kiss to the tip of my nose and then to my lips. "Well, whatever got you into my bed, I'm glad."

For a beat the air seemed charged between us, the playfulness of the moment before turned serious. I was suddenly afraid where it might lead—to conversations of us sleeping together and where that might lead, and since I already knew the answer, I didn't want to risk having to hear it out loud.

"We should get started with dinner," I said.

He paused for a beat before nodding, and we turned to the task of prepping the meal, quickly slipping into the now-familiar cadence of working together in the kitchen. Even though we'd barely known each other a couple of days, being together was comfortable in a way I hadn't felt with someone else in a long time. The closest friend I had was a carriage driver named Ardi. He was from Albania, so the language barrier was sometimes a problem, but the man was hilarious and sweet. Since he lived in the same area of Queens I did, most days we found each other on the same bus and train. He'd even offered to have me stay over at his place when I got kicked out of my rented room, but his brother was homophobic as hell. Since they lived together, that was a no-go.

"You got quiet all of a sudden," Roman said. "Cat got your tongue?"

"I was just thinking... This is nice. I've never really done this, like... fixed a big meal with all this fresh stuff. We—my mom and I— usually made meals out of boxes or cans. I mean, don't get me wrong. We cooked chicken and vegetables, but never like this. I don't know how to explain it. It just feels so normal."

Roman kept his eyes down on the frying pan where he was sautéing chicken pieces in olive oil. "Yeah, I feel the same way. You were right before, when you accused me of having meals brought in. I do, normally, but it's not really for the reason you think. When I'm filming, I tend to work long days and come home exhausted. What do you eat when you're too tired to get off the sofa?"

"Chips and beer?" I teased.

"Yep. And delivery takeout like pizza and burgers."

"Mm, pizza and burgers..." I groaned. "Now you're making me hungry."

"Well, directors don't take kindly to lead actors ballooning up in weight during filming. So when I was able to afford it, I had healthy meals delivered to force me to eat well. It made a huge difference to my energy level on set."

He set the spoon down and took a sip of his beer before looking back at me with a grin. "So I don't get a chance to cook anymore. And

I kind of like it. It's nice having someone else to cook for. It's no fun to cook for one person."

"Very true," I said. "I'm the king of frozen dinners. It's depressing as hell. Nothing makes you feel more single than those little plastic trays stacking up in your recycling bin."

Roman set down his beer and stepped toward me, cupping my cheeks in his hands which he seemed to like to do often. "Why are you single?"

It wasn't at all a question I'd been expecting, and I was caught a little off guard. It didn't help that his eyes were laser focused on me, causing my stomach to flip in all kinds of delicious ways. "I told you," I said, trying not to stammer. "About Ian, the guy I dated in high school. It kind of put me off relationships."

"That was a long time ago. You need someone to look after you." His voice was deliciously deep, and his warm eyes searched mine.

"I can look after myself," I told him. But the moment the words left my mouth, I realized that they weren't necessarily true. After all, the whole reason I was here in Vermont was because I'd lost my job and was too broke to afford to take care of my own horse. Which I'd then had to sell so I could send my mother money. I dropped my eyes, not wanting him to see the truth of his words there.

He ducked until he was in my line of sight. "Of course you can, Scotty," he said. "I never doubted that. But you wouldn't have to all the time if you had someone. That's what I'm saying. You have so much to give. I don't like the idea of you alone, without someone to give back."

Before I could respond, before the words had even found their way into the corners of my brain and settled, we were interrupted by a loud banging noise that came from the direction of the front door. It broke the moment between us, and Roman blinked, pulling back.

"Christ, what now?" he murmured. "Do you mind keeping an eye on the chicken while I get that? I think it's close to being done," he asked. I nodded and he kissed me on the forehead before striding toward the door like he owned the place. I was starting to realize there were moments when Roman flicked on the switch to his star power. One minute he was regular Roman, the next he was *Roman Burke, Superstar.*

I checked the chicken, keeping my ear tuned toward the direction of the entry hall. I was not disappointed.

"Where is he?" a male voice screeched from the front door. "Oscar, get out here you home-wrecking cocksucker!"

I made sure the chicken was cooked through before pulling the pan off the heat and turning off the stove. The low rumble of Roman's voice was interspersed with more screeching.

"I know he's in here, motherfucker. Oscar! *Oscar!*"

I rounded the corner to the entry hall and nearly tripped over my feet at the sight of the tall, beautiful man standing just inside the front door. He was honestly one of the most striking men I'd ever seen in real life. He looked like a cross between an elegant swan and a ballerina, but the male version. He was so lovely, I almost didn't realize there was a little toad next to him. And the toad was clearly the screecher.

Swan Man placed a slender-fingered hand on the screecher's shoulder.

The screecher shook off the hand with a violent shake of his shoulder. "Don't touch me, Lolo. There's nothing you can say to stop me from punching that fucker in the face. How dare he touch you! How dare he touch my sweet Dilly Bar."

Swan Man, or Lolo, rolled his eyes and looked at Roman. "My apologies. My partner seems to be forgetting we were on a break when Oscar and I—"

"Fiancé!" Screecher said. "Partner? What the fuck?"

Lolo didn't even blink, just turned slowly toward the toad and sighed as if completely put out. "Honey, we've talked about this. Stop reaching for the stars." He patted the toad on the cheek and then wiped his palm against his leg as he turned back to us.

"Forgive him. We aren't actually engaged," he explained. "It's more of a... well, never mind. That's information you don't need. Did you say Oscar was here?"

Roman noticed me standing next to him and moved to put himself between me and the screecher. "No. Oscar isn't here. Sorry."

Lolo turned to speak to his screecher when the toad launched himself at Roman. Everything happened so fast, I barely had a chance to push Roman out of the way. Unfortunately, when I did, the short man barreled into me and sent both of us staggering back into the circular table in the large entryway. My back hit the table and took my feet out from under me. I heard shouting and the sound of things falling to the floor, but I realized belatedly, I wasn't one of them. I was on my back on the table covered in a screeching toad.

I shoved him off and scrambled to follow him, prepared to beat the shit out of the asshole for coming at Roman like that. Before I could throw the first punch, strong arms wrapped around my middle and yanked me back against an even firmer body. A familiar body.

"Let me go," I growled. "Roman, let me go. That fucker tried to—"

Warm lips landed on the shell of my ear, and a low rumble of laughter snuck down my ear canal. I tried to fight the gooey feeling threatening to pull me back from the brink of violence. First, I needed to teach that toad a lesson.

"Why are you laughing?" I asked, fighting Roman's hold on me. It was impossible. He was way bigger than I was and in prime shape. "Let go."

I noticed Lolo standing tall by the front door, inspecting his fingernails. I'd never in my life met such a cool cat. He sniffed. "Larry, are you done?"

I joined in. If I couldn't hit him with my fists, I could hit him with my smack talk. "Yeah, *Larry*, are you done?"

Larry feinted toward me like he was going to hit me, and an arm shot out so quickly from behind me, I simply stared as Larry took the punch to the jaw and went down.

"Ow," Roman muttered, pulling his fist back and shaking his hand out. "That man has bricks for teeth."

Lolo rolled his eyes again and toed Larry's shoulder. The man groaned. "Oh. Still alive then. Hmm." He stood contemplating his companion for a moment before shrugging and stepping over him, "accidentally" tripping over Larry's nuts in the process, and making the guy cry out and curl into a ball in pain.

"Oops," Lolo said with a put-upon sigh. "I guess now he won't be in the mood to make any phone calls for a little while. Regardless," he added with a wave of his hand, "I'm going to need a vodka gimlet before this goes any further. Anyone care to join me? I know where Oscar keeps the good stuff." He looked down his long, elegant nose to the heap of whining on the floor and raised an eyebrow at his partner. "From when he and all his friends took naked body shots off me at New Year's."

Larry howled something in response, but it was completely incomprehensible given the pitch and extent of his rage.

Lolo simply smirked and sauntered past us, deeper into the house. Roman and I glanced at each other with matching looks of surprise on our faces.

"You're really going to have to introduce me to your friend Oscar," I said with awe. "I think I'm in love."

The groaning from the floor suddenly ceased. The two of us looked down at Larry. He was staring up at Roman with wide eyes.

"Holy crappin' crawdads. I recognize you now. You're Roman Burke."

"Shit," Roman said under his breath. "This asshole is not outing my location to the fucking media. Grab his legs, Scotty. We're going to have to lock him up until I can get a hold of Oscar."

I stared at him.

Roman Burke had just instructed me to commit unlawful imprisonment on a complete stranger.

Maybe Marigold had left us some magic 'shrooms after all. And I'd accidentally eaten the whole lot.

# 16

## ROMAN

*Hiding The Body: When Cat Fights Turn Feral*

SCOTTY LOOKED at me with such an expression of complete horror that I almost started laughing again. Something about being around him made me so fucking giddy, it was insane. I couldn't remember the last time I'd had so much fun with a partner in crime.

"Just for the record, I was kidding about locking him up," I said, knocking my shoulder gently against him. "Grab his legs so we can take him to the kitchen and get a bag of ice. I'd carry him by myself, but my hand is already swelling."

Scotty moved around to grab the guy by the ankles. "Am I on some kind of reality show? I should have asked you sooner."

I glanced up at Scotty after getting my arms under Larry's shoulders. "Would you believe me if I said no?"

His grin was goddamned adorable, and I wanted to eat it. "Absolutely not. There's no other explanation for the past twenty-four hours. Hell, the past two weeks, if I'm being honest."

We dragged the moaning shithead into the kitchen and plunked him down. Lolo was somehow already perched daintily on a stool with a martini glass in his hand. As I looked more closely at the glass, I realized there was even an artsy twist of lime on the edge.

"I need a Lolo in my life," I heard Scotty mutter under his breath. "Dragging assholes across mansions is thirsty work."

Lolo flicked the back of his fingers toward an area of the counter that held the ingredients for the cocktail. "DIY, fellas. Help yourself. Once I get a couple of these down, I'm going to have to find some tapas."

He said the word with a clipped Spanish flare before taking another glug of his drink.

I lifted a brow at Scotty. "Want me to make you one?"

"Hell yes. I'll finish the casserole thing."

We wound up next to each other while I made the drinks and he put the dinner fixings together into a baking dish. Scotty spoke softly out of the corner of his mouth. "No offense, but I'm not sure a chicken veggie casserole is going to cut it for princess over there."

"Definitely not," I agreed. "Ideas?"

He looked up in thought. "I worked as a busboy at Boqueria for a while. The trick with tapas is to serve tiny portions on tiny plates and call it something fancy."

"Can't we just make portions of that look tiny and fancy? Call it... blistered pepper poulet et pâtes?"

"I think that's French, not Spanish."

"French tapas is the new tapas," I said with a sniff. "Everyone knows that."

Scotty's eyes opened in recognition of the made-up bullshit. "So true. Everyone who's anyone knows that."

We continued joking around while he slipped the casserole in the oven and returned to help me fill up a couple of bags of ice for me and the shithead.

"Let's go into the den," Scotty said. "There's a fire in there."

"Ooo! Goodie," Lolo said, extricating his long legs from the pretzel twist he'd had them in. "We can leave Larry here. Just kind of... lean the ice bag up against his face. Yes, like that." He nodded and began walking out of the kitchen.

When we got into the den, Lolo had already dropped sideways into one of the chairs with his slender feet closest to the glowing embers. They were encased in a brightly colored pair of velvet slippers. He must have changed into them when we weren't looking. I vaguely recalled a large black leather handbag slung over his shoulder when the two of them had first arrived.

"Be a love and toss a few logs on, won't you? I would but..." He didn't bother finishing the sentence, instead taking another swig of his cocktail. Which seemed somehow miraculously full again. I glanced around the den, spotting a bar tucked away in the back corner. The man worked quick.

Scotty started toward the fireplace, but I snaked my hand around his elbow, nudging him to the couch instead. "I'll do it." While he sat, I grabbed several logs from the stack off to the side and crouched to place them on the grate.

Once I had the fire going again, I turned to stand and noticed two pairs of eyes that had clearly been locked on my ass for the last few minutes. I lifted my eyebrow. Lolo lifted his glass in return in a cheers. Scotty smirked and raised his glass as well.

I let out a mock beleaguered smile and joined him on the couch.

Lolo closed his eyes and let his head fall back. "This is divine. Oscar always has the most exquisite taste, doesn't he?" He sighed. "That man... I swear..."

Scotty and I both gawped at him before meeting each other's eyes.

Scotty was the braver of the two of us.

"So..." Scotty began. "You and Oscar..."

Lolo flapped a hand in the air. "Oh, Oscar and I go way back. I went to school with Basil, you know."

Scotty snorted out his drink and looked at me with mirth in his eyes. "Let me guess, another brother?"

"Oh, right. I forgot about Basil," I admitted. "He lives in Iceland."

"Of course he does," Scotty said, wiping his mouth with the back of his hand.

We heard what sounded like Larry finally stirring in the other room. He moaned and cursed but didn't appear in the den.

"Ignore him," Lolo said. "He'll be fine. Stubborn, you know?"

Scotty leaned forward from where he sat next to me on the love seat. "If you don't mind me asking... Why are you with him? I don't mean any offense, but... no, like, why are you with him? Really? The guy seems like a..."

He seemed to be struggling to find the right word, so I supplied it for him. "He seems like an ass."

Lolo smiled down that aquiline nose at Scotty with a bemused expression. "Oh, he's for *sure* an ass, darling. A right royal one at that. But his body is snug and hot like a virgin teenager. When I'm inside him, it's like—" He held out the slim fingers of one hand in a tight fist and was about to enter the fist with the long index finger of his other hand.

Scotty choked on his drink again. "What?" he squawked, throwing his hands over his face and almost dumping the gimlet in his own lap. "Never mind."

I could tell this was about to go into a very personal direction, and frankly, I couldn't bear to imagine this beautiful creature anywhere near Larry the Tightass Bottom. "What do you do for a living, Lolo?" I blurted, desperate to turn the conversation to safer, less viscerally visual ground.

He paused with his glass halfway to his lips and gave me a quizzical look. "Do?" he asked.

"You know, for a job," Scotty said.

Lolo tilted his head to the side. "Huh," he said, as if he'd never heard such an odd question.

Scotty looked at me out of the corner of his eyes, but I knew that if I met his glance, I wouldn't be able to hold in my laughter. So instead I pulled him against my side and wrapped my arms around him, wanting him close. I found that I couldn't be near him and not want my hands on him.

Lolo tilted his head in the other direction, his face crinkling as he pointed a talon at us. "Aren't you two cute together. Are you two..." He waved his finger back and forth.

Scotty abruptly sat up and scooted as far away from me as

possible on the little love seat, which wasn't very far at all. "Us? Together? No! Of course not. No. Don't be ridiculous."

Lolo and I stared at him.

"What?" Scotty asked. "We only just met. And you... have that thing."

Lolo lifted a waxed brow. "What thing?"

For a moment I was offended, wondering if Scotty just didn't want to be associated with me. But then I realized I had it backward—he didn't want *me* to have to be associated with *him*. He was giving me an out so that Lolo wouldn't realize we'd been sleeping together. He was trying to protect my reputation, which left me feeling a little melty with affection for him. Okay, a lot melty.

"There is no thing," I said very clearly, making sure to meet Scotty's eyes.

His face flushed a little, and he glanced over at Lolo before turning back to me. "I didn't want... I..." He sighed. "Don't feel like you have to..." He waved his hand between us.

He was obviously so unsure of what he could and couldn't say in front of a stranger that I decided to make it very clear.

I leaned in and kissed him. He was hesitant at first, stiffening and almost pulling away. But then I threaded my hand into his hair and tilted his head to get a better angle. Our mouths explored each other for a few moments before I pulled back and met his eyes. "If you don't want people to know that I like you enough to touch and kiss you, speak up now, and I'll make sure Lolo knows it was my misunderstanding."

Scotty's pupils were blown, and his lips glistened from our kisses. He looked beautifully dazed and deliciously kiss-drunk.

"No. I mean, they can know. Anyone can... know. You know?"

Lolo snorted. "You must be a damned good kisser, Roman Burke."

"He is. He *sooo* is," Scotty said with a sigh, still staring at me like I invented chocolate. I couldn't help leaning in and kissing him again.

"Do I need to leave the two of you alone?"

"Uh-huh," Scotty murmured while I said, "No, it's fine."

Lolo chuckled into his glass. "Tell you what. I'll make us another round and check on Larry while you two finish the porn show. Just know that if I were a lesser man, I'd have my camera out right now."

I remembered wanting to confiscate Larry's phone. "Hey, Lolo?"

"Yes?"

"Can you please grab Larry's phone for us? I really don't want my location being leaked to the press."

"I would love to. Larry, darling," Lolo called as he sauntered out of the room on flamingo legs. "How are you feeling, boo boo?"

I shuddered, still unable to determine the attraction there. Tight asses could be found on decent men, and I didn't believe for a second that Lolo was only into someone for the sex. I'd have to ask Oscar what their deal was when I saw him next.

Scotty sat silent for a moment, watching as he drew a fingertip around the top of my hand. "Did you mean what you said about liking me and not caring if other people know?"

"Yes," I said immediately. I didn't want him to have one single second of insecurity about me. "Is that okay with you?"

He nodded, not looking up at me. "I just didn't want you to have more trouble if word gets out..."

"I'm inclined to trust Lolo's discretion," I admitted. "I don't think Oscar would have had him here in his home before if he thought he was the kind of guy to sell his story to the media. Also, those ridiculous velvet slippers he's wearing are Versace which means he may not be money motivated like most people who blab to the tabloids."

Scotty still wasn't meeting my eyes. I tilted his chin up. "Hey," I said softly. "Is that all you're worried about, or is there something else?"

He paused, as if trying to figure out how to say something. "Don't feel like you have to... I don't know... claim me or whatever. I mean... I get it. It's just a hookup. You don't have to pretend we're dating, you know?"

His words shouldn't have surprised me since I'd caught glimpses of his insecurity before, but they did anyway. I couldn't determine whether Scotty was still trying to give me an out or whether he was trying to tell me he saw this as just a convenient hookup. It was the second time he'd made a point of saying something that implied this was just a little bit of fun and nothing more.

I realized the thought made me feel a little... disappointed? Was that the right word? It wasn't like I'd given a lot of thought to dating Scotty. The idea seemed foolish on its face: he was a regular person, not at all involved in the frenzied Hollywood life. He had no idea what he would be getting into dating a movie star: the relentless pressure and attention. The scrutiny. My last serious boyfriend hadn't been able to handle it. I didn't know that anyone outside the celebrity culture would be able to.

Which was a shame, because a part of me thought it might be nice to date Scotty. See where this connection between us took us. But I'd had that kind of fantasy before, and it hadn't been strong enough to withstand the pressure.

"I didn't pretend we were dating, I simply didn't want to not be able to touch you in front of him," I pointed out. "I like touching you. In case that wasn't obvious." To illustrate the point, and hopefully lighten the mood a little, I grabbed at him and tickled him in the ribs until he was laughing and squirming underneath me on the love seat. His blue eyes danced, and his laughs turned to higher-pitched giggles until he was out of breath.

Scotty Pinker was simply gorgeous, and I kissed him yet again.

Because I really couldn't stop.

My phone buzzed in my pocket with an incoming call and I ignored it, not wanting to interrupt my make-out session with Scotty. There was a brief respite before it started buzzing again. Scotty was the one to pull away from the kiss. "Sounds like someone's trying to reach you."

"It can wait," I growled, dipping my head to reclaim his lips. "I'm busy." But then it started vibrating for a third time and I couldn't ignore it any longer. Groaning, I sat up and fished my phone from my pocket. An old photo of Polly filled the screen. If she was being this insistent, it was important. But I didn't want to answer it and have Scotty think he wasn't important to me either.

Thankfully, he resolved the dilemma for me. "Go ahead and

answer," Scotty told me. "I'll go find us some wine." He stood and left while I swiped open the phone and pressed it to my ear.

"Everything okay?" I asked.

"You absolute piece of shit," she said.

My eyes widened. It was not the response I expected. "Ooooh-kay, I'll take that as a no, then?"

"Of course things aren't okay, Roman," she said testily. "They're terrible! Why in the world did I listen to you? About dating no less? What the fuck do you know about keeping a man?"

I winced. "Low blow, Polly."

She let out a sigh. "Sorry. I just... ugh."

I settled back on the couch. I had a feeling this conversation might take a minute. "Does this have anything to do with Howard by any chance?"

"Yes." The answer came out muffled as though she had her head in her hands.

"I take it you had the talk?"

"Yes."

"It went that well, huh?"

She let out another groan.

It was obvious how upset she was, and my heart ached for her. She'd been a close friend for a long time, and I knew how badly she wanted to settle down and raise a family. I also knew just how hard that was given the scrutiny we received in our day-to-day lives. "I'm sorry, Polly. If he doesn't know what a treasure you are, then he wasn't worth it in the first place. You're an amazing person, and you're going to be an amazing mother with or without him in your life."

"He wants to make it work."

Her tone was so dejected it took a moment for her words to filter through. "Wait, what?" I asked, sitting straighter on the couch. "So you told him the truth and rather than run he wants to stay? Then why do you sound so upset?"

"Because you and I both know it will never work, Roman," she said. "He's a regular guy. He lives in the suburbs for fuck's sake. He still gets a newspaper delivered every morning. Like actual printed words on paper that a kid on a bike throws onto the front porch. He owns a lawnmower and coaches a junior girls rec league soccer team because he did it once a decade ago when his twins were that age and just never stopped. And don't get me started on his kids. They'd be subjected to just as much scrutiny as he would be and sure they're in college so practically adults but still. Their father got an actress pregnant out of wedlock—can you even imagine what the tabloids are going to say about him? I can't do that to them, Roman. I just can't."

I could hear the misery in her voice. "I'm sorry, Polly," I said again, softer.

Just then Scotty came in, a glass of red wine in each hand. He glanced at me hesitantly, silently asking whether he should leave so I could continue the conversation in private. I waved him in and patted the spot next to me on the couch. He set the wineglasses down on the coffee table and then settled against my side. I draped my arm around his shoulder, drawing him closer, enjoying the warmth of his comforting presence.

She sighed. "I know. It's just... it feels so unfair." Her voice broke on the last word, and I heard her sniffle.

"Maybe you should give Howard a chance," I offered.

At the mention of the man's name, Scotty stiffened beside me. He pulled out from under my arm and started to stand. "This is private. I should go," he murmured under his breath.

I snagged his wrist. "Stay," I mouthed.

"What if I'm able to figure out who you're talking about?" he asked. "That's like state-secret-level information right there."

It wasn't likely Scotty would be able to guess Howard's identity, but even if he did it wouldn't matter. "I trust you," I told him. And it was true.

He hesitated a moment longer before easing back against my side. I traced my fingertips idly up and down his arm as I pressed my point. "I'm serious, Pol," I told her. "Howard's a grown man. He can make his own decisions about his life. If you've told him what it will be like for him to date a celebrity, and he knows what he's getting into, then it's up to him whether he wants to take that on or not."

She barked a laugh. "You know as well as I do that no one can truly know what they're getting into," she said. "Look at Pete. He thought he could handle it. He couldn't."

At the mention of my ex-boyfriend, I scowled. She had a point. But I still wasn't willing to concede that easily.

Before I could respond she said, "Sorry, I shouldn't have brought Pete into this. It's just, how do you take a regular guy like Howard and meld him into the chaotic life of Hollywood? He has yard art, Roman. Real, honest-to-god yard art. The tabloids are going to eat him alive."

"Maybe he's stronger than you give him credit for," I suggested.

"He's been through enough in his life. His wife's death ripped a hole in him that's taken years to heal." She sounded defeated.

"Maybe that's part of what made him stronger, Polly."

She didn't argue the point, which meant she was considering it. "And what if it doesn't work out?" she asked. This time I could hear the fear in her voice. "What then? What if we start dating and they stomp all over his life and I get my hopes up and we don't end up together after all?"

"What if it does work out?" I countered.

She didn't have an immediate answer to that.

"Do you like him, Polly?" I asked.

"Yes," she said without hesitation.

"And he cares for you?"

"He..." She paused and drew a breath. "He told me he loves me. But we've only spent that one long weekend together. Who falls in love that fast?"

I became acutely aware of Scotty resting against my side, the steady rise and fall of his breathing, the warmth of him seeping through my shirt. I continued running my fingers lightly up and down his arm, watching goose bumps trail in the wake of my touch.

He must have realized that I was looking at him because he tilted his head back and looked up at me. He smiled before snuggling closer against me.

My lungs felt devoid of air, my heartbeat a thundering cacophony in my ears. I swallowed, my throat suddenly dry. "I think love can be unpredictable and it's not up to us to dictate its terms. If it happens fast, it happens fast. We just get to choose to embrace it or push it away."

There was no way Scotty wasn't listening; no way he hadn't heard what I'd just said. I wondered if my words made him think of me.

They certainly made me think of him.

Polly broke the moment. "Was that pretty little speech from one of your movies?" she asked dryly.

I scowled. Polly never missed an opportunity to bring me down a notch and make sure my head never got too big, a common problem in our industry. "No, that's a 100 percent original Roman Burke-ism. You're welcome. Anyway, how did you leave things with Howard?"

Polly sighed. "He wants to come visit. I have an ultrasound in a couple of days and he... he wants to be there for it. Even if we don't end up together, he wants to be there for the baby."

I smiled. He sounded like a good guy, which gave me hope. "So you're going to see him again soon?"

"No. I told him not to come."

"Polly," I groaned.

"I know, I know," she said defensively. "I'm just..."

She couldn't seem to find the right word, so I said it for her. "Scared."

"Yeah." Her voice was soft, resigned.

I let one of Scotty's blond curls twist around my fingers as an ache spread through my chest. "I know how you feel."

Polly laughed. "The day Roman Burke is scared of anything..."

I didn't let her deflect. "Give him a chance, Polly."

There was another sigh and a beat of silence before she grumbled, "I'll think about it. That's the best you're going to get."

Just as we were getting ready to say our goodbyes, Lolo came careening back into the room, his slippers literally slipping on the hardwood floor. Whatever it was, it looked like it was going to require all of my focus.

"Crap. Polly, I gotta go," I said quickly, disconnecting the call.

Lolo pressed a hand to his chest, sucking in several exaggerated breaths before dramatically proclaiming, "Call the police!"

I straightened, my heart pounding. "What is it?"

Scotty bolted upright. "Is it Larry? Is he okay?"

Lolo's brow crinkled. "Larry? No. Who cares about him? It's our car. It's been stolen."

Scotty slumped back against the seat. "Oh sweet Jesus. Seriously?"

"Hand to god," Lolo said, flashing three fingers in the Boy Scout salute. Or was it the Vulcan salute? I always got them confused.

I groaned, rolling my eyes. "Fucking A—how many cars is Marigold's boyfriend going to steal?"

Lolo placed a hand on his hip and cocked it to the side. "Shit. Is Marigold dating again? Well, that explains that." He swiveled and called over his shoulder. "Larry, honey. Looks like we'll be staying the night. I hope you brought in the essentials when we arrived. So help me if you forgot the lube, you're going to be feeling it—"

He glanced our way and winked. "Not that Oscar doesn't have some stashed in almost every room, but I like to keep Larry on his toes. Makes him eager to please if you know what I mean." Then he pressed a hand against his chest and slid it down his body, including his genitals. "Plus, I have sensitive skin. Particularly in the area of my—"

"Yep, got it," Scotty said, cutting him off.

Just then Larry came storming into the room. He went straight for Lolo, his hands clasped in front of him and his eyes beseeching. "Snookie, I'm sorry, sweetheart. Will you forgive Big Papa?"

Lolo crossed his arms over his chest and looked down his nose at Larry. "Is that any way to apologize to your Dilly Bar?"

I choked. Scotty's voice rang out in the small room, making me jump. "No! No my god, *no*! No. Spartacus, make it stop."

I stepped forward. "Before we go too far down this path, perhaps we should discuss accommodations?"

They swiveled toward me. Lolo lifted a perfectly arched eyebrow. "What's there to discuss?"

"Well, I mean, there are hotels and—"

Lolo waved a hand. "Oh you're sweet to consider our comfort, but we won't be put out at all staying here."

I glanced at Scotty. He opened his mouth. Closed it. Opened it again. And closed it. We both seemed at a total loss for words.

"We're fucked, aren't we?" I murmured to him.

"Looks like it," he agreed.

"If only we could send them to the spa." I sighed and started toward the door. "Come on, let's find a spare room."

Lolo trailed long elegant fingers across my shoulder to keep me from leaving. "No need, love. I know my way around."

"I thought you said you didn't spend the night!" Larry squawked, chasing after him.

"Oh Snuffles, I was lying. Of course I spent the night." He crooked a finger toward the toad. "Come along, then."

# 17

## SCOTTY

*High-Maintenance Houseguests And The Men Who (Don't) Love Them*

AFTER GETTING Lolo and Larry settled, which involved sourcing a bottle of Pellegrino as well as a particular eye mask that Oscar seemed to keep scores of in a special minifridge, Roman and I were exhausted.

Well, at least I was. Roman always looked like he could go straight into a magazine cover shoot at a moment's notice. The bastard.

Not that I minded. He was constant eye candy and boner fodder. And when we fell into his bed together again, I realized I'd been following him blindly.

"If you were hoping for me to sleep somewhere besides on top of your hot body, too bad," I mumbled, draping myself across his chest and inhaling his scent.

Roman looked at me like I was crazy. "Why would I want you to sleep somewhere else?"

I shrugged. "I didn't want to assume."

He snickered. "You know what they say about that word."

"No, what?" I asked with a straight face.

"I don't know, but I'm pretty sure *u* need to give *me* your *ass*."

I narrowed my eyes at him. "I don't think that's how it goes."

Roman rolled on top of me. We were both stripped down to our underwear, and I could feel his big heavy cock hard against my thigh through the smooth cotton of his boxer briefs. His body was so warm and solid above me. I wanted him to pound me into the mattress, but I wasn't sure I had the patience or stamina for anything more than a quick frot or suck.

His grin was goddamned adorable, and it softened when he met my eyes so that when his lips landed on mine, the kiss was gentle and sweet. It didn't at all match the intensity of the wrestling and tickling we'd done earlier. This was something different, something intimate. Our eyes were still open despite the kiss, and it struck me that it was the first time I'd ever looked at a man while kissing him.

I brought my hand up to touch his face with the tips of my fingers, to feel the softness of the whiskers he'd never bothered to shave off that day. The rolling of his hips had changed from grinding to teasing. It was too light to give me any satisfaction. I brought my legs around him and pushed my dick up into him, seeking more.

Roman's hand came down between us to squeeze me through my briefs. *Fuckkkk* it felt so good when he touched me. I moaned into his mouth.

"What do you want, sweet Scotty?" he murmured against the skin of my jaw.

"You," I said breathlessly. "You inside me. You sucking me. Touching me. Anything. You making me come. Please."

His big hand reached inside my briefs and grasped my shaft, tugging enough to make my head spin and my cock fill even more.

"Oh fuck yes, like that." I moved my own hand down to do the same to him, reaching into his boxer briefs until I could take hold of his own warm cock. Roman groaned against my throat.

"Fuck, baby. That feels good." The deep rumble of Roman's voice vibrated against my chest, and the wet trail of his openmouthed kisses snaked down my neck to my collarbone.

We jacked each other, panting and exclaiming how good it felt until I knew I couldn't hold back anymore.

"Roman," I gasped. *"Fuck—"*

When the orgasm hit, he surged up and took my mouth, continuing to stroke me through my release. As soon as the wet fluid hit my belly and his hand, he came too, shooting all over my stomach and chest and hand. Something about being pinned down and covered in our combined releases made me feel completely dominated and owned by Roman. There was something erotically primal about it. With a touch of the forbidden as well knowing just how off-limits he would be to me under normal circumstances. Knowing how crazy the tabloids would go if they found out Roman Burke was sleeping with the likes of me.

Roman's thick muscled thigh pressed between my legs as he shifted part of his weight off me. I could have sworn I heard him mumble something about not being able to get enough of me, but maybe that was just my brain indulging in a little wishful thinking.

I lay there a few more minutes to catch my breath before shimmying out from under him to clean up.

"Stay." His voice was sleepy and rough. I looked back over my shoulder to see him propped up on an elbow. His body was magnificent, like something out of a centerfold. His hair was sticking up in a wild tangle that made him look less than perfect, and it endeared him to me, as if the man needed more endearing.

"I'm just going to take a quick shower." I turned back and made my way through the darkened room to the warm tile floor of the fancy bathroom. I'd never known tile to be warm before, but Roman had explained that there were heating elements in it. I wondered how much heated bathroom floors added to the home's heat bill, and that led me to wondering what the heating bill for this monstrosity was. I couldn't even begin to imagine.

I tried forcing thoughts of money out of my mind and focused instead on figuring out how to work all the switches and dials on the wall of the shower. I finally got at least one waterfall to start pouring from the myriad showerheads and spigots and stepped carefully onto the strange wooden decking to rinse off.

The hot water felt amazing, and I stood under it forever simply enjoying the ability to do so. After a while, I felt a slight draft followed by the warm dry hands of a sleepy giant step up behind me.

"Having fun?" he mumbled into the back of my neck as he pressed a kiss there.

"How much do you think it costs to have your own waterfall?" I asked without turning around or moving out from under the wide tumble of hot water. "I'm asking for a friend."

"Hmm," he said, running his hands down my sides. "I feel a bit put on the spot like when the presidential candidates are asked about the price of a gallon of milk."

I tilted my head to the side, giving his lips better access to my neck. "Well, I've never bought a full gallon," I told him. "But a half is just under three bucks at my local market in Queens. The problem is, you can't get out of there without buying a Reece's Cups which is another dollar. So really, milk is at least four bucks."

The now-familiar rumbling laughter made its way through his chest to my back. Roman reached past me to find a bar of soap on the shelf and used it to slick up my chest and stomach. Just looking down at his large, capable hands against my skinny body made my dick stiffen again. I'd seen these hands pull the trigger on machine guns in a war movie and caress the small of a woman's back in a rom-com. I'd seen them clasp the throttle of an airplane in an action adventure film and gesture passionately to the jury in a legal thriller.

I'd spent so much time the past couple of days seeing Roman as just regular Roman that when I was suddenly struck by the fact he was *the* Roman Burke, it took me by surprise. And honestly scared the fuck out of me.

I was playing with fire.

And living in a fantasy world.

But as long as Roman himself was fine with it, I was going to enjoy it while it lasted.

I turned to slide my soapy self against him, front to front. Roman's hands instantly found my ass and started kneading it. He slipped a thick thigh between my legs again and I began to ride it, imagining sinking onto his big cock in bed and riding him instead, not that I had the energy for that.

I looked down to see water sluicing down his thick erection, soaking the dark brown curls at the base of it, and dripping off his heavy, low-hanging sac. I swallowed a moan and slithered down his body until I was on my knees before him, dragging my tongue along the hot water on his hard cock.

Roman's hands landed in my wet hair as he gasped and grunted his gratitude. My tongue danced along his length, circling the head and teasing him before I looked up and met his glassy eyes.

In that moment he was all mine. It wasn't fantasy; it was real.

And I was going to drink it all down as long as I could.

# 18

## ROMAN

*Grand Theft Auto: Special Stowe Edition*

THE NEXT DAY was blissfully calm. After I whipped us up some pancakes, we found Oscar's office and used his computer to create a Western Union account so I could send the money to Scotty's mom. With that out of the way, we had the entire day to ourselves—no obligations, no schedules, nothing. We took advantage of it, whiling away our time gaming, watching movies, talking for hours in front of the fire, and taking a couple of long walks outside with Nugget in the snow. It was glorious.

Lolo and Larry were conspicuously absent through most of it. The only trace of them was a bizarre rhythmic squawking sound that came from the direction of their room around lunchtime and was quickly followed by Lolo's voice snapping out a tight, "Settle down."

Scotty and I had exchanged startled glances across the kitchen table before both shaking our heads in a mutual silent agreement not to even speculate on what those two were up to.

It wasn't until very late that night, when we were trying to get up the energy to relocate our lazy asses from the movie room to the bedroom, that the doorbell rang again.

We both looked at each other and groaned, "*Fuck*," at the same time.

"That cannot be good, Spartacus," Scotty mumbled from beneath the plush blanket we'd been snuggled under. "Nothing good comes through that door. Haven't we learned that?"

I stood up and stretched. "Maybe it's just Marigold looking to borrow a cup of sugar."

"Or a fifth of vodka," he said, pushing off the ground with a groan. "Or a bag of weed."

"Or maybe it's Lolo returning from burying Harry's body," I suggested.

"Larry," Scotty corrected with a snort. "And the fact we haven't seen those two today concerns me greatly."

I reached for his hand to help him up, and he followed me up the stairs and through the house to the front door. "Oscar texted a while ago. Said those two were at the spa for mani-pedis."

Scotty stopped and yanked my arm to get me to do the same. I looked back at him. "Can you please, once and for all, explain this spa shit to me? I thought it was a spa, then I thought it was a summer house, now it sounds like a spa again."

"Does it matter?"

He blinked at me before shrugging. "I mean... I could go for a facial..."

I pulled him against my chest and gave him a lecherous look. "I can do that without you having to leave the house. All you have to do is ask."

"Eww," he said, pushing me away and laughing. "Don't be crass. If jizz did anything good for skin, my right hand would be featured on the cover of magazines already. Here, feel it. Tell me if it's soft." He started poking and grabbing at me with both hands, and I swatted at him to get him to stop as I unlocked the front door.

I swung it open to find Officer Flirt waiting on the other side. I half stepped in front of Scotty, blocking him from view, and crossed my arms. "What do you want?" I asked.

Scotty elbowed me and ducked out from behind me. "He means, hi, Trevor, any news on the stolen car?"

Trevor lifted a bushy brow. "Which one? I'm here to take a report for a second stolen car, and I'm wondering what the hell kind of crime ring the two of you brought to our sleepy town."

"Oh thank god, the police are here!" Larry bellowed from the staircase. "Fucking finally. I called you people last night."

Officer Beardy swiveled his upturned eyebrow to little Larry, who stomped toward the door, followed elegantly by Lolo in a long, flowing white robe.

"Larry, darling, don't forget your heart condition," Lolo warned.

"What the fuck? I don't have a heart condition," Larry stammered.

"Shame," Lolo murmured under his breath as he floated past me. When he caught sight of Trevor, his entire demeanor changed. "Well, well. Who have we here?"

"This is Officer..." I realized I didn't know Trevor's last name.

"You can call me Trevor," he said to Lolo with a thousand-watt smile. "Nice to meet you, beautiful. And you are?"

Larry sputtered up at Trevor. "He's none of your goddamned business is what he is. You're here about the car."

Trevor studied Larry with narrowed eyes. "Are you the owner of the vehicle?"

Larry's face turned an unhealthy shade of red. "Not, uh, technically..."

"The car is rented under my name," Lolo said, strolling past Larry to offer a pale, slender hand for Trevor to kiss. "I'm Lloyd Lovegrove," he purred. "But you can call me Lolo."

Scotty and I stared at him. I thought I heard a slight breath from Scotty that sounded like, "Wow." I reached for his hand without thinking and threaded my fingers through his. I liked having someone to share this insanity with.

"Why don't we move into the kitchen?" I suggested.

Before we even got away from the open front door, headlights flashed and a car fitting the description of Lolo's rental pulled to a neat stop in the circular drive. A familiar woman got out. Marigold caught us all staring at her slack-jawed.

She waved. "Thanks for the loaner! There's an extra dozen donuts in the front seat for you. Cheers," she added happily before turning and setting off in the direction of the spa with two boxes of donuts under one arm and a handle of vodka dangling from her other hand. After a beat, she called back over her shoulder, "Oh, and the keys are in it. Don't worry, no one would steal a car around here, so it's safe."

No one said a word until she'd disappeared into the wintry Vermont night.

"Anyone know who that was?" Trevor asked.

"Oscar's sister," I said.

"Well, fuck me," Lolo said with a laugh.

"Yes, please," Trevor muttered under his breath.

"Other way around, doll," Larry said proudly.

Scotty made a soft gagging noise beside me, and I bit back a laugh. "Well, now that that's solved... Okay, everyone. Party's over. Good night."

I tried to nudge Trevor out the door, but he dug in his heels, resisting. "You need anything else or have any problems, feel free to give me a call." He said it to all of us, but he handed his business card to Lolo.

Lolo took the card, his eyes holding Trevor's as he slowly ran the tip of an elegant finger along the edge of it, before slipping it into what looked like an intricately laced bra.

"What the—" Larry gurgled in rage.

But Lolo ignored him. "Come along, Pom Pom," he said, pirouetting elegantly on the ball of one foot and hooking a finger in the collar of Larry's shirt, tugging him along behind him as he glided to the staircase.

"Sweet dreams, Officer," he called over his shoulder. "Unless they're of me, in which case I hope they're very, *very* naughty."

Trevor let out a laugh and started toward his car. I quickly closed the door behind him, making sure to lock it. Then I turned and met

Scotty's eyes. "Can you help me push that big table in front of the door?" I teased. "I'm not sure we can handle any more surprise visitors."

"No shit," he said with a snort. "Although you... or maybe *Oscar*... get extra points for being entertaining. I'm not sure the last time I laughed so much."

I agreed wholeheartedly. Being with Scotty was so much fucking fun. I couldn't imagine our time together coming to an end.

*Maybe it doesn't have to*, a small voice in my head said.

I let the thought linger in the back of my mind as I led him up the stairs to our room and curled around him in bed. I fell asleep to candy-coated daydreams about making Scotty mine, about bringing him back to the city with me and setting him up in my brownstone. I'd help him get another job at the stables if that was what he wanted or even tell him he didn't have to work if he didn't want to.

It was all so perfect and easy, so when a high-pitched screech hit my ears and an elbow clocked me under the chin, it shoved me face-first into a very different reality.

"Scotty?" I called out, gasping and reaching for the pain shooting through my teeth. "Fuck!"

I opened my eyes and saw him standing on top of the mattress over me, his little butt sexy as fuck in navy boxer briefs. His fists were clenched and his blond hair wild.

"Get out," he screamed, pointing at a figure standing in the door. "Get out!"

I followed his finger, still cupping my tender mouth. There stood a man I recognized. I scrambled to sit up, reaching for Scotty to pull him down next to me. "Shh, it's okay. I know him, baby."

Scotty looked at me with crazy eyes. "How many times is some random person going to sneak into this room? What the hell, Sparta-cus? Is this normal for you? Why didn't we move the table like you suggested?"

The man in the doorway chuckled. "I tried calling. Just wanted to let you know we were here early, okay? Diana's making breakfast. We're starved. That piece-of-shit plane you chartered only had peanuts on it. I always assumed there was caviar and stuff on private planes. What a letdown."

With that he turned and left, closing the door behind him.

Scotty blinked several times. "Who the hell was that?" he asked. Then his brain seemed to catch up with what the man said, and he frowned. "Wait, Diana as in your sister Diana?"

I nodded. "That was my brother-in-law, Earl."

"Did you know they were coming?" His frown deepened. "Wait, I guess so if you chartered a plane? Did I hear that right?"

"I invited them—Diana, Earl, and their two girls," I said, nudging him off the bed. "And yes, I chartered the plane for them. It's not easy flying from middle-of-nowhere Nebraska to middle-of-nowhere Vermont without making a million stops." I stood and stretched, enjoying how Scotty's eyes traced down my body, lingering on my abs before dropping lower.

He seemed to realize he'd gotten distracted and shook his head to focus. "Okay, but why are they here? Why didn't you tell me they were coming?"

I grinned. "Because it was a surprise."

He didn't follow. "A surprise for who?"

"You."

He still didn't get it. "Me?"

I wanted to bounce on my toes I was so excited to finally share the news. "Yes you. I asked him to come out and give you horseback-riding lessons."

Scotty said nothing. He just sat there, forehead furrowed in confusion. It wasn't at all the reaction I'd been hoping for. The moment Scotty'd told me he'd never learned to ride and how much he'd wanted to, I'd thought of my brother-in-law, Earl. It had seemed crazy at the time, but I'd asked Diana what she thought about bringing the family to Vermont for a visit, and she'd been all for it. She'd take any excuse to escape the arctic tundra of Nebraska, espe-cially if it meant seeing me.

I'd been hoping Scotty would be thrilled by the news. But so far he just seemed confused. I wondered if maybe I'd overstepped my bounds, if this gift was too much, too extravagant.

"I don't understand," Scotty finally said.

"Horseback riding. You said you wanted to learn. My brother-in-law raises Tennessee Walkers. I'm told that's a kind of horse even though I could have sworn it was a kind of whiskey. Anyway, when you mentioned wanting to learn, I figured who better to teach you than a professional horse trainer?"

When his eyes met mine, they were guarded. "For me?"

He looked so damn cute and vulnerable that I wanted to reach out and tousle his hair. "Of course for you."

"No, I mean... you flew your sister and her family all the way out here just so I could learn how to ride?"

I nodded.

"Why?" His voice was soft, breathy. Hesitant.

I smoothed a thumb over his pink cheek and down across his soft morning stubble. I wasn't sure how to answer the question. It was too complicated to put into words. So I settled with the easiest answer, even if it wasn't a complete one. "Because I thought it would make you happy."

Scotty hesitated a moment longer, thinking through my answer. Then he surged to his feet, his arms threading around my neck to pull me down to his level. My thoughts went fuzzy with lust and desire as his soft lips and prickly whiskers started in on mine. When he pulled back, I didn't want to let him go.

He looked up at me, his eyes glistening. "No one's ever done anything like that for me," he said. "Thank you, Spartacus."

I cleared my throat, feeling a little uncomfortable under all the gratitude. I hadn't done much, other than make a few phone calls the day before while he'd been in the barn checking on Nugget. And Scotty deserved so much more than that. I didn't know how he couldn't see it.

I lifted a shoulder. "Of course. No problem," I said, deflecting his praise. "It's a slow time of year on their farm. I'm sure they'll take advantage of being here and take the girls skiing." I pulled away from him and grabbed my pants from the back of a nearby chair. "We should get dressed and get down there, though. My sister makes a killer french toast."

He watched me for a moment before nodding and moving to the dresser where he'd put his meager stack of borrowed clothes. He'd washed some of them yesterday and folded them to use again. Despite Oscar having closets full of clothes, Scotty hadn't wanted to take more than the bare minimum. He'd also refused to let me send his mother more than a couple of hundred dollars the day before. I didn't even know it was possible to stay anywhere in New York for less than two hundred dollars a night, but he'd insisted sending her more than that would have been a mistake.

He slipped into some jeans and a henley shirt before pulling a thick sweater on over it. I watched his body as he dressed. My eyes were glued to him like little twin perverts, but I truly had never seen a man more mesmerizing. When he turned and caught me staring, I finally had to snap out of it and finish dressing myself.

"By the way," Scotty said as we started downstairs. "We need to move rooms. This one is hexed."

I was still laughing at the comment when we reached the cacophony in the kitchen. I recognized Earl and my niece Sonya singing "Head, Shoulders, Knees, and Toes" together at top volume and increasing speed. My younger niece Naomi, or Nay-Nay as we called her, was sitting on a stool, kicking her legs and giggling along.

Diana was at the stove already cooking the french toast. I smelled bacon coming from the oven too. It was a domestic scene that made me miss home. I'd been back to Nebraska for Christmas, but I hadn't been able to stay very long since we'd been in the middle of filming.

"Uncle Roman!" Sonya shouted when she saw me. She came flying around the counter and threw her arms around my waist. I picked her up for a real hug and relished the feel of her little body in my arms. The girls were such unadulterated sweetness and light, they never failed to bring me joy.

"Sweet Sonya, how is your new hamster?" I asked, setting her down so I could pick up Nay-Nay and give her a hug. "And how is this giant girl doing?"

Sonya proceeded to go right into updating me on the state of the Christmas hamster, and Nay-Nay nodded along like a bobblehead. I met Scotty's eyes over Nay-Nay's head and winked at him.

When the pace of my niece's chatter finally slowed, I introduced Scotty. "Girls, this is my good friend Scotty. Scotty, this is Sonya, who just turned five, Naomi, who is three *and a half*, my sister Diana, who is—"

"Don't you dare do it, Roman Anthony Burke," Diana warned with a laugh. "My husband taught me how to work a bullwhip, and I won't hesitate to use it on you."

I walked over to kiss her on the cheek. "And that is Earl. The man who's lucky enough to live with these lovely ladies. And who apparently has tastes in the bedroom I didn't need to know about."

I shifted Naomi to one hip and pulled Scotty in with the opposite arm. "Guys, this is Scotty Pinker. He's the man I told you about who drives the horse and carriage in Central Park."

Sonya came up to Scotty and tugged on his sweater. "Can we meet your horse? Daddy says you have a horse who pulls the carriage and that Uncle Roman brought her with you here on vacation."

Scotty crouched down until he was at face level with her. "Absolutely, why don't we help your mom with breakfast, and then I'll take you out to the barn and introduce you to Nugget?" Sonya nodded earnestly. "Should we set the table, then?" Scotty asked.

I set Nay-Nay down, and both girls took off toward where Earl was holding out silverware and napkins.

"Finding everything okay?" I asked, moving to grab a serving platter and setting it down at Diana's elbow. "I didn't mean for you to show up and start cooking for us."

She turned and pressed a kiss to my cheek. "It's fine. The girls wanted french toast, and I wanted something to keep us busy till you got down here. This place is amazing, Roman," she said, waving her spatula around. "How come you'd never been here before with Oscar?"

I watched Scotty wander off toward the kitchen table to help the girls. When he couldn't seem to get a word in edgewise with Sonya, I figured my chatty carriage driver had finally met his match in my niece.

"Roman?" Diana prodded.

"Huh?" I asked, turning back toward my sister, whose eyes were twinkling. "What was that?"

Her eyes shifted to Scotty and back to me. Her lips twisted into a knowing smirk. "Who's the kid?"

I felt my cheeks warm. "He's not a kid."

"Who's the *man*?" she asked with a quirked eyebrow.

"I told you," I said petulantly. "He's the carriage driver. From, you know, the *incident*."

Diana snorted and met Earl's eyes. The two of them exchanged a knowing look. "He's cute," she said.

"Yeah," I agreed without thinking. It came out as more of a lovesick sigh than anything else.

She threw her head back and laughed. "Oh my god," she said in an excited whisper. "You've got it bad. Tell me everything."

Scotty was still listening to Sonya ramble on about hamster habitats while they carefully and meticulously set each place at the table.

"I really like him," I admitted, keeping my eye on him as he moved around the large table.

"Duh." Diana rolled her eyes. "Jesus, Roman," she said, elbowing me. "Get to the good stuff."

I fiddled with a fork, running my fingers across the tines. "It can't turn into anything, can it? I mean, after what happened with Pete…"

"Fuck Pete," Earl said. "He wasn't good enough for you."

"He loved me," I reminded them.

"Not enough," Diana said softly. "And he wasn't right for you anyway. He was too… I don't know… soft, maybe?"

"I like soft," I said. "What's wrong with soft?"

She pushed the french toast pan off the heat and turned to fully face me. "You have a strong personality, Roman. You need someone who can stand up to you. Pete took all your bullshit and swallowed it wholesale. And he didn't have the balls to stand up to the media and tell them where to put it."

I stared at my sister. She'd never said one negative thing about Pete in the time we dated.

Earl's hand came down on my shoulder. "What she means is, it's good to see you so happy and relaxed. You've been working too much lately. It's about time you took some time off and enjoyed yourself with a nice person."

"Also," she said, pointing a wooden spatula at me, "Pete would have never stood up on the bed and defended you the way Earl said Scotty did."

Earl's face cracked into a wide grin. "He hissed at me, Roman. *Hissed*. And his fists were like angry little..." He made two fists and shook them at me. "Like this. He wasn't going down without a fight. That man was going to defend you to the death."

I glanced back toward Scotty, who was now sitting in a chair with both girls on his lap telling him how to fix his hair. Two sets of little sticky fingers tugged and pulled at the blond curls, and something about the scene made me feel like my chest might explode right there and then.

"You *do* like him," Diana said in a surprised whisper. "Look at your face. Aww, Roman."

I don't know why I felt the need to deny it. What was the point? She was right—why was I fighting against it? "You might be right," I conceded under my breath. "I think I've got it bad, Di. He's such a sweetheart."

Diana handed the spatula to Earl and came over to hug me. She must have been the same height as Scotty because her head fit under my chin the way his did. I squeezed her tight, reminded once again how grateful I was to have such a supportive and wonderful sister in my life.

She squeezed me back and then stepped away, patting me on the shoulder. "Then let's get this breakfast done so we can show that sweetheart how to ride a horse."

The girls must have heard that last part because they started chanting, "Ride a horse!" Nay-Nay even began bouncing up and down on Scotty's knee like she was already riding a horse.

I winced, expecting to see Scotty calmly putting up with my nieces' exuberance, but when I caught his eye, there was nothing in it other than pure happiness. It caused my heart to catch.

Who knew how long I stood there staring at the stunning man, but suddenly I felt the sting of a spatula across my ass. "Ow! What was that for?" I asked, rounding on my sister.

"Breakfast is ready. Take this to the table," Diana said with a smirk, handing me a giant platter of french toast.

Once we were all seated around the table, passing orange juice, platters of bacon, bowls of fruit, and bottles of syrup, I realized how happy I was. I'd enjoyed Christmas morning breakfast with my family and hadn't really expected to see them again after that until a visit in the summer for Nay-Nay's birthday. So having them here, along with Scotty, was a special treat. And it was a reminder that my "normal" life in the city was very, very solitary.

I didn't like being alone, I suddenly realized. Perhaps I'd convinced myself I did out of necessity, because I preferred spending time at home out of the eye of the paparazzi, and being home necessarily meant being alone. But wanting to avoid reporters wasn't the same as wanting to be alone. I preferred being surrounded by this sense of family, the low buzz of kids and teasing, the clink of glasses and dishes.

Scotty caught my eye across the table and winked. It was like a cupid arrow into the fucking heart. I thought about what my sister had said.

Scotty wasn't Pete.

Clearly this was a bubble situation unlike real life, but that didn't mean I had to assume someone like Scotty would balk at the media attention the way Pete had. At the very least I could give him the benefit of the doubt to at least be willing to try.

I could at least talk to Scotty and let him decide whether or not he wanted to try to make things work between us longer term than a Vermont vacation fling.

Scotty's smile faded and his eyebrow went up. "You okay?" he mouthed.

I nodded and smiled in reassurance. "I'm okay," I mouthed back. And I was. Honestly, I'd never been happier.

Until Lolo and Larry turned up that is.

# 19

## SCOTTY

*Ski Season's Hottest Styles On The Slopes In Stowe*

"OH THANK THE LORD, we're saved," Lolo claimed, arriving in a blur of bright red synthetic fiber. "I'm so hungry, I could eat cow... *boy*."

"What are you wearing?" Roman asked.

Lolo looked down his nose at him. "Rossignol. Larry and I are hitting the slopes after breakfast. So kind of you to have someone come in and cook for us."

He sat at an empty seat and began serving himself from the platters and bowls in the center of the table.

Larry shuffled in a moment later, fighting the zipper in a pair of tattered ski bib overalls that looked like they were from the 1980s. Overstretched elastic suspenders held them up on his shoulders over an off-white waffle-weave long-underwear shirt. It couldn't have been more opposite of the sleek, designer outfit his significant other wore.

"How did the two of you meet, again?" I asked. There was no explanation for their pairing. It was like seeing Angelina Jolie hook up with Mr. Bean.

Larry opened his mouth. "Grind—"

"Zzzzzt!" Thankfully, Lolo cut him off with giant exaggerated eyeballs toward Roman's nieces. "Christian Mingle dot com!"

Diana, Earl, Roman, Larry, and I all stared at Lolo.

He let out a huff. "Okay, fine. A dating app. No need to name names," he muttered, spearing a cube of cantaloupe with a fork.

"But how did any app…" I was going to ask how any dating app made these two a compatible pair, but then I remembered that Grindr had nothing to do with compatibility in *that* way. "Never mind."

Roman's eyes twinkled at me knowingly.

He then cleared his throat and gestured to his sister. "Lolo, Larry, this is my sister, Diana, and her family," he said, making the introductions and explaining that Diana was the one who'd graciously cooked the big breakfast. As soon as Lolo realized he'd made some insulting assumptions, he began his charming apologies. I ignored him and bent to face Sonya, who'd been tugging at my sleeve.

"Mister Scotty," she asked in her little voice. "Will you please help me get more toasties?"

I reached across to the platter and forked another slice of french toast onto her plate, cutting it into bite-sized pieces before adding a generous glug of syrup.

I notice Roman watching me as I helped his niece with her breakfast. For a split second, it seemed like the buzz of everything and everyone else faded away, leaving the two of us there staring at each other across the large wooden table. I had a stupid dreamy moment of imagining this was real life, that Roman and I were together and had a house full of family and guests. No more solitary nights in a rented room in Queens where the closest thing I had to company was my own Grindr hookup or a Netflix marathon on my phone.

I'd never had this. I'd never known what it was like to sit around a breakfast table with heaps of plentiful good food and even better company. Even my best childhood memories only featured my mom, my grandfather, and me sitting at a card table in my grandfather's apartment. He'd had a handful of neighbor friends who came over on

Sunday afternoon to watch football games, but that was as close as I ever got to this kind of feeling.

It was nice. More than nice. My heart ached from wanting more. I remembered watching television shows and wondering if those big Thanksgiving scenes were real. Did families actually get together like that, or was it all made up for TV?

And here I was sitting among friends and family just like from one of those shows, all because the man across from me had let me barge into his life and make myself comfortable as if it was no big deal.

But it was.

Roman didn't have to trust me. I was no one. More than no one—I was someone who was clearly desperate for money. Yet he trusted me to sit here among his family, to see him naked, to hear about the most vulnerable moments in his life, and to not sell any of it to the tabloids.

Why? Was he simply gullible and trusting?

I didn't think so.

"What're you thinking about over there?" Roman asked softly, reaching across the table for my hand. "Your forehead looks like an accordion."

"Thank you for this," I said around the lump in my throat. I looked down at where his thumb traced over my knuckles. It was such a small gesture, such a quiet reassurance, but it struck me to my very core. He gave of himself so willingly and easily, and I didn't understand how I could be so lucky as to be the recipient.

"It may not seem like much to you," I continued. "But..."

I was interrupted by Larry's exclamation as he glanced at the time on his phone. "Balls...ack... Balzac!" he cried, glancing worriedly at the girls. "Was a French novelist. But, uh, more importantly, we're going to be late for our ski lessons. Lolo, shake a tail feather."

One of Lolo's perfectly manicured eyebrows shot up in indignant surprise. "I do not have tail feathers. And my ski instructor cannot begin instructing without pupils." He waved a hand in Larry's general direction. "Finish your coffee, love chunk."

Larry's eyes glanced furtively around the table as he took a final guzzle from his mug. "Uh, thanks for breakfast, Diana. Lovely to meet you all. Sorry to eat and run." He set his mug on the table beside his dirty plate and started backing from the room.

Lolo dabbed a napkin at the corners of his mouth and elegantly rose, like a merman rising from the sea. "Yes, we must away. Many thanks for such a rustically aesthetic meal."

Diana blinked, not quite sure whether to take the statement as a compliment or insult.

"Uh, aren't you forgetting something?" I asked them.

Larry froze, dancing from foot to foot. "Uh..."

Lolo pressed a hand to his chest. "Oh, of course, aren't you a dear for pointing it out." He snapped his fingers at Larry. "Be a doll and make me a tea for the road? Chamomile. Loose, not bagged. Two lemon wedges. Elderflower honey. And..." He tapped his finger against his lips, thinking. "195 degrees water. No, make that 200. It's nippy out there."

That wasn't at all what I meant. "I meant, aren't you going to help clean up?" Growing up, that had always been the rule. We may not have had much, and dinner might have consisted of a pan of water and a box of mac and cheese more often than not, but we'd still adhered to the "he who doesn't cook, cleans" rule.

"I don't do dishes, darling," Lolo said with an indulgent smile. "This sweater is Dale of Norway."

"I don't care who your sweater is," I said, standing up and collecting my own plate. "You're cleaning up after yourselves."

"It's okay," Diana said, waving a hand. "I don't mind."

"You're not doing the dishes," Earl insisted. "I'll clean up."

"See?" Lolo said, flitting toward the door. "Problem solved. Thanks bunches, handsome." He blew Earl a kiss. "We'll be in charge of dinner to make it up to you. How's that?"

"Roman takes his filet medium rare," I called out to their backs. "And the girls want ice cream. With sprinkles!"

The girls started cheering and chanting about ice cream with sprinkles. It seemed anything worth cheering for was worth chanting about too. When the door finally closed behind the two freeloaders, I turned to Diana. "I'm so sorry," I told her, collecting empty dishes from the table.

"What for?" she asked with a laugh. "You're not responsible for the actions of others."

Earl also started to gather up dishes, but Roman waved him away. "I'll help Scotty. Why don't you head on out to the barn and get things set up for the lesson?"

The girls shifted their chants from demanding ice cream to wanting to go meet the horsey.

"That okay with you, Scotty?" Roman asked me. "Or would you rather go with them? I don't mind handling all this on my own."

I was touched by the offer, but it wouldn't be fair to leave Roman with the mess. Plus, I liked being around him. "No, I'll stay and help." I turned to Earl. "Feel free to go on out and meet Nugget. That horse has never met a stranger, so you'll be fine."

The girls made little fists with their hands, pumping them in the air. "Nug—get, Nug—get," they shouted, emphasizing both syllables of the name.

Diana glanced between us and winked at Roman. "I'll get the girls out of your hair."

The family left in a flurry of coats and scarves and hats and laughter. Once they were gone, the house seemed oddly empty and quiet.

I gathered another load of dishes from the table and carried them to where Roman had already beat me to the sink. "It was so nice of your sister to do this."

Roman waited until I set the dishes down before drawing me into an embrace and kissing my cheek. His scent still carried traces of sleep mixed with coffee, and I imagined sneaking back to bed with him for another hour or so of snuggling under the covers and feeling him up at leisure.

"I'm glad you're okay with the surprise," he said, threading his fingers through my hair. "I probably should have warned you before inviting them—the girls can be a handful."

I leaned into his touch. "A wonderful handful," I told him. "They have so much energy."

Roman let out a laugh. "Tell me about it. It's from visiting them that I realized nap time is for the adults more than the kids."

I nuzzled my face into his neck and wrapped my arms more tightly around his back. I loved the feel of him—so strong and solid and comforting. And sexy as hell. "I'm looking forward to nap time with you today," I said, trailing a kiss along the column of his throat.

Roman hummed in appreciation. "Are you now?"

"Mmm-hmm." I let my hand drift to his waist, my fingers dancing just under the lip of his pants. "Maybe I can put my riding lessons to good use."

A laugh rumbled through his chest. His touch danced down the center of my back before splaying wide over my ass. "I'm definitely looking forward to that."

I pushed up onto my toes, pressing a kiss to his mouth. His lips parted, and I tasted the sweetness of syrup and the bitterness of coffee. Roman sucked in a breath, tightening his arms around me and deepening the kiss. I lost all thought, my only awareness his touch and taste and smell. The sound of his breath catching in his throat when my teeth nibbled at his bottom lip.

His hands circled my hips, lifting me onto the counter. Roman stepped between my legs, and I wrapped them around his waist, digging my heels into his back to pull him closer. I let out a whimper, wanting more. Wanting the feel of his skin under my nails and his cock pressed against my own. God I could never get enough of this man.

I pulled my mouth from his, panting heavily. "Roman—" I gasped. There was so much I wanted to say, but I couldn't find the words. Even for myself. I just knew that I wanted him and not just physically. I wanted all of him. I wanted to know him. Be a source of comfort for him, a refuge from the relentless pressure. I wanted to be the one he came home to, the one he confided in, relied on.

I wanted to be the one he wanted.

But it felt like too much to ask. And so I said nothing, just sat there, trying to catch my breath and keep my emotions from growing so large they choked me.

Roman must have seen something in my eyes because he reached out and drew his fingers down the side of my face and then cupped my cheek in his palm. "Are you happy, Scotty?"

It was obvious in the way he asked it that the question was important to him. And the answer was so complicated. So much in my life had fallen apart recently: I was homeless, jobless, broke, with a mother getting released from jail who needed help I couldn't give. It should have all been so overwhelmingly awful and yet, I realized, I'd never been happier.

Because of Roman.

"Yes," I told him simply.

His lips pressed together, and he nodded. His hand slid into my hair, fingers curling around the back of my head. The touch was almost possessive in its strength. "Could you be happy with me?"

That feeling in my chest, the wanting and the needing, grew larger, almost swallowing me. "I already am."

His eyes searched mine. "Don't leave. Stay with me here. Come home with me after."

My breath caught in my throat. This was everything I wanted. More than I could have imagined. It was too much, too perfect. And that was the problem.

I looked away, steeling myself to tell Roman the truth. "I have a past."

"We all do."

God I didn't want to tell him this. But I had to. It wouldn't be fair to mislead him. If he wanted to date me, he had to know what he was getting into. "Mine involves a criminal record."

He let out a breath of air. "Oh."

"I was a teen—juvie. It's sealed. But... it could still get out..."

His hands dropped to his sides, and the absence of his touch felt like a physical blow. "I understand." He sounded wounded, and it struck at my very core.

I wanted to reach for him, but I was afraid he would pull away and I wouldn't be able to bear it. "I'm sorry, Roman. If I could change it I would. Trust me. I want nothing more than to be with you."

"It's okay," he said. He looked everywhere but at me. "I understand. You have a right to your privacy. You shouldn't have to risk having your secrets exposed just to be with me. It's not fair of me to ask. I'm sorry."

He started to turn toward the sink and I snagged his wrist, keeping him in place. He had it all wrong. "Wait, it's not having my past exposed that I'm worried about. I couldn't care less about that coming out. It's what it would mean for *you* if it did," I told him. "You'd be dating someone with a record, someone whose mother just finished a stint behind bars. The tabloids would have a field day with that information. It would be terrible for your reputation."

Roman's eyes finally met mine again. "You're worried about my reputation?" He seemed genuinely surprised.

"Of course I am! I care about you—I couldn't stand the thought of your career suffering because of me."

He took my hand in his and lifted it to his lips, pressing a kiss to the inside of my wrist before placing my palm against his chest. His heart thundered under my touch. "Sweet, sweet Scotty," Roman murmured.

I swallowed, my throat tight with emotion.

He smiled. "Dating a guy with a record will just add to my street cred when it comes to landing the grittier movie parts. Haven't you noticed that Hollywood likes a bad boy?"

I couldn't help but laugh. "Oh yeah, and I totally fit the Hollywood image of a bad boy. Straight out of central casting, that's what I am."

Roman's eyes twinkled with humor for a moment before turning serious again. "It's not easy being with me... the paparazzi... the scrutiny..." He shook his head. There was an edge of pain in his voice when he said, "I can't ask you to subject yourself to that."

I pressed a finger to his lips. "You wouldn't have to ask me. I'd do it willingly."

"Why?" His voice cracked on the question.

How could Roman even ask me that? Didn't he understand how amazing he was? "Because you're worth it."

"Scotty." The way he exhaled my name sounded like a prayer, and I closed my eyes, absorbing it into my soul. His breath caught in his throat, as though he was about to say something more, but before he could, the back door slammed open and the sound of Roman's chattering nieces blew in on a draft of frigid air.

The girls tumbled through the door from the mudroom. Diana deftly snagged them both by their scarves before they could track muddy snow into the kitchen. "Take your gear off in here," she reminded them. They began de-layering in a flurry of mittens and hats.

Diana draped her coat on a peg and stepped into the kitchen, pausing when she caught sight of us. She looked pointedly at the stack of dirty dishes and the way I still sat on the counter, Roman standing between my legs. "I see you two have been hard at work," she said with a knowing smirk.

I slipped off the counter, ducking around Roman and moving to the sink. My cheeks blazed with heat. "Right. Yes. We were just ah... discussing strategy. You know. How best to tackle the beast."

She lifted an eyebrow. "Oh really? Is that what the kids are calling it these days?"

Roman threw back his head and laughed. Just then, Sonya burst out of the mudroom, racing straight toward me, her eyes bright. "Uncle Scotty!" she called. "Daddy said his saddle fits Nugget!"

I had to admit being called "uncle" made my own chest pinch a little since I'd never known what it was like to really have family. As an only child, I'd never expected to be anyone's uncle one day.

I squatted down to Sonya's eye level. "Really? That's great, sweetie. Are you going to show me how to ride?"

She nodded firmly. "I promise it's easy."

I glanced up at Diana, who'd taken up a position at the sink and was rolling up her sleeves. "No way, you're not cleaning up."

She ignored me, turning to Roman instead. "Dear brother, how well did it go for you growing up when you tried to tell me what to do?"

"Terribly."

She grinned. "Exactly." She made a shooing motion at me. "Now you get out there. Earl's already gotten everything set up out there and wanted us to come fetch you." I started to argue, but she shook her head. "You'd better hurry before my husband seduces your horse away from you. He's a sucker for a sweet Percheron. If it was up to him, we'd have all kinds of draft horses on the farm."

I smiled. "I'll bet. There's a pair of Clydesdales at the stables where I work... *used* to work... that are sweet as kittens. But all that leg feathering is a pain to keep clean. We call them our bathing beauties because they're always getting cleaned."

Sonya and Nay-Nay each took one of my hands and began tugging. "C'mon, let's go!"

I gave one last look to Diana and she mouthed the word "go." I nodded and let the girls drag me to the mudroom to put on my cold-weather gear. As I slid on my coat, I realized it smelled like laundry detergent, and I wondered who'd thought to wash it. It had to have been Roman. Considering I would have assumed the man didn't even do his own laundry, it surprised me he'd thought to do mine. I wondered if maybe he'd been grossed out by the horse smell enough to sneak away while we'd been watching movies the day before.

But then I caught a whiff of his own coat and realized it smelled like detergent too. So if he did throw mine in the wash, he washed his own as well. I glanced at Roman out of the corner of my eye and caught him reaching for my gray scarf from a nearby hook. Before I had a chance to take it from him, he looped it around my neck and used it to pull me in for a kiss.

Despite the kiss being quick and chaste, Sonya noticed it. "Oooh! Uncle Roman kissed Uncle Scotty on the lips!"

I felt my face heat and noticed Roman's do the same.

"I gave Scotty a quick kiss to say thank you for helping with the dishes, sweetie," Roman explained.

Nay-Nay reached her arms up to me. "I kiss too!"

I picked her up and planted a loud smacking kiss on her cheek before turning and doing the same to Sonya. By the time we made it out onto the snowy path, the girls were giggling from the raspberries I'd planted on their cheeks.

Roman and I chased them through the snow, throwing small soft snowballs at them and dodging the ones they tried to throw back at us. When we arrived at the barn, everyone's cheeks were flushed and Roman's brown eyes were dancing. I could tell he was loving the chance to play with his nieces, and it was nice seeing him so... carefree. He deserved to have fun like a regular person without always looking over his shoulder and feeling like he needed to be "on" for whoever was watching.

When we got close enough to see Nugget in the small ring next to the barn, I stopped and stared. She was saddled and stood proud as a peacock against the side rail of the ring.

I felt a hand on the small of my back, nudging me forward. Roman, always there when I needed him.

Earl rubbed up and down Nugget's long neck while murmuring to her under his breath.

"Hey, Nug," I said, reaching out to let her smell me. Nugget let out a happy *pbbbbt* sound and tossed her head, jangling the metal tack and pulling the loose reins in Earl's hands.

"She's a good one," Earl said with a grin. "But she does not like peppermints."

"She loves carrots the most. Then apples," I said, smiling back at him. "I never tried peppermints."

"I've never met a horse who doesn't like them," Earl admitted with a chuckle. "But she's a good-looking beast, Scotty. Clearly you take good care of her."

I nodded and mumbled my thanks for the compliment, but inside I was clutching the words to me like a tiny piece of spun gold. There wasn't much left in my life these days, but I'd have been damned if I'd have let Nugget bear the brunt of my stupid, irresponsible life situation. To know that a horse aficionado recognized I did my best to care for my horse meant the world. If my dire straits hurt Nugget, I'd...

well, I didn't know what I'd do. Sell her, I guessed. Like I was already doing.

Roman had offered to write me a check for the full purchase price. He'd even done the research on how much Percheron mares Nugget's age and size sold for. But I'd been too nervous to accept that much money from him all at once. I'd never had several thousand dollars before, and it scared me to death. I'd asked Roman to send two hundred to my mom and then asked if we could do the rest later. And then I'd promptly relegated "later" into a pocket of my brain that had a heavy steel door locked closed with rivets.

"Scotty?" I looked up and saw Roman frowning at me. "You don't have to do this if you don't—"

"No!" I blurted. I wasn't about to look a gift horse (man) in the mouth. "I'm just... I'm just so grateful to all of you for this. I can't even begin to thank you for this incredibly kind gesture."

Roman's face softened back into a relaxed smile. "Good. I'm glad."

"Okay," Earl said with a clap of his gloved hands. "Let's get started."

We spent the next few hours chilly but happy as could be. Nugget loved the cold, which I already knew, and she was totally ambivalent about being ridden. She was so docile, Earl even let the girls take turns riding her around the ring after I was finished with my lesson. Seeing Roman's nieces on her big wide back was like having a piece of some puzzle snap home. It felt so good. After all the little kids who'd begged to ride her during carriage rides, now here we were, on a spacious farm in Vermont where there was time and space to let her walk them around proudly on her back. It hit me dead center in the heart and made me feel so incredibly lucky to have that moment there with all of them.

When we were all done and it was finally time to give poor Nugget a break, we took her into the barn and put her in cross ties to brush her down.

Diana helped the girls take turns giving Nugget chunks of carrots while Earl walked me through removing the tack and explaining the adjustments of the saddle again for next time.

Once Nugget was fed, watered, and put back in her stall, we made our way to the house where Roman and Diana began making soup and sandwiches for lunch. I helped the girls wash up in the sink in the mudroom before pouring them the milk they asked for.

Again, I found myself at the kitchen table surrounded by the boisterous comfort of a family meal. The girls chatted excitedly about their horse adventure, and Roman teased them about the snow "horse" they'd tried building while I was riding. It was so domestic and warm, I wanted to close my eyes and simply live in it for as long as I could, imprinting it on my memory to bring out later when I was all alone again in a murky rented room in Queens. Despite Roman's sweet words about a future together, it still seemed too good to actually come true.

"Baby," Roman murmured in my ear. This time he'd chosen to sit next to me instead of across the wooden table.

"Hmm?"

"Everything okay?"

I nodded and turned to him, opening my eyes and hoping he could see my emotion without asking me to verbalize it. His hand clutched my thigh, and he leaned in to press a kiss next to my mouth. "Too much?" he asked softly.

I shook my head. "The perfect amount."

And it was. The day continued in family bliss with a Disney movie marathon in the theater room in which I snuggled against Roman and the girls snuggled against me. Once it was over, Diana, Earl, and the girls headed to their rooms. Roman had put them in a family suite up over the garage. It was like their own little apartment with two bedrooms and two bathrooms and a small play area where they could spread out and still have privacy. It also kept them away from Lolo and Larry, wherever they happened to be (a question I chose not to ask).

Roman and I weren't quite ready to retire, so he set a fire in the den while I opened a bottle of wine. I sighed as I sunk onto a pallet of blankets Roman had arranged in front of the flames.

"Everything okay?" he asked, pulling me against him and trailing his fingers through my hair.

I couldn't stop the grin from spreading across my face. "Everything is perfect."

"Oh, I don't know that I'd go that far," he said, his voice low and rumbly.

"Really? Why not?" I twisted to look up at him and noticed that his pupils were blown wide, his expression naked with desire.

"Because no day is perfect unless I've had you in my mouth." He dipped his head toward mine, capturing my lips with his. I surged against him, straddling his lap and looping my arms around his neck to draw him against me.

"Getting closer," he growled, nipping down the column of my throat.

And it was too. Until the doorbell rang and my almost perfect day came to a screeching halt.

# 20

## ROMAN

*Pros and (Ex) Cons*

THE DOORBELL RANG AGAIN and I groaned.

"Let's ignore it," Scotty murmured against my mouth. "Nothing good ever comes through that door."

As much as I wanted to, this wasn't my house and I wasn't comfortable not answering it. "We can't," I said, reluctantly pushing to my feet.

Scotty tugged on my wrist, trying to pull me back down beside him. "We totally can. Ignore it and they'll go away. That's my philosophy on life and people who arrive at Oscar's cottage after dark." He used air quotes around the word *cottage*.

The doorbell rang a third time. "Don't think that approach is going to work." I held out a hand to help him up, and we started threading our way through the house. "Plus, it could be Marigold needing something."

Scotty snorted. "Like vodka? We might be out. Which is a pretty impressive feat. That man had enough liquor stashed away to survive the zombie apocalypse. No, I'm guessing it's that cop again. Officer McHotBeard."

I froze, pulling Scotty to a stop beside me and draping a possessive arm over his shoulder. "Maybe we shouldn't answer it, then," I growled.

Scotty smirked. "Oh he wouldn't be here for me, I can guarantee you that. I think he's got his cuffs set on someone else, if you know what I mean." He waggled his eyebrows as he mouthed the word *Lolo*, and I shuddered at the thought of the burly cop cuffing the slender egret of a man.

"You're going to regret planting that image in my head," I said, tickling my fingertips over his ribs and making him squirm. He let out a squeal of laughter and twisted out of my grasp. He danced backward just out of reach ahead of me, teasing me with his smile.

"Though speaking of Lolo, that's probably who it is," I said, advancing on him. "I doubt either he or Larry remembered to take a key with them earlier, so I'm guessing it's them."

Scotty froze and grabbed my arm before I could reach for the handle. "No! That's even more reason not to answer!"

I placed a kiss on his nose. "You're adorable, you know that?"

He grinned, his eyes bright with mischief and cheer. "And you're sexy as fuck and I can't wait to get you back in my bed and—"

The doorbell rang again. This time longer and more insistent, cutting him off. Scotty clapped a hand over his mouth. "Oh my god, do you think they heard?" he asked with a giggle.

I had no idea, but the embarrassment turning his cheeks a blazing red was absolutely worth it if they had. "I guess we'll find out," I said, reaching for the door. He shook his head, burying his face in his hands in mortification and ducking behind the door as I swung it open.

A woman I'd never seen before stood waiting on the other side. She was in her late forties, petite with wavy blonde hair and wearing drab clothes.

Instantly, my guard went up. I glanced past her, searching the darkness for evidence of any cameras or reporters hidden out of sight. "May I help you?" I asked rigidly.

She frowned. "Yes. I'm..." She trailed off, craning her neck to look past me. "Is Scotty here?"

Scotty's head jerked up, his eyes going wide. "The fuck?" He grabbed the door, yanking it wider until he could see the woman.

"Mom?" he asked, his voice incredulous.

Her face brightened. "Scotty—"

Before she could finish the statement, Scotty swung the door, slamming it closed in her face. The bang of it echoed through the house, followed by silence.

He stood rigidly still, arms stiff by his sides, mouth open as he dragged in lungfuls of air as if he'd just finished sprinting a mile.

I stared at him a long moment. "Um, Scotty?" I finally asked.

He didn't take his eyes from the door. "Yeah."

"That was your mom?"

"Yes."

He said nothing more. "Do you... maybe want to invite her in?"

"No."

I wasn't really quite sure how to respond to that. The entire situation was utterly confusing. I'd never seen Scotty as anything other than gregarious, outgoing, and welcoming. This seemed completely unlike him. "I thought you and your mom had a good relationship?"

"We do. I mean, more or less."

Well, that made even less sense.

"Scotty, honey, let's talk about this," his mother called, her voice muffled by the thick wooden door.

Scotty's eyes closed and he let his head fall forward. "Fuck."

"Didn't she just get out of jail yesterday?" I asked.

He ground his teeth together. "Yes. And she was supposed to stay in the city."

"Scotty? Honey?" she called again.

He shoved a hand through his hair and turned to look at me. "What the fuck is she doing here?" he asked, as if I would somehow know.

"We could... open the door and ask her," I offered.

He shook his head. "Absolutely not."

I racked my brain, trying to understand why Scotty was acting so out of character. He and his mother had shared an apartment before, and he'd never said anything that made me think he had a problem with her being in his life. He'd even sold his horse to send her money the day before. If he hated her so much that he couldn't even stand to be around her, why would he give up his most precious possession to help her?

"Scotty..." I reached out and placed a tentative hand on his shoulder, approaching him the way I'd approach a feral cat or stray dog. He was acting so strangely I was afraid he might bolt at the slightest touch. But instead he sagged, the tension seeping from his muscles.

"You don't understand, Roman," he said. "She can't see us together. She just can't."

Oh. So the issue wasn't her. The issue was me. Specifically, him being seen with me. What I didn't understand was why. "Are you not out?" I asked him.

For the first time, his eyes met mine. His forehead crinkled in confusion. "Out of what? What are you talking about?"

"The closet," I explained.

Scotty threw up his hands in an overly dramatic way. "Do I look like I'm trying to hide the gay? Jesus, Roman, don't be an idiot. I'm too pretty to be straight."

He was very pretty. That was true. I wasn't sure what that had to do with being gay, but he didn't seem like he'd be receptive to me asking clarifying questions.

"Then what—"

Scotty blew out an aggravated breath. "She's a con woman, Roman. She'll rat you out to the paparazzi soon as look at you."

Oh. So he was doing this to protect me. A part of my heart warmed at the thought that he cared so much. "Why don't we just ask her not to?"

He stared at me a long moment and then blinked. "Yeah. That'll work. Laws, she'll break on a whim, but a pinky swear—now that's some serious shit right there."

I reached for him, drawing him against me and pressing a kiss to his temple. "Scotty, I appreciate that you're trying to protect me from her or from the media, whatever. And that's very sweet of you. But this is your mom. And she's come a long way. It wouldn't feel right to turn her away when we have 10,000 square feet of extra room here. At least for the night and we can figure out what to do with her tomorrow. How much trouble can she get in in one night?"

"A lot, Roman," he said, eyes wide. "Like metric crapton levels of trouble."

"We'll just make sure she won't have anything interesting to share with the press," I told him. "The worst she'll be able to do is give them my location, and while that would suck, it wouldn't be the end of the world."

"But your sister and her family are here," he pointed out. "What if one of them says something they shouldn't?"

"My sister knows better than to share personal details about me with a stranger. I'm not worried about her."

Scotty let out a long sigh and pressed his face against my shoulder. "This is a bad idea, Roman."

I slipped a finger under his chin and tilted his head back. "I'm not going to force you to let her in. She's your mother, and I'm the last person to dictate your relationship with her. But if we're going to try this dating thing, I don't want you to have to choose between us. It's not fair to you, and I would hate that you cut someone important out of your life just to protect me."

He pressed his lips together, still considering.

"Hello?" came his mother's muffled voice again. "Scotty, honey. It's very cold out here, and it's late. I've already sent the taxi away and don't have a cell phone to call another."

He let out a sigh of defeat. "Fine. But can I tell you I told you so ahead of time?"

I brushed a kiss against his forehead and then placed another on his lips. "Of course, baby." I smiled at him. "You're not going to regret this. I promise."

He snorted, rolling his eyes. "Famous last words."

I reached for the door and swung it open. "My apologies, Mrs. Pinker," I said. "Come on in."

Beside me, I heard Scotty grumble, "Suuuuuch a bad idea," as I stepped to the side to let her pass.

The moment she stepped into view, Scotty forced a smile and raised a hand, twitching his fingers in a half-hearted wave. "Mom. Hi. Sorry. There was a... thing. That... got in the way. Of the door. Anyway. Hiyeee."

At the sight of her son, Scotty's mom exclaimed, "Oh my poor Scottybear missed his mommy," and pulled him forcibly in for a hug. I noted that he didn't hug her back, just stood with his arms limp by his sides, a pained expression on his face.

"Nice henhouse. Who's the fox," his mom whispered, perhaps louder than she meant to because I didn't think she'd intended me to hear.

"No. Absolutely not," Scotty hissed back. "There are no hens, and he is most definitely not a fox. I mean, okay, he's hot and all," he corrected. "But not in a foxy way."

His eyes met mine and I couldn't help smirking. His cheeks flushed.

His mom ended the embrace and turned to face me. "And who might you be?"

I put on my most polite smile and held out a hand. "Hi, Mrs. Pinker, I'm Roman. Scotty's—"

"Friend," Scotty cut in. "He's a *friend*."

She narrowed her eyes, appraising me with a calculated look. "You seem familiar... have we met?"

I ducked my head. "No, ma'am. I'm...uh... an actor. You might have seen me in a movie." I didn't know why I was suddenly embarrassed at the admission, but my cheeks flushed anyway.

Her eyes widened comically the moment she recognized me.

"Well, aren't you the sly one, Scotty Pinker," she said, elbowing him in the side.

"Mom," he groaned.

She ignored him, stepping forward and taking my outstretched hand. "And it's not Mrs. Pinker, Roman. I was never married to Scotty's daddy. I'm Cyndee Brady. And no, not that one. Mine is spelled with a *y* and two *e*'s."

I should have remembered that from when I'd filled out the money transfer the day before, but Scotty had been rolling my balls in his hand at the time, and, well, things had gotten fuzzy after that.

I cleared my throat. "My apologies, Ms. Brady." I held out an arm, gesturing to the house around us. "Welcome. Please, make yourself at home."

"Or not," Scotty said, stepping up to fit his arm through hers and steering her toward the staircase. "I'm sure you're exhausted and want nothing more than to go to bed, so I'll just take you straight there."

She dug her heels in. "No need to be hasty. It's been a long day and I could go for a bite to eat."

Scotty closed his eyes and blew out a breath. "Fine. Eat and then bed." He turned and started tugging her toward the kitchen, but she wouldn't allow herself to be rushed.

"This is a beautiful house," she said, eyeing the dining room as Scotty dragged her past it. "Is it yours, Roman?"

"No, ma'am," I told her. "It belongs to a friend. He's letting us stay for a while."

"Hmmmm... shame," she said.

When we reached the kitchen, Scotty steered his mother toward one of the stools at the counter and ordered her to sit. He then moved to the fridge and started digging around for leftovers. I grabbed a glass out of the cabinet and filled it with ice water for her.

"So, Roman," she said, eyeing me. "Tell me a little about yourself. I assume all the nonsense in the tabloids isn't true. What are you really like?"

I suddenly felt put on the spot. "Um..."

"Mom," Scotty said. "Can you just—"

"Hush, darling, Roman is a grown-up. He can handle some basic get-to-know-you questions. Can't you, Roman?"

I chuckled. "Of course I can. I guess I just don't know what you mean. What's my life like? What's my personality like?"

"Yes," she said with a wink. "All of that."

"Well," I began, pulling out a napkin and utensils for her, "my life is oftentimes all about work. I'm either preparing for a role or actively filming it. If not, I'm promoting a release. When I do get free time, I enjoy being outside. Believe it or not, I have a little kitchen garden behind my place in the city. I spend more time than is normal taking care of my plants."

"Kitchen garden?" Scotty asked in surprise. "You don't even cook."

"I... well... it's mostly herbs. I read an article that gardening is supposed to be good for managing anxiety."

Scotty's face turned from shock to a knowing smirk.

"Your fence didn't really get pulled down by the paparazzi, did it?"

*Shit.*

I felt my face heat. "It did, but that wasn't the only reason Nugget couldn't..."

He smirked, quirking an eyebrow. "You just didn't want her messing up your precious garden, did you?"

I cleared my throat and looked away. "Some of those things are delicate in the winter."

He shook his head, his smile knowing. "You're so fucking adorable. I can't even with you right now."

"Shut up," I mumbled. "All I could picture was Nugget stepping on my chives and flooding my rosemary with horse piss. It was a nonstarter."

He barked a laugh. "You would have rather her shit in the foyer than in your kitchen garden that you don't even use to cook with? That is hysterical."

"Marble is easier to clean than organic soil," I said with a sniff, moving past Scotty to grab a place mat from the drawer.

Scotty smacked my ass as I passed, and when I turned to gripe at him about it, I caught the instant of remorse that flooded his expression. His eyes darted over to his mom and back to me before he noticeably winced.

Regret. He hadn't meant to be so intimate with me in front of his mom for fear of giving her information she could use against me. I hated seeing the moment he realized he couldn't be open and free with me, and I knew it was only the beginning. If he stayed with me, there could be many more moments like that in his future.

I couldn't give him a nice, steady relationship like almost anyone else would be able to. Being with me meant horrific invasions of privacy, no detail of life or someone's past left unexamined, and no future in which someone could even go to the corner coffee shop in ratty sweats without being photographed.

I shook my head, trying to remind myself to stop worrying about those things when they weren't a problem right now. Right now, we had privacy and space to enjoy each other. It was temporary time in a bubble, maybe, but I was going to try and enjoy it without wasting it with worry.

I pulled the meal out of the microwave, transferred it to a nice plate, and set it in front of Cyndee before turning to fix her a drink. "Would you like something in addition to water?" I asked. "Soda? Wine, beer?"

She gave me a knowing smile. "You have any hard liquor? I would kill for a shot of anything strong right about now."

I turned to her in surprise. Those were hearty words coming out of a sweet little woman.

She smiled at me. "I don't normally partake, you understand, but I'm still feeling a little jittery from my awful experience. You wouldn't believe what kind of people there are in the prison system." She whispered the two words like contraband.

"Of course," I said, moving to the liquor cabinet. "I can't imagine."

"And thank god for that," she said. "I'll never go back, I promise you that."

My gaze flicked to Scotty in expectation of seeing him smile with approval or relief. Instead, his eyes were narrowed in suspicion at his mom. I decided to give them some time to themselves to catch up.

I dropped a kiss on top of Scotty's head. "I'm going upstairs so you two have some time together. I'll see you after you help your mom get settled?"

He looked up at me with an expression of gratitude and a little insecurity. "You sure?"

I clasped the side of his neck and angled his head with my thumb under his chin so he was looking at me.

"Very."

# 21

## SCOTTY

*WikiHow To Deal With Your Mother*

As soon as Roman left the room, I snapped my head around to glare at my mother. "Explain yourself," I hissed. The last thing I wanted was for Roman to hear this conversation.

"Don't be like that, Scotty. I didn't have anywhere else to go." Her whining voice grated on me, and I wondered how other people didn't see right through her bullshit.

"I sent you two hundred dollars!" I said, exasperated. "You could have rented a room anywhere with that money. That boarding house I told you about by the detention facility is like thirty bucks a night."

She pulled a face, wrinkling her nose and turning down her lips. "Those places are disgusting. No way was I staying there when I knew you were in cushy Vermont."

"How did you even know where to find me?" I asked, still feeling off balance by her sudden appearance.

"You told me, remember? I needed the address for my discharge paperwork."

I mentally kicked myself. How had I not seen this coming? "Oh yeah," I grunted.

"As soon as I heard you say swanky Stowe, Vermont? Please." She waved a hand through the air. "I'm not an idiot, Scotty. I figured you had something real good going on here." She reached out and placed her hands over mine, smiling. "And I want in."

I yanked out of her grasp. "No. Absolutely not. This is not what you think."

She lifted an eyebrow. "You're in bed with Hollywood's biggest star and you're going to tell me you don't have some kind of endgame planned? Pfft. No boy of mine would be that stupid."

I closed my eyes, forcing myself to take a deep breath before continuing. Otherwise I was afraid of what I might say. Because what I wanted to do was grab her and toss her ass back out into the Vermont winter.

"Mom," I pleaded. "That's not what this is. Please don't fuck this up for me. I really like him."

She gaped at me, a forkful of food forgotten halfway to her mouth. "You... what? Do not tell me you have feelings for him." She snorted and set her fork down. "Honey, don't be ridiculous. Men like that do not end up with men like you. And that's even assuming he ends up with a man at all. Ten bucks says he ends up with some beautiful woman on his arm who can give him equally beautiful babies."

I crossed my arms, trying to ignore the ache in my chest her words created. I didn't want to believe what she'd said, but her words continued echoing around in my head, taking up space, and I knew they would be difficult to forget. What if she was right? Sure Roman had said all sorts of wonderful things about the two of us having a future together, but that was because we existed in a bubble. In the real world, things might look different.

"Even more reason for you to get out of here and let me enjoy whatever it is while it lasts," I said, suddenly feeling sullen.

She made a *pffft* sound and quirked an eyebrow. "If you think for one minute I'm going to let you squander this opportunity, you're fucking nuts. Scotty, we have one chance at a million-dollar take here." She leaned closer, dropping her voice. "This could set us up for *life*. We need to strategize. And what the fuck with the two hundred bucks? You couldn't send me a thousand? I'll bet the man has more than that in cash in his wallet right now."

"Keep your voice down," I growled. "And stay away from him. His money is not our money."

"Not yet," she said. "Just you wait. I'll think of something."

I dug my fingertips against my temples in aggravation. I'd never been on board with her plans to scam people's money away from them, but targeting Roman? No fucking way. I had to think of a way to get her out of there. The clock on the microwave ticked over to half past one in the morning. There was no way to kick her out at this hour, especially in an unfamiliar town.

I placed my hands on the counter to keep them from trembling with anger. "First thing in the morning, you're going back to the city, you hear me?"

She rolled her eyes.

"I mean it, Mom. If you even think about stealing one single thing from this house, or of selling one piece of information about Roman to the press, I'm calling the cops on you," I warned. "Don't think I won't."

"I'm not about to fuck up something big for a trinket, Scotty," she said, an incredulous look on her face. "How stupid do you think I am?"

I buried my face in my hands, wondering if I should try warning Roman about my mom again or not. It was humiliating having a scammer and a thief as a parent. There had been years when I'd agreed with her schemes because she'd done such a good job of convincing me it was the only way to support the two of us. But then I'd started driving the carriage and realized how many people we knew who were able to support themselves even with low-paying jobs and tips. No, it wasn't easy. But it was possible to support yourself legally, even if you had a shit education like my mother. She'd had to drop out of high school when she found out she was pregnant with me.

And maybe that had been part of it. I felt guilty. Like... she wouldn't have had to scam people out of their money if she didn't have me. She would have had a better chance at a decent life.

But there was no amount of guilt in the world that would allow me to let her scam Roman Burke out of his money, no matter how much he had to spare.

I tried one more time. Dropping my hands and letting every bit of hope and fear show in my face I said, "Mom, please. I think... I think Roman could be the one."

She studied me for a long moment and then let out a sigh. "Oh, Scottybear." She sounded defeated and sad and exhausted. She reached out a hand and laid it over mine, squeezing gently. "I wish I could tell you it would work out—"

"Then do," I told her, cutting her off before she could tell me all the ways I was being stupid and naive. "I don't need to hear all the potential downsides. I don't need you to tell me how ridiculous I'm being to think that Roman Burke might fall for me the way I've fallen for him. Trust me, I'm very well aware of all of that. What I need is for you to be happy for me. To give this relationship a chance to work. And for fuck's sake, I need you to not fucking steal anything or fuck this up with one of your fucking schemes."

She pressed her lips together. Then, finally, she nodded. "Okay."

I waited for her to say more. She didn't. "Seriously?" I asked.

"Seriously."

I narrowed my eyes suspiciously, wondering what her game was. I was about to ask her if she was just telling me what I wanted to hear, but then decided that I didn't want to know. If this was just another elaborate con, there was nothing I could say to talk her out of it. All I could do was find her a room, get her to bed, and make sure she left first thing in the morning before she could cause any real trouble.

I nodded. "Okay. Thank you."

She pushed from the stool and slid her arms around me, pulling me close for a hug. "I've only ever wanted the best for you, Scottybear. You know that."

I returned her hug, biting back the response hovering on the tip of my tongue: that what she thought was best for me didn't always line up with what I thought was best and that was the problem.

Eventually I pulled away and grabbed her plate, placing it in the sink to worry about in the morning. "Let's find you a place to sleep."

I led her to a guest room clear on the other side of the house from the one Roman and I were sharing, wanting as much distance as possible between us. The moment she stepped into the room, she gasped. "This is fucking gorgeous," she said, slowly turning to take it all in. "I'll bet this whole damned thing is bigger than that rec place you used to hang out at after school. Remember that place? You thought it was so big?"

I thought back to the youth center I'd gone to years before. Since it was the place where I'd met Ian, my first crush who'd eventually turned into my first boyfriend, I remembered it well.

"Yeah," I said with a smile. "It was a long time ago, and it was certainly bigger than this bedroom."

"I'm not so sure," she murmured, wandering around and touching everything. "Sure is fancy. Any chance Roman's wealthy friend is single?"

"Yes, and he's gay, so don't get your hopes up." I took a little statuette out of her hands and placed it back on the dresser. It was two birds huddled together under an umbrella. The trinket didn't seem to mesh with the rest of the house and seemed another odd piece of the Oscar puzzle.

She reached for another statuette and I batted her hand away. She wandered toward the bathroom, letting out a low whistle at the sight of it. "How did you meet these people?"

"Roman rode in my carriage," I said, vastly oversimplifying the explanation.

"Oooh! Who with?" she said, eyes dancing. "Another actor? An actress?"

I backed toward the door of the guest room. "No one, Mom. It was just him."

Her face scrunched in confusion. "Roman Burke just went out for a Central Park carriage ride by himself? Was it like some kind of publicity stunt?"

I almost snorted. "You could say that. Feel free to ask him about it tomorrow, but it's late now. Good night, Mom. See you in the morning."

I stepped out, closing the door behind me and wishing I could somehow lock it. Wishing I could believe that she wasn't going to somehow fuck this up for me in the end like she always did.

As I made my way down the long hall to Roman's room, I contemplated simply choosing another room and sleeping alone. Whether Roman realized it or not, things had changed when we'd answered that door. A hole had appeared in our safe little bubble and a piece of the real world had seeped in.

And this was just the beginning. It wasn't just my mom I was going to have to worry about, but the rest of the world too. They'd all look at my relationship with Roman and wonder if I was only in it for the money and attention. They'd find a picture of me mucking Nugget's stall and post headlines that Roman was slumming it and take odds on how long he'd roll around in the hay with a nobody before finding someone more appropriate to get serious with.

By the time I slipped into Roman's bedroom, my jaw ached from clenching it so tightly and my shoulders were wrenched up to my ears with tension. He was already in bed, the top of his bare back just poking out above the bedding. I could hear light snores coming from his direction, and something about it made my chest tight.

I closed the door behind me and padded over to him. The only light in the room was from the bathroom. He must have left it on for me so I wouldn't be completely in the dark. It glowed warmly on his honeyed skin. He'd mentioned having such a natural tan that the makeup crew on his last film had been forced to use a light foundation on his skin to make him paler for the winter scenes.

"Come to bed, baby," he murmured into the pillow. I hadn't even realized the snoring had stopped.

The endearment seriously fucked with my equilibrium, so much so, my eyes felt raw and a lump formed in my throat. I wasn't sure I'd ever met such an easy, affectionate person in my life, and I was damned sure I hadn't ever been on the receiving end of this kind of sweetness.

In my world, everything came at a price.

But Roman seemed to give his affection freely, without expectation. And it caused me to wonder what the catch was.

"Scotty?" he asked, turning over to squint at me. "Everything okay with your mom?"

"Um, yeah." I had to clear my throat to keep my voice from cracking. "Yeah. She's fine."

He rolled over the rest of the way and opened the covers in invitation. He was wearing only his underwear, and I could see the irresistible planes of his chest and abdomen leading down to his happy trail. "You getting in?" he asked in a sleep-roughened voice.

I stripped out of my clothes and left them in a pile on the floor before sliding in beside him. His skin was warm and inviting, and he reached out immediately to draw my cooler body against his, wrapping arms and legs around me to warm me up.

"Sleep," he murmured into my ear. "Everything'll be okay. Promise."

I wasn't even sure he was awake enough to know what he was saying, but just knowing he didn't want me to worry about anything made me feel cared for. Being enveloped by his bigger body made me feel protected and safe. It had only been a few nights, but I was already falling for him like a desperate fool. But I refused to expect or demand more from him than he could give. Roman already had way too many people in his life who seemed to do that.

I wouldn't be another person who put his reputation in jeopardy. Except that I already had. What would happen if my mom contacted the tabloids? What if she sold his location, or god forbid something even more personal like a photo or news of our relationship, to the paparazzi?

Could he ever forgive me?

I thought back to the conversation he'd had about his career. I remembered the stories about him in the news when he'd accidentally smashed a real antique guitar on set rather than the replica or when he'd been featured in a Rolex magazine spread but then was photographed wearing a Breitling at one of his premieres, but I'd never thought about how that might have affected his career or whether or not certain people in the industry would want to work with him.

He'd come to Vermont to lie low, to avoid any negative press. His agent and PR people had warned him that he was close to an unofficial "three strikes" rule. They worried that one more bad story in the news would solidify his reputation as being too much of a risk to work with in Hollywood.

The idea we could continue to stay here—that *he* could continue to stay here—without the paparazzi finding out was becoming less and less likely. With my mother here, it was downright impossible.

And even if we were able to finish out his time in Vermont without making waves, what were the chances we could move forward and build a life together without me or my mom somehow fucking it up? Zero. Nada. Zilch.

I'd brought a horse to his front door for god's sake. I was the epitome of fucking it up.

As I lay there pressed against him, my brain whirring at top speed, I realized his breathing had changed. Roman's fingers danced lightly along my shoulder and down my arm. I wondered if we'd just been too naive to think we could truly try to have a real relationship. If it had all just been wishful thinking.

"Your brain is literally putting off heat," Roman murmured into my hair. "Your hamster wheel must be spinning like crazy."

"Sorry," I said, letting out a breath. "Didn't mean to wake you."

He pushed up onto his elbow. "Want to talk about what's bothering you? I assume it's your mom."

I curled tighter around myself, my back still to him. "Anything I say would be beating a dead horse," I admitted. "But I can't let it go."

"Tell me. What part specifically has you in knots?"

When I didn't answer, he tugged gently on my shoulder, pulling me onto my back beside him so he could see my face. He kept a hand on my chest, the weight of it a comfort against my thundering heart.

"She's going to sell you out for a quick buck," I told him. "I just know it. You don't realize that it's not an issue of *if*, it's more a matter of *when*. And from everything you told me, you can't afford for that to happen right now. So I'm worried."

Roman smoothed his hand up my chest to run the back of his index finger down the side of my face. "Then let's talk about it. I didn't mean to make you feel like I was dismissing your concerns earlier, but I also didn't want you to feel like you couldn't have your own mother come stay with you."

I sighed, frustrated I couldn't make him understand. I appreciated how willing he was to give her a chance, and it meant more than I could say that he was doing it for me. But he didn't know her like I did. He didn't know that I'd already given her more chances than I had fingers to count them.

"I get that," I told him. "I do. But it's... she's not like regular moms. She's a con artist. And she'll smile and profess her love to you at the same time she slides the knife in."

I stopped with a jerk, my own words and tone surprising me. Roman's face showed a similar response.

I quickly began backpedaling. "I mean..."

Roman grasped my chin and forced me to meet his eyes. "You're not alone in this anymore, Scotty. You have me now. We're together. A team. And I'm not about to let her or anyone else hurt either one of us. Do you understand?"

My stupid eyes filled. I nodded, too afraid to speak in case my voice broke. This was all too good to be true. No one had ever made me feel like that before, especially not someone so kind and funny.

"Why don't I arrange for an apartment in Queens and get her on a bus back there tomorrow?" Roman's voice was quiet but determined. "She probably shouldn't be out of state right now anyway, right?"

"I don't know, but I can't let you—"

"Stop right there. I'm not spending my own money on it. I'm spending your Nugget rent."

I was confused. "Nugget rent?"

"Yep," he said with an adorable smile. "I've decided not to buy Nugget after all, but rent her instead."

I narrowed my eyes at him in the dim moonlight coming through a nearby window. "That's not really a thing."

"Not rent, I meant *lease*. I'm going to lease her. That way, you retain ownership."

"Let me guess. You're going to lease her for an absurd amount of money."

"Of course. Babe, horse leasing in Manhattan isn't cheap. Everyone knows that." Roman's eyes twinkled and his grin spread.

"You're not leasing a horse in Manhattan," I muttered. "We're in semirural Vermont."

"Correction, dear one. We're in *Stowe*, Vermont. That's like Lifestyles of the Rich and Famous right there. Plus, I'm leasing a world-famous Central Park carriage horse. This gal has a reputation and has been on covers of magazines all over the world."

I snorted. He wasn't wrong.

"What if I don't want to spend my lease income on an apartment for my mom?" I challenged.

Roman lifted an eyebrow. "Spend it on one for yourself, and let your mom stay there until she gets on her feet. Oh, and by the way, you don't get to stay there with her since you'll be staying over at your boyfriend's place most nights."

I stared at him, my chest feeling impossibly tight. "My boyfriend?"

# 22

## ROMAN

*How To Know When To Leave*

I'd FELT the tension in Scotty's body the minute he'd slid into bed next to me and knew his brain was spinning a million miles a minute. As soon as I'd gotten him to open up about his fears, I'd finally understood that reassuring him wasn't what he needed. He needed action.

He needed proof.

"Your boyfriend," I repeated firmly. "And my first official act as Scotty Pinker's boyfriend is going to be arranging to send his mother away from our little... *big*... love nest. Understand?"

Scotty's shy smile was a visual reminder he hadn't had many people in his life willing to actively look out for him. That was going to end right this minute.

"So," I continued. "In the morning, we're going to have breakfast and then sit her down and make the arrangements. If she wants to spend more time with you, tell her we'll be back in the city in a couple of weeks and will see her then. In the meantime we can arrange for a phone for her and you two can FaceTime or whatever. Okay?"

"A couple of weeks?" he asked, a frown furrowing his forehead. I wanted to reach out and smooth away the lines, to smooth away everything in his life that caused them to appear. He was born to smile and smirk and laugh, not to worry and frown.

"If that's okay with you," I told him. "I guess I should have asked before presuming, but will you stay here with me? I can't stand the thought of how empty this house would feel without you in it. How empty my bed would feel."

He glanced away, his top teeth scraping over his bottom lip. Something was bothering him.

"What is it, baby?" I asked.

"I want to stay here, I really do..." He trailed off.

Something in my chest turned cold, and my heart began to pound harder in fear that he might have changed his mind. "It sounds like there's a but coming, and not the good kind of ass."

The corner of his lip twitched, but he didn't smile.

I swallowed, my throat tight. "Do you not want to stay with me?"

His eyes flared wide. "Are you kidding me? Oh my god, Roman, how can you even ask that?" Scotty pressed a hand against my chest. "Of course I want to stay with you. If I had my way, I'd handcuff you to my wrist so we would never be apart."

I liked the idea of that. "Then what's the problem?"

"I still don't have a job," he explained. "It feels wrong to stay here rather than pounding the pavement back in the city. I just don't want to be seen as a freeloader or that I'm just using you for your money and fame."

"What about my good looks and charm?" I teased him. He still didn't smile. I knew how much pride he took in having made his own way in the world.

I took his chin, tilting it until he met my eyes. "I know how hard you work, Scotty Pinker. And I know you're not a freeloader. But the reality is that I make a lot of money, and I like to spend that money on people I care about, which means I'm going to be spending money on you."

He opened his mouth to protest, but I cut him off.

"Scotty, I *want* to take care of you. I know you can take care of yourself—I've *seen* you take care of yourself. But the idea that I can ease your burden and lighten your load... you don't understand how much that means to me."

I shifted my fingers, running my thumb along his cheekbone. "Please, baby. Let me take care of you. I'm not saying you can't work if that's what you want—of course you can. I'm just saying that you don't have to worry."

His jaw clenched and his Adam's apple bobbed in his throat several times. He nodded. "Thank you." The words were whispered so softly, they barely made it the short distance between us. I reached out to run my fingers through his tousled curls.

When I spoke, my voice sounded different. Deeper and rough. "You're not walking through life alone anymore, Scotty. I'm here beside you, and I plan on staying beside you as long as you'll let me."

His eyes shone. "So help me, if you make me cry in front of the star of *Back Passage*, I'm going to—"

I didn't let him finish. I leaned in and took his mouth in mine to shut him up before he could tease me anymore about that fucking movie. I could feel both of our smiles against each other as my tongue sought entrance to his mouth. We rolled around kissing and teasing each other for what seemed like hours until something changed between us. Suddenly we were panting while staring into each other's eyes, and everything went from playful and fiery to profound and intense.

He reached up and traced a finger down the side of my cheek. The expression on his face, the look in his eyes... it was impossible to describe. There was trust and lust and wonder and awe.

"Roman," he whispered.

So many words fought for dominance on my tongue. Want, need, take, give, protect, and yes, even love. It was new and wobbly maybe, but it was there. I wanted him everywhere and in every way. Naked, underneath me. Laughing, beside me. And growing, along with me. It was different from what I'd felt for Pete. My love for Pete had been a quiet, still thing—something calm and predictable. My feelings for Scotty were loud and wild. They grabbed me by the throat, the balls, and especially tight-fisted my heart. I never knew what was coming next with Scotty, and it was thrilling.

I smoothed a palm down his face and around the back of his neck before pulling him in so our foreheads were touching.

"I need you more than I've ever needed anyone or anything," I admitted in a low voice. "It's terrifying. I'm scared I'm going to fuck it up or you're going to run as soon as the media finds out about you."

Scotty's lips brushed along my jaw until they reached my ear.

"Then don't let me."

It was all I needed to hear before kissing him again. This time there was power and purpose behind our joining. Our lips tangled together, both of us trying desperately to delve deeper, connect something inside each of us to the other.

Scotty's sharp intake of breath spurred me on like a lit fuse, and I wrestled him onto his back before looming over him, hands everywhere on his smooth skin and lithe muscles.

He moved his mouth down my neck to my shoulder and arm, anywhere he could reach from where he lay pinned underneath me. My cock pressed hard into the softness of his belly, and his legs came up to wrap around my ass.

"Baby, look at me," I urged. Just watching his half-lidded eyes and the flush of arousal on his neck made me breathless.

He pulled his lips off my arm and looked at me with glassy eyes. "Huh?"

"What do you want?" If Scotty wanted my ass, it was his. But I wanted whatever would make him happiest. He'd mentioned earlier preferring to bottom, but we hadn't been together long enough for me to assume anything. Honestly, we'd be lucky to even get to that stage since I felt like a few more pulses against his stomach might be enough to make me come.

"You inside me," he said. "Please, Roman."

I leaned down to kiss him again, more gently this time. His lips felt puffy against mine, and I sucked his lower lip into my mouth, enjoying every little moan and whimper that escaped him.

I ran a hand down his chest, past the hard pebble of his nipple, and to the waistband of his boxer briefs. My fingers slid easily beneath the elastic and down over the round, firm curve of his ass. I squeezed appreciatively and felt his legs tighten around me in response.

Everything about his body excited me. He was trim but strong, smooth and rough depending on where my hands happened to be exploring. When I dipped a finger into his crease, he moaned sweetly in my ear. I hadn't even realized my lips had moved down to nibble along his collarbone while my fingers searched for his hole.

Scotty's hands mirrored mine. They delved into the back of my shorts and grabbed my ass, pulling me tighter to him. He began mumbling to himself about pesky underwear and damned boyfriends needing to sleep in the nude as he shoved my waistband down with both hands.

Sex with Scotty was like that. It could go from intense to light and back to profound in an instant.

I moved down his body to strip his underwear off before taking care of mine as well. Seeing Scotty laid out completely naked and hard on the bed was like someone taking a firm swipe of my prostate. I felt precum leak out of me as I crawled back onto the mattress and tried to decide what part of him I wanted to devour next.

"Roll over, sweetheart."

His eyes widened before he flipped onto his stomach and arched his adorable butt back toward me like a cat stretching in the sun. I moved up behind him and immediately grabbed those gorgeous cheeks, spreading them apart and leaning in to taste him.

I moved my tongue from his sac up to his hole and circled around before sucking and nibbling his tender skin.

"Fuck, oh fuck!" Scotty cried, suddenly unable to remain still. He pressed back into my face, and I increased the tempo, licking and sucking aggressively at his hole while holding his hips firmly to keep him as still as I could. Scotty cried out my name over and over until it was more of a broken, begging sound. When I'd finally had enough and felt like I'd loosened him up with my mouth, I smacked his ass lightly and flipped him back over.

He gazed up at me, unseeing. His face was deep pink, and his bottom lip was pinned by his top teeth. His chest heaved with the intake of breaths, and his hands automatically reached for his dick.

I moved his hands away and leaned in to suck the head of his cock into my mouth.

"Ungh," Scotty croaked. "Stop or I'll come!"

I looked up at him and noticed the tendons straining in his neck and the clenched fists by his side. He was riding the edge of his orgasm, and I could tell he wasn't sure if he wanted me to stop or continue.

I made it easy for him.

With my eyes locked on his, I leaned in, swallowing his cock all the way into my throat and sliding a slick finger inside him.

"*Roman!*" he gasped as his climax hit all at once. His back arched, his eyes rolled back, and the thick liquid of his release began pegging the back of my throat. Every muscle in his body seemed to contract, spasming through his orgasm. He was so fucking beautiful, and making him feel like that was amazing.

I sucked lightly while he came down from his high, and eventually I moved to kiss the smooth skin over his hip as his legs sagged down beside me on the mattress.

"Why didn't you wait?" he asked in a semi-slurred voice. "'Till you were inside me?"

I moved up and brushed the hair from his forehead, taking in his blissed-out expression and the soft grin overtaking his lips. "Not that I'm complaining," he added.

"I wanted to see you fly," I told him. "You're gorgeous when you come. You don't hold back, and I love that."

Scotty gazed at me like I was the second coming of Christ. It was a heady feeling to be the focus of such appreciative attention.

His eyes slid from half-mast to three-quarters-mast as he fought sleep. "Still want you inside me," he murmured.

"And that will happen. But first, sleep."

"Hm?"

I continued to run my fingers lightly through his hair and along the side of his face, simply enjoying the sight of a sated Scotty in slumber. I leaned in and pressed a kiss to his warm cheek. "Sleep, baby."

He was asleep in two seconds.

I lay on my side watching his chest rise and fall. At some point I must have fallen asleep myself because I woke up with the warm pink light of sunrise illuminating Scotty's messy curls as he ran a tongue up my hard dick.

"Oh fuck," I gasped, reaching a hand into his hair. "Fuck, Scotty, god. *Mpfh.*"

It felt so good, the hot wet suction of his mouth around me and his hands wandering along my inner thighs. I watched him suck me off as my brain tried to click into gear. It was impossible. The feel of him, the sight of him, it was all too much. So I lay back and enjoyed the attentions, sucking in a breath every time he got me close to the edge and pulled off.

His light blue eyes watched me as he lavished my cock with attention, until suddenly he sat up and reached for something in the bedsheets. The sound of crinkling condom packet hit my ears and when he reached for my cock, it jerked in anticipation.

Scotty rolled the condom on me before pumping out lube and reaching behind himself to prep. The look of pleasure on his face as his fingers found his hole made my dick jump again.

"Scotty," I groaned. "I want to see."

His grin was adorable. "Too late, Spartacus. I'm ready."

He added another pump of lube to my dick before moving up and kneeling over me to position himself over my hard shaft.

I groaned again in anticipation, wanting nothing more than to feel his body's hot squeeze around me. As soon as he sank down over the tip, we both let out cries of bliss. He felt so fucking good, it was hard to keep still when all my body wanted was to shove up inside him hard and fast.

As Scotty worked himself onto me with little pulses up and down, I hissed out a breath and tried not to notice the delectable dark blond treasure trail on his belly, the dusky discs of his nipples, or the sexy curve of his shoulders and biceps muscles.

Suddenly, I was seated all the way inside him. My hands grasped his hips and held him there as I ground up into him, locking eyes with him to watch his pupils edge out the blue of his irises.

He leaned down to kiss me, so I curled up to meet him. Scotty's mouth was tender and gentle, asking for a connection I was eager to give him. He rocked his hips, pulling his body off me before sinking back on again slowly. It was languid and sweet, reminding me of the many flavors of sex with Scotty, but this one was different. I wasn't sure I'd ever felt so connected to another person.

"*Scotty*," I breathed against his mouth.

He pulled back from the kiss and met my eyes again. We stayed that way for a long time, moving our bodies together and speaking without words. When the emotion between us reached a breaking point, I flipped him onto his back and began slowly sliding in and out of him, changing angles until he cried out my name.

Scotty began babbling then, begging for release, begging for me to stay right there, to make him come, to never leave. His eyes fluttered closed, and his breathing hitched. I reached for his cock and stroked it to push him over the edge since I was close too.

As soon as his orgasm hit and his body squeezed me in a vice grip, I lost it. Waves of pleasure moved through me, stealing my breath and blanking my vision. I pressed deep inside him as my body released, and when my brain started clearing, I realized Scotty was wrapped tightly around me like a four-limbed boa constrictor.

I kissed him and gently released his hold on me before pulling out of his body to dispose of the condom. Before I could even pull the condom off, Scotty sprang into action and did it for me, jumping up and making his way to the bathroom. He came back with a hot, wet washcloth and fluffy towel and smiled serenely while he tended to me before cleaning up his own body.

"That's my job," I said with an appreciative smile. "What're you doing?"

He tossed the towels away and climbed back in bed, snuggling in close.

"It occurred to me that you're a service top."

"Explain."

"Every time we've had sex, you're the giver. You give, give, give."

"I want you to feel good," I said, defensively. "Is that bad?"

Scotty's face softened. "No, Spartacus. It's not bad. It's very, very good. But I want you to feel good too, you know?"

I pulled him closer. "Seeing you happy makes me feel good."

"Shhh!" Scotty hissed. "Don't let anyone else hear that, or they'll bump me off so they can take my place. Jesus Christ. It's bad enough you're gorgeous and successful and famous. You gotta be kind and generous in bed too? Fuck me."

I laughed and pulled him on top of me, enjoying his fake frown. The sunlight hit him again, causing him to glow like an angel. It was impossible to take him seriously.

"We still on board for Operation Cyndee Dump today?" I asked.

"Ew. That sounds nasty." Scotty shivered in disgust. "But yes. To use Lolo's phrase: she must away."

"That man is a character," I mused. "Wonder where Oscar found him."

"Some kind of used diva store; I'm sure of it." He frowned. "Though I still want to know why he's with that toad."

I sat up and faced him, realizing I'd forgotten to tell him about Oscar's text from the day before. "Omigod, I got a little intel on that. Scratch that. *Big* intel."

Scotty crossed his arms behind his head on the pillow and smiled up at me. "Here for it. Continue."

"Supposedly, our Larry is none other than Lawrence Porterfield, a state senator from Louisiana most famous for an anti-gay rant on the senate floor two years ago. He'd sponsored a bill against LGBT adoption, and when it subsequently passed, Lolo lost his shit. He was adopted himself by shitty parents who later kicked him out. So the idea that a kid like him would have no chance at adoptive queer parents made him see red."

Scotty sat up and leaned forward, anger flushing his face. "God, Roman! Why the hell is he with someone like that? That makes me want to go beat the toad to death."

I held up a finger, smirking. "Before you do that, wait," I told him. "You might like this part." I paused, building anticipation before saying, "Lolo deliberately set out to seduce him."

I saw the reality dawn on Scotty's face and a sly grin appear. "No shit. Smart Lolo. Very, very smart."

"Right?"

"So what's his endgame do you think?" I asked him.

I shrugged. "No idea. But given what we've seen of Lolo, I wouldn't underestimate him. I'm sure things aren't going to end well for Larry."

# 23

## SCOTTY

*Storm Strands Stowaways In Stowe*

AFTER ROLLING AROUND in bed a little longer, we exchanged soapy hand jobs in the shower and made our way downstairs. Roman was whisper-giggling his way through an impression of Lolo playing prisoner to Trevor's cop when I recognized the sound of my mother's voice in the kitchen.

"Shit," I hissed, nudging Roman to go faster. "She's already up. Hurry."

My mother had never been known as a morning person, so it hadn't occurred to me that we'd have to wake up early so we could warn Diana and her family not to share anything my mom could sell to the tabloids. But sure enough, when we entered the kitchen my mother was begging Diana to tell her more little-boy Roman stories from their childhood.

The moment I saw her, I went straight to her, forcing a smile. "Mom! You're awake. How... great," I said, false cheer dripping from my voice.

She turned to me, a familiar gleam in her eye. "There you are,

Scottybear." She air-kissed my cheeks. "Of course I'm awake—jail isn't really known for letting inmates sleep in," she added with a wink.

I blinked, glancing toward Diana to see if she'd react to my mother's admission she'd just gotten out of jail. But she didn't even bat an eye, just continued hulling strawberries for a fruit salad. I cleared my throat. "So... I guess you shared details about your recent... accommodations?"

Mom waved a dismissive hand. "Oh of course. Diana and I are old friends by now, aren't we, dear?" she asked, sending a smile Diana's way.

"We've been trading embarrassing stories about the two of you," Diana said, waggling a finger between me and Roman. "I had no idea you'd performed a full reenactment of *All The Single Ladies* for your school talent show."

Oh dear god. I winced and glanced at Roman out of the corner of my eye, desperately hoping he hadn't just heard that. I could tell from the smirk on his face he totally had. "I didn't know that either, *bae*. You'll have to tell me more about that later," he said, brushing a kiss along my temple before whispering in my ear, "Or even better, show me."

My cheeks turned fire-engine red. Everything about the moment was so tranquil and ordinary, it was almost possible to forget that my mother was a con artist always on the lookout for her next score. And she'd clearly set her eyes on Roman.

"I'm so glad you two have gotten to know each other," I told my mom through ground teeth. "Shame you're leaving so early this morning," I added pointedly.

She opened her mouth to protest, but Earl beat her to it. "'Fraid that's not gonna happen. Big storm coming." He nodded to the window. Sure enough, the last of the morning sun was being chased across the snow-covered backyard by dark clouds and intermittent flurries.

My stomach churned with anxiety. This could not be happening. No way was my mother going to be trapped in this house with Roman and his family. "I'm sure it will be fine," I said, taking her arm and steering her toward the mudroom. "This is Vermont; they have snow plows."

Just as I reached for the door, it banged open and Marigold blew in lugging a heavy plastic shopping bag and chatting a mile a minute. "Sorry to barge in, but whoever's rental Tahoe was in the driveway this morning, you're out of gas." She tossed a set of keys toward a ceramic bowl on the counter and continued into the kitchen where she set her bag down on the island with the unmistakable sound of clinking bottles.

I frowned at Roman. His car had been stolen by Marigold's boyfriend their first day here, and Lolo's rental was a luxury sedan. Which left Diana and Earl's car. Roman must have come to the same conclusion. He fisted his hands on his hips. "Marigold, you didn't."

"Of course I did. Someone needed to get more vodka," she said, unloading several bottles from the bag. "Didn't you hear about the storm? Anywho, never fear, I've already put in a call to AAA, and as soon as the storm clears, they'll tow it back. No harm no foul."

I wasn't going to let that deter me from getting my mother out of there. "Fine," I said, nudging my mom back toward the mudroom. "Then we'll borrow Lolo's car to get to the bus station."

Marigold paused her unloading and let out a long, "Ehhhhhh-hhh, I wouldn't."

"What did you do to Lolo's car, Marigold?" Roman asked.

She widened her eyes innocently. "Blame Collins. When the Tahoe ran out of gas at the liquor store, I made him come get me, and let's just say he apparently never learned you're supposed to turn *into* the skid when you hit ice. No worries," she said, flapping a hand. "AAA said they'll pull it out of the creek when they drop off the Tahoe."

I was about to ask for details before deciding I didn't want to know. The end result was still the same. "So we're stuck."

"Unless you can get my brother to fess up where he's hidden the keys to the Hummer or the Bugatti." Marigold brandished a vodka bottle in each hand, beaming. "But at least we have supplies!"

"I don't think that will be enough," I grumbled under my breath.

"Oh, ye of little faith, don't think I didn't plan ahead," Marigold laughed. "There's plenty more where this came from. I mean, have you met me?"

"Actually," my mother said, stepping around me and holding out a hand. "I haven't. I'm Scotty's mother, Cyndee. Did you say that your brother is the owner of this delightful property?"

I could already see the familiar gleam in her eyes at having found a new potential mark. The two began chatting, and I couldn't decide whether that should terrify me or make me feel relieved that it might take her attention away from Roman. I let out a sigh, dropping my head in my hands.

A warm, familiar hand landed on my shoulder, squeezing gently. "Hey," Roman breathed into my ear, pulling my back against his chest and wrapping an arm around me. "It's going to be okay." Surrounded by his strength and comfort, I almost started to believe him.

At least until the mudroom door banged open again and Collins, aka pink polo shirt guy, staggered in, stumbling under the weight of several more shopping bags from the liquor store. "Jesus fucking Christ, Marigold, what the hell? Didn't you hear me calling for you to wait up? This shit is heavy as cra—"

He froze, mouth open when he noticed all of us staring at him. Including Roman's two nieces, who sat at the kitchen table, crayons held forgotten in midair as they stared at Collins in fascination.

"Uh-oh," Sonya said in a hushed, serious tone. "He said a bad word."

"He's in trooouuubbleeeee," Nay-Nay added in a singsong voice.

"Seriously, Collins," Marigold scolded, rolling her eyes. "Language."

"Uh. Sorry," he mumbled.

Marigold waved a hand at him. "Drop those bags over there, and then go see if you can find that space heater so we can thaw out the Ferris wheel."

I looked over at Roman, mouthing the words "Ferris wheel?"

He leaned in to murmur in my ear. "I think she means the water wheel at the Mill."

I wasn't sure what the fuck he was talking about, but I nodded anyway. "Yeah, sure. Makes sense."

It didn't make sense.

Roman winked at me, revealing his ability to see right through my bullshit. Smart man.

"So how long is this storm going to last?" I asked weakly.

"Looks like it's going to be pretty serious accumulation," Earl said, looking up from a weather app on his phone. "They're anticipating quite a few inches in the next hour alone."

"Aren't we all?" Lolo called out, gliding into the room in a sheer peach nightgown barely covered by a purplish flowy robe.

"Ooh-la-la! What are you wearing?" Marigold asked with a gasp. "That robe is divine."

Lolo beamed at the compliment. "Isn't it? It's the Adriana Degreas fig-print kimono but only because someone got cum..." His eyes skittered over to the girls, who had returned to chattering happily at the table. "*Kumquat* juice on my Rianna + Nina checkerboard one. I could have throttled that mother... *lover*."

Larry shuffled in, sporting tattered gray sweats complete with a red-and-navy-blue-striped terry cloth headband. I wondered if he was going jogging back to the 1980s.

"Wasn't my fault," he muttered, scratching his stomach. "You did that thing with the—"

"Earmuffs!" Diana called across the room. The girls automatically dropped their crayons and put their hands over their ears as Larry said something that sounded an awful lot like *Trump dildo*.

I lifted an eyebrow at Diana, who shrugged. "Learned that trick from a Will Ferrell movie. Comes in handy more than you'd think. Earl, tell them they can uncover."

"Twenty-four inches of snow expected," Earl finished, pulling the girls arms down. "The airport is already closed, and they're advising everyone to hunker down."

"Shit," Roman muttered, taking the word right out of my mouth.

"Oh what fun," my mom said, clapping her hands together. She looked like a woman who'd just won the lottery. And from her point of view, she probably had. "We can build a fire and roast marshmallows," she continued. "Won't that be fun, girls?"

Roman grunted, making me realize I'd squeezed the hell out of his hand until my nails dug into his skin.

"Sorry," I muttered under my breath, letting him go. "This is a disaster. I'm pretty sure Mom's looking at this situation with dollar signs in her eyes. Think we can put her in the barn with Nugget?" Before my anxiety had a chance to ramp back up, Roman grabbed my elbow and pulled me around until my face was buried in his chest.

"Shh. Take a breath. We're going to be fine," he said softly. "We're a team now, remember?"

"Yeah, that's why I said *we*." My voice was muffled in his shirt-front. When laughter rumbled through his chest, I closed my eyes and smiled. It felt so good having someone, being able to touch someone, finding comfort in someone.

Roman pulled back and cupped my face before kissing me full on the lips in front of everyone. My mother squealed and clapped, making my stomach clench with nerves. The girls giggled and tittered, and I swore I heard Collins mutter, "Duuuude. Hot."

"Lawd, don't stop," Lolo drawled when Roman pulled away. "The show was just getting good. This is better than that scene in *Death Pawn* when he and Polly Macari—"

He stopped suddenly and stared at me, bringing his delicate, long-fingered hand to his chest. "Did you just growl at me like a little baby tiger cub?"

I felt my face heat and looked away, mumbling, "Of course not."

I refused to think of the hot-as-fuck sex scene between Roman and Polly in that movie. It was so iconic, there were still gifs of it everywhere all the fucking time. It had been good spank bank material until the dude became my boyfriend and the entire world thought he was the father of Polly's baby. Now it was... *grrr*.

Roman's warm chuckle hit my ears again as he nuzzled against my neck. "You make an adorable tiger cub, for what it's worth."

"Shut up," I growled.

The mudroom door banged open and Oscar's mother trotted in. "Just dropping Rosie off to play with the girls before heading to the Hutch. Cheers!" Oscar's mom called out before turning and disappearing again.

Oscar's niece Rosie, the one who'd woken us up a few days before, trotted in happily to join the girls at the kitchen table. They'd met the previous day while out for a walk in the snow and apparently become fast friends.

I looked around. No one else even batted an eye that another person had joined our chaotic household. As if at this point it was just expected that random people would arrive out of nowhere. At least the impending storm meant our numbers wouldn't be growing anytime soon.

"Can someone please tell me what the Hutch is?" I asked. "I need a map and a dictionary, as well as Oscar's phone number."

Marigold ignored my question and clapped instead. "So, mimosas for breakfast?"

"Yes, please." Lolo floated farther into the room and gave Diana air-kisses on each cheek. "Good morning, doll. What's for brunch, and how can I help?"

Roman and I looked over in shock at Lolo's offer to do actual work.

Diana, however, took it in stride. "I have an egg-and-sausage casserole in the oven, but I'd love some help cutting up fruit."

Before we knew it, she'd set him up with a cutting board, a huge knife, and a cantaloupe. He'd clearly never seen a real cantaloupe in the wild before and blinked at it a few times in confusion.

"Do I... skin it first?" He poked at it with the tip of the knife, accidentally sending it rolling. It fell from the counter and hit the floor with a squelching splat that sent melon guts flying.

Lolo shrieked, leaping back and clutching his robe tighter as though the fruit had intentionally attacked him. "Egads—it lives!" he cried, brandishing his knife at the poor broken melon.

I jumped in, hoping to calm the situation. "Here," I said, gently prying the knife from his fingers. "Let me."

He clutched me against him, his long arms surprisingly strong. "My hero."

"Now wait a minute—" Larry started to growl.

Lolo pushed me away and drifted past Larry toward the hall leading upstairs. "Come along, Powder Puff. If you want to see me naked today, now's your chance to watch while I change into something a little more—and perhaps a bit less—appropriate."

With Lolo gone, I ended up on cantaloupe duty next to Diana as she finished hulling strawberries. My mom sat with Earl and the girls at the table, cutting up snowflakes while Roman gathered plates and silverware to set the places. So for a moment, Diana and I were more or less alone.

"I'm sorry about my mom," I mumbled, keeping my eyes on the melon.

"She seems nice," she said carefully.

I let out a sigh. "She's a con artist." I winced at how terrible the words sounded, how blunt. But Diana deserved to know the truth so she could protect herself and her family. "She'll sell Roman out the first chance she gets."

Diana nudged me with her elbow playfully. "This ain't my first rodeo, Scotty. You don't have to worry; I didn't tell your mother a single story that hasn't already been printed in one magazine profile or another."

I blinked up at her, impressed. "Seriously? That was pretty smart."

She grinned. "My little brother's been a famous movie star for years. Thankfully, his agent brought in PR and media training for all of us early on. It's made all the difference. I'm sure he'll hook you up with them soon too."

The casual mention of PR and media training brought me up short. While she continued cutting up fruit, I placed the knife aside and pressed my palms against the counter, trying to control my breathing.

Shit was getting real. This was actually happening. Nerves tickled my gut, but I tried my best to tamp them down. I cared about him enough to do this, to face whatever challenges at home or in the media. I wasn't about to let those fuckers break us apart like they did with Roman and Pete.

But then again, Pete had actually experienced it, and I hadn't yet. Not really. There'd been a few paps who'd tailed me after the carriage incident, but they'd quickly realized my life wasn't exciting enough to document. It was nothing like what would happen once news of our relationship became public. What if I couldn't handle it? What if I failed him?

Diana must have noticed my anxiety because she reached over and placed a hand over mine. "Scotty, I want you to know that this is the happiest I've seen my brother for a long time, if ever. And whatever your mom may or may not have done, doesn't reflect on *you*. I can tell you have a giant heart. The way you are with my girls, the way you are with Nugget... hell, the way you don't call that Larry guy out on his shit... you're steady. Patient. Sweet."

"But Roman can't be seen in public with someone like me," I said miserably, shaking my head. "It'll ruin him."

Her smile was knowing. "It'll make him."

I had no idea how she could say that so confidently. "How?"

"Because he'll finally be comfortable in his own skin. He'll finally know how to prioritize his work and his personal life. And you're not the kind of person to let him hide away in that brownstone in fear. Remember when you were in the middle of the riding lesson and you hopped off Nugget to pull the girls over to the edge of the woods to show them the way that one icicle was hanging off the tree limb?"

"It looked just like a carrot. I didn't want them to miss it," I said defensively. "Earl didn't mind."

"Pfft, of course he didn't mind. Because you were teaching his children how to embrace life in small moments. How to see fun and beauty everywhere. You didn't stay in the saddle to continue what was expected of you. You took an opportunity you saw to enrich others, to share the joy of life with others. That's what Roman needs, Scotty."

My heart felt full from her words. "Thank you," I whispered. "That... that's amazing. Thank you."

"You're going to do just fine," Diana reassured me. "Trust me. You're not only going to be okay, you're going to shine. Mark my words. The press is going to fucking love you."

I still wasn't sure I agreed with her, but I decided for the moment to at least try to entertain the possibility that she could be right. It wasn't like I was a complete social nincompoop—as a carriage driver I'd interacted with strangers all day long. Since a hefty amount of my income was based on tips, I'd quickly learned how to be gregarious and entertaining. It hadn't always been easy—just like everyone else, I had bad days and rude passengers, but I couldn't let it show. I couldn't let one bad ride cascade into the next. Instead I'd learned to hide behind a smile and an offhand joke.

Maybe I just had to apply the same lessons to dealing with the paparazzi. After all, if I could survive tourists in New York at Christmas, I could pretty much survive anything.

Or so I thought.

# 24

## ROMAN

*She Came In Like A Wrecking Ball*

AFTER BREAKFAST I cleaned the kitchen while Scotty helped my nieces and Rosie cut snowflakes out of folded paper. Earl and Diana had snuck away somewhere, and I was happy to be able to give them a break from the girls for a little while. Plus it was fun listening to Scotty make up stories about "special snowflakes" for the girls.

"This one is missing one of its points," he said, holding up a wilted paper snowflake. "Which is a little bit like another special snowflake we know who serves in Congress. And this one over here is extra holy like another special snowflake who runs a mega church and flies in a private airplane."

I snorted and met his eye as I wiped down the counter. "I believe the technical term for what you're doing is brainwashing."

He winked at me. "You gotta turn 'em early, Spartacus. It's the only way forward."

Before I could respond, Nay-Nay tilted her head to the side and scrunched up her nose. "What dat noise, Uncle Scotty?"

I paused, listening. Sure enough, I felt the *thump thump* of something rhythmic and low through the floorboards. The beat was familiar, but I couldn't quite place it.

Scotty must have heard it too. "Is that Lolo and Larry again?" he asked. "What the he... ck are they doing now?"

"I'm not sure I want to know," I told him.

"So help me if I hear barking coming from their room again..." he grumbled.

The sound continued to grow louder, enough that the walls had begun to shake. If that was Lolo and Larry, they were having some truly epic wall-banging sex. Scotty looked at me with wide eyes, clearly sharing the same thought. "Maybe that explains why they're still together."

I snickered. But it was obvious by that point that the sound was coming from outside the house. I realized then what it was: a helicopter, the rhythmic beat of rotors unmistakable now.

And it was coming closer.

The girls realized what it was at the same time because they bolted out of their seats and raced across the kitchen to press their noses against the cold glass panes. Scotty and I trailed after them. "Speaking of special snowflakes," Scotty murmured as a bright red helicopter hovered into view over the treetops.

It began to circle the open patch of ground between the house and the pond, clearly intending to land.

"What the fuh... reak?" Scotty murmured. "Who is that? Oscar?"

Lolo's voice came from behind us. "No, darling. His helo is purple."

"How do you know that?" Larry scoffed, following Lolo like a lost puppy. "Princess, you told me—"

"Hush, jingle bell. Don't worry about it."

"Then who do you think it is?" Scotty asked, ignoring the lovers.

I shook my head. "I have no idea."

As we watched, the helicopter touched down and the rotors began to slow, coming to a stop. Beside me, Scotty grew agitated. "Should we call the cops?"

Just then Marigold came strolling into the room, Collins at her heels. She waved her glass of vodka-spiked orange juice at the windows. "Hey, did anyone else notice a helicopter just landed in the backyard?"

"No shi... itake, Sherlock," Scotty said, wincing when one of the girls glared back at him, clearly noticing that he'd almost said a bad word.

"Any idea who it is?" Marigold asked, taking a swallow of her drink.

We all shook our heads and stared as the door swung open. Out climbed a ball of bright white skiwear topped with familiar golden-blonde strands of hair flying out from a grass-green wool hat of some kind, pulled low over her ears in a stylish way.

I recognized her instantly. "It's Polly," I murmured to Scotty in surprise. "What in the world is she doing here?"

As the pilot began unloading her luggage, Polly turned to look up at the house, her hand tented over her eyes, blocking out the nonexistent sun.

"Oh my god," Collins squealed. "I recognize her! It's the woman from that thing!" He started dancing from foot to foot, unable to control his excitement. "You know who I'm talking about," he said, snapping his fingers at Marigold. "Fuck, what's her name?"

"Oooooh, I'm telling Daddy you said a bad wooooord," Sonya sang while Nay-Nay giggled.

"I should go help her in," I said with a sigh.

Scotty touched my elbow. "You want me to come with you, or should I stay?" His eyes were full of anxiety, and I dropped an appreciative kiss on his nose. "It's okay, no need for you to get snowed on."

"I'll go!" Collins shouted. He scrambled toward the French doors leading to the back patio, his drink splashing everywhere as he fumbled with the lock. The little girls skittered out of the splash zone, squealing.

Collins finally got it unlatched and stumbled outside. "Hey, Movie Lady!" he cried, the remains of his drink splashing over his hand as he slipped and slid across the ice-slicked patio. "Hey, you! I know you! Hey!"

"That guy's an idiot," Marigold mumbled under her breath. "Wasting perfectly good vodka like that."

Lolo wandered closer and toed the edge of the orange juice puddle from Collins's spilled drink. "Someone should really clean that up."

"Agreed," Marigold said, nodding. Neither one of them moved to take care of it.

I was about to say I'd handle it when the doorbell rang. Marigold brightened. "I'll get it! It's probably my parents here to get Rosie," she said, spinning away from the mess, clearly happy to have an excuse to avoid cleanup duty.

I let out a sigh and started toward the kitchen to grab paper towels when my phone buzzed in my pocket. I glanced at the screen: Oscar. I knew if I ignored him, he'd just keep calling, so I answered it. "Hey, I can't really talk now," I said in lieu of a greeting.

"Won't take but a second," he said. "Just wanted to give you the heads-up that Polly's on her way up there."

I twisted my lips. "Information that would have been useful five minutes ago."

"Oh, she's already there? Capital!" Only Oscar would use that word and get away with it.

I noticed that Scotty had settled my nieces back at the kitchen table to work on their snowflakes before grabbing a dish towel to blot up the spilled drink. I held the phone away from my ear to tell him, "Scotty, you don't have to do that, I'll take care of it." He waved me off and continued cleaning.

"Who's Scotty?" Oscar asked. "Is that Marigold's new boyfriend? God I hope so—that last one was a complete dud. Kept stealing my cars, so I had to start hiding the keys."

I grinned. "No, Scotty's *my* new boyfriend."

I purposefully said it loud enough for Scotty to hear and saw him smile, a blush tinging his cheeks. It made me want to drag him back upstairs to our bedroom and never let him leave.

"Ooooooh, Uncle Roman has a *boy*friend," Sonya chanted. Nay-

Nay and Rosie quickly chimed in. Scotty's blush deepened. It was fucking adorable.

There was silence on the other end of the line. "Since when did you get a boyfriend?"

Before I could answer, Marigold rounded the corner out of breath. "It's the cops! I'm not here." She bolted toward the mudroom and cursed roundly when she opened the door. "Crap! We're out of cars." She turned, a panicky look on her face.

Lolo unwound from where he'd been lounging on the couch. "The police, you say? Did one of them happen to have a deliciously full face of hair?"

Marigold threw up her hands. "I don't know. I saw the badge through the window and bolted."

"Wait, is that my sister?" Oscar asked. "Did she just say the cops are there?"

"Hold on," I told him. To Marigold I said, "You didn't even let them in?"

"Of course I didn't!" Marigold shouted. "I'm not an idiot! Tell them to come back with a warrant."

"Oh, I'll be more than happy to convey that message," Lolo said. He dabbed at the corners of his lips with his pinky and began gliding toward the front door.

Larry grabbed his arm. "Oh no you don't."

Lolo's eyes went wide before narrowing to dangerously glittering slits. He looked at Larry's fingers on his arm and then up at Larry's face. Larry blanched, dropping his hand. Lolo said something under his breath that I couldn't hear, and Larry began to quiver. I tried to tune out their disagreement.

"Jesus," I muttered under my breath. In the background the girls continued their off-key chant, growing louder when they felt that no one was listening.

In a word, it was chaos. I glanced toward Scotty, who'd finished cleaning the orange juice and was now trying to temper the volume of the girls' chant.

"Did you hear me, Roman?" Oscar shouted into the phone. "Why are the cops there?"

"Oh, it could be any number of things, really," I told him. I glanced outside and noted that Collins had reached Polly and was talking to her animatedly, his hands gesturing wildly. In normal circumstances I would have gone out to rescue her, but these weren't normal circumstances.

Scotty must have noticed my concern because he left the girls and came over to place a hand on my arm. "Do you want me to go intervene?" he asked quietly, gesturing outside. It had started to snow again, and I hated asking him to go out in it to clean up my mess. I appreciated his willingness to help, but it wasn't his job to try to control the craziness in my life, and I was afraid that if I asked too much too quickly, he'd get overwhelmed and bolt like Pete eventually had.

"No, I can handle it, thanks," I told him. I turned back to the phone. "Oscar, look," I told him, cutting him off midrant about his sister and her past with the police. "I really need to go—"

"Is that Oscar?" Marigold asked, pointing at the phone. "Ask him where the keys to the Bugatti are."

I did as told. "Marigold wants to know where the keys to the Bugatti are."

Oscar let out a string of curses. "The last time she drove that car, it ended up in the pond. Plus it has zero clearance—it wouldn't even make it out of the garage this time of year."

"He says no," I told her.

She fisted her hands on her hips. "Tell him it's important."

Oscar must have heard because he said, "Oh for Chrissakes, put me on speaker." It was just easier to do as asked rather than continue as their go-between. I pressed the Speaker button and held the phone out.

"Listen to me very carefully, Marigold," Oscar instructed. "Go find the fox figurine in the music room. Inside of it, there's a key. Take the key into the conservatory and find the statue of the gladiator who's freeballing. Somehow the sculptor elected not to put him in a battle tunic, but whatever. Another story for another time. At the base of the statue is a hidden cubby."

"The keys are in the cubby?" Marigold asked excitedly, leaning down toward the phone.

"No. Don't be ridiculous," Oscar scoffed. "But you'll find a really nice ball gag in there that you might find useful. Avoid the handcuffs though. The key to those is somewhere else. Oh, actually... Lolo might have them. You can ask."

Lolo paused from berating Larry and put a fingertip to his chin. "Is that what that goes to? God, it's been bugging me for absolute ages."

Marigold glared at the phone. "Thanks, *darling* brother."

I closed my eyes and pinched the bridge of my nose. "I... I don't even..."

"Shit, Farish is here with the doves. Gotta go." Oscar hung up before I could figure out what the hell he was talking about.

I kept my eyes closed a beat longer, hoping that when I opened them again the chaos of the day might have eased, but I wasn't so lucky. Because just then Marigold hissed, "Cheezit! It's the cops!" I looked up to see her scrambling out of the room as Trevor came strolling in from the front hall, decked out in all his Vermont State Trooper glory.

"Morning," he said, touching the brim of his hat as he headed toward the fridge in the kitchen.

Lolo placed his hand to his chest. "Holy hot blowjob on a biscuit," Lolo breathed as the trooper sauntered past. "I think I broke a law and need to be cavity searched. Aggressively."

He cleared his throat and started toward the trooper. "Officer HotBeard?" Lolo called. "I believe I've done something very bad, darling."

I turned to tell Scotty I'd totally called it, but he wasn't beside me. I glanced around, wondering where he'd gone, and saw that he was outside, juggling several of Polly's suitcases as he tried to bring them in from the helicopter. My heart swelled. It was obvious he was jumping in to try to control the mayhem wherever he could, but as much as I appreciated it, I didn't want him thinking it was his job to try and tame the chaos in my life. That way lay madness. I started out to help him but was met at the door by Polly.

The moment she saw me, she fell into my arms and burst into tears. I froze, unsure what to do. "Um, Polly?" I asked, tentatively patting her shoulder. "You okay?"

"No," she wailed in my ear. "I really, really need to pee."

It was not at all the answer I'd been expecting. "Okay, um. The bathroom's through there." I pointed down the hallway and she shuffled off, still sniffling.

I started again toward Scotty but Collins came tumbling through the door next. "Polly Macari! I knew that's who it was. She's like my favorite," he babbled to Scotty, who trudged along behind him. I quickly reached out, taking the suitcases from Scotty and setting them on the ground.

A man I'd never seen before squeezed past us through the door. "Name's Lee," he said, not even bothering to stop for a proper introduction. "I'm the pilot. The bird's grounded, so looks like I'll be here a while. Got any snacks?" He continued to the kitchen, making himself instantly at home.

I watched him, speechless. I felt like I'd been struck by a Mack truck, my entire world spinning around from the chaos of the past few minutes. I reached for Scotty, needing the reassurance of his touch to center me. Just knowing he was within holding distance eased the panicky fluttering in my chest.

I noticed when I pulled him into a hug he was a little stiff. "You okay?" I murmured in his ear.

He didn't answer immediately. "Yeah," he finally said. "It's just... a lot."

I drew back so I could read his expression. I noticed fine lines had appeared at the corners of his eyes and his lips were pressed tightly together. He was overwhelmed. I could tell. My heart began to trip in trepidation. This was too much at once.

"It's not always this crazy," I told him, pressing a palm to his cheek, "I promise."

He smiled, but it didn't reach his eyes. "It's okay, it's just—" He hesitated, searching for the right words.

Before he could finish, his mother came strolling into the room. "Who was at the door? And was that a helicopter I heard earlier?"

"Shit," Scotty mumbled under his breath. He pulled out of my embrace and started toward her.

I turned to follow him, determined to keep him by my side, but just then Polly burst out of the bathroom. She was still sobbing, and she made a beeline right for me. "God, Roman, I fucked up bad. Howard showed up at my brownstone in New York and told me he wants to be with me and help me raise our kid and I didn't know what to do so I ran and I need your help fixing it."

Beside me, I heard Scotty let out a choked kind of gasp. His eyes went wide, his cheeks paling as he glanced at his mom. It was obvious from her expression Cyndee knew exactly who Polly was and exactly what she'd just overheard—the biggest, most sought-after piece of celebrity gossip in years.

Scotty cursed under his breath and raced to his mom, taking her by the arm and trying to lead her from the room. "Mom," he said under his breath.

But she held her ground. "Aren't you going to introduce me to your friend?"

Polly seemed oblivious to the tension in the room. "And I also need carbs," she continued. "Like a really eggy bread? Challah or brioche? Hell, I'd even take an English muffin, honestly. Oh, and do you have—"

"Pol," I hissed under my breath. Didn't she know better than to spill her secrets in front of strangers? I shoved my hands in my hair, grabbing hold and yanking.

Just then the doorbell rang. Again. "Jesus fuck," I muttered under my breath.

"I'll get it," the helicopter pilot said, appearing from the kitchen.

"Ignore it," I snapped. I couldn't handle anything more at the moment. Not with Scotty on the edge like he was. The pilot shrugged and sauntered back into the kitchen.

I was past the point of caring. My heart raced a million miles an hour and my chest felt tight. It was all just too much at once.

And the look on Scotty's face: panic and terror. It struck me to my very core. Because they were not expressions I'd ever seen on him. They were not who he was to me. Scotty was light and air and joy, and it was my fault he now bore creases across his forehead and tension in his jaw.

It was too much. All of this—my life, the chaos of it. I believed him when he told me he was strong enough to face the scrutiny that came with being with me, and I didn't doubt that. Scotty was one of the strongest men I knew. He'd endured more hardship than I could ever imagine. He'd fought for everything he owned, everything he earned, every dream he'd achieved.

If I asked him, he would fight for me. Fight for this. Fight for us. But this was what it would look like. I realized that now. The constant pressure, the unrelenting stress would dull the brightness of him. It would take its toll, bearing down on him. The weight of it a constant burden.

That's what loving me was: a burden. Something to be endured rather than celebrated.

It wasn't just that Scotty deserved better than that, it was that I couldn't bear the thought of being the one responsible for dulling his sparkle. I wouldn't be able to live with myself.

"Scotty." I took a step toward him, my hand outstretched, my voice breaking on his name.

But then, two things happened at once. First, Marigold appeared in the doorway, dragging the statue of the freeballing gladiator behind her. It made a terrible grating sound as the base of it gouged against the wooden floor. "I can't find the fucking hidden cubby," she growled. "I think Oscar might have been lying."

Second, I heard the front door open and glanced down the hallway to see a swarm of photographers stampeding toward us.

*Fuck.*

If Scotty got attacked by the paparazzi right now just as everything was going crazy, there wasn't a chance in hell he'd stay. They'd scare him off. I was sure of it.

It was Pete all over again.

"Scotty, I need you to go to the den. Take your mom too." My voice came out short and brusque because I had about half a second before the paps overran the room and I needed him gone. I needed him *safe*. "Now!"

His eyes widened in surprise tinged with hurt. I didn't have time to explain, so I met Cyndee's eyes and gave her a pointed look. She understood instantly, grabbing his elbow and pulling him away down the hallway.

As they left she glanced back at me. But Scotty didn't. It was more painful than any physical blow. My chest grew tighter, my lungs squeezing until there was no air left.

Just then a man with vibrantly blue hair sauntered into the room gesturing over his shoulder. "These guys were all waiting outside for some reason? And it was cold so I, like, let them in? Hope you're cool with that." He chucked a set of familiar car keys onto the coffee table and collapsed onto one of the couches. "Also, dude, whoever loaned me their car? You have shitty taste in music. Like, the *worst*."

At the sight of him, Marigold shrieked, "Cyan, you motherfucker!" as she let go of the gladiator to storm over to him. The statue wobbled, catching for a moment against the wall. It stayed that way for a heartbeat, teetering, looking like it almost might stay standing. Until it finally tipped, crashing to the floor with a massive bang that shook the walls and sent vibrations surging through me.

The wave of paparazzi hit then, snapping pictures, firing flashes, missing nothing.

And suddenly all I saw was white. All I knew was panic. I was a child back in the car as a thunderstorm surged around me, my father forever unreachable outside. I turned and bolted, the familiar sound of camera shutters clattering behind me, capturing it all.

# 25

## SCOTTY

*Mama Said There'd Be Days Like This*

THE MOMENT I'd heard the angry tone of his voice I'd known it was over between Roman and me.

I'd wanted to stay, to face the craziness of the day at his side, but instead, I'd run like the coward I was. And when I'd turned, I'd seen what had caused him to bark at me: a man with blue hair leading a swarm of photographers right to him.

I'd tried to go back to him, to stand by his side and support him—prove to him how strong I was, that I could handle it so long as we were together—but my mother had clutched my elbow and dragged me away. "We can't let them see us," she'd hissed.

And I'd suddenly understood.

I'd thought the look of anger and resignation on his face had been because of the sudden appearance of the paparazzi. But in that moment, I'd realized I'd been wrong, It was because of me. And my mom. The tabloid press had arrived and Roman's first thought had been to get me and my mom out of sight. It wasn't that I thought he was embarrassed by us. I knew better than that at this point. But we were still trouble. We were a complication he didn't need right now even if he didn't think the worst of us. He needed steady, and I was anything but.

The realization cut me deep.

It was all my fault. Every ounce of chaos bombarding him was because of me. I'd been the one to encourage Marigold in her loony schemes. I'd been the one to invite Larry and Lolo to stay, I'd been the one who told Roman to invite Polly to Vermont, I hadn't been able to get my own mom to leave, and I'd even been the reason Diana, Earl, and the girls were here to get mixed up in it all. Roman had come here to relax and lie low.

And now his entire world was caving in on him and it was all because of me.

I was trembling by the time I reached the den. I went straight to the empty fireplace, hoping that the memory of heat and light might warm the chill that was slowly swallowing my heart. Behind me, my mother quietly closed the door and stood for a moment. I knew she was watching me, considering me, waiting for me to turn and yell at her for selling Roman out to the tabloids. After all, how else would they have known where to find him?

But I was suddenly too exhausted.

It was too much, all of it. It was the kind of chaos that always followed me, that found me no matter where I hid. I thought that if I was careful, I would be able to keep it at bay, keep it from interfering in Roman's life, but today had been a sobering wake-up call.

Roman wanted security and peace. I was anything but that. I was boisterous and trouble and loud and inappropriate in every way. The notion of me on the red carpet, or at a high-end restaurant—even the barest thought of having to learn how to travel in those circles made my chest tighten with anxiety. I wasn't made for that kind of life. I was a kid from the streets—no formal education, no polish, no money.

"I didn't sell Roman's location to the paparazzi," my mother finally said quietly.

I lifted a shoulder. What did it even matter anymore? They were here. Me and my mom couldn't be trusted. That was that.

She moved farther into the den, drawing closer. "Scotty, I know you think I did, but I didn't."

"If not this time, you would have next time," I said, my voice sounding weak and tired. "I saw the gleam in your eyes when you heard Polly talk about her baby's father. You're always going to look at the world with dollar signs attached to everything."

She didn't say anything for a long moment. I glanced over to find her staring at me, her eyes bright with unshed tears. The woman could cry on a dime. It was one of her more effective cons. "Don't," I warned her.

"You love him, don't you?"

I looked back at the empty fireplace, the ashes still scattered across the stone hearth. The answer was yes. I knew it instantly. Like a lock clicking open, a truth finally acknowledged. It seemed impossible that I could fall in love with someone in such a short period of time, but sometimes that's how love worked.

I'd fallen in love with Nugget the moment I'd smoothed my hand down her neck and felt her nose nudge my shoulder.

"It doesn't matter," I told her.

She pressed her lips together and started to slowly circle the room, her eyes taking in the bookshelves, the decor, the artwork. I wondered if she was looking for something to filch, so I was surprised when she said, "I didn't love your father."

I snorted. "Great, that makes me feel better. Thanks, Mom."

"In fact I've only ever been in love with one person in my life," she said.

She was behind me now, so I had to turn to ask the question. "Who?"

"You, of course."

I rolled my eyes. "That doesn't count."

"It does too," she insisted. "There isn't a thing in this world I wouldn't do for you, Scotty."

"You mean like give up grifting?" I asked bitterly.

She took a sharp breath, and I noticed a flash of irritation in her eyes. "It's the only thing I've ever been good at, Scotty. And it was the only way I could keep us safe and put food on the table."

"Sure," I said, crossing my arms. "Blame me. It's my fault you had to defraud people so you could take care of me."

She'd come full circle around the room and now stood next to me. She held out a hand and tentatively rested it on my shoulder. I realized belatedly the familiar acrid scent of cigarette smoke that had always drifted around her was missing. In fact, she hadn't smelled like cigarettes since she'd arrived. Before I could ask her about it, she spoke. "I would never intentionally hurt you. I saw the way you looked at Roman, I figured out how you felt about him. Love like that is priceless—I wouldn't sell it for anything."

I looked away, blinking away the sting of tears. I wanted to believe her, but I couldn't bear to have my heart broken twice in the same day. "Well, it doesn't matter now," I said, the words sounding watery.

"That man loves you," she said.

God I wished it were true. I shook my head. It was too painful to have to deny it out loud.

"He does, Scotty," she insisted. "You know what being a con artist taught me? How to read people. You have that gift as well; it's what makes you so good at your job. You know what people need, what they want, and you figure out how to give it to them. You can read Roman as good as I can—better even. You know he loves you."

I dropped my chin to my chest. "If he loves me it's only out here—when we can exist in this bubble. But in the real world..." I trailed off, sighing.

"In the real world is where the work begins," she said. "It's easy to love someone when life is good, when food is plentiful and money isn't a concern. But true love—real love, the kind you know will be there through thick and thin—that kind of love is forged in the real world. When you're hungry and tired and scared and you know that when you reach out your hand, someone will be there to take it and hold you and support you and know you and love you. If you can love and be loved in the real world, you know that love is truth."

My throat tightened. Tears pricked the backs of my eyes. I wanted to believe her, about all of it, but I didn't know how.

Her hand still rested on my shoulder and she squeezed. "Now I'm going to go talk to that helicopter pilot and see about hitching a ride back to the city so you can continue to enjoy your man without your mom hovering around."

She started toward the door, but I reached out and grabbed her hand, stopping her. The kind of love she was talking about, the kind that existed in hunger and fear, I understood that she was describing how she felt about me. And regardless of all the pain she'd caused me in my life, my mother had truly always been there for me.

"Thanks, Mom," I told her. And I meant it. "I believe you about the tabloids," I added. I wasn't quite sure how much I meant that, but there was enough truth to the statement that I felt comfortable saying it.

She pressed her lips together, her chin quivering for a moment before sniffing and forcing a smile. "I mean, I'm not gonna lie and say I didn't think about selling him out. But you got a good thing going here. You and Roman end up together, I'm set for life, baby." She held up a finger, wagging it. "But you better lock that shit down, or I'm gonna start getting antsy."

Her eyes twinkled with that familiar glint, and I laughed, knowing that though she made it sound like a joke, there was still an edge of truth to it. With that, she patted my hand and slipped out of the den, leaving me alone with my thoughts.

I hated being alone with my thoughts. I was used to being surrounded by the hustle and bustle of kids and parents at the park, asking about Nugget and sharing their enthusiasm for adventure with me. At the thought of my big, sweet girl, I knew exactly where I needed to be. The place that always brought me peace and clarity.

I slipped out through one of the den doors. The snow was thick, my boots sinking deep, and I shivered as flurries swarmed around me. It had probably been stupid of me to come outside without a coat, but my winter clothes were in the mudroom and that was practically chaos central. I'd rather brave the cold than Roman at the moment.

My mother's words still swarmed through my head as I shouldered my way through the storm to the barn. Inside was warmer, but not much. I didn't stop shivering until I reached Nugget and wrapped my arms around her neck, letting her heat seep through me.

She nudged at my shoulder with increasing pressure until I was forced to let go. "I know, I know," I told her, reaching for a carrot from the nearby bucket and feeding it to her. The soft fuzz of her nose tickled my palm as she sniffed for any bits of food she might have missed. I laughed and fed her another.

"All I have to do is keep offering you carrots and you love me without question," I laughed. "If only it were that easy with people."

I understood what my mother was saying about love and the real world, but what she'd been missing was that sometimes love might not be enough. Roman could love me all he wanted, but if all I did was bring chaos into his life, if all I did was make him more miserable and more resentful of the tabloid scrutiny, what kind of happily ever after would that leave for us?

You could love someone and still not end up with them. That was the tragedy of love that all the songs and movies and books failed to show. And the thought of loving Roman but not being able to be with him was more painful than I could bear.

But at the same time, I had to admit, I was terrified of trying. Of giving my heart away and trusting the other person to care for it as if it were their own. I was used to being alone in my heart. I'd made my peace with it. What if I came to rely on Roman? What if I leaned on him and then one day he wasn't there? What if I became too much for him: my chaos, my brashness, my over-the-topness?

What if he left and I had to be alone again and I didn't remember how? What if loving him left me broken and unable to live without him?

Nugget nudged me again, shifting her feet. She was restless. She hadn't stretched her legs since the morning before, and as the storm grew worse, it would only get more difficult to take her out. I decided

I should do it now while there was still daylight and visibility was decent.

I shuffled down to the tack room and rummaged around for an old coat, a hat, and gloves. Then I grabbed the saddle Earl had found in a storage room and lugged it to Nugget's stall. It took me a while to get her tacked up, but finally she was ready and I led her out of the barn and into the winter afternoon. She'd pulled my carriage through weather way worse than this and didn't even blink a long-lashed eye at the swirling snow.

It took three tries and a whole lot of grunting and cursing before I finally hoisted myself up into the saddle. I clicked my tongue against my teeth, squeezing with my knee to nudge Nugget toward a trail that looped through the trees around the property. She shifted under my weight, getting accustomed to me before plodding toward the path.

As we made our way through the snow, I thought about everything I was going to lose. My chin tightened until my jaw began to ache.

It wasn't like me to throw a pity party for myself. My mom had a saying that always snapped me out of melancholy moods and helped me spring into action to fix it.

*You're not a victim, you're a victor.*

I repeated that phrase in my head like one of Sonya and Nay-Nay's chants. What would victory look like in this case?

*Roman and me together and strong, facing the paparazzi side by side.*

I thought about it some more, envisioned a strong, united front. What if I was looking at it all wrong? What if, instead of a half-cocked, homeless freak of a boyfriend, I was Roman's steady, centering life partner? What if, instead of the two of us retreating to our lonely lives of separate solitude, we helped each other find a different way forward? Together.

I blew out a frosty breath and shook my head. I was an idiot. Maybe instead of trying to get Mom and me out of sight of the paps because we were an embarrassment, he was trying to save me from their pushy interfering ways.

That sounded much more like the Roman Burke I knew.

And what if, instead of my mom leaking his location to the photographers, they'd somehow been tipped by Polly or her helicopter pilot?

I wasn't about to give up on Roman Burke. If he wanted me gone, which I was starting to suspect he didn't, he was going to have to tell it straight to my face.

After turning Nugget around to head back, I felt the saddle shift under me like it had suddenly loosened. It felt exactly like what would happen if I didn't wait for Nugget to let out her breath before cinching it again, but I knew I had.

I hopped off quickly and examined the saddle straps, noticing the flank cinch had frayed almost completely apart. That's what I got for using someone else's old saddle. I hadn't wanted to use Earl's nice one without permission, so I'd grabbed the random ancient one from the tack room.

"Shit," I muttered. It was going to be a cold walk back. "Sorry, sweet girl. Narrowly averted a disaster there because I wasn't using my head."

I followed Nugget's tracks back the way we came, keeping my face down and out of the wet flurries. I spied a stripe of weak sunlight up ahead and lifted my head to see a lovely clearing I hadn't noticed on the way there.

I slowed Nugget to a stop and took a deep breath, moving into the beam of sun and closing my eyes. Before wandering back to face Roman and the media, I decided to take one last moment of quiet solitude to gather my strength and become the man Roman needed me to be.

# 26

---

## ROMAN

*Inside A Celebrity Meltdown: Roman Burke Hits Rock Bottom*

I STOOD with my hands braced on the bathroom sink, my face dripping from where I'd splashed myself with cold water, hoping the shock of it would calm my racing heart. When the photographers had swarmed in, my first thought had been of Scotty. Once he'd turned and fled, my only other thought had been of escape.

I'd ducked through the first door I'd come across which had landed me in the downstairs powder room. It was a small space, every surface covered with mirrors for some reason I couldn't understand, and the sight of my panicked expression staring back at me from every reflection had me flicking off the lights and standing in darkness while I'd struggled to catch my breath.

My mind had spun a million miles a minute, and I'd forced myself to stop and focus. *Breathe*, I'd told myself. Just breathe. I was okay. Scotty was okay. My family was okay. We were safe. I just needed to breathe.

After several moments, my lungs had loosened, the pain in my chest had eased, and my heart rate had slowed, the flood of adrenaline working its way out of my body. I'd let out one last long trembling breath and flicked on the lights.

An infinity of my own reflection stared back at me from all the mirrors. It was a startling and overwhelming effect, and I was just glad I didn't have to pee because I couldn't imagine anyone wanting to watch themselves on the toilet from so many different angles. "Jesus fuck, Oscar," I muttered as I turned on the sink. "What were you thinking?"

Splashing cold water on my face helped, and I was just drying off when there was a knock at the door. "Roman?" my sister asked, her voice tight with concern. "You okay in there? It's safe to come out now, the photographers are gone."

I opened the door cautiously, peeking out to find the main room practically empty, only Lolo and Trevor talking quietly at the kitchen table with mugs of coffee between them. "Where... where the hell is everyone? How long was I in there?"

"Not too long, believe it or not," Diana said, taking my arm and leading me to a nearby chair next to the kitchen. "Earl took the girls to our suite for naps, Marigold and Preppy Dude snuck out the back when they realized there were three additional state troopers here, Polly is on the phone with her man, and Cyndee went to get you some juice. The troopers came in right behind the paparazzi and started threatening to take them into custody. In the process, apparently Larry was outed as a Louisiana state senator who'd done some naughty things—"

"Don't call me that," Lolo chastised her from across the room. "Besides, it was the other way around. And I only did it for the photos. His wife hired me. I had to take the blue pill to even make it through, for god's sake. *Ew.*" He shivered and closed his eyes. Trevor reached out a hand to squeeze his shoulder.

Diana continued. "—and whose son was involved last night in a convenience store robbery."

"Good god," I said, shaking my head as I tried to keep up with the flood of information. "Quality family."

"Needless to say, he left."

Cyndee approached cautiously with the juice. "Here, see if this helps."

I reached out a shaky hand and took the small glass from her, relishing the sweet, cold taste on my tongue. "Thanks. Where's Scotty?"

Cyndee and Diana exchanged a look.

I sat straighter in the chair. "Where is he?"

Neither answered and my heart immediately began to hammer again. "Di, where is he?" My voice was high and panicked. I looked around but didn't see him anywhere.

"Did he... did he *leave*?" I asked, the words barely a whisper.

"No," Cyndee said firmly. "He'll be back. I'm sure of it."

I looked frantically at Diana. "He'll be back means he left. Where is he?"

She gave me a helpless look. "I don't know."

I turned toward Cyndee and she shook her head, making it clear she didn't know either.

I spun, intending to tear the house apart from top to bottom—all ten thousand square feet of it—when I realized that I knew exactly where he'd gone. To the barn. To Nugget. He'd told me that growing up the barn had always been the one constant, the most stable environment. It was where he went when he needed to center himself or to think or to wrap his arms around his horse's neck and remember he was loved.

My jaw clenched. If I had my way, that man would never question that he was loved ever again. I would spend the rest of my life making sure he knew it to be true.

I stood up, ignoring the leftover unsteadiness. The mudroom had my boots and coat, so I headed there. "I don't understand why he left."

"Roman," Diana said, following after me. "He saw the paparazzi here and bolted."

I froze a moment, letting that sink in. Hearing that the photographers had scared him away shouldn't have surprised me, but it did.

Yes, it had been my biggest worry, but I'd truly thought he was different from Pete. I'd thought he was stronger and feistier.

"He couldn't fucking take it?" I spat. "The first sign of trouble and he bolts? Jesus. That's exactly why I sent him to another room—so this wouldn't happen!"

I shoved my arms into my coat and stomped into my boots. My teeth clenched in anger. "That motherfucker better run. He'd better run far away from me. Fucking coward. I'm going to find him and give him a motherfucking piece of my goddamned mind."

I was angry enough to punch something, and I almost ripped a hole in my palm pulling my boot laces tight.

Diana's eyes brightened and a smile appeared on her face.

"What?" I growled at her.

"You're pissed." She said it like it was a good thing. It wasn't.

"Damned right I'm pissed! He doesn't get to give up that easily. He doesn't get to promise me pretty words and make me think he's different and then he bails at the first sign of trouble. Fuck that, Di." My voice rose until I was practically shouting. "Fuck him."

A giggle escaped her throat, and she clamped both hands over her mouth. Her eyes danced, and it brought back memories of when she used to tease me for having a crush on the kid who'd brought the fancy rooster to the county fair.

I glowered at her. "Stop laughing, dammit," I hissed, standing back up. "This is awful. He's breaking my fucking heart, Diana!" My voice broke and I refused to lose control.

"He's not Pete," she said with a grin.

"Of course he's not Pete," I spat. "Pete was nicer than him! He didn't cause trouble like this."

I grabbed a scarf and wrapped it around my neck several times before belatedly realizing it was his super-soft gray one, the one he'd worn the day we'd met. It smelled like him and almost brought me to my knees.

"And you let him go," Diana said, her voice gentler.

I turned to her in confusion. "Huh?"

"You didn't once fight to keep Peter."

My nostrils flared. I couldn't concentrate on what she was saying. "Whatever. Fucking coward," I grumbled again. Because if I didn't stay angry at Scotty, I'd curl up into a ball and die.

Cyndee stood behind Diana, worrying her hands together, looking unusually contrite. "He thinks it was all his fault."

I snapped my eyes to her. "What?"

"The paps coming. The chaos," she explained. "He thinks it's all his fault. That's why he ran."

I didn't understand. "Why would it be his fault?" I asked. "They're always fucking here! They're everywhere! It's what they do."

"And you always hate it," Diana broke in. "And he knows that. So if he thinks they were here because of him, he thinks he's the cause of your unhappiness."

Fuck. I dropped my face into my hands. She was right. That's what I'd seen in his eyes when I'd told him to leave the room earlier: guilt. Remorse. Pain.

And it was all my fault.

"I have to go," I croaked.

I pulled the door open and stalked out into the twilight of the stormy late afternoon. Drifts of new snow piled up everywhere, and the temperature had dropped to bitter levels. But I didn't feel the cold because I was too worried about Scotty. Too focused on getting to him, holding him.

I followed faint bootprints toward the stable, expecting to find him holed up with his best girl. But when I stepped inside, neither one of them was there.

"Fuck," I muttered to the empty stall. "Such a fucking idiot. That sweet fucking man."

I sprinted out of the barn, searching for hoofprints that might indicate where they'd gone. I found a faint trail of them leading toward the woods, a pile of partially frozen poop indicating they'd left not too long ago.

I set out after them, hoping like hell he hadn't gone too far for me to get there on foot. I plunged into the woods, the canopy of firs overhead blocking the worst of the wind and turning the swirling flurries into dancing specks of snow. It was eerily still and quiet, the snow muting all sound. Except for one. I paused, the crunching of my boots falling silent, and tilted my head listening.

Was that... Lady Gaga? Being sung by a man? A very familiar, sexy man? My heart surged in relief. Only Scotty, I thought, would belt out "Born This Way" in the middle of a frozen forest during a snowstorm. And surely you couldn't belt it out the way Scotty was if you were half-frozen.

I slowed my steps, catching my breath and taking a moment to enjoy the sound of Scotty's voice. The pure vibrance of it. Scotty sang those words like he didn't give a fuck about what anyone thought.

Because that's who Scotty was: someone who lived life with no apologies.

And I loved him all the more for it.

He broke off singing mid-refrain and started talking to Nugget. "You know, I keep saying we're on the right track, baby, but I'm not so sure anymore. The hoofprints are hard to see in the shadows. And, like, no offense, but if it comes down to us spending the night out here, you're going to have to be the big spoon."

I put my hand over my mouth and bit back a sob. I loved this man so fucking much.

Scotty continued. "Do you think he's going to be mad?" The rest of his words were muffled, but the tone of his voice was enough to make me start to run. I couldn't bear him spending one more minute feeling guilty.

"Baby?" I called out.

Silence for a beat.

"Spartacus?" He sounded so unsure, it hurt my heart.

"Yeah, I'm here." I took the last part of the path at a sprint and came out into a clearing to find him standing next to Nugget.

We both froze and stared at each other for a split second before Scotty dropped the reins and flew at me. My anger had evaporated the minute I'd heard him singing to his horse, but when I felt him crash into me and remembered how it felt when I'd thought I'd lost him, it all came flooding back.

I shoved my hand into his hair, holding him against me. "You aren't allowed to leave me!" I cried into his neck. "God, Scotty, I thought you'd left me. You can't leave me, dammit. That's not how this works. You said... we said... and you... you can't..." The sobs came out for real, finally, and I could barely catch my breath.

He wriggled around until he could grab my neck and yank me toward him, smashing our lips together just long enough for me to know we were okay, and then he pulled away to let me breathe.

"I love you," he said urgently, meeting my eyes with his own bright blue ones. "I love you so much and I don't want to be the reason you're—"

"You're not," I said in a rush. Incredulous he could think such a thing. "Jesus, you're the best thing that's ever happened to me, you idiot. I needed you with me. I *need* you with me. I can't do this without you anymore."

I pulled him closer, pressing my forehead against his. "I was missing something huge and I didn't know it, Scotty. It was you. It was always you I was missing. Please. Please don't leave me. I'm not sure I'll survive it."

He pulled back so he could look me in the eyes. "I don't want to ever be a burden," he warned.

I cupped his cheeks. "I don't want to ever be alone."

"I don't want to be dependent."

"I don't want you to ever resent me."

We grinned stupidly at each other.

"My mom didn't sell you out," Scotty said.

I smiled, running my thumb along his cheekbone. "I know, baby. One of the photographers bribed the info from an employee at the helicopter company."

"Oh good. But, um..." He bit his lip, and I wanted to run my mouth along the mark his teeth had left. "I can't promise Mom won't... I mean, in the future—"

I cut him off. "I don't care. I love you," I said. Happiness bubbled out of me. "I love you so fucking much, Scotty Pinker."

He jumped back up and kissed me, throwing his arms tightly

around my neck and his legs around my waist despite our bulky winter gear. I spun around while we kissed and kissed and kissed in the snowy clearing in the woods.

It was magic.

Until we heard the clicking and saw the flashes go off.

I instinctively set him back down and curled around him, trying to keep him out of sight and protect him from them, but he pressed a hand against my chest.

I looked down at him questioningly.

"We can't hide from them forever," Scotty said softly.

I clenched my jaw, wanting to protest. Wanting to tell him that it wasn't fair—this was our moment, and it shouldn't belong to anyone else. "But can't we hide a little longer?"

He ran his thumb along the back of my hand. "Baby, this is part of your life. Part of *our* life now. You think they're going to drive me away, but they're not."

"You can't say that." My voice broke and I swallowed. "You can't know that. What happens if in a month or a year or a decade it becomes too much?"

"Oh, Roman." There was such tenderness in his eyes, such love. Scotty reached up and brushed his fingertips along my temple, threading them into my hair. "There is nothing that will ever drive me away from you. You are worth it in every way imaginable."

"But—"

He didn't let me finish. "And I intend to make sure the whole world knows that." Scotty dragged my head back down to his, sealing his lips over mine.

I resisted, for just a moment, surprised by his boldness. "You're mine," he growled into my mouth.

I nodded, holding him tighter, my tongue sweeping into his mouth before whispering. "Yes. I'm yours."

And all the while the cameras clicked and flashed around us. But I didn't care because all that mattered to me was in my arms in that moment.

When we finally broke the kiss, both of us gasping for breath, the questions started. They came at us fast and loud, and I tensed, waiting for Scotty to balk at the intensity of it. But instead he took my hand in his and leaned in.

"Here's the deal," he said, addressing them directly. "I get it. You're trying to make a living, and this is the best way you know how. Trust me, I understand what it is to hustle. Trust me," he added, his eyes focused and clear.

"But this"—he gestured his fingers between us and them—"us, it's a two-way street. If you guys push too hard, Roman and I can start using anti-flash scarves, or wearing the same clothes day in and day out so your photos look dated and reused, or we can beat you to the punch selling our own pics, or we can stay holed up inside all the time, but then where will that get you?"

The photographers shifted, unsure how to react to this unknown newcomer confronting them. A few still snapped photos, but most listening too.

"I totally understand wanting to get pics of Roman—I mean, look at the man," he said, gesturing toward me. "He's a *gorgeous* individual, and that face sells magazines. His body sells even more," he said, laughing. "Hell, I've probably bought half of them just so I can gaze at his adorable face."

I blushed madly while several of the photographers snickered.

"So why don't we do each other a solid and maybe work together on some of this stuff?" Scotty suggested.

I tensed, wondering if he really understood what he was saying, but he just clenched my hand tighter, indicating that he knew what he was doing and I needed to trust him. Which I did.

"We'll make sure you get the photos you need—good ones too, like tonight," he said. "And when we're on the street, I get it— we're fair game. That's the way this works. But when we ask for privacy, we expect to get it."

Several of the photographers eyed each other, unsure how to feel about the request. That they were still listening surprised me. They were sharks, and to them Scotty was chum.

"One more thing," Scotty continued, holding up a finger. "And this is important. If any one of you runs into trouble in life, and I mean real trouble like you can't put food on the table for your kid or you're about to miss a mortgage payment, you let us know and we'll get you what you need."

My eyes bulged at the request, and Scotty just gripped my hand tighter. "I mean it," he continued. "Like I said, I've been there. You wouldn't be hiding out here in the freezing snow if you had other options. I respect what you're doing, and I respect how hard you're working, and in return I'm asking you to respect us as well." He paused, eyeing them each individually. "Got it?"

They glanced at one another, still unsure about this new guy making demands on them. "Now, in a minute we're going to invite you all into the house where it's nice and warm and we've got plenty of food and drink and enough rooms for you all to bunk up until the storm passes. *But,*" he said, "that's on the condition you leave your cameras outside. Any one of you breaches that trust, you all lose out. Are we all on the same page?"

To my astonishment, every single one of the photographers nodded, several of them mumbling their agreement. It was astonishing. I'd never seen anything like it.

Scotty then clapped his hands and flashed a million-dollar smile. "Great. Now that we have that sorted, we'll take a few questions before heading back inside. Who's first?"

"Are the two of you a couple?" the first woman asked.

"Yes," I answered with a big smile, beating Scotty to the punch.

"He's trying to lock it down," Scotty said with a laugh. "You heard it here first. We're going steady. And what's your name?" he asked the woman.

She frowned, clearly surprised by the question. "Um... Amanda."

"Great, thanks, Amanda. Who's next?"

"Why are you in Vermont?" another reporter asked.

"And your name is?" Scotty asked.

"Zachary," he said.

"Thanks, Zachary. Roman finished filming *Deep Cut* and was going to take some time off to unwind. When he realized the place where he was staying had a stable for my horse, he offered for us to join him."

Total lie, but I would have done just that if I'd truly understood how much he needed it. And he knew it.

"Scotty, is it true your mother just got out of prison?" another asked.

Scotty looked at the man, clearly waiting for something else, and the man shuffled a moment before saying, "Oh, yeah, I'm Ralfie."

"Thanks, Ralfie. Nice to meet you. Yes, it's true," Scotty said confidently. "She and I have both struggled with poverty since she dropped out of high school to raise me, and that's led to some poor decisions. Thankfully, Roman has been very understanding since he himself has made poor decisions in the past like we all have. Cough, *Back Passage*, cough. We both agree that our past is what helps inform our future, and we can learn from our mistakes to become better people. Roman, did you have anything to add?"

"Mostly that I love you. Like, a lot. A staggering amount, really."

He stared at me in surprise, the pink of his cold cheeks blooming into the deeper red of a blush.

"You're beautiful and kind and real, and I'm..." My throat thickened, and I tried swallowing. "And I'm so lucky to know you."

Scotty's eyes filled and he cleared his throat, trying to fight the emotion. He turned back toward the group of reporters, who looked shell-shocked at my public admission. "That's all fair game to print," he told them, and they laughed. I realized he had them eating out of the palm of his hand. Because he saw them as people, individuals with names and families and jobs and responsibilities.

It was the same thing he'd done to me. He'd looked past the superstar persona to find the real me. Because that's who he was: genuine, and kind, and attentive, and generous, and loving, and hot as fuck.

And mine. I reached up a hand to his cheek, drawing my thumb along his jaw. I leaned in close, pressing my lips to his ear so only he could hear. "I love you, Scotty Pinker."

I felt him tremble, and I tightened my arms around him. "I love you too, Roman Burke," he murmured against my neck. For a moment we stayed that way, inseparable. And there were no camera flashes, no sound of shutters closing. They were giving us this moment because they knew it belonged to us alone.

I took a moment to inhale the scent of Scotty, of hay and outdoors and new love. Then I pulled back and dropped a kiss on his nose, basking in the adoration in his eyes, before turning to the paparazzi. "You'll want to have your cameras ready for this one," I told them.

As soon as they were ready, I took Scotty in my arms and kissed him again for all he was worth.

# 27

## SCOTTY - SEPTEMBER

*Superstar And Stable-Boy Partner Settle Near Summit Hill*

WHEN YOUR BOYFRIEND comes running out of your new barn at top speed, hops in your carriage, and screams, "Go!"—you go.

You don't stop and ask for a kiss. Or a hug. Or an explanation of why he's naked. You simply follow his shouted orders about where to drive.

At least, that's what I did when it happened to me.

After the sexy man jumped in shouting, I snapped the reins on Nugget's big brown ass and felt the carriage lurch along the dirt trail into the woods. Fat rabbits and terrified squirrels leaped out of the way, spilling mouthfuls of nuts and tripping over their tails and feet to skitter into the underbrush.

Onward we surged. It was a race toward the swimming hole, or so I assumed. I hunkered down in my seat and sallied forth up Summit Hill toward the waterfall. There was blessedly nothing around us. No press, no lookie-loos, no friends or family or meddling neighbors anywhere within the hundred-and-fifty-acre property we now owned in Connecticut.

"Are we heading to the swimming hole?" I called back with a laugh. "And why are you naked?

"Just go!" he shouted. I could hear the smile in his voice.

When we reached the edge of the swimming hole, I turned around in time to see Roman climb over the seat to join me in the front. Sun angled down through the trees and lit up his handsome face as well as his chest, which was unfortunately still bare from the waxing he'd had to do for his new film. I reached out and smoothed a hand across it.

"I can't wait till I get this hair back. You look weird without it," I admitted, letting his stunning body distract me.

Roman ran sneaky fingers up the inside of my shorts and discovered my lack of underwear.

"Mmm, naughty boy," he teased, leaning in to nip at my earlobe. "Lose the clothes."

We made out like teenagers on the bench of the carriage Roman had managed to procure from my old boss and have transported to our new farm. Apparently the asshole had agreed to let us have it in exchange for me coming back to do a few "celebrity" carriage rides at the park during the holidays. This was after he'd repeatedly begged me to come back to work as his driver and Roman had nearly lost his shit at the guy, accusing him of wanting to use me for my status as Roman Burke's other half.

Without taking my lips from Roman's skin, I wriggled out of my clothes and began pulling him toward the edge of the bench so we could move this lovefest down into the cool water. Understandably, I got distracted by his hands on my ass and lost track of time again until he finally pulled back with a grunt and said, "What's that?"

I swiveled my head and saw the piece of outdoor furniture Kip had helped me install the day before. We'd had to use the farm utility vehicle to haul it out here, so I'd been grateful once again for Kip's experience on his parents' farm growing up. There was still so much I had to learn about managing a large property like this, but I loved every minute of it. I was pretty sure Roman was getting as much joy out of it as I was. Despite the intermittent travel of his film schedule last month, when Roman was home, he always insisted on being the one to mow the lawn on the big fancy riding mower.

"That's a surprise for you," I said, nudging him down so I could show it to him. "Remember when we were looking at properties and you fell in love with this spot?"

"Of course I do. All I could think about was skinny-dipping with you on hot days after your riding lessons were done."

"Well, there's a woman in town who does woodworking, and I hired her to make this. Come see."

I led him to the large granite slab–topped bench with a carved wooden storage cubby below. I crouched down and showed him how to open the hidden compartment.

Roman knelt in the dirt next to me. "Is that lube?"

"Towels, suits, lube, baby wipes, bottled water, first aid kit, and even a flashlight if we lose track of time," I explained. "Everything I could think of to ensure our ability to have spontaneous rendezvous out here whenever we wanted to."

Roman leaned in and ran his finger over the carved inscription on the wooden panel.

*Life is a joyful adventure, and we will live it like no one is watching.*

It was a motto we'd decided on after the incident in Vermont. We'd spent hours talking about how we wanted to handle the media's intrusion into our lives. I'd explained to Roman that it wasn't fair to allow a fear of stupid headlines to imprison him in his own home. Moreover, it wasn't the way I was ever going to live my own life. I was a people person, and I wanted to live out loud no matter who saw and judged me.

We'd discussed worst-case scenarios in which Roman ultimately came to the conclusion that he had enough money to live on for the rest of his life, even if he never got another role in another movie. So what was he so afraid of?

Coming to that realization was like allowing the sun to shine unimpeded on his life. Roman's shoulders didn't seem to carry the same burdens as before, and he was less likely to let directors and producers control his media contact. He'd lost one potential movie deal because of this new attitude, but another had come along to take its place within days.

After all, he was still Roman Burke—box office heartthrob and silver-screen superstar.

"Can we use the lube right now?" Roman asked sheepishly, stroking his already hard dick. "Just to make sure it works?"

"Duh," I said, pulling out one of the extra-large towels to spread on the grass nearby. "Get your horny ass over here."

"It's not my ass that's horny," he muttered. "But it's your ass that's making me horny. And your fucking thigh muscles since you started riding so much. Jesus."

I felt my face heat. It was true. Since Kip and I had been spending hours prepping the horses for our after-school riding lessons this fall, I'd spent most of the past two months in the saddle. Something about me on the back of a horse had triggered all kinds of fantasies in Roman. One night I'd gotten out of the shower to discover a pair of assless chaps laid out on our bed and an already hard Roman blushing furiously next to them while holding a lasso.

That had been a fun night, but the next morning, my mother hadn't been able to make eye contact with us in the kitchen and had announced her move to the guest house would be completed a week earlier than expected. Win-win.

I lay back on the towel and made the gimme gesture toward him with my fingers. Roman crawled on top of me with a predatory grin. Within seconds, we were back to making out and rubbing against each other like horny teens. Thank god we weren't actually fucking yet, because the familiar low titter of Lolo's laughter came through the trees.

"No, darling, they won't mind. They said I could use their love hole whenever they weren't here."

There wasn't even time to gag at the term *love hole* before we scrambled up and wrapped towels around our waists.

"Lolo, what the fuck?" Roman barked as Lolo stepped into the clearing with a man who was definitely not Officer SexyBeard.

"Where's Trevor?" I snapped. "Who the fuck is this?"

Lolo looked down his nose at me like I was an inconvenient rodent. "If you must know, this is Pascal Charbonneau—*the* hottest star in boudoir photography right now."

"Lolo, are you back here somewhere? You forgot your aubergine peignoir," a shrill voice called through the trees. "Holy shit, did I just step in horse poop?"

Marigold stepped into the clearing, limping so as not to further poopify her shoe. "There's not enough Grey Goose in the world to make up for this sh—" She looked up and caught us all gawping at her. "What?"

Roman's jaw clenched. "Why are you all here?"

"In your fuck hole?" Marigold asked.

"*Love* hole," Lolo muttered. "Don't be crass."

"Ew," I said with a shudder. "Neither. Please."

Roman stepped closer and pulled me against his side. The faint scent of his sweat and deodorant battling for dominance made my head spin and my cock fill again despite the mixed company.

It deflated the second I saw Polly and Howard stroll hand in hand into the fray. Howard had little Charlotte in a baby carrier on his chest like the proud papa he was.

"There you are," Polly said with a sigh of relief. "Your moms are looking for you two, and Diana said she can't hold them back much longer."

Before we had a chance to ask why, Collins stumbled out of the trees and almost tripped over a tree root. "You left me behind," he whined at Marigold. "I told you I wanted to see sexy stork dude get naked for whatshisface."

He seemed to realize the rest of us could see and hear him because he suddenly stopped speaking with a squeak.

Lolo spoke dismissively. "You do know I have *close* connections to law enforcement, yes?"

"Sorry," Collins muttered. "Um... Scotty, your mom says to come back because she's throwing you a surprise engagement party tonight and you two need to be there. Obviously."

I stared at him.

Everyone else stared at him as well.

"Seriously?" Marigold asked. "Did you even listen to the words coming out of your mouth?"

His eyes went wide. "What?" he asked, clearly confused at why he was suddenly the target of so much ire.

"The secret part, dear," Lolo stage whispered, loud enough for us all to hear. "Pretty sure someone here didn't know about a certain something."

He scrunched up his face, still not understanding. "But I already knew about the party."

Marigold rolled her eyes. "Dear lord. I swear, sometimes..." she muttered.

Before they could continue the argument, Roman threw up his hands. "Oh for fuck's sake," he grumbled before turning to the group of crazies we, for some ridiculous reason, called friends. This time he shouted at full volume. "Everyone, get the fuck out of my fuck hole right the hell now!"

There was silence for a beat, and then everyone began scrambling around in circles like a damned comedy sketch. I could hear Marigold continuing to scold Collins as they retreated back toward the main house, while Lolo suggested some creative posing he could do using the wooden fencing surrounding one of the paddocks. Polly just blew me a kiss and winked, linking her arm through Howard's as they wandered away.

Finally, fucking *finally*, we had the area to ourselves again.

I turned around to find Roman spreading out another towel on the grass. I clasped my hands in front of me and then rubbed my palms against the towel, suddenly nervous. Because there was another key detail Collins had seemed to miss about announcing the secret engagement party that evening: Roman and I *weren't* engaged.

And that's what had me pressing my fingers to my lips to keep from blurting out questions. I was too terrified to believe what Collins had implied.

"Do we have money in the budget to electrify our property fence line?" Roman grumbled, moving over to grab my hand and pull me down next to him.

"I warned you," I said defensively. "I told you my mom was trouble. 'Give her a job,' you said. 'She can do admin for the riding school,' you said. Well, now you know, she's nothing but tr—"

Roman snorted, building quickly into unstoppable laughter. I watched him let go and enjoyed the ride. When he finally calmed down enough to catch his breath, he cupped my chin and forced me to meet his eyes.

"We have the best life ever, and I wouldn't want it any other way," he said with a sweet smile. "You're crazy and chaotic and our friends are even worse. And you... this... makes me laugh every single day. Scotty... I don't ever want to be lonely and bored and isolated again. I want this... all of this... with you. Forever."

My chest tightened painfully with hope, and I tried not to hold my breath as my heart threatened to burst from my chest.

Roman moved to his knees and grasped both of my hands in his. His eyes shone with love and adoration as he looked up at me, his lips curving into a smile. "Scotty Pinker," he said, his voice rough with emotion. "Will you do me the honor of becoming my partner for life, my husband?"

He barely had the words out of his mouth before I tackled him onto his back on the ground and kissed the fuck out of his face. "Yes," I told him. "Yesyesyesyes!" I repeated, just to make sure my answer was clear.

And from somewhere deep in the trees, we heard the unmistakable sound of a shutter clicking.

For once I was glad. The photo of our engagement would join the other invaluable memories framed on our walls, memories we had permanent records of thanks to the media: our carriage ride, Nugget's butt walking through the front door of our brownstone, and the famous kiss in the Vermont snow. It was a good thing our house had so many walls because I planned on spending the rest of our lives adding more photos to the collection.

Our life together was a joyful adventure, and we were living it like no one was watching.

And later that night when Oscar texted Roman to explain why he hadn't made it to the party, he summed it up perfectly:

**Oscar:** *Congratulations!! I take full credit for the two of you, you know.*

**Roman:** *I'd have given you credit if you'd been here, but alas... you snooze you lose. BTW, what happened? You said you were on your way?*

**Oscar:** *There was a thing. With a guy.*

**Roman:** *Isn't there always?*

**Oscar:** *Shut up, I don't want to talk about it.*

**Roman:** *Well, you missed Cyndee teaching my nieces three card Monte, our new neighbor showing up with a gift of dancing chickens, Lolo wearing one of those clear raincoats with nothing on under it, and your sister's newfound declaration of sobriety that lasted all of ten seconds.*

**Oscar:** *And? What else is new? This is your life now LOL.*

**Roman:** *OMG, I just had a horrible thought.*

**Oscar:** *... and?*

**Roman:** *What if LOL stood for Larry/Oscar/Lolo? Like a naughty, nasty sex sandwich...*

**Oscar:** *STFU.*

**Roman:** *Heh, gotta repeat that one to Scotty—BRB.*

*Thank you for reading LOL: Laugh Out Loud! For a bonus deleted scene, visit http://www.lucylennox.com/l/4035434 to enjoy a little more Scotty and Roman.*

*Want more After Oscar love? Up next is BTW: By The Way, the story of James Allen who we last saw being mistreated by his boyfriend Richard in IRL: In Real Life... Turn the page for a sneak peek or grab BTW: By The Way here → https://readerlinks.com/l/1437623*

# SNEAK PEEK OF BTW: BY THE WAY
## JAMES

After fighting early summer traffic from Boston to the Cape, including a massive backup on the bridge and a jeep full of rowdy teens nearly sideswiping me into the sign for Mashpee, my nerves were shot, and I finally understood why my ex had always insisted on vacationing at Fire Island instead of Provincetown. I should have flown straight into Hyannis instead of Boston, but then I would have missed out on the chance to visit the big costume store on Mass Ave that carried custom Geralt wigs.

My friend Conor and I had won a bet against his husband, and the prize had been Wells dressing as the Witcher at an upcoming gaming convention. Hopefully the stressful detour would be well worth it when Conor saw the facial scar makeup and the Witcher's medallion the young woman at the checkout counter had added to my haul.

I drew in a deep breath and let it out as I noticed, thankfully, mine was the only car taking the turnoff for McBride. It took me a minute to wonder how there could be *any* seaside village on the Cape not completely packed for the early summer weekend. There should have been tourists streaming into McBride in droves, considering it was perfectly positioned on one of the nicest points on the south coast of the Cape with views in all directions. But as I pulled into the tiny town just as afternoon turned to evening, I noticed it was almost like stepping back in time. There was a red general store at the corner of the main street and the cross street that led to the public beach. A small grocery store named Bedwicks had hand-printed signs in the windows advertising cheap cuts of meat, but it was clearly already buttoned up for the night.

Even the ice cream shop, that would have had a line around the corner this time of night in any other coastal town, only had one family inside from what I could see through the plate glass window. The small redbrick library still took a prominent spot on the main drag which indicated more expensive tourist shops hadn't come in yet and forced it to a more remote location.

The town had potential, though. I could see that right off the bat. I'd been sent there by my largest client to negotiate the purchase of an old motel that sat out on the tip of a peninsula jutting into Gannet Bay. The minute I drove past it, I understood exactly why it had caught my client's eye. Despite his oftentimes overbearing nature, Dick Sr. was savvy about real estate investment potential, and he'd latched onto this particular coastal property as the next site of a luxury resort. From the looks of it, he was about to strike gold.

Because of its location, the land itself had had an unobstructed 180-degree view of the bay, the surface of which currently glimmered with an explosion of color from the setting sun. It was breathtaking. So much so that I found myself pulling to the side of the road and letting the light wash over me and warm me. Instantly I felt my shoulders relaxing, the tension of the drive and the traffic easing out of me.

Then my eyes shifted to the motel itself, and I almost wanted to laugh. From the look of things, it had slid past disrepair and into derelict sometime in the 1980s. During my drive out here I'd been a little worried about the negotiations for this place—it had been in the same family for eighty years and had recently transferred to the next generation after the grandparents passed away several months ago. From experience I knew estate battles could turn ugly, old family tensions surfacing and throwing emotional wrenches into already settled deals.

The last thing I wanted to do was find myself in the middle of a family battle, not because I shied away from confrontation, but because it wasn't my place to trespass into someone else's private life like that. It felt intrusive and wrong. I'd had enough of my own family drama growing up to know that outside appearances rarely told the whole truth.

From the outside, the dismal state of the Sea Sprite Inn might make it look like easy pickings, but that didn't necessarily mean it was going to be easy to strike a deal. I thought about this as I made my way back toward the little town, following my GPS to the address of the Airbnb my assistant had booked for me.

I pulled my rental car into the gravel lot of a small bar topped with a driftwood sign that said *By the Way*. I snorted since the building was located on the corner of Main Way and By Lane. It was like something out of a Hallmark movie except much, much shabbier.

A set of weathered wooden steps bolted along the side wall of the building led up to a small porch where another small sign hung that read *On the Way*. I glanced again at the itinerary my assistant had printed up, confirming that was the name of the apartment she'd rented for me.

At least it seemed the folks in the town had a sense of humor, I thought to myself as I grabbed my bag from the trunk and made my way up to the apartment. It was nice inside, clean and minimal with wide windows that looked out over the town. I stood for a moment, trying to decide what my next move should be. I'd gotten a good sense of the town itself from driving around, but I was still curious about the people who lived here. I figured the best place for that would probably be the bar downstairs.

Plus, I was craving a Mai Tai.

Even though it had been several months since the breakup, I still heard Richard's voice in my ear. *Maybe you should get a vodka soda instead. Those Mai Tai's are going to cost you another hour in the gym tomorrow.*

I gritted my teeth, trying to force my ex's voice out of my head as I made my way outside and back down the stairs. Fuck it. I was getting a Mai Tai, I decided, in part because Richard wasn't here—wasn't even in my life anymore—which meant I could do whatever I wanted. And what I wanted was a Mai Tai. I was on the Cape for god's sake. And what the hell did I care if I was carrying a few extra pounds of weight around my middle these days? Some people starved themselves through a breakup, and others spent too much time at Zabar's. It was fine. Even though I was here for work, I still hoped to sneak a little time on the beach to at least put some color back into my skin from a long, cold winter.

I reached the gravel lot and circled around to the front of the bar. The place was very old Cape Cod. Weathered boards from the exterior gave way to a similarly weather-beaten look inside. Old painted wooden buoys hung from rough hemp rope on the walls, neon beer signs dotted the front windows, framed black-and-white photos of fishing boats and proud fishermen holding record catches held place of pride behind the bar, and a few of the barstools had old wooden ship wheels as their backs as if that had been a theme of the place at one point.

The bar was crowded—more so than I'd expected from how sleepy the town had appeared on the drive in. But it was a Friday night, and maybe this place was the only nightlife option in town. There was an open stool at the far end, and I slid into it, wedging myself between the wall and a pack of older men in matching softball shirts laughing and giving each other hell about a game they'd played earlier that evening.

I leaned forward, searching out the bartender, and sucked in a breath when he came into view. I'd expected to find some old grizzled fisherman type behind the bar, but instead I found a much younger man. Correction, a much younger, sexy as hell man. He had a wide, dimpled grin and dirty-blond hair flipping out from underneath a well-worn Red Sox cap. His tanned, muscular forearms flashed as he moved between pouring draft beers and reaching out for people's credit cards.

Well, hell. I hadn't expected to get that little weirdness in my gut from seeing an attractive man. And yet, there I was, stomach twisting and pulse hammering. It had been a while since my interest had been piqued. Even before Richard and I had broken up, things hadn't exactly been on fire in the bedroom for months. It was good to know I wasn't dead.

The kid glanced my way and gave a quick nod to indicate he'd seen me and would be down to take my order next. It gave me just enough time to get myself under control so that I wouldn't make a fool out of myself ogling him. Which was important because I wasn't here to check out sexy young men, I was here for work.

Though it occurred to me that perhaps I could mix the two together a little. After all, pressing this kid for information about McBride and the old Sea Sprite Inn property might net me some information that could help in the negotiations tomorrow.

"What'll you have?" he asked with eyes flashing. He'd just finished laughing at something his previous customer had said.

"Mai Tai," I said automatically, wincing a little at the frivolous order. I glanced down the bar. Most folks were drinking draft beer or basic mixed drinks. There wasn't an umbrella or pineapple garnish among them. For a second I wondered if I should have ordered some-thing more manly, but then, of course, I had to stop and lecture myself about internalized sexism.

"You sure?" There was a note of hesitation in his voice.

I blinked up at him, ready to defend my drink order now that I was properly re-feminist-ed. But his furrowed brows weren't teasing. They were concerned.

I frowned. "Yes. Very sure. Why?"

"Your face did a whole thing just now, like..." He paused and then shook his head. "Never mind," he said, clearly deciding not to pursue the line of thought. "One Mai Tai coming right up." His easy grin reappeared as he turned to make the drink.

I couldn't help but watch. After all, he was standing right in front of me. Despite the summer weather, he wore blue jeans that were clearly in love with him. They hugged him close and caressed every damned inch of his long legs and tight ass. It was impossible not to notice the way the muscles of his butt moved underneath that soft denim.

My stomach did that flip again, except this time something squeezed even lower in my gut. Something close to desire.

"The view costs extra," he said over his shoulder. My face ignited as I realized he'd been watching me in the mirror behind the bar and had noticed me staring. I immediately dropped my eyes to my clasped hands on the lacquered surface of the bar. Since when did I perv on bartenders? Especially young ones who were clearly so outside my age range that it bordered on embarrassing.

When the drink appeared in front of me, I forced myself to look up. "Sorry about that," I said, still feeling hot in the face.

He winked at me. "I was just kidding." His grin spread slowly across his face, and he leaned in ever so slightly before adding, "For you, the view is free." He held my eyes for a beat longer before turning to help the pack of softball players next to me who were clearly ready for another round.

It was about five minutes before I could even draw breath again. And I spent that entire time trying not to watch the guy like some horny barfly.

Which I failed at, utterly.

There was something about him, about the way he moved. He'd obviously been doing this job long enough for most of it to be muscle memory. He seemed at home behind the bar, and he certainly knew most of the locals since he called them by name and asked about their families or jobs or offered a joke if they looked like they needed cheering. The faded T-shirt he wore said Barwich High School Lacrosse which seemed to confirm both his youth and his local ties.

I focused on my drink, needing to find something—anything—to take my notice off the bartender. Richard would have had a field day if he'd seen me panting after such a young pup. *You're closing in on forty, old man. Maybe lower the bar a little.*

I sucked vigorously at the Mai Tai. My friend Conor had warned me to stop giving so much mental real estate to my ex, but it was hard. After being with someone for several years, their voice was pretty well burned into your internal monologue.

"Ready for another?"

I blinked up at the bartender. My head felt a little bit lighter, and before I could stop myself I asked, "How old are you?"

He let out a soft snort but didn't seem offended by the question. More amused. "Twenty-six. How old are you? Are we in some kind of competition?"

I shook my head and held up a hand. "Sorry. That was rude. Forgive me." I cleared my throat and added, "And I'm thirty-eight. So... clearly I win. Or lose, depending on how you look at it."

He grew serious, his eyes widening. "Ahh, ancient. Have you looked into reverse mortgages yet? I hear they're all the rage with your set."

I couldn't help but bark out a laugh, which made his eyes brighter and his dimple deeper. "I'll check it out. Thanks for the tip."

"You just visiting?" he asked.

I nodded. "Just here for a few days."

"Let me know if you have any questions about our little neck of the woods. I'm a McBridey, born and raised." His smile was genuine. "Ask me anything."

It seemed the perfect opening, so I jumped in. "Thanks." I glanced around, taking note of the crowd that had started to finally thin a bit as the night grew later. "This place seems to do a brisk business. Is it mostly locals?"

His eyes flicked around the space as if reminding himself of his own clientele. "Well, it's not usually this crowded, actually. There was a softball game tonight. Everyone always comes here after. It's tradition."

"Not as many tourists?" I pressed. "You're kind of off the beaten path here."

He seemed to bristle a little. "We get tourists. McBride has a reputation as one of the Cape's best-kept secrets. You can still get away from the hustle and bustle of the crowds and have a true old Cape experience." He sounded like a brochure, and I wasn't sure who he was trying to convince: me or himself.

"But there aren't any resorts to really draw in the big money," I pointed out. "I'd imagine if there were more hotels and such, this place would be busy every night."

His face kept its easy grin, but he shook his head firmly. "No, thanks. We already have a small B&B in town and the Sea Sprite. Between that and the public beach access, it's enough to keep us plenty busy during the season."

I turned around as if I could see the shabby seaside motel from here. "That... that old place on the point? There are actual guests that stay there?" My surprise wasn't fake. I truly didn't realize the inn was still hosting enough guests to be considered a viable tourist destination in McBride.

His expression turned defensive. "Well, I mean... most of the guests are ones who've been coming for years. They have a sentimental connection to McBride and the inn. I'll admit it needs some fixing up, but once that happens..." He was distracted by a server calling for him at the other end of the bar. He blew out a breath, replacing the furrowed eyebrows with an easy grin. He turned back to me with another flirty wink that made the Mai Tai in my stomach fizz. "Excuse me."

I wrapped my fingers around the tall, cold glass of my fresh drink, wondering what this guy's response would be once he learned about the new resort going up in town and the effect it would have on businesses like his.

Seemingly on their own accord, my eyes drifted back to the bartender's ass in those jeans. God, he was hot as hell. His T-shirt was worn enough that I could easily see the muscles of his back stretch and bunch as he reached for a bottle above the bar. And the muscles along his arms clearly attested to his continued fitness even though he was well past his high school lacrosse days.

Twenty-six.

*Hm. Not exactly jailbait.*

After all, Richard had been in his mid-twenties when we'd started dating. Sure I'd been in my early thirties, but there'd still been enough of an age difference that it had become a problem, especially as I'd grown older and wanted to settle down and he was still enjoying being young and irresponsible.

I downed another gulp of my drink. Thinking of Richard made me think of his father and was a cold reminder that I wasn't here to flirt. I was here for intel. For the deal. For Richard's father, who remained my biggest client at the law firm by far. Now that Richard and I were broken up, I knew I was on thin ice. If I lost Dick Sr.'s business, the firm wouldn't be pleased. With the number of real estate transactions he did every year, Dick Sr. was one of the firm's mainstay sources of income. The fact that I'd landed him as a client was one of the reasons I'd been promoted to equity partner. If he switched firms, I'd lose the respect of my peers and possibly my status at the firm. Maybe even my job.

When the bartender came back over, he had a wet cloth in his hand and began wiping down the already clean bar. "Want another?" He nodded to my empty glass.

The smart thing would be to say no and go to bed. Turn in early so I could be top of my game at the meeting in the morning. "Yes, please," I found myself saying instead.

Okay, so maybe the smart thing was to stay at the bar and probe the bartender for information. After all, I prided myself in being more prepared than most when it came to negotiating deals, and going into the meeting with intel about the town would only help my client.

At least it sounded like a viable excuse when I knew the reality was that I just wanted to keep looking at the pretty bartender. Feeling compelled to at least give a nod to the excuse I'd given myself for sticking around, I asked the bartender about the inn while he mixed my drink. "So, you said the inn needs renovations... Is that... what does everyone around here want to see happen to it?"

Maybe I wasn't as good at my job as I'd thought. I wasn't sure I'd ever sounded so stupid in my life.

The young man's face lit up completely. "There's a really cool vintage motor inn in Arizona—and others all over the country, really—that's been done over with this funky retro vibe. I can totally see the same thing for the Sea Sprite. If done right—and I have lots of ideas for this—it could help revitalize McBride and bring in lots of new jobs. But, it wouldn't be like what happened with some of those other towns where like all the chichi stores came in and priced the locals out of the market. I mean, McBride wouldn't be McBride without Flamingo's and Nanny's, obviously..."

He seemed to realize he'd been talking a mile a minute. It was endearing, especially when he blushed.

"Sorry," he said with a soft chuckle. "I didn't mean to—"

I cut him off. "I liked it. Please continue. It sounds like this town means a lot to you."

He shrugged, and suddenly the man looked less sure of himself, less like the flirty bartender I'd noticed when I'd first sat down.

"My family has always encouraged me to spread my wings and go have some big-city experience, but that never really felt like my thing. I think..." He looked down at the damp bar rag he'd folded and then refolded as if wondering how much to share. I held my breath, realizing that I wanted to hear what he was about to say and not wanting to do anything to spook him away. "I think they want me to be sure of what I want before deciding to settle down in McBride for good, but sometimes you already know, you know? And this place... it just... it's perfect for me. My family is here, friends from school... I mean, not everyone, of course. Most of my cousins have gone off to Boston and stuff, but I've always seen myself in McBride for the long haul. I'd love to be a part of the town's revitalization, and I think the Sea Sprite getting a big facelift would go a long way toward bringing in the money and tourism that we'd need for that to happen."

He shook his head and scratched self-consciously at the back of his neck as he grinned at the floor. "My family thinks I'm crazy. They think it's too far gone and needs one good swing of the wrecking ball, but..." He shrugged again. "I know I'm right. I feel it... I feel it here, you know?" His eyes met mine, and I could see the earnestness and conviction in them as he put his hand over his heart. I noticed his long fingers were work-worn and flecked with little nicks and scratches. I couldn't help but imagine what those fingers would feel like on my skin.

Or what it would feel like if he looked at me with that same amount of passion and conviction that he talked about McBride.

I mentally shook my head, trying to rein my overly active imagination. The bartender was clearly waiting for me to respond, and I could already tell from the hint of hesitation and doubt crowding into his expression that he was wondering if perhaps he'd overshared.

"You've given this a lot of thought," I pointed out.

His grin turned lopsided. "Hazard of living through the off-season —lots of time to think," he said with a chuckle. "But yeah, I guess I have given it a lot of thought." A slight frown marred his forehead, his expression turning contemplative. "I think sometimes it's easy to let things get stagnant, you know? Maybe stagnant isn't the right word, but you start to accept the status quo without question. You keep doing things the way you always did because that's the way they've always been done. Don't get me wrong, I love tradition and all, but sometimes you have to find a way to respect the past while still embracing the future."

He gestured in the general direction of the bluff I'd driven past earlier that day. "Take the Sea Sprite, for example. That inn has been the anchor of this town for so long, and I think people have just gotten so used to it being there that it's easy to take for granted. Sure it would take serious investment and a shit ton of elbow grease, but you revitalize the inn, and the town will follow. It's just going to take someone with vision to make it happen."

I thought about other properties my client had purchased and how the luxury resorts he'd built on them had inevitably impacted the nearby towns. High-dollar tourists expected a high-dollar experience, and that extended beyond the walls of the resort itself. They came on vacation with money to spend, and they weren't looking for the standard kitschy souvenirs and bric-a-brac you might find in a small-town general store. They wanted diamonds and couture bathing suits and restaurants with unpronounceable items on the menu.

I traced my fingers down the condensation on my glass, trying to figure out how to best formulate my question. "Do you ever worry that the opposite might happen? That more tourists might lead to McBride losing its small-town charm?"

The bartender chuckled. "Nah. Most of us in McBride have lived our whole lives here, and when you live in a place all your life, it seeps into you. It becomes a part of you in a way. Your neighbors aren't just people who live next door, they're family. You shop at Don's Book Nook down the block because Don's mom knows who your favorite author is and has their latest book already waiting for you the day it comes out, and you know buying the book there rather than somewhere else means Janet can keep fostering dogs. You walk into the pharmacy and order jalapeño pickles on your patty melt because Precious keeps a jar in the kitchen just for you."

His words struck a chord in me. It was the absolute sense of belonging somewhere. I realized suddenly that it was something that I'd never experienced before and hadn't realized I'd been missing until that moment. I felt a sharp pang of longing and forced myself to focus on my half-empty glass, gripping it tightly and letting the biting cold of the melting ice seep into my palms.

"I can see why you love it here." I cleared my throat, hoping he hadn't heard the loneliness that had crept into my voice.

"I do. This place isn't just my past, it's my future." His eyes met mine, and there was an intensity to them, a lingering passion from talking about McBride.

It made me wonder when I'd last felt that kind of passion. Not anytime recently that I could remember.

The moment felt charged between us, a casual conversation that had unexpectedly turned deep and personal. He seemed to realize it at the same time I did because his cheeks flushed pink. "You're easy to talk to," he said, sounding a little sheepish. "I don't usually spill so much of my personal shit to the customers. Sorry about that."

I flapped a hand in the air stupidly, so I reached for my drink and took a gulp for something to do. Of course it went down the wrong pipe and I choked, trying to stifle a cough. "Happy to be of service," I wheezed before falling into a fit of coughing.

*Smooth, James*, I thought to myself. Nothing sexier than a man half choking to death on a Mai Tai.

Once I finally got my breathing under control, I looked up to find the bartender smiling at me. "You okay?"

I nodded.

The dimple appeared again, and I wanted to lick it. "So, what are you up to while you're in town? Doing anything interesting?"

I almost choked on my drink again. Three Mai Tai's in quick succession had loosened my thoughts enough that my brain immediately wanted to fire back with *I'd like to be doing you.*

Even thinking the words made my cheeks burn, and I cleared my throat. "Just checking out the place." Was it just me, or did my voice sound gruffer than usual?

"Need someone to show you around?"

I blinked. He asked it so offhand and casually that it took a moment for the words to sink in. Was he actually asking me out? Was that even possible?

I thought about an old Bible story I'd heard when I was little about Satan tempting Jesus during his time in the desert. I wondered if Satan had taken the form of a twenty-six-year-old hottie with twin freckles over his wrist and a scar on his chin. If so, maybe I needed to reconsider my atheism. If Jesus was able to resist, he had to be a god.

"Maybe," I said, hedging. But I couldn't help indulging my curiosity. "What would you show me?" I realized how dirty that sounded and quickly amended the question with, "What are McBride's best features and hidden secrets?"

I hadn't heard myself flirt like this in years, and it felt strangely freeing. Maybe I needed to get out of the city more often and relax for once. If this is what it felt like, I definitely wanted more.

The bartender leaned a hip against the edge of the bar. "Well, let's see... all of the best sea glass can be found on the far side of the point. But you have to look up in the sea grass for it because all the good stuff by the water is already taken. What else?" He pressed his lips together and looked up as though mentally touring the small town. He snapped his fingers. "Oh, you can rent the best cruiser bike from Nanny's ice cream shop down By Lane. It has a big enough basket to carry your goodies home from the farmer's market on Friday mornings. Also, if you visit the lighthouse during a new moon, you can usually hear the ghost of Tonny McBride herself moaning out to the tides that took her dear Franklin away from her three hundred years ago."

He leaned across the bar and lowered his voice. I caught a whiff of something fresh and outdoorsy, like sunshine and salt, maybe even freshly mown grass. Without realizing it, I'd moved in to hear him better.

"But the real cause of the sound is McBride's Wiccan society doing their New Moon Ritual." He held a finger to his lips, drawing my attention where it definitely had no business going. "Shh, don't tell anyone. It's our little secret."

"And all the Wiccans," I couldn't help pointing out.

He chuckled. "Nah, they're usually so sloshed by then, they hardly remember anyway. McBride Wiccans like to ratchet up the power of their spells with a little liquid courage. Bev Mulrooney mixes up a fresh fruit sangria that would make you cry."

I laughed, the stress of the day—hell, the stress of the last few months—easing from my shoulders. Whether it was the strong drinks, the cozy atmosphere, or the attention of the hot, young bartender, I wasn't sure, but suddenly I felt more at peace than I had for the better part of a year. I let myself sink into the feeling, to enjoy it as I continued to watch and listen, spellbound, as he told me more stories of McBride and recounted all the things about the tiny town that made it special.

And I tried not to think about how the deal I was bringing to town was going to ruin everything.

GRAB *BTW: By The Way* here → https://readerlinks.com/l/1437623

# LETTER FROM LUCY & MOLLY

Dear Reader,

Thank you so much for reading *LOL: Laugh Out Loud*, book two in the "After Oscar" series! We would love it if you would take a few minutes to review this book on Amazon. Reader reviews really do make a difference and we appreciate every single one of them.

Lucy and Molly are pen names of a real pair of sisters who have joined together to create the After Oscar series. While Molly has been a full-time author for a decade, this is her second novel in the gay romance genre.

There are five stories in the After Oscar series, and you can enjoy them all back-to-back! Up next is the story of what happens when James' Richard from *IRL* turns out to be a Dick. *BTW: By The Way is available on Amazon now.*

Be sure to follow us on Amazon to be notified of new releases, and look for us on Facebook for sneak peeks of upcoming stories.

Feel free to sign up for our newsletters, stop by www.LucyLennox.com, www.MollyMaddox.com, or visit Lucy's Lair on Facebook to stay in touch.

To see fun inspiration photos for this book, check out the Pinterest page for LOL.

Happy reading!
Lucy & Molly

# ABOUT MOLLY MADDOX

Molly Maddox is the romance pen name for a New York Times bestselling author who started writing at an early age because her older sister, Lucy Lennox, was a writer and Molly wanted to be like Lucy in all ways (she still does).

When she's not writing, Molly likes to cook, read, take pictures of her dog and cat cuddling, and finds an odd satisfaction in folding sheets so that the top sheet is indistinguishable from the bottom sheet.

She loves all things romance and is grateful every day she gets to write for a living.

⤳

*Connect with Molly on social media:*
www.MollyMaddox.com
AuthorMollyMaddox@gmail.com

**f** facebook.com/molly.maddox.16752754

**a** amazon.com/author/mollymaddox

# ALSO BY MOLLY MADDOX

After Oscar Series (with Lucy Lennox):

IRL: In Real Life

LOL: Laugh Out Loud

BTW: By The Way

ISO: In Search Of

HEA: Happily Ever After

Also be sure to check out audio versions on Amazon, Audible, and iTunes.

# ABOUT LUCY LENNOX

Lucy Lennox is the USA Today bestselling author of over fifty gay romance titles including the GoodReads Hall of Fame winner Wilde Love. Born and raised in the southeast USA, she is finally putting good use to that English Lit degree she earned before the turn of the century.

Lucy enjoys naps, pizza, and procrastinating. She stays up way too late each night reading romance because it's simply the best.

For more information and to stay updated about future releases, sales and audio news and to grab some free and bonus reads, please sign up for Lucy's author newsletter on her website at LucyLennox.com or to stay in the know, join her exciting reader group, Lucy's Lair on Facebook.

facebook.com/LucyLennoxMM

instagram.com/lucylennoxmm

amazon.com/Lucy-Lennox/e/B01N0IOYPT

bookbub.com/authors/lucy-lennox

pinterest.com/lucy_lennox

# ALSO BY LUCY LENNOX

Made Marian Series

Forever Wilde Series

Aster Valley Series

Virgin Flyer

Say You'll Be Nine

Hostile Takeover

Prince of Lies

Short Stories

Twist of Fate Series with Sloane Kennedy

After Oscar Series with Molly Maddox

Licking Thicket Series with May Archer

Champion Security series with May Archer

Honeybridge series with May Archer

Visit Lucy's website at www.LucyLennox.com for a comprehensive list of titles, audio samples, freebies, suggested reading order, and more!

Printed in Great Britain
by Amazon

41588561R00179